GRAHAM MASTERTON

SACRIFICE

A TOM DOHERTY ASSOCIATES BOOK

SACRIFICE

Copyright © 1985 by Graham Masterton

Reprinted by arrangement with Wiescka Masterton

First TOR printing: June 1986

A TOR Book

Published by Tom Doherty Associates
49 West 24 Street
New York, N.Y. 10010

ISBN: 0-812-52197-8
CAN. ED.: 0-812-52198-6

Printed in the United States of America

0 9 8 7 6 5 4 3 2 1

With special thanks to Arja Salminen

———————————

"In my view, the defense of Europe is principally an issue of *European* defense. We have a duty to help our allies, for a secure Europe serves our common interests. But this should not mean an American guarantee to take up the slack whenever Europe is unwilling to make the required sacrifice."

Senator Larry Pressler,
Chairman of the U.S. Senate Foreign Relations
Subcommittee on Arms Control, *June 24, 1984*

"To achieve victory for Communism throughout the world, we are prepared for any sacrifice."

Mao Tse-tung, 1944

"When bad men combine, the good must associate; else they will fall, one by one, an unpitied sacrifice in a contemptible struggle."

Edmund Burke, 1794

ONE

He was washing the lunch dishes when the gray Mercedes 350 SL drew up outside on the cobbled forecourt, and he knew at once they had found him. He accidentally tugged the stopper out of the old-fashioned porcelain sink and the soapy water drained away with a sharp and sudden gurgle. He said, "Karin!" and when there was no answer, *"Karin!"* again, and reached behind to untie his apron.

Outside, in the wavering May sunshine, the Mercedes had drawn up beside a yellow Volkswagen camper and parked, its engine still running. The sun reflected so brightly from its windows that it was impossible for Nicholas to see who was in it, but he could guess: the three men who had been waiting for him by the fish stand on Gammel Strand in Copenhagen on that foggy morning of February 10, the three men who were his nemesis.

Karin banged open the old wooden door and said, "Mrs. Nexø's furious! The laundry has lost half the pillowcases."

"Listen," said Nicholas without taking his eyes off the Mercedes. "Do you think you could carry on doing the dishes for me? I have to make a phone call."

"A phone call?" She frowned. "I'm supposed to be vacuuming the dining room." She peered unenthusiastically at the stack of blue-and-white Bing & Grondahl plates smeared with

1

congealing mayonnaise and whiskered with fish bones, and at the crowd of empty beer glasses patterned with froth.

"Just for a moment," Nicholas asked her. "Please."

Karin frowned out the window—a red-haired, freckled girl with an uptilted nose and a long braid down the back of her neck, standing in a gloomy, tiled kitchen, her hair shining the same color as the copper pans hanging over the blue-and-white ceramic range. To Nicholas she looked for a moment like a portrait by Jørgen Roed, the Danish realist. It was a real moment, caught in time, but other, more urgent realities were pressing in on it from all sides. The clock striking three in the inn's hallway. The heat of the day. The three men waiting outside in their Mercedes.

And even more pressing was the reason the three men were here.

Karin said, "Are you all right? You look as if somebody just stepped on your grave."

"I have to make a phone call, that's all."

"Mrs. Nexø will want you to drive into Randers and find those pillowcases for her."

"Karin," said Nicholas. "I love you."

Karin said *pffff* and pursed her lips in amusement as she tied her apron.

"Just because you are an American, you think you can twist any girl around your finger."

Nicholas was moved to kiss her but there was no time left for romantic gestures. A car door slammed outside, leaving a solid echo like a picture frame, and two gray-suited men crossed the forecourt toward the entrance to the inn. Nicholas glanced quickly around the kitchen and picked up a large chef's knife, still sticky with herring. Then while Karin watched him in bewilderment, he crossed to the door that led out to the hallway and listened. Karin started to say something but Nicholas hurriedly waved his hand to quiet her.

Voices talking in Danish. One of them thick and heavily accented, like water washing through gravel.

"We have been told that you have an American working here. Don't worry, we're not from the *Tilsynet med udlaendinge*. We're just friends of his. Nicholas Reed?"

"I don't know. I don't have any Americans working here.

Why should I?'' (That was Mrs. Nexø, being evasive. Mrs. Nexø had been taught by her late husband that there are only two kinds of people in this world, sellers and buyers, and that sellers should never give anything to buyers for nothing because that would destroy the integrity of world commerce, not to mention the balance of payments at the Hvidsten Inn.)

"He's a tall fellow, six feet; slim though; thin face, with fair, curly hair. You know the American movie star Donald Sutherland? Looks like him.''

A silence. Somebody coughing and the shuffling of feet. Then Mrs. Nexø saying, "No. Nobody like that here. Are you sure it's the Hvidsten Inn you want? Have you tried farther up the road?''

"The Hvidsten Inn, that's what we were told. No mistake.''

"Well, I'm sorry. I can't help you.''

Somebody saying something quickly in another language, indistinct but probably Russian. Then the gravelly voice saying again, "It's most important that we talk to Mr. Reed. It's his mother, you see. She's been taken critically ill. She doesn't have long, and if we can't find him . . . well—''

Another pause. Nicholas strained to hear what was going on but the Volkswagen camper had suddenly started up in the forecourt and if the three men were saying anything to Mrs. Nexø, it was impossible for him to make it out.

Karin said anxiously, "Nicholas, what's happening? What is that knife for? *Nicholas!*''

Again Nicholas waved her into silence. The Volkswagen's engine coughed and died and the driver almost immediately started it up again, but in that brief intervening second of silence, Nicholas heard Mrs. Nexø say, "Three thousand kroner? What do you expect me to tell you for that?''

Nicholas moved away from the door, stepping as quietly as he could on the kitchen's shiny, tiled floor. He took Karin's wrist and said to her quickly, "Don't worry about the dishes. I have to go. But make that phone call for me, would you? Call a man named Charles Krogh in Copenhagen. You can usually find him at the Københavner bar on Gothergade. Here—write the number down, twenty-one eighteen oh-one. Or if he's not there, try him at home on Larsbjørnstrade.''

"What do I have to say?"

"Tell him Lamprey called. Tell him the old code. 'The old code.' Can you remember that? That's all you have to say."

"Lamprey?" Karin had difficulty in pronouncing it. "The old code?"

Nicholas kissed her. She was yielding, soft-skinned, and she tasted of flower-scented soap and Danish salami.

"I'll come back when I can," he told her. They had done nothing together apart from bicycling occasionally on Sunday afternoons to Asferg, where Karin had an aunt, a smiling woman with big arms; and once they had driven to Randers Fjord and picnicked on the shore in a strong wind, with the sea dancing like smashed windows. Now she kissed him back, worried, uncomprehending. He had always been so calm, so laconic and so unfailingly gentle, treating everybody around him with such American civility, that she could not understand why he should have to run away from anything.

He said, "They may come in and ask you questions. Act, you know, dumb." Then he smiled and went quickly out through the wooden door and along the dark, flagstoned corridor that led to the back of the inn. He hesitated when he reached the door at the end of the corridor and then eased up the wrought-iron latch. He could hear voices in the forecourt at the front of the inn, but they sounded like tourists. The sun shone warmly on the cobbled steps and a marmalade cat that had been sleeping among the geranium pots turned and looked at him narrow-eyed. Cats could always recognize prey.

He waited a moment or two longer, then stepped outside into the sunshine and made his way cautiously along the half-timbered, lime-washed wall. The Hvidsten Inn was thatched—a picturesque, old-fashioned Jutland *kro*—and he could hear mice rustling in the eaves. He reached the rear of the building and took the risk of looking around the corner to see if any of the three men had been sent to cover the garden. But it was deserted. Only the white daisies ruffled by the wind. Only an old wooden wheelbarrow filled with gardening tools.

He was about to cross the corner of the garden into the

shadow of the white-flowering chestnut trees that surrounded the inn on the northwestern side when another door abruptly opened and one of the gray-suited men emerged, smoking a cigarette. He was talking to somebody inside the inn whom Nicholas was unable to see.

"She says he was supposed to be washing the dishes."

"He's been here all right, and he hasn't taken anything with him."

"Well, maybe he just went out for a while."

"You think so?"

The man looked around the garden and coughed. "Nobody could have warned him we were coming."

"So where is he?"

"How should I know? That girl was as thick as two bricks."

The man said nothing but remained on the steps smoking and staring at the garden. He had short-cropped hair the color of sand and was wearing large black business shoes. Nicholas couldn't see much of his face but it seemed pale and lumpy, like a turnip.

Nicholas waited, sweated and shifted the chef's knife from one hand to the other. The man coughed again and sniffed.

Nicholas was confident that they weren't going to catch him. Not this time at least. But it had been a shock to see them turn up outside the inn in that gray car of theirs, as undistinguished and as uncompromising as an illness that refuses to be cured. They must know that he hadn't managed to pass on anything of what he knew, yet they still wanted him. He had imagined spending a lazy and idyllic summer at the Hvidsten Inn and then surreptitiously trying to leave Denmark during the winter.

Now, however, he was going to have to think of some other way of eluding them. A clever disguise perhaps, or a complicated program of doubling back and changing names just to shake them off. Even a plain out-and-out run for it. The trouble with running for it, though, was that the information he had learned made it difficult for him to think of anyplace he could possibly run to.

There are some secrets, like some passions, that are greater than those who are chosen to carry them, and the burden of carrying them, passions or secrets, is ultimately overwhelming. This afternoon, as he stood with his back pressed to the wall of the Hvidsten Inn, Nicholas began to clearly recognize that the secrets he knew could kill him.

The gray-suited man went back into the inn. The door hesitated, then closed. Nicholas walked smartly away from his hiding place at the corner of the inn and across the short stretch of bright green grass that separated the inn from the chestnut trees. A dove started warbling and startled him, but he kept on walking.

He had almost reached the trees when a rough voice called out, "You! Hey, you! Just a moment!"

Nicholas didn't turn around but called out, "Gardener, going for a pee! Won't be a second!" Then he started running through the trees, down a crackling, leaf-choked gully dappled with light and shadow and flickering bushes, along by an old half-dilapidated picket fence, until he was suddenly clear of the woods and out in a dazzlingly yellow mustard field.

He still didn't turn around but ran as fast as he could, plunging into the mustard as if he were throwing himself into a blinding, primary-colored lake. He was fit and he could run. With any luck, he could make it to the far side of the field where there was a tile-topped wall and beyond that, a whitewashed, red-tiled church, St. Jorgens, where he could find cover among the orchards and outbuildings.

The mustard whipped against his legs as he ran. His breath sounded like the breath of someone running close behind him and when he was a third of the way across the field, he had to turn around to make sure it wasn't. One of the gray-suited men was standing in the shadow of the trees, his hands on his hips. There was no sign of the other two.

He kept on running. The sky above his head was like a blue-and-white jigsaw. His feet rustled swiftly through the mustard stems; insects droned past his ears. He hoped to God that Karin would manage to call Charles, although he didn't really know what good it would do. Charles might not even understand. He might understand but refuse to care. He hadn't seen Charles for a long time and he knew that Charles was fond of his Jack Daniel's, and fond of his lady friend too. Too fond of them, perhaps, to want to jeopardize them.

He was only a hundred yards short of the tile-topped wall when he saw the gray Mercedes dipping its way toward him through the mustard. As it ploughed through the field, its windshield sent out warning heliograph flashes from the sun. Nicholas realized that it would reach him before he could reach the wall. It sent up a drifting cloud of dust and yellow mustard and approached him in an oddly dreamlike way.

His chest tightened. He was fit but he was fully clothed, it was suffocatingly hot and he was already cramped and tired. His first instinct was to run diagonally away from the Mercedes but then he saw that it would easily catch up with him if he did. So, instead, he began to run toward it, hoping to pass it as close as safety would allow so that it would have to drive around in a U turn to follow him.

He prayed that they wanted to question him, that they didn't want him immediately dead. A single lucky shot could drop him as he ran. His throat was thick with phlegm and he was gasping now with every step.

The Mercedes began to steer toward him. It was only forty yards away now. He could see that his original idea of running past it wasn't going to work. He ran six or seven more steps and then pitched himself sideways onto the dry, stalky dust and immediately began to worm his way on his knees and elbows through the mustard, veering sharply off to the right.

He crawled a good twenty yards before he stopped. He spat into the dust, cleared his throat and wiped his mouth on his shirt sleeve. Then he lay where he was and listened. He could hear the whining of the Mercedes' transmission and the crunching of its wheels through the field. Then it stopped and its engine was switched off. It couldn't be far away because he could hear the slow ticking of its bodywork as it cooled down. He heard the doors open, creaking on their hinges.

"Did you see where he went?" This, surprisingly, in American-accented English.

"He's lying low. But don't worry about it, he can't get away. Axel will find him."

Nicholas supposed that Axel was the lumpy-faced man

whom he had seen smoking in the garden, the man who had followed him through the trees. He lay with his cheek against the earth, trying to suppress his panting. An amber centipede climbed up a mustard stem only an inch in front of his nose. He supposed that this would be as good a place to die as any. He wondered what his mother would have thought on the day he was born had she been told that her new baby would die in Jutland in just over thirty-two years, under a May sky in a mustard field.

Even now, all those miles away, his mother must be thinking something, doing something, tidying, or tending her garden; for a moment Nicholas shut his eyes and wished it were possible to travel through time and space just by thinking about it. To open his eyes again and find that he was standing in the garden in Colonial Heights, Virginia: that would be a miracle for which he would light a candle every day for the rest of his miraculously preserved life.

He could almost hear the garden swing creaking and his mother saying, "Nicholas never eats enough, never did. All scrag, that boy. Good brains but no body even worth arguing about."

But the creak of the garden swing was the creak of the Mercedes' door, and the sounds of summer in Virginia were the footsteps of the two men in gray suits who were now crossing the field looking for him. He cleared his throat again and wiped the sweat from his mouth with the back of his hand.

"He can't be far," said one of the men. They stopped, then started walking again.

"Axel!" called the other.

"All right, all right," replied the one called Axel, impatiently. "I saw him fall. He can't be far away."

At that moment the single bell in the red-tiled steeple of St. Jorgens Church began to peal steadily, clearly, into the warm afternoon. Nicholas raised his head a little and saw that the three men had now met up. One of them was physically vast, a huge-headed man whose suit stretched across his back like a tarpaulin over a truckload of packing cases, but it was impossible to see his face because he was too far away and because he was wiping his forehead with a large blue handkerchief. The other two were quite ordinary; middle-aged, one of them wearing glasses. The one called Axel was lighting another cigarette. The smoke hurried off to the east, over the tile-topped wall.

Nicholas thought: if I make a run for it now, chances are that I might surprise them. They might shoot at me, but probably they only have handguns and by the time they've taken them out and tried to aim them, I'll be well out of accurate range. Tula-Tokarev automatics probably; couldn't hit a hippo unless it was sitting on your lap. He tried to think of who had told him that and then remembered with a wash of bitterness. Charles Krogh.

Well, he thought, it's now or it's definitely never. And he was up and running before he even realized what he had done. Through the mustard, around the car and across to the wall. None of the men shouted at him, although he heard their heavy footsteps in pursuit. He reached the wall, gripped the edge of the tiles on top of it and dragged himself up the whitewashed rendering, his feet scrabbling against dust and grit. Then he rolled over, cracking two or three tiles as he went, and dropped straight into the churchyard. The bell was still pealing loudly, although he hadn't heard it while he was running. He ran across the brick-paved yard and around to the low, open doorway.

Inside, it was cool and so dark that he had to open his eyes wide to see what was happening. Down at the far end of the church, ten or eleven people were gathered, all dressed up in summer suits and flowery hats, and a baby was crying. A priest in a white smock was standing by the font reading the words of the christening ceremony.

Nicholas walked down the length of the church. Because the floor was tiled, his footsteps clattered and echoed and everybody in the christening party looked around at him in irritation.

"Father," he said. "Father, excuse me."

The pastor looked up. He had white eyebrows and eyes as pale as gulls' eggs. "Please," he said. "This is a christening."

"Father, I need your help."

"Here now," said a young man with a long mustache. "This baby is being christened. Wait your turn."

"Please," the pastor asked him. He pointed to one of the pews close by. "Sit there and I will attend to you just as soon as this baby has been christened."

"Father—"

The priest pointed again at the pew. Nicholas, chilled, sweating, nodded and went to sit down. The christening ceremony continued. The baby panted and cried and panted and cried. On the wall behind the font there was a benign statue of St. Jorgen smiling beatifically toward the church's open door. Welcome inside, all those who seek sanctuary and peace.

Nicholas heard squeaking footsteps. Rubber-soled shoes on tiles. At least two men, one on each side of the church, approaching him slowly and with great deliberation. He lifted his hands and began to pray. Our Father, for God's sake, help me. Hallowed be Thy name. Thy kingdom come.

The man called Axel reached the end of the line of pews and worked his way sideways toward Nicholas, holding in his stomach with one hand to prevent it from bumping the backs of the chairs in front. At last, breathing heavily, he sat down next to Nicholas, folded his arms and said, "You should have known there was no place for you to hide. Especially not here. A church! Do you think they will give you divine protection?"

Now the other man approached from the other side of the church, the huge man whom Nicholas had only managed to glimpse across the field. He sat down, too, and rested his hands on his knees: massive hands, grotesquely large. His shoulders were higher than Nicholas' ears and Nicholas felt completely dwarfed. It was when he turned to look at the man's face, however, that he was frightened the most.

Not only was the man a giant, but his face had been hideously burned. His skin was mottled and stretched, and his mouth was dragged down at one side so that he seemed to be perpetually snarling. His eyes were as taut-lidded and expressionless as those of a turtle, and his nose was nothing more than a lump of tissue that must have been borrowed from some other part of his body by the surgeons who had reconstructed his face. His hair was tufted and sparse and both ears were shriveled.

"We wanted to speak to you," the giant said and sucked in saliva to prevent himself from dribbling.

Nicholas said, "I don't know who you think I am or why you're chasing me."

"No, no, *we* are not chasing you," smiled the one called Axel. "*You* are running away from us! Naturally we are interested to know why. People run away only if they are guilty, only if they have something to hide. We are concerned that you might be feeling overburdened, that whatever it is you are hiding is becoming too much for you. So we wish to relieve you of it."

The members of the christening party were looking around in annoyance and the pastor said sharply, "*Sssshhh!*"

"Well, we won't disturb them more than we have to," said Axel in a friendly mutter. "Here, Novikov, the wire."

Nicholas said, "I don't understand what it is you want."

Axel shook his head and continued to smile. There was dandruff on the shoulders of his jacket, spread out as if he had sprinkled it there on purpose. "You don't have to understand, my dear Mr. Reed. Neither you nor I nor Mr. Novikov here are paid to understand. You are a capitalist, you should understand that. What you are not paid to do, you do not do. Moral and political commitment is measured in money. And why not?"

While Axel was saying this, Novikov had drawn out from around his huge waist a coiled length of steel wire, thin and shiny, with a white-nylon handgrip at each end. Nicholas said, "What the hell is that?"

"A precaution, that's all," replied Axel. "Here, Novikov, my friend, give me that handle."

Novikov passed one of the handles across to Axel, who immediately passed it back to Novikov behind Nicholas' back. Novikov then passed it back to Axel so that by now the thin steel wire was circling Nicholas' waist.

"What the hell are you doing?" Nicholas demanded. "Listen, if you so much as—"

"It's a precaution, that's all," Axel repeated. "Now, please, I want you to tell us a little about Lamprey."

"Lamprey? I don't know what you're talking about."

"Well? Should I remind you? What about Klarlund and Christensen? What kind of bells does that ring?"

Nicholas noisily cleared his throat. He was sweating and shaking. "I'm warning you now," he told Axel. "If you don't take this wire off me and leave me alone, I'm going to scream my goddam head off until that priest brings the police."

"Not recommended," said Axel, puckering his lumpy face into a frown. "It would be much better for you to talk to us a little, tell us what you know; and also, where is all your information?"

Novikov sucked in more saliva and said, "We have no desire to be cruel, Mr. Reed."

"I'm going to scream," said Nicholas.

"No, no, please," smiled Axel. "That would be most ill-considered."

"Damn it, I'm going to scream. I'm giving you five and then I'm going to scream."

"Mr. Reed, please! Look at that baby there! Do you have children of your own? It would be much better if you were reasonable."

"One," said Nicholas, trembling but firm.

"Mr. Reed, I appeal to you. Please see reason."

"Two," said Nicholas.

Axel leaned forward to catch the attention of the burned Novikov and they exchanged a curious look between them, almost mischievous, like trolls.

"Three," Nicholas intoned in time with the bell that was ringing from St. Jorgen's steeple.

"Four."

Axel nodded. He gripped his nylon handle as tight as he could, still smiling, while Novikov gave a grunt of exertion and wrenched his handle sharply to the right.

Nicholas felt an agonizing pain in his spine, cold and cutting, as sharp as glass. He found that he was completely unable to speak but he stared at Axel in perplexity. He kept trying to say, "What was that pain? What have you done to me?" but somehow none of his nerves seemed to coordinate, as if they were telephone wires that had been ripped out of their sockets and left in multicolored disarray. Then he tried to turn to Novikov but found that he was totally paralyzed. Something else was happening to him too, something inside his brain. He could feel a fading, a darkening, as if one by one the cells inside his mind were being switched off. Goodnight, gentlemen, time to leave. You're dying, Nicholas, that's what's happening to you. Dying to the sonorous, monotonous clanking of a Calvinist bell.

He couldn't quite grasp why he was dying. He didn't know what Axel and Novikov had done to him. But then they moved away from him; he was conscious of their leaving—pale, gray shadows on a dim afternoon—and the bell sounded echoing and faint, until he wasn't sure if it was a church bell or the distant clanking of a railroad crossing far away in Colonial Heights.

He fell. The pastor, finishing the christening ceremony, looked up and suddenly understood that something was terribly wrong. The baby was crimson now, crying with that enraged, wavering cry that only a feed and a cuddle can control. The pastor said to the christening guests, "Please, just for a moment, wait here. I'm sorry."

He walked with echoing footsteps to the pew where Nicholas had been sitting. He peered through the gloom at the shape he could see there and for a long moment he couldn't understand what it was. Then as he began to make sense of it, he slowly raised his hand to his face as if to reassure himself that he was still alive and that he was still human.

Nicholas' torso, from the waist up, had fallen sideways onto the pew. One arm was half-raised as if he had been reaching out to stop the upper half of his body from losing its balance. The lower half of his body remained where it was, sitting upright. Axel and Novikov, using their thin steel wire, had cut Nicholas almost completely in half, right through to the spine, and now his insides were piled into his exposed pelvis like yards of bloody spaghetti poured into an eggcup. Blood and bile were running onto the tiled floor in a steady black river and following the pattern of the grouting.

The pastor turned around and stared at the christening guests. They stared back at him. The bell above them continued to ring, on and on and on.

The pastor said, "I regret that something has happened. A tragedy. I will have to ask you to leave by the vestry door."

They remained where they were, staring at him. The baby cried and cried.

"Now!" roared the pastor apoplectically. "You will have to leave *now!*"

TWO

"Mr. Townsend!" called Janice through the hammered-glass partition. "Mr. Beasley on line one!"

"Tell him I've come down with elephantiasis," said Michael distractedly. He swallowed the chilly dregs of his morning coffee, said *"Urrgh"* in disgust, gathered up the catalogs he needed and pushed them untidily into his briefcase.

He heard Janice saying, "I'm afraid Mr. Townsend isn't very well today, Mr. Beasley. Can I take a message? Oh. Well, I'm sure he's read it. Yes, I know it's been a long time. Well, can you call back tomorrow?"

Michael came out of his office and said, "I've got to go out to Slough first. If Mr. Lilley comes in, can you tell him that I'll try to phone him this evening? Oh—and would you phone Norwich Transmitters and ask them where those semiconductors are? I should be home about eight. If there's anything else you need, you can leave a message for me there. Ask Margaret to put it on the recorder. She always gets hopelessly confused when anyone starts talking about computers."

Janice gave Michael one of her tart, knowing little smiles. "Don't worry, Mr. Townsend. The great industrial wheels of Townsend and Bishop will continue to turn, very well-lubricated, even when you're tossing back the vodka and the caviar sandwiches and doing the twist with two-hundred-pound lady road pavers."

Michael nearly laughed but stopped himself. Janice was the daughter of a locomotive engineer; she was blonde and big-nosed and busty, a chain smoker of strong cigarettes and a chain eater of jelly doughnuts, all short skirts and fluorescent T shirts and dangly plastic earrings, yet her turn of phrase was consistently articulate and droll.

Michael often wished that he could be just half as funny; but then from boyhood he had always been seen as a "serious fellow." His last prep-school report had said, "Michael is persistent and grave and will succeed through determination as much as talent." His father had frowned and said, *"Grave?"*

He closed the door behind him and walked along the tiled corridor to the staircase. In another office, with the door open, two teenage girls, both recent school dropouts, were packing computer games in plastic-bubble wrapping and singing along disharmoniously to the latest rock hit, blaring out of their transistor. "Morning, Mr. Townsend," they called cheerily as he passed. He gave them a little finger wave. "Good-morning, Corinna. Good-morning, Doris." They both adored him. He had overheard them telling a friend of theirs that he was "ever so sensitive."

God, he thought, clattering down the stairs to the green-painted reception lobby, anybody would be sensitive if he had twenty people's livelihoods to take care of, not to mention all the costs of overhead, and research and development and end-of-year tax returns.

Sheila, the switchboard operator, was reading *Smash Hits* and painting her fingernails purple. "That Mr. Beasley's a bit of a nut case, don't you think?" she asked Michael as he put down his briefcase to sort through the second mail. Most of the envelopes were buff. Two of them said *On Her Majesty's Service.* He dropped them back in the tray without opening them.

"Mr. Beasley," he told Sheila, "is a true eccentric."

The switchboard buzzed. Sheila flicked a switch with the tip of a finger. "Townsend and Bee-shop, good-mawnin'," she said in an exaggeratedly posh accent. "Neow, I'm afraid that Mr. Bee-shop is away today, awl day. Would yew cayuh to speak to 'is secre-terry? Neow?"

Outside, in the yard, the sky was beginning to spit with rain. The facade of Townsend & Bishop was as unprepossessing as its interior. A square, orange-brick building with green-painted metal windows, backing onto the railway line just south of the East Croydon station. Next door there was an auto-repair works, its sagging doors sprayed with every conceivable color from Vauxhall Crimson to Ford Ivy. All around, hundreds of slate rooftops lay submerged among the green plane trees of suburban Surrey. Children played in the streets; their distant voices sounded like the chattering of birds.

Michael walked across to his four-year-old Ford Granada and unlocked the door. He was just about to climb into the driver's seat when someone whistled to him. He looked around and saw a short man in a green-suede hat and a tan raincoat come hurrying across the yard, one finger raised to hold his attention.

"Mr. Townsend?" he panted. He was round-faced, late middle-aged, with a white, bristly mustache. "I'm so glad I caught you. Wallings is the name."

Michael shook his hand. "I'm afraid I have to be in Slough by twelve."

"Well, that's quite all right. I'll come with you."

"I'm sorry, Mr.—"

"Wallings. HM Customs and Excise."

"Well, I'm sorry, Mr. Wallings, but I have three or four other calls to make after Slough. Then I'm going home. I don't really see how you can expect to follow me around all day."

"I don't," said Wallings briskly.

"Is it tax reports?" asked Michael. "I don't have my books here. Why don't you make an appointment with my secretary; then I can make sure we can be ready for you."

"Ah, but you're going to Moscow tomorrow."

"Yes. Only for ten days though. Surely Her Majesty can wait until I return."

"Sorry," said Wallings with a smile.

"Well, this is quite ridiculous," said Michael. "You can't possibly come to Slough with me. Now listen, Mr. Wallings, I'm late. Go into the office there and ask to speak to Janice. She'll fix something up for you."

"Security," said Wallings.

"I beg your pardon?" It was beginning to drizzle now and Michael held his coat collar close around his neck.

"Security," Wallings repeated. "National security."

"You mean you're not really Customs and Excise at all?"

"General drift," said Wallings. Then he nodded at the car. "Shall we . . . ?"

Slowly Michael opened the door and reached across the front seat to unlock the passenger door for Wallings. Wallings climbed in with an appreciative nod, took off his hat and promptly fastened his seat belt. Michael closed his door and started the engine. The windshield wipers groaned a rubbery complaint across the glass.

"Didn't mean to spring it on you," said Wallings. "Would have come earlier, you know, but nobody told me you were going out."

Michael drove through the back streets. Wallings said, "Which way do you usually go? Mitcham, Putney, Mortlake, Kew?"

"That's it," said Michael. He was beginning to feel uncomfortable and irritated, and anxious too. He had never liked any intrusion in his life, never liked anybody telling him what to do. That was why he had left Sperry Guidance Systems when he was twenty-seven and started up in computerized toys with his best friend, John Bishop. That had been four years ago, four years of worry and work and near-bankruptcy, but at least all the decisions, right or wrong, had been theirs, all the late hours had been worked for their own benefit and not for the lordly dismissal of a departmental manager who sniffed at their work as if they should never have bothered. Now they had two popular computer games on the market, *Robot Crisis* and *King Dinosaur*, and they were going to the Moscow Toy Fair tomorrow with the intention of launching a computerized spelling instructor for Russian schoolchildren, called *Tovarish!*

Four years of self-employment had left Michael thinner and with a spray of gray hair on the left side of his head, but he felt that he was better looking when he was a few pounds underweight, and so did Margaret. He was just six feet tall, narrow-faced, with dark-brown eyes that Margaret had de-

scribed as "perpetually hurt." That was presumably why
Corinna and Doris thought he was "ever so sensitive." That
and the fact that he wore reading glasses. He was aware that
he was becoming old-fashioned in the way he dressed (pastel-
colored shirts with button-down collars, and charcoal-gray
slacks); and he was also aware that his tastes in music and
food and movies were slowing down toward early middle
age. But what did you do about it? Dress like a punk? Go out
and buy *Wham* albums and eat hamburgers every evening?

There was little enough room these days for the young and
the desperately fashionable, let alone for Michael's generation—
all those bewildered refugees from the early 1970s who had
been born two years too late to enjoy the boom of the 1960s
and two years too early to be accepted as members of the new
tribes of the 1980s. There was nothing more dispiriting than
having reached maturity between eras. That was part of the
reason he had taken up computers. A frantic bid to catch up,
a frantic try to get ahead of the game. It hadn't really worked
though, not socially. He still ate spaghetti Bolognese. His
mother had bought him a Hostess platewarming trolley for
Christmas and he was embarrassed whenever he thought of it.
Owning a platewarming trolley was only two stages away
from retiring to Bournemouth and wondering whether anybody would come to your funeral.

They drove through Thornton Heath, a dreary valley of
cut-rate furniture shops, discount stores and small supermar-
kets, congested with red double-decker buses and builder's
trucks. It was raining harder now and the windshield of the
Granada was beginning to fog. Wallings said, "The news'll
be on in a moment. Eleven o'clock."

Michael switched the radio on. The news was the same as
usual. Russia had at last agreed to return to the nuclear
disarmament talks in Vienna, although Soviet forces continued to mass in East Germany and Poland as part of the
Warsaw Pact exercises. The pound had fallen against the
dollar to a new low. A farm worker had lost his leg in a
baling machine and crawled half a mile with it to seek
medical help.

"Seems like a new détente," said Wallings, switching off
the radio without being invited.

"As long as they place an order for my spelling program, I don't honestly care," Michael told him.

"There's actually something we want you to look at," Wallings remarked offhandedly.

"What do you mean? Where?"

"In Moscow, of course."

Michael drew up behind a bus and waited while its passengers disembarked. Rain drummed on the roof of the car with sudden fury.

"You don't mean spy?"

"No, of course not. Goodness me, *spy*. But since you and your pal know something about guidance systems and computers, well, we thought you could be useful."

Michael rubbed the back of his neck. "Who's *we?* M-Sixteen or something?"

Wallings laughed, although it was more like a shout than a laugh. "You've been watching 'The Professionals,' " he said. "Either that or you've been taking *The Sunday Times* too seriously. No, no. This is purely commerce. Department of Trade and Industry. The Russians have built a new guidance complex, that's all, out by Central Airport. All we want you to do is take a look at it. Just externally, no risk. You don't have to break in or anything like that. Just cast an eye over it and tell us what you think."

They had reached Streatham now. Michael turned left toward Streatham Common and Tooting. The rain began to ease and a garish yellow sunlight could be seen through the clouds.

"You can't learn much about any kind of electronics installation from the outside," he told Wallings.

"*You* can't but we have people who can."

"Then why don't you send *them* to look at it?"

"No cover, old man, not like you. No legitimate reason for being there. The Russians would pick them up in a minute."

Michael drew up at the traffic signal. "I really think the answer has to be no," he told Wallings. "I don't want either of us to end up arrested. Come on, we've both got families. We don't need to take risks like that. And what would we say if they caught us? 'Oh, we just fancied taking a look at your brand-new guidance complex'?"

"We'd tell you what to say," said Wallings. He sounded rather testy now.

"Well, I'd rather not say anything. I'd rather not do it at all. Thanks all the same, but no thanks."

"Oh," said Wallings as if Michael's refusal was an unpleasant surprise.

"Why 'Oh'?" said Michael.

"It creates a problem, that's all, your saying no."

"Well, it might, but it's not *my* problem. I'm only going there to sell electronic games. I never liked James Bond anyway."

That last remark was supposed to be a joke but Wallings took it in bad humor. He kept brushing the top of his green-suede hat and bulging his upper lip so that his white mustache prickled up. "I did expect some cooperation," he said.

Michael blew the horn at a boy on a bicycle wavering around in front of him on Tooting Broadway but the boy was wearing headphones and couldn't hear him. "Very dangerous, that," remarked Wallings irritably.

They had reached the north end of Garratt Lane before Wallings said anything more. The rain had started again and Wandsworth looked drowned. A man stood on the corner with rain pouring from the peak of his sodden cap in a steady stream, his cigarette extinguished, staring out at nothing.

Wallings said, "If you won't agree to take a look at the guidance complex, you see, we can't let you go."

"What did you say?" Michael asked. He didn't quite understand what Wallings meant.

"I said, we can't let you go. Can't have chaps going to Russia if they don't show one-hundred-percent patriotism. Who knows what might happen?"

Michael savagely pulled the Granada over to the side of the road and slammed on the parking brake. "Now listen here," he said furiously. "What the hell is this all about?"

"Thought you would have understood, old man. Helping one's country, that's what it's all about. You didn't have to join the army, did you? You would have had to in Russia. Eighteen years old and they would have had you marching and drilling and digging tank pits and cleaning out toilets with your toothbrush. Didn't have to suffer anything like that, did you? Nor will you because other chaps are prepared to do what you won't do. All we're asking is that you get on the Moscow metro, ride a few stations north and then go for a walk. You don't have to carry cameras, you don't have to make any drawings. Just keep your eyes open. Now that isn't hard, is it? Nor dangerous either.''

"This is unbelievable," Michael raged at him.

"Well," sniffed Wallings, "you either go to Moscow and do it or you don't go to Moscow at all."

"I've spent two years and seven thousand pounds developing *Tovarish!*" Michael snapped.

Wallings began to smile again. "Precisely," he said. "Pity to throw the whole lot in the trash can just because.you're feeling stubborn."

Michael stared at the raindrops spattering the windshield. He couldn't believe that any of this was real. But a policeman was slowly approaching him from the other side of the junction and so he released the brake, shifted the Granada into gear and pulled away from the curb.

"Jesus," he said to himself.

He returned home that evening exhausted. He turned the Granada into their steeply sloping driveway in Sanderstead and sat in front of the wheel, feeling the back of his shirt sticky with sweat. His beard was beginning to grow, too, and felt irritatingly prickly. At last he climbed out of the car, retrieved his briefcase from the backseat and walked up the four steps that led to the front door.

He and Margaret had lived here for six years now, two-thirds of their married life. Before this it had been a modern flat in Basingstoke so that he could be close to the Sperry Guidance Systems factory at Edison Road. But this was a small, mock-Tudor semidetached with leaded windows, fir trees in the garden and a fish pond. There had once been a gnome fishing in the pond but as soon as they had moved in, Michael had knocked off its head with a five iron. He didn't seem to be capable of doing spontaneous things like that anymore.

Duncan's bedroom light was on. Michael opened the front door and there was a warm smell of cooking. Chicken casserole probably. He set his briefcase down on the patterned carpet and closed the door behind him unusually firmly. Margaret's voice called from the kitchen, "Mike? Is that you?"

"I hope so," he said. He walked through to the kitchen and there she was, smiling and piping out fresh whipped cream onto two glass dishes of chocolate mousse. A pretty, dark-haired girl with wide, appealing eyes and a snubby nose. A little more suburban-looking now than she had been when he first met her; her hair was bobbed in a flicked-back Princess Diana style and her blue eyeshadow looked as if it had been issued by the national society for making all grade-school mothers glamorous. Not erotic anymore but that was probably because he was dog-tired. He kissed her and she said, "Mmmm," and he said, "What's cooking?"

"Poulet," she told him. It was a standard routine between them.

"That's funny," he replied. "It smells exactly like chicken."

"Hard day?" she asked. She finished piping the whipped cream and then put the dirty dishes in the sink. "Duncan's waiting for you if you want to go up and say good-night."

He nodded. For some extraordinary reason, he felt a lump in his throat as if he were about to burst into tears. But he managed to smile and say, "Fine. Yes, I'll go up."

She followed him to the foot of the stairs. "You're all packed except for your shaving things."

"Oh, thanks. You're an angel."

"I do wish you'd buy yourself some new underwear."

"What, in Russia? We could probably all go camping in the smallest pair of shorts they make over there."

"You know what I mean. Marks and Sparks do some quite nice brief ones."

He blew her a kiss. "For you, anything. Let me just say good-night to Duncan."

Duncan, dark-haired, tired-eyed, was sitting up in bed reading. On the walls of his small, brown-wallpapered bedroom there were dozens of cutout pictures of war planes. They hadn't managed to get around to decorating Duncan's bedroom yet, especially after all the money they had had to spend on new gas heating.

"How are you?" Michael asked him.

"Okay. I got a hundred in math today."

"You're a genius. Here, time to settle down now."

Duncan snuggled into his quilt. "Is there time for a story?"

"I'm sorry, not tonight. Mummy has supper ready, and I have to get up first thing tomorrow."

Of course, he thought as he leaned over his son and kissed him, it was always possible not to go at all. He had no idea of what Moscow would be like apart from a few horror stories Alan Taylor had told him about waiting for hours for a meal, even at the so-called "international" restaurants, and the restrictions on traveling anywhere outside Moscow. But it was ridiculous to be frightened. Why should he be frightened? Wallings had assured him that taking a look at the new guidance complex wasn't going to be dangerous.

Mind you, they had probably told Greville Wynne, too, that spying wasn't going to be dangerous.

Supper was waiting downstairs on the Hostess trolley. There were avocados for starters. Margaret said, "I hope you don't mind. I opened the wine." Michael nodded, kissed her forehead and poured them each a glass of Sainsbury's Liebfraumilch.

"I saw Sally today," said Margaret, eating tidily. "You remember Sally Hutchinson?"

Michael ate his avocado without tasting it. In his mind he was already on that metro ride north to Central Airport. Wallings had even told him the stations: Sverdlova Square, Gorkovskaya, Mayakovskaya, Byelorusskaya, Dinamo, Aeroport. Margaret said, "Are you all right? You look tired."

On *News at Ten* that night, which they watched in the living room with Margaret sitting on Michael's lap, Alistair Burnett said that the huge Soviet maneuvers in East Germany were being regarded by Western experts as nothing more than "saber-rattling" in order to give greater significance to the disarmament talks in Vienna.

A Foreign Office spokesman with a creased forehead said, "In fact, we regard these exercises as a sign of the Soviet Union's concern that the discussions in Vienna should be really effective. I have to say that we are encouraged by them rather than alarmed."

Michael and Margaret went to bed at eleven o'clock. Margaret set the alarm for seven-fifteen. Michael's suitcase stood by the wardrobe as a reminder that tomorrow was the day. Margaret snuggled up close to him and said, "I hope it isn't too awful. Russia, I mean."

"I'll bring you back one of those fur hats."

He kissed her, then slipped his hand inside her nylon nightgown and caressed her small breasts. They made love in silence while the springs of the bed went *squonk*, *squonk*. Up above the head of the bed there was a reproduction of Renoir's "Le Moulin de la Galette."

Michael dreamed that night that he was having an argument with Wallings. Then he was riding on a brightly lit, echoing metro train but the doors of the train refused to open and he was unable to get out. He knew that he had traveled a long way past Aeroport Station and that he was in serious trouble.

Wallings said, "You're sweating. What's the matter?"

He opened his eyes. Margaret was propped up on one elbow looking at him, although he couldn't see her face in the darkness.

"I had a dream, that's all. Overtired, I suppose."

She kissed him. Far away, a train echoed its way south along the main line that led to Purley, Coulsdon and all the clustered dormitory communities where London's clerks and office managers now lay sleeping, or worrying, or making love to their wives. Michael lay for a long time with his eyes open and thought: God, is the world really so dangerous?

THREE

It had been drizzling all morning in Zossen-Wünsdorf and when Marshal T.K. Golovanov arrived at the headquarters of the Western Strategic Direction in his huge black Volga limousine, three officers came running out with large, multi-colored golf umbrellas to protect him from the wet.

The marshal made a point of ignoring them. A soldier who had fought with Konstantin Konstantinovich Rokossovskiy at Kursk during the Great Patriotic War scarcely had need of multicolored golf umbrellas to protect him from the weather. "Learn to love the foulest of storms and the bitterest of blizzards," he often told his subordinate officers. "Bad weather has saved Russia more than once; it will save her again."

The headquarters at Zossen-Wünsdorf was a lichen-streaked concrete building surrounded by lines of bedraggled linden trees. Marshal Golovanov crossed the puddly yard and, as bulky as he was, quickly and athletically mounted the wet stone steps that led up to the main entrance. He was followed closely by his military aide, Colonel Lev Chuykov, and his newly appointed secretary, Major Valentin Grechko; and they were followed in turn by the three dithering officers with their multicolored golf umbrellas.

Before Golovanov could reach the glass doors, however, they were swung briskly open and out strode General of the Army Ivan Yeremenko, who rapped his heels, snapped a smart salute and then held out his hand. "Comrade Marshal," he greeted him.

"Well, now," said Golovanov, taking off his cap and banging it against his coat to shake the rain off it, "you could have done better with the weather, Comrade Yeremenko. Just because I believe in the strategic value of rain, just because I am impervious to it, that doesn't mean to say that you have to put it on for me specially."

Yeremenko shook his hand. "How was your journey?" He wrinkled his nose up at the gray clouds. "Yes, I'm sorry about the weather. Not like Tbilisi, I'm afraid."

They went inside and walked noisily across the marble-tiled foyer, under a huge, angular portrait of Lenin, his sharp chin pointing to the west. Golovanov said, "Germany's always the same. I spent the last year of the war soaked to the skin. Wet right through to my underwear. I can't remember a single day when it didn't rain. But I suppose, well, memory can play tricks."

The elevator doors rumbled open and Yeremenko ushered Golovanov inside. Colonel Chuykov and Major Grechko did not attempt to join them but waited in the foyer for the elevator to return. They knew that Golovanov didn't like to be crowded too closely by his subordinate officers. "If I want to be breathed on, I can take a ride on the metro," he always said.

As the elevator rose, Yeremenko said, "You shouldn't have to worry about the rain this time, Marshal. It will be over in eight days at the most, and the long-range forecast is excellent. Sunbathing weather."

"Hm," said Golovanov. Then, as the elevator whined to a stop on the third floor, "You did remember to call Inge?"

Yeremenko nodded.

Golovanov clasped Yeremenko's arm. "I've been thinking about her, you know."

Yeremenko said, "Everything is arranged, Marshal. We have dinner tonight with Commander Kiselev and Admiral Perminov; then Major Poplavskiy will drive you to Herbertstrasse. Fraulein Schültz has been told to expect you."

"I bought her a necklace in Tbilisi. Diamonds and hematite."

"I'm sure she'll be delighted, Comrade Marshal."

Yeremenko's tone was close to a parody of lubricity but Golovanov knew how vulnerable he himself was when he spoke of Inge. Yeremenko had visited the Golovanov *dacha* often enough during the summer months to have become well-acquainted with Katia Golovanov, and Golovanov knew that if she were ever to hear about Inge, her reaction would be volcanic.

Apart from that, Yeremenko had made an outstanding success of his recent appointment as Commander-in-Chief of the Soviet forces in Germany in place of the disgraced General Voroshilov, and Golovanov suspected that Yeremenko's promotion to marshal was imminent—even before B-Day perhaps. Yeremenko was efficient, calculating and smart, and for the time being, he was one of the Defense Council's favorites. Better not to make an enemy of him, especially now that events were beginning to move so rapidly. This summer would make or break the careers of many high-ranking Soviet officers, even of those who had come to consider through thirty years of peace that they were reasonably safe from political purging.

"She's a bright girl, Inge," said Golovanov as if he were trying to justify his eagerness in asking about her so soon. "Very bright! She talks, she dances, she can cook too!"

"*Galubtsi?*" asked Yeremenko obliquely. Golovanov frowned at him but said nothing. *Galubtsi* was Russian stuffed cabbage and it was conceivable that Yeremenko was being sharply suggestive.

They walked the rest of the way along the corridor in silence. Their shoes echoed on the wax-polished floor. There was a distinctive smell in the building of electronic equipment that had been switched on for too long, and insecticide, and Balkan tobacco smoke. Every Soviet staff building seemed to smell the same.

It was exactly two hundred and ten yards from one end of the corridor to the other and they had walked it at a smart pace, but Golovanov wasn't even breathing heavily when they reached the doors of the strategic conference room. Although he was sixty-three years old, he exercised ruthlessly every day, engaging in an hour of weight training and aerobics. He was short and squat, with immense shoulders that were emphasized by his lavish marshal's epaulettes. His head was like a small boulder of brown granite on which somebody had scratched two slitted eyes, a slitted, lipless mouth and thin lines to represent sparse, brushed-back hair. All that was expressive about Golovanov's features were his white, brambly eyebrows.

T.K. Golovanov had been born in 1922 in the old Russian town of Staraja Russa, the son of a shoemaker. His father Nikolai had been called up in the First World War and had fought as a private alongside the celebrated Konstantin Rokossovskiy. During the Great Purge of 1937, Rokossovskiy had been imprisoned, tortured and beaten, and Golovanov's father had been called as a witness against him, but despite having his fingers hammered flat as an "inducement" to give testimony, Nikolai Golovanov had refused and later "disappeared."

When Rokossovskiy had been released from prison to command the Soviet tank forces against Hitler, he had not forgotten his old friend from the days of the Terror. He had made sure that young T.K. Golovanov (then a lieutenant in the 9th Mechanized Corps) was immediately promoted to major, and later to colonel in the 16th Army. Under Rokossovskiy's paternal eye, T.K. Golovanov had risen through the ranks of the Soviet Army until by the end of the war, he was a colonel-general and a Hero of the Soviet Union.

Now he was First Deputy of the Ministry of Defense, one of the most powerful men in the most powerful army in the world.

Despite his unreadable face, Golovanov was an ebullient man, emotional and demonstrative in the company of friends, passionate and round-tempered. He enjoyed his vodka and he enjoyed young women, but that didn't mean that he didn't adore his family too: his wife Katia and his four sturdy daughters. Every year he made a point of spending two weeks with them at their *dacha* at Zhiguli and inviting scores of friends. He was ebullient, a party-goer, but he was also a survivor; he had kept his place in the elite ranks of the Red Army by being a dogged exponent of orthodox Soviet military strategy, by holding no political opinions of his own but interpreting the fierce and heavy-handed policies of the Kremlin Defense Council down to the last letter.

It had been Andrei Gromyko who had first called him "The Bear with the Broad Back."

Yeremenko, on the other hand, was calmer, wilier, but an equally astute survivor. He was tall, thin-faced, almost emaciated, a hawk to Golovanov's bear, with bleached-blue eyes and a nose as sharp as any bird of prey's. Yeremenko was fifty-five, a professional soldier whose father, Y.V. Yeremenko, had been a leading *Stavka* officer before his recent retirement due to multiple sclerosis. Yeremenko had caught the eye of Leonid Brezhnev when he was serving with the 24th Samaro-Ulyanovsk Iron Division in Czechoslovakia in 1968. He had recommended several ways in which the blatant crushing of the Czechs could be made to seem more digestible to the West and his suggestions had earned him a speedy promotion to the Directorate of Strategic Deception under the famous General (later Marshal) Ogarkov.

It had been Yeremenko who had masterminded the building of a massive "antimissile complex" on the northern Moscow Ring Road—in full view of Western diplomats and journalists—in order to convince the West that the Soviet Union was far ahead of it in defensive electronics. Unnerved, the West had agreed to new disarmament talks, SALT 1, not realizing that Yeremenko's "antimissile complex" was completely empty and that later it would be used as a paint warehouse.

Yeremenko's appointment as Commander-in-Chief in Germany had come as no surprise to his fellow officers. It was the most influential posting in the whole of the Soviet Army and gave Yeremenko command of four strategic fronts, a tank army and the Baltic fleet. Yet Yeremenko shouldered his responsibilities calmly, almost icily. He was one of the few senior officers in the Soviet Army who wasn't married or even known to have a mistress. Nobody had ever seen him lose his temper; nobody had ever heard him raise his voice. His coldness was enough.

Golovanov and Yeremenko reached the doors of the strategic conference room. An armed sentry standing outside gave them a sharp salute and crashed one boot onto the floor.

Golovanov said unexpectedly as Yeremenko held the door open, "Were you ever frightened?"

"Frightened?" asked Yeremenko, impatient to get into the conference room. Eddies of tobacco smoke swirled out into the corridor.

"Yes," Golovanov persisted. "Frightened of what you were about to do, frightened of the great scale of it. We will be changing history, my friend, and geography too."

Yeremenko gave him a taut smile. "Only because we are paid to, Comrade Marshal."

"Being paid is no protection from fear."

"No," Yeremenko agreed. "But at least we will be able to die in a decent pair of trousers."

A long way behind them, Colonel Chuykov and Major Grechko came clattering along the corridor in their dazzlingly polished boots, their thick briefing folders tucked under their arms. They were so alike they could have been brothers: brown-haired, fair-skinned, with rounded faces, and dark eyebrows that met in the middle.

"I don't think I've ever seen the Bear so cheerful," Grechko remarked. He had been on Golovanov's staff for nearly six weeks now and today was the first time he had ever seen him smile.

"He's always happy when he visits Wünsdorf," said Chuykov. "General Yeremenko has a way of making his superiors happy." He made a suggestive circle with his finger and his thumb. "Semonov told me that he'd seen her once, the wonderful Inge. The Bear was dancing with her at Sternhalle, of all places. Almost six feet tall, Semonov said, a good head and shoulders taller than him. Ash-blonde hair and knockers like Eight K Eighty-fours."

Grechko grinned. 8K84s were one of the largest of Soviet missiles. "The pleasures of being a marshal," he said.

"Well, who knows?" Chuykov replied. "The way things are going, you could make marshal yourself in a few weeks' time."

"I *could* be fertilizing the plains of North Germany," said Grechko. It was the first time since the beginning of the East German exercises that either of them had acknowledged the danger of what was about to happen.

They hesitated for a moment outside the conference room and ruffled through their papers. Yeremenko was notorious for asking his superiors awkward and persnickety questions, and Golovanov would be furious if his aides were unable to provide him with every fact and every statistic, from the number of front-line missiles in the whole of East Germany to the time it would take to order up a fresh supply of bandages from the depots in Poland.

"I could do with a drink," said Grechko, swallowing dryly.

"I'll stand you one later," said Chuykov. "Yeremenko doesn't believe in liquor. He thinks it saps the virility or something."

"Sergei said that Yeremenko was—well, you know, a bit of a ballet dancer."

"Yeremenko? Not him. Just because he never got married. Actually, he *did*—he married the army. He eats, sleeps and farts army, twenty-four hours a day. If he fornicates with anything, it's a one-twenty-mm mortar."

Grechko said, "I don't know. He just looks a bit that way."

Chuykov pinched his cheek. He was being playful but it hurt. "And what do you think *you* look like with that pretty little *usi?*" He was making fun of Grechko's mustache, which Grechko had grown after seeing Stacy Keach in *The Long Riders*. Grechko was a keen Western fan; he adored J.T. Edson. It had never struck him as ironic that the popular culture he enjoyed the most was the one his army was in existence to destroy.

They pushed their way into the strategic conference room. It was high-ceilinged and smoky, and the only illumination came from rows of desk lamps so that the room had a mysteriously barbaric appearance, like the inside of Genghis Khan's battle tent, blurred by the fires of pillaged Khorezm. On the far wall there was a vast, large-scale map of Western Europe, as wide as a Cinemascope screen, covering Europe from the west coast of Ireland to the foothills of the Urals. Beneath this map there was a long mahogany desk around which Golovanov and Yeremenko were already talking to the four front commanders of the Western Strategic Direction as well as to the group commander of the Western Tank Armies and the admiral of the Baltic fleet.

Facing this desk were seven rows of smaller desks at which sat thirty or forty other high-ranking officers: Grechko recognized divisional commanders, divisional intelligence officers, commanders of the rocket services, motor-rifle troops, air-defense forces and SPETSNAZ commandos. Each of them had their deputies and their assistants and all of them were smoking furiously.

Chuykov nudged Grechko and discreetly pointed out B.Y. Serpuchov, the white-haired political commissar of the Western Strategic Direction, standing at the far end of the main desk leafing through a folder of papers and slowly and systematically wiping his nose.

Chuykov and Grechko went around and took their places a little to the left of the large chair in which Marshal Golovanov was going to sit. They were greeted by Lieutenant-Colonel Gulayev, an old friend of Chuykov's from the military academy at Frunze.

"Drop a bomb on this lot and you'd finish the war in three minutes," smiled Gulayev. He had always been known for his irreverent jokes and they had slowed down his promotion. Most of his superiors in the *Stavka* took themselves extremely seriously.

At last, after a bout of last-minute handshaking, Golovanov came and sat down and Yeremenko raised his hand for silence. There was a flurry of coughing and then Yeremenko said, "Marshal Golovanov has come to visit us today with the message from the Defense Council that we have all been preparing ourselves for. It was considered desirable for the Marshal to speak to you in person so you will understand quite clearly the historic dimensions of what is about to happen and what your part will be in the greatest advance in the course of the World Revolution since the days of Comrade Lenin."

There was healthy applause and Golovanov noticed that the political commissar was nodding in approval. Yeremenko would go far, he decided. He just hoped that he himself had the stamina and the cunning for what was to come. He stood up, pushed back his heavy chair and walked across to the huge illuminated map. All that the officers in the conference room could see of him was his stocky silhouette and a slight glint of gold on his shoulder boards.

"I have spent the past month visiting in person each of the military districts of the Soviet Union," he said hoarsely. "I have flown from Khabarovsk in the Far East to Tashkent in the south, from Sverdlovsk to Tbilisi. In fact, I arrived from Tbilisi only this morning, my last port of call before coming here. As you know, every military district has been on full-scale exercise and every front has been brought up to maximum combat strength and full preparedness. It has been my duty to satisfy myself and the Defense Council that the Soviet Army is at its peak—fully armed, fully alert and in a condition of high individual morale.

"What you may *not* know is that this tremendous military exercise has been done in conjunction with secret and vital diplomatic negotiations, which, when they are successfully concluded, will dramatically alter the military picture to our advantage. I can say nothing further about these negotiations at this stage except that I received a message in Tbilisi last night from the Supreme Commander of the Soviet Armed Services, Marshal N.K. Kutakov, who informed me that only a few minor diplomatic details remain to be resolved.

"We are on the brink of Operation *Byliny*, comrades. The very brink. We have already settled on a provisional date for its commencement and everything is in readiness. Your efforts in bringing your divisions and your battalions up to scratch will be rewarded not just by recognition from your Supreme Commander and the Defense Council, but by swift victory on all fronts."

Golovanov cleared his throat and came around to the front of the large desk, where he stood with his hands clasped behind his back, his chin belligerently lifted. Chuykov, even though he could see him only dimly from the rear, thought that he looked rather like Mussolini, and he noticed the political commissar lean over and say something confidentially to Yeremenko. The world is about to change, Chuykov thought; history is about to be turned upside down and already the predators are elbowing their way forward.

Golovanov said, with more staccato now, "Operation *Byliny* will largely follow the standard plan for the military liberation of Western Europe, which you already know well. However, the outcome of the secret diplomatic negotiations that I mentioned will render many parts of the plan unnecessary and whole sections of it irrelevant. Perhaps the most significant departure from the original plan is that no nuclear carpet will be used. The tactics will be entirely conventional. I am telling you this now so you can make appropriate adjustments in requisitioning ammunition and deploying your armored vehicles."

He returned to the map and indicated with his stubby finger five points along the border that divides West Germany from East Germany. "Five points of maximum thrust, comrades. From Czechoslovakia to Regensburg and Munich; from Czechoslovakia to Nürnberg and Stuttgart. From the southern border of the GDR through the Fulda Gap to Frankfurt and Bonn; from Berlin along the autobahn route to Hanover. And last, along the coast to Hamburg. Five concentrated points, five fingers with which our hand will thrust its way into the heart of West Germany."

One serious young intelligence officer at the back of the conference room raised his hand. Golovanov impatiently wagged a finger at him and said, "What is it, Comrade Colonel?"

"Forgive me for interrupting, Comrade Marshal," said the intelligence officer. "The time scale of the standard plan for military liberation of the West is ten days. Will this still apply to Operation *Byliny?*"

Golovanov folded his short, muscular arms melodramatically and looked around at his audience. "We have a contingency plan for eight days," he said. "However, if our diplomatic negotiations are successful, and we have every reason to believe they will be, it is possible that we will be talking in terms of five days, or even fewer. The speed of the victory, comrades, will be up to you!"

There was a moment's pause and then General Yeremenko stood up and began to applaud. All the other officers and staff in the room rose to their feet, too, and clapped for two or three minutes. Golovanov applauded them in return and shouted in his hoarse voice, *"Pobyeda! Pobyeda!* Victory!"

"Pobyeda!" shouted his commanders, clapping more loudly. *"Pobyeda!"*

At last Golovanov lifted his hands for silence.

"Comrade Lenin said that in its struggle for power, the proletariat has no weapon but organization. Today, on the eve of this historic struggle, we have much more. We have rockets and guns and ships and aircraft—everything we need to overwhelm the oppressive occupying armies of Western Europe. But it is still our determined organization that makes us invincible. It is our great army, marching forward as one man, shouting out our battle cry with one overwhelming voice!"

There was more applause. Golovanov eventually sat down and Yeremenko clasped his hand and said, "Very stirring, Comrade Marshal." But both of them somehow sensed that Golovanov had looked too old and too dictatorial, a belligerent geriatric who had suddenly lost his teeth. Shifts of influence within the upper echelons of the army could be felt by experienced officers like Golovanov and Yeremenko as if they were warnings of impending earth tremors. Even Colonel Chuykov found himself frowning and glancing across at Yeremenko and Political Commissar Serpuchov, strangely alerted to the subtle tilt in the balance of personal power.

The remainder of the morning was spent in a long and detailed briefing. Each front commander made an exhaustive report on the readiness of his troops and his armor, the balance of his land forces and his air-defense forces, the distribution of his reserves and his ordnance. There were reports from the Baltic fleet, from the SPETSNAZ diversionary forces, from the divisional tank commanders, from the rocket army. Gradually, like a massive jigsaw, a picture emerged of an unstoppable military machine: nine tank divisions, ten mechanized infantry divisions, four rocket brigades, two engineer brigades, two bridge-building brigades, an artillery division with more than seven hundred guns, all supported by the 16th Air Army with over two thousand aircraft, outnumbering the forces of NATO two to one.

Yeremenko had organized the forces of the Western Strategic Direction with such efficiency that when the day came for Operation *Byliny*, it would take only a few key military signals to reorganize the troops, apparently on nothing more threatening than their annual exercises, into an invasion force of awesome momentum and concentrated strength.

FOUR

After dinner that evening in Yeremenko's house on Falkenstrasse, when Commander Kiselev and Admiral Perminov had left, Golovanov said, "I'm very impressed, Comrade General."

"Hilda has a way with pork," replied Yeremenko, deliberately misunderstanding him. He was drinking *kvass* and eating black grapes, collecting the pips in his hand. A George Shearing record was playing quietly on the stereo.

Golovanov knocked back the last of his Pertsovka peppervodka and wiped his mouth. "I never thought I would live to see this happen, you know."

"*Byliny?* No, I don't think any of us did. But you can sense the excitement, can't you? Did you sense it today? It's almost as if everybody were getting ready to go off on holiday."

"It's hard to think of the world changing so drastically," said Golovanov. "In six days, you know, we will alter the map more than Hitler did in six years."

Yeremenko spat out more pips. "That's what we were trained for, after all. You can't build an army like ours and then expect it to sit on its backside doing nothing. An army has to fight. You can't deny any organization its basic function. Would you start a ballet company and train it to perfection and then forbid it to dance in public?"

"Some ballet company," grunted Golovanov in amusement.

They sat in silence for a while, listening to the music. Golovanov felt uncomfortable in Yeremenko's house. It was modern but in a heavy, Germanic way. There were big square armchairs and big square tables and big square abstract paintings on the walls, in black and orange. Golovanov hated orange and he hated black. There were no plants in the house, no ornaments, none of the feminine touches that Golovanov enjoyed around his own flat in Moscow and in his *dacha* at Zhiguli, for all that most of his own furniture was massive and traditional. In Yeremenko's house he felt as if he were waiting to go somewhere else, as if it were an airport or a doctor's waiting room. It was a key to Yeremenko's state of mind, just like his cold, stilted, army-textbook conversation.

Yeremenko said, "More vodka?"

Golovanov lifted his finger and thumb to show that he wanted only a little. "I don't want to go around to Herbertstrasse rolling drunk."

Yeremenko poured him another and then they raised their glasses. *"Za vahsheh zdahrovyeh!"*

Yeremenko didn't sit down but prowled around the room, his fingers drumming on the backs of the chairs, on the tables, on the walls.

"Byliny," remarked Golovanov. "I wonder who thought of that." *Byliny* were the great historical cycles of songs that characterized early Russian folk culture. *"Byliny* makes the liberation sound almost sentimental."

"Somebody seems to have a sentimental turn of mind," said Yeremenko.

"Oh, yes?" asked Golovanov. He sensed that Yeremenko was preparing to get something off his chest that had been disturbing him all day. "Is it me? Do you think *I'm* sentimental? I assure you I'm not. But you can always try me, Comrade. Life is competitive, after all."

"I'd just like to know who decided that we shouldn't go nuclear," said Yeremenko. "We could clear Germany in a single morning if we used nuclear warheads. You know that as well as I do. Instead, I'm going to have to risk scores of tanks, hundreds of guns and use up tons of ordnance and fuel."

Golovanov squinted at Yeremenko through his vodka glass.

Yeremenko's image was peculiarly distorted, like a pale-faced fish swimming around in a bowl. Golovanov decided he had probably drunk too much already. Curse Yeremenko for being a teetotaler. But he managed to slap his thigh and say with great geniality, "If our diplomatic negotiations go well, we won't have any need of nuclear weapons."

"What about the ax theory?" Yeremenko asked. The ax theory was fundamental to Soviet military thinking. It simply propounded that if you happen to be holding an ax, you shouldn't bother to punch your enemy on the nose with your fist; you should hit him with your ax straightaway. In other words, if you have nuclear weapons, use them, and quickly.

"The ax theory is all very well as far as it goes," said Golovanov, still beaming. "But of course the trouble with nuclear weapons is that they are not axes. They have a tendency to linger and to do as much damage to those who have dropped them as to those upon whom they were dropped. My instructions are that if we can possibly avoid using them . . . well, we're not to, and that's all there is to it."

"I can't imagine how any diplomatic negotiations can alter the strategic situation so dramatically," said Yeremenko, displeased.

"No, well, I don't expect you can," Golovanov replied. "But, Comrade General, I assure you that the Supreme Commander is highly optimistic." He thought to himself: you should drink a few grams of vodka every now and then, Comrade Yeremenko. Kvass never put fire in anyone's belly.

"Well, I suppose I'm just keyed up," said Yeremenko. "I don't want anything to go wrong. My father was at Kharkov. He used to have nightmares about it, the rockets shrieking through the streets."

Golovanov said companionably, "You can't base a strategy on your father's nightmares. Our task is to liberate Europe, not destroy it."

Yeremenko said nothing. At the moment there was nothing he could say. Golovanov was the First Deputy. Until Operation *Byliny* began to move, the best that Yeremenko could hope for was that Golovanov would be too demanding, too arrogant, too old-fashioned, and that eventually he would arouse Kutakov's displeasure.

There was a subdued ring at the door. Yeremenko said, "That must be Major Poplavskiy. Do you want another small one before you go?"

"No, no," said Golovanov, shaking his head. "You have been far too hospitable already."

He eased himself out of his armchair and stood up. His uniform jacket was rucked up like a ballet skirt. "You have achieved wonders here in Germany," he said. "I shall make a special point of mentioning to the Supreme Commander how efficient you have been."

Yeremenko escorted him to the door. Major Poplavskiy had been let in by Yeremenko's housemaid Hilda and now stood uncomfortably in a corner under a splashy turquoise-green abstract painting that reminded Golovanov of seasickness.

At the door Golovanov briefly hugged Yeremenko and said, "Remember, my friend, these are momentous days. This may well be the last great political upheaval in the world for the next hundred years, the last great task."

"These diplomatic negotiations . . ." said Yeremenko.

Golovanov gave him a broad smile. "As soon as *I* know, Comrade, *you* shall know! Now, sleep well."

"You too," said Yeremenko in a tone so flat that Golovanov couldn't tell if he was being sarcastic or not.

Inge Schültz lived on the west side of Wünsdorf in a small, exclusive estate of red-roofed private houses, most of which were occupied by East German civilians employed in important jobs with the GSFG headquarters: the privileged middle class in a so-called classless society. There were new Volvos and Mercedes parked outside, an occasional Skoda, no Ladas. Major Poplavskiy drove the black Volvo with an engaging lack of expertise, bumping the rear wheel over the curb whenever he turned a sharp corner and parking almost in the middle of the road when they eventually arrived at 17 Herbertstrasse. Major Poplavskiy had been chosen for his discretion rather than his driving ability.

"Tomorrow morning, Marshal?" asked Poplavskiy hesitantly. "Seven o'clock perhaps?"

"Six," Golovanov told him and tugged on his gloves.

He walked up the stepping-stone path until he reached the

varnished front door with its yellow hammered-glass window. From inside, he could hear the sound of rock music, he didn't have any idea of what. His idea of music was Tchaikovsky and *chastushki,* ribald four-line folk songs. Good hearty stuff you could stamp your feet to. He rang the doorbell, although he could see that Inge had already heard him.

Inge opened the door and stood silhouetted by the light in the hallway. Chuykov's description of her had been accurate but not evocative. Whenever he set eyes on her, Golovanov's breath was biffed out of his lungs and he found himself unable to speak. What could you say, in any case, about a woman like Inge? He stepped into the hallway, flapped his hat around and nodded, and that was all he could manage.

She smiled, the legendary Inge, and walked ahead of him into the sitting room. The gray-velvet curtains were drawn tight, the white carpet was immaculately smooth, the gray-leather furniture shone with polish. It looked as if professional cleaners had been here, and they probably had. There was a glass room divider on which were dozens of glass statuettes, Lalique and Wärff and Daum, crystal fishes and dancing ballerinas and purple vases.

Inge turned and stood in the center of the room, her hips cocked, and smiled at Golovanov with that smile that always drove him mad: taunting, provocative, mysterious. He was not a child. He knew that she was either employed by the KGB or that she reported to them every time he visited her. If the Politburo had wanted to destroy him on moral grounds, they could have done so years ago. But Inge, he knew, was one of his continuing rewards for being conservative and loyal, and for being powerful enough to dominate executive officers as skillful and political as Yeremenko.

Inge was twenty-eight or twenty-nine years old; she had never told him her exact age. She was tall, broad-shouldered, white-skinned, with enormous Olympian breasts and a pinched-in waist. Her legs sometimes looked to Golovanov as if they were longer than he was tall: lean and shapely, with a triangular space between her thighs through which he could have passed a fifty-gram glass of vodka. It was her face that always transfixed him though. Her clear-cut Germanic chin; her straight, thin nose; her pale lips that rose in a bloodless bow shape. Those translucent gray eyes that stared at him and made his prostate gland tingle with fear and arousal. That white, white hair, immaculately braided around her forehead. She looked as if she had stepped out of a Wagnerian opera.

She was everything that aroused him and everything that unnerved him. Strong, erotic, passionate, dominating. He had never known a woman like her. She made his skin burn with a sexual hunger like napalm. He had to blot out of his mind the thought that she probably had sex with scores of other men, that to her he was just another "uncle."

This evening she was wearing a black-satin evening suit with high, padded shoulders and a deep décolleté that exposed her startlingly white cleavage. Her calf-length skirt clung to her long legs, and he could see that she was wearing black fishnet stockings and black open-toed shoes with high, stiletto heels.

"Well, Inge," Golovanov swallowed, tugging down his jacket. "You look as eatable as always." His German wasn't very good; they usually spoke to each other in a ragbag of Russian, German, Swedish and English.

"Comrade Marshal," she smiled. She stayed where she was in the center of the room. "Why don't you come and kiss me?"

Golovanov lifted his hat, hesitated, then tossed it onto one of the chairs. He walked up to Inge, cautiously put his arms around her slippery black-satin body and lifted his face to kiss her. Their mouths barely touched but then she kissed him again and again—his forehead, his cheeks, his eyes—and her thin nostrils flared with something that might have been desire, or might not.

"I didn't expect you back so soon," she said. "I heard that you had gone east to Khabarovsk."

"I've been everywhere, traveling. You know what chores they give us old men to do: inspecting, saluting, looking into pots of *kasha*."

"Something's happening," she said without preamble. "There are so many officers here this month, so many more than usual."

"Annual maneuvers, that's all. They haven't been a bother to you, have they?"

Inge kissed his forehead absentmindedly. Her perfume was musky and intense, and Golovanov could feel the body heat radiating from her milk-white cleavage. "Maybe a drink," he suggested. He walked across the room, loosening his necktie. "What's this music? More decadence, I expect?"

"Oh," she said. "*Frankie Goes to Hollywood.*"

"That's the name of the pop group?"

Inge went to the glass shelves and took the stopper out of a pear-shaped glass decanter. "*Wyborowa?*"

"Anything." Golovanov unbuttoned his jacket and eased himself out of it. In his khaki shirt, the sheer squat bulk of his body was even more obvious. He was proud that he didn't have to wear a corset. He knew at least two other marshals of the Soviet Union who did, including Kutakov. He sat down on the gray-leather sofa and rubbed the palm of his hand over its shiny surface. "You haven't heard anything to make you worried?" he asked her.

She brought him his drink and knelt on the floor beside him, resting her thin, sharp elbow on his knee. Her gray eyes stared into him unsettlingly. "Something's happening," she said. "I know it. All you Russians have been excited, like horses in heat."

"Nothing," he said, shaking his head. He raised his glass and said, "*Za vasheh zdahrovyeh e blagapaluch'yeh!*"

Inge ran her long fingers over the top of his head, lifting his thin, swept-back silver hair. "You wouldn't lie to me, would you?"

"About what? There is nothing to lie about. We are having our summer exercises, that's all. Very tedious it is too. One division here, one division there. Tanks, trucks, BMPs. Come on, my dear, I didn't come here to talk about the army."

Inge thought for a moment, then smiled slowly and said, "No. Of course you didn't. Do you want me to dance for you?"

Golovanov lifted his drink again and nodded. "A dance, why not?" But as she stood up and turned away from him, he felt a twinge of suspicion and concern. Had she really sensed that something was up? She couldn't be telling the truth when she said that "all you Russians have been excited." Only those who had attended this morning's meeting in the strategic conference room had been told of Operation *Byliny:* thirty-one senior officers with impeccable security clearance. A woman like Inge should be aware of nothing at all unusual, only of the comings and goings of the officers and staff who attended every summer exercise. She was stunning to look at, she was wily, but she was only a whore.

Perhaps her questions had something to do with her connections with the KGB. Perhaps the KGB was testing him. He sipped his vodka and watched her as she put on another record, and for the first time since the last days of Khrushchev, he felt insecure.

She put on Culture Club's latest. To Golovanov's ear, the music was nothing more than dissonant jangling, with those strange, whining voices that Western singers always seemed to adopt. But the way in which Inge danced made the music hypnotic and peculiarly compelling.

To begin with, she walked up and down the room in front of him, her hips and shoulders moving in time to the music in that particularly arrogant fashion-model stride that had become popular in Paris haute couture. Then she turned and as she turned, she unbuttoned the front of her black-satin jacket and swung it open to bare one breast. Big, creamy-skinned, with a wide, pale nipple and mobile with its own weight. Golovanov watched her in fascination as she strode down the room again, moving rhythmically, dancing like a sophisticated animal, and then she turned again and this time bared both breasts, enormous and rounded, and her flat, white stomach.

Golovanov was breathing heavily. Already his marshal's trousers were feeling crowded. He sipped more vodka and wiped his mouth with the back of his hand.

Inge slowed down now, dancing on the off beat. Expressionlessly she slipped off her black-satin jacket and let it slide to the floor. Then she loosened the sash of her skirt and turned her back on Golovanov as she gradually eased the garment down over her hips.

Golovanov stared at her, mesmerized. The muscles in her long back moved, her hips rotated with sensual insistence. She edged the skirt farther and farther down, baring her wide, white bottom, and at last let it drop to the floor. She was now wearing nothing but her black fishnet stockings and high-heeled shoes. She bent over with her back to Golovanov to untangle her skirt from her heel and as she did so, he glimpsed between her thighs the pouting lips of her vulva.

She danced with her back to him for a minute or two longer, teasing him. Her breasts were so large that he could see the half-moon curve of them on either side of her back. He began to unbutton his shirt in quick, jerky movements, baring a brown, deep-set chest marked by a crucifix of thick white hair.

"Inge," he said thickly.

She turned around, still dancing, her chin raised, her eyes dispassionate. Her breasts bounced and flowed in time to the music; her nipples had risen, pale and unusually long. She was like a goddess poured out of milk and moonlight, and Golovanov found that again he was holding his breath. Her thighs stirred with each beat from the drums; her hips swayed with that unending erotic demand. Her pubis was shaved bare except for a small plume of ash-blonde hair that rose just above her clitoris like a white flame. Her lips were neat and tight but glistened with the first suggestion that she was aroused.

Singing softly to herself, she came over and unfastened Golovanov's shoes, then drew off his socks and at last helped him to lift himself out of his trousers. His body was scarred and chunky, bunches of muscles and tight sinew. From between the hardened curves of his thighs, his erection rose gnarled and crimson, a great Russian tree.

Inge climbed onto the sofa and stood astride him while he sat there looking up at her. Then gradually she lowered her hips until her vulva was only two or three inches from his face. She opened her legs a little farther and the pink, sticky inner labia parted with the faintest of fluid clicks, revealing the dark-red moistness within.

"Inge . . ." he said. "You know I can never resist you. You know I never shall."

He reached forward, his tongue protruding, but she swayed back a little so that he missed her. He lunged again but still she swayed back.

"Will you do anything for me?" she asked.

He stared at her vagina and tensely licked his lips. "You know I will. I've already brought you a present . . . a necklace from Tbilisi. You know you can have anything you want. Money, clothes, liquor. I can arrange anything."

She leaned forward again so she was within reach. Slowly, with infinite relish, his eyes closed, Golovanov began to lap with his tongue at her clitoris, now and again allowing his tongue to run down and slip into the warm sweetness of her vagina. She tasted like *shampanskoye*.

Now Inge raised first one leg over the back of the sofa, then the other, sitting astride Golovanov's face so that his head was forced back onto the gray-leather cushion. Her eyes half-closed, crooning quietly to herself, she rotated her hips so that Golovanov's tongue massaged her all around her vulva. She anointed his face all over, his forehead, his eyelashes, his cheeks, his nose, his mouth; and then at last her breathing began to quicken. Her hips began to shudder; her huge breasts shook. She stayed still for a frozen moment while her fluids ran down Golovanov's chin. Then athletically she raised herself up off the back of the sofa and walked around until she was kneeling in front of the marshal, her expression as erotic and calculating as ever.

"You are a man of great passion, Marshal. Now I would like to return your compliment."

Golovanov stared back at her. She clasped his erection in a long-fingered hand and slowly and tantalizingly stroked it up and down.

"If the devil was ever white, as white as an angel, then it must be you," breathed Golovanov. He knew he was talking nonsense, the result of too much vodka, but Inge made his brain flare up.

Slowly, slowly, Inge massaged him. Once she leaned forward on her haunches as if she were going to take him into her mouth but she drew back again.

"You are afraid to speak to me, aren't you?" she said. "Just in case the house has ears. Just in case I will pass on what you say to the KGB."

Golovanov said nothing but frowned at her. She stroked his erection even more slowly.

"Well," she said, "it is true. I am paid by the KGB to

pass on whatever you say. I have a tape recorder in the bedroom, and I have passed on everything you have ever said to me when we were making love, every single grunt, every single groan. They probably have a great time listening to the great Marshal T.K. Golovanov having a finger stuck up his backside!''

Golovanov remained unmoved, masklike and calm, his eyes slitted. ''I suspected that this would be so. I would do the same myself if I were you. I am not a fool, Inge. You have not surprised me.''

Inge stopped rubbing him. ''I have to ask you if there is going to be war,'' she said.

Golovanov lifted an eyebrow. ''If you work for the KGB as you say you do, you know I cannot possibly give you any classified military information. I have never done so in the past; I cannot start now.''

''Timofey,'' she whispered, an urgent expression in her voice that he had never heard before. ''I work for the KGB and that means I have to keep my ears and my eyes always open. I am like an animal that has to protect itself. I know that something is happening. These are not your usual summer maneuvers. And what are you doing here, back so quickly? When General Yeremenko's man told me you were coming back, that confirmed my fears at once.'' She used the Swedish word for fear, *nervositet*.

Golovanov took a deep breath. ''Whatever happens, Inge, you yourself have no need to be alarmed.''

''It's soon, isn't it?'' she urged him.

''Inge,'' he protested, both at her persistent questioning and at the teasing stroking of his penis.

She let go of him, rose and sat on the sofa beside him and grasped his shoulders. Her nails were like black-painted claws. ''Timofey,'' she said, ''you are the most influential of all the officers I know, the most important. Please help me.''

''But what do you want? I can't help you if I don't know what you want. Listen, my dear, I have always said anything, anything at all.''

She lowered her head. He found himself looking at her severe blonde parting, her tightly wound braids and the large, pale curves of her breasts.

"I want to go to America," she said. She looked up at him again and those gray eyes were intense. "Timofey, I beg you, before the war begins. After that, there will be no chance. I beg you to help me get away."

Golovanov looked down at himself. His reddened erection was gradually diminishing. After a while it fell over sideways and curled up.

"Well," he said grumpily. "Look at what you've done now."

FIVE

The phone rang somewhere on the galaxy of Ursa Major. Light-years away, echoing and far. Charles Krogh turned over in space and time and tried to make himself believe that he hadn't heard it, that it didn't exist, that everything was darkness and silence and celestial peace.

The phone continued to ring. It was getting nearer too, and louder, traveling through the eons at unimaginable speed. Suddenly it materialized right beside his bed, on his bedside table, and he lashed out at it so that it crashed to the floor along with two empty wine glasses, an ashtray crowded with cigarette stubs and a paperback copy of Huysman's *Against Nature*—about "an unbalanced, neurotic woman, who loved to have her nipples macerated in scent." He sniffed, roared, shouted and sat up in bed, his face as crumpled as the Danish duvet.

"Agneta! Tager du da aldrig den forbandede telefon?"

A woman's voice retorted sharply from the kitchen, *"Den kan du selv svare."*

On the floor, the telephone was saying, tiny and plaintive, "Hello? Hello?"

"Oh, shit," said Charles and buried his face in the pillow.

"Hello?" said the phone. "Mr. Charles Krogh?"

At last Charles climbed out of bed, treading barefoot through

50

the scattered cigarette stubs, and picked up the receiver. "Do you know what time it is?" he demanded.

"Ten after ten," replied the voice on the other end. A man's voice, Danish, but a good English speaker.

"That's *dawn*," Charles complained. He scratched his shoulder blades and then ran his hand through his unkempt gray hair so it stuck up wildly. "Jesus, Agneta, what are you doing with that blender? Grinding up the cat?"

"Making you some fresh orange juice, you ill-tempered bastard," Agneta called back.

"Well, put some schnapps in it," Charles shouted. "If I can't be sober, I might as well stay drunk."

Agneta came to the door of the bedroom. She was blonde, small, pixie-faced, but the smudges under her eyes betrayed her age and her experience. She was wearing one of Charles' shirts, a pale-green Van Heusen, and nothing else. She said, "Talk to him, whoever it is. Who is it?"

Charles had temporarily forgotten that he was on the phone. He growled, "Hello? Yes? I'm supposed to ask who you are. Not that *I* give a shit."

"You are Mr. Charles Krogh?"

"That's me," replied Charles less irascibly. Light and order were gradually beginning to penetrate his brain. "Who wants to know?"

"My name is Christian Skovgaard, Mr. Krogh. I have a message for you from Jeppe Rifbjerg. He says he cannot call you direct because of particular circumstances but he would like you to meet him at Fiskehusets at twelve."

Charles noisily cleared his throat. "Did he say what he wanted?"

"He says he will explain everything later."

"Did he say who's paying for lunch?"

Christian Skovgaard, whoever he was, put down the phone. Charles stared at the receiver for a moment and then tossed it onto the tousled bed. He didn't want to take any more calls until his head had cleared, particularly any more calls as mysterious as that. He stood up, scratching himself, and shambled through to the kitchen. Agneta was buttering wholewheat bread for him and arranging slices of smoked ham on it. Charles came around the counter and kissed her noisily on the ear. "I don't deserve you, you know," he told her. "Where's that orange juice?"

Agneta had poured the juice into a tall glass and set it on the counter. Sniffing, Charles opened the large Amana icebox and took a bottle of schnapps out of the freezer. He poured a hefty measure of schnapps into the orange juice and a smaller measure into a shot glass.

"I didn't do anything crazy last night, did I?" he asked Agneta. They had been to a party thrown by Danny Neilson, one of Copenhagen's most influential gangsters. Neilson's contraband automobile business—mainly in brand-new luxury Volvos and Saab Turbos, all unregistered—had made him a millionaire at the age of thirty-one. The party had been held on his luxurious private yacht, which had been moored for the occasion in the Christianshavn Canal. Charles remembered drinking more schnapps than was good for his equilibrium, or his soul, or the future of mankind.

Agneta said matter-of-factly, "You told the superintendent of police that his wife reminded you of a porcupine. Apart from that, nothing much."

"Not too bad, then," said Charles, hoisting himself onto a stool. The breakfast counter was directly below a long skylight, with plants hanging all around; on the walls of the white-and-beige kitchen there were glazed clay figures of trolls and mermaids. The decor was plain, clean and modern. Nobody who walked into this kitchen would have guessed that an untidy and obstreperous middle-aged American lived here. The style was entirely Scandinavian.

"He can't blame me," said Charles, stirring his orange juice with the handle of his fork.

"Who can't blame you? And for what?"

"The superintendent of police. For saying that his wife looks like a porcupine. She does. It's that spiky hair and that fat little tummy."

"You should learn to be polite," Agneta admonished him.

Charles nodded, swallowed orange juice and schnapps, coughed and then nodded again. "You're right, of course. Even my course director at Langley told me that I should learn to be polite. 'Mr. Krogh,' he said, 'an intelligence agent is not a high-profile character.' I guess in the end that's why they never promoted me, and why they retired me. Imagine that, retired from the CIA. And my father was afraid they'd suck me in for all eternity. Some eternity. Some suck.''

Agneta sat down and watched him eat his breakfast. She liked to watch him eat; he looked vulnerable then, like a small boy. Scruffy-haired, bulbous-nosed, irresistibly ugly. She knew just how much strength he had though. His character was like flexible steel: often bending but never breaking. He had worked for the CIA in Denmark for fifteen years before his "retirement," and she knew that he was responsible for catching and killing two Soviet spies who had been infiltrating the Danish military base at Århus in 1976. There had been an international furor about it: two Russians found on the island of Tunø with their heads beaten in. One evening when he was drunk, Charles had said to Agneta, "Remember that Tunø business? Well, you want to know what I'm made of? They didn't cry out, either of them. They just looked at me. Think about it.''

He hadn't mentioned it again; he may not even have remembered the following morning what he had said. But Agneta knew that he had killed those men, sledgehammered them to death like culled seals. She also realized that there had probably been many more. In spite of the peace, the war went on silently, violently, like men struggling in the dark.

Charles, at fifty-two, had felt too old, too displaced, to return to the United States. Also, he was still bitter about having been taken off the active list so early. He was good, he knew he was. His knowledge of Soviet agents and their techniques was encyclopedic, more comprehensive and more interpretive than any computer's memory bank. He had known many of them personally, just as they had known him. He used to have lunch once a month with Ivan Yerikalin, head of the KGB in Copenhagen. They had eaten at the Café Victor on Ny Østergade, indulging themselves at the expense of their respective countries in caviar and smoked salmon, all the time probing and prodding each other with provocative questions. Charles missed those lunches. He also missed Yerikalin, who had been recalled to Moscow without warning. Shot probably.

After his retirement, Charles had traveled around Scandinavia but eventually had returned to Copenhagen simply because he felt he belonged there. There was something about its steep orange rooftops, its green copper spires, the way it lay stretched out so flat in summer, like a map, with its dark-blue canals and interlacing bridges, Langebro and Knippelsbro and Dronning Louises Bro; the way it closed in upon itself in winter when the skies were black and overwhelming and furious with snow.

He had made his home on Larsbjørnstrade in the Latin Quarter, at the top of a narrow, yellow-washed building that smelled of cheese and laundry. From his bedroom window he had a view of Studiestrade and Vor Frue Kirke, the Church of Our Lady. He had gathered around him as friends all those people he had known during his CIA days: gangsters and diplomats and prostitutes and policemen; and after he had lived there for four months, Agneta had moved in with him. She was thirty-seven years old, a former nightclub dancer, sex-show artiste and casual prostitute. Their friendship had grown into a loving and comfortable relationship; plenty of wine, plenty of food, plenty of laughter, sex when they felt like it and no questions asked about the past, the present or the future. He never asked Agneta if she loved him; if he did, she might have had to answer. He knew that he loved her. God Almighty, he would have died for her. But what a strange death that would be for his father's son, the boy who had grown up over a dry-cleaning store in Minneapolis, the lanky youth who had joined the navy and eventually found himself inducted into the intelligence services and then into the CIA.

He arrived at Fiskehusets ten minutes late. He had showered and his untidy gray hair was still wet. He wore a gray summer suit, a yellow shirt and an expensive silk tie he had bought on a day trip to Oslo. Fiskehusets was one of the more expensive fish restaurants on Gammel Strand, overlooking the canal; personally Charles preferred Krogs. But Jeppe was there waiting for him at one of the tables at the back, talking to the manager, Arne Larssen. Charles shook Arne's hand, then Jeppe's and said to Arne, "What's good today? The plaice?"

"If Mr. Rifbjerg's paying, the turbot," smiled Arne.

Charles sat down. Jeppe said, "You look as if you swam here."

"Oh." Charles raked his wet hair with his fingers. "I took a shower. It was either that or a bath, and I couldn't stand the idea of immersing myself in hot water."

"Bad head?"

"I went to Neilson's birthday party last night. The liquor flowed like liquor."

Jeppe beckoned to the waiter and said, "Bring this man a Carlsberg Special Brew, please."

"Do I look that bad?" asked Charles.

Jeppe smiled and laced his fingers together. Charles recognized that gesture. It meant that Jeppe had something complicated to say; either that or he wanted to ask a favor, or both.

Jeppe was an agent for the Danish Intelligence Service: thin-faced, blond-mustached, agitated. A brilliant agent, intuitive but methodical. A man who lived on his nerves but was never nervous. Through a combination of inspired guesses and methodical calculation, he had broken two Soviet spy cells in Denmark and had subsequently arrested fifteen major dealers who were using Copenhagen as a warehouse for American electronics hardware, which they were intending to sell to the Russians in exchange for gold and drugs.

Partly because of his success, however, and partly because of his unorthodox methods, Jeppe was not a popular figure in the intelligence service; his superiors thought he was too idiosyncratic and his subordinates thought he was too smart.

Charles lit a cigarette and blew out smoke. "Who's Christian Skovgaard when he's at home?"

Jeppe smiled. "He's my deputy. A policeman once. He used to be stationed at Store Kongensgade. He seems like a quiet chap until you get to know him. Then—the stories he can tell you!"

"All policemen have stories," said Charles. The waiter brought him his Special Brew and set it down in front of him. "Agents too."

"Well, that's why you're here," said Jeppe. "I want a story out of you."

Charles cleared his throat. "Do I owe you any favors? I mean, what's the score? Or are we equal and starting again from scratch?"

Jeppe rearranged his stainless-steel cutlery and said in a low voice, "A man was killed the day before yesterday in a country church in Jutland. St. Jorgens Church at Hvidsten, just a few miles north of Randers."

"What do you know about him?" asked Charles, swallowing the cold, sweet beer and grimacing.

"Not much except that his name was Nicholas Reed and that he was an American. He was working for Klarlund and Christensen, architects; they have an office opposite the station on Vesterbrogade. Something to do with a new retirement village they're designing, outside Roskilde. Apparently Reed had had experience with retirement communities in the United States and that's why they brought him over."

Charles said, "What was he doing in Hvidsten?"

"Well, it seems that he'd been living there since about the end of February, working at a small *kro*. He was last seen at Klarlund and Christensen on February ninth. He came in to work as usual that day; everything seemed to be fine, but the next day he didn't show up. That was the last they saw of him. They tried to contact his family and his business partners in the United States; no luck. They informed the police and the *Tilysnet med udlaendinge*, but there wasn't much else they could do."

Charles said nothing but drank more beer and waited for Jeppe to continue. At that moment Arne Larssen came up and said, "You've decided?"

"The eel," said Charles.

Jeppe thought for a while and then said, "The sole will do for me, Arne. Plain-grilled, maybe a little lemon."

Jeppe waited for a second or two, stroking his blond mustache. Then he said, "The police at Randers were obliged to send me a report about Reed's murder. It's part of normal procedure whenever a foreign national comes to grief, especially a Russian or an American. There may be intelligence connotations, however innocent or accidental the death may seem, and Reed's was a particularly nasty murder, particularly strange. But on the whole, when I checked, he seemed legitimate. Nothing more than an ordinary American architect working in Denmark on an ordinary commercial contract. No intelligence background as far as I could tell. No trace of 'Nicholas Reed' on any of our computers. I was on the point of filing the information away and forgetting about it.''

''But?'' asked Charles.

''But,'' Jeppe echoed, ''I received that morning a visit from a gentleman who had extremely high-powered credentials from the Defense Ministry. He gave me no explanation but said simply that I was to proceed no further with my investigations into the Reed murder.''

''That was all?'' said Charles.

Jeppe nodded. ''I asked him why. After all, I have the highest security clearance, I should be entitled to know. But he refused. He said the matter was over and I was to forget that I had ever heard the name Nicholas Reed.''

The waiter brought fresh rolls wrapped in napkins. Charles broke one of them open with his thumbs and tore it to pieces, which he ate without butter. In Denmark, eating bread without butter was a small heresy Charles enjoyed. Likewise, he refused to eat Hereford *beefstouw*. It was rather like refusing to eat rice in India, or spaghetti in Italy.

''Tell me how Reed died,'' he said. ''Were there any clues, any witnesses?''

Jeppe said, ''It appears that he was working in the kitchen of the Hvidsten Inn at lunchtime on Tuesday when three men turned up outside in a gray Mercedes-Benz. One of the girls who works at the inn said Reed seemed to be very agitated and that he ran out of the building as quickly as possible. That was the last anyone saw of him until he turned up at St. Jorgen's Church about a mile away. There was a christening taking place there and so the police were able to interview several of the guests, and the pastor too. From what they say, Reed came and sat in the church as if he were seeking sanctuary. Then two men followed him in and sat down on either side of him. After a few minutes they left; it was only later that the pastor found out what they had done. They had cut Reed in half, can you believe that?—leaving his legs sitting where they were and his torso lying sideways on the pew. Yes, my friend—somehow, in silence, in a church, they had managed to cut him in half and leave without anybody realizing what it was they had done.''

Charles sat back, chewing a crust of bread. "Did you get a description?''

"Not a clear one. Nobody really took much notice of them; they were all too busy with the christening.''

"Was one of them very tall with a badly scarred face?''

Jeppe looked up. "I hope you don't know what this business is all about, my friend.''

Charles said, "Our medical-examination department at Langley had a name for it. Hemicorporectomy. That means cutting somebody in half. It's a trademark. Some killers are arrogant enough to have trademarks. Carlos, he was one. Wolper, he was another, always shot his targets in the ear; in one ear, out the other. But cutting people in half, that's something different. I mean, it may be a blind. It's so distinctive, it could be a deliberate attempt to put you off the scent.''

"But you are right about the scarred man. Burned, one of the witnesses said, as if in a terrible fire.''

"I think I'll have another beer,'' said Charles.

Jeppe beckoned to the waiter. "One more Special Brew, please. And bring me a schnapps.'' Then he turned back to Charles and said, "You know this man, then? This killer?''

"As I say, it may be a blind. All our information was that he was dead. Killed in Afghanistan, so we were led to believe, when he was trying to take out one of the rebel leaders at Qu'al-eh ya Saber. You should be able to pull a file on him yourself if you talk to Monson nicely enough.''

Jeppe said, "I'm not sure I want to alert Monson yet.''

"Hmh?'' asked Charles, sucking in smoke.

"Well,'' said Jeppe, "after the visit I received from the gentleman from the Defense Ministry, I asked one of the girls I know at Christiansborg to do a little digging for me. She talked to one of Nyborg's secretaries and the indications seem to be that the Defense Ministry was instructed to put a lid on what happened to Reed by no less an authority than the State Department in Washington, highest level.''

Charles looked at Jeppe for a long while without saying anything, his eyes narrowed thoughtfully.

Jeppe said, "I've had orders before to cancel investigations

for what were obviously political reasons. But never before
have I received a personal visit from a deputy minister such
as I did this week. And never before has it been apparent that
the cancellation came not from the Danish government, but
from abroad. It is very unusual, my friend. Very unsettling.''

"And that's why you don't want to ask Monson?''

"Well, of course. If my superiors were to discover that I
was continuing to look into this affair—well, the least I
would lose would be my job.''

The waiter brought their drinks and then Arne Larssen
personally brought their fish: eel stewed in white wine, decorated with dill, and a plain-grilled sole. Fragrant and fresh,
both of them.

"Arne, you're a genius,'' said Charles. "The way you
treat fish, I would have thought you had a mermaid in your
ancestry somewhere.''

They started to eat. Fiskehusets was crowded now, and the
sunlight filtered in through the streaked glass windows, tumbling through the aromatic steam of turbot and plaice, herring
and sole.

Charles said, "Cutting people in half, that was the trademark of a Soviet assassin who rejoiced in the code name of
Krov' iz Nosu, which literally means 'Nose Bleed.' Appropriate under the circumstances, don't you think? His real name
was Aleksei Novikov and he was a shock worker at Kuibyshev
during the fifties, one of the *udarniki*. As far as we know, he
was working in a smelting plant when he was accidentally
splashed with molten iron ore.''

Jeppe's fork remained poised above his fish. Charles, with
his mouth full, said, "Go ahead. Don't let a little *Krov' iz
Nosu* spoil your lunch.''

He swallowed and then said, "The story goes that Novikov
was so severely burned he almost died. His face was burned
away, his hands, most of the skin on his chest, his thighs. But
somehow he managed to survive. He was incredibly powerful, incredibly fit. Something like six feet four. He went
through years of skin grafts; then he started a physical-therapy
program that would have killed anybody else: weight lifting,
running up and down mountains of slag. He ended up so
powerful that the army began to take an interest in him as a

special kind of killer. He was trained in the SPETSNAZ for three years, then appropriated by SMERSH for military counterintelligence work. I believe he was responsible for twenty-two hits during the late sixties, early seventies. But most of his work was inside the Soviet Union, dealing with traitors in the Soviet Army and army generals who were found to be on the take. That's why he developed that rather flamboyant style of wasting people, *pour encourager les autres*. Marshal Zhukov once called him 'the conscience of the army.' Quite a conscience, huh? Come on, eat your fish.''

Jeppe said, ''I don't think I'm hungry.''

''Have another drink, then.''

''I don't know, Charles, this worries me,'' said Jeppe. ''Why should a killer like—what did you call him? *Krov' iz Nosu?*—why should a killer like that be called in to Denmark to deal with a man like Nicholas Reed? Usually if the Soviets want to take out one of your agents, they do it discreetly. No fuss, no bother. But this man is grandstanding.''

Charles sucked dill weed off his front teeth. ''You sound more American by the minute,'' he remarked. ''Watch less TV. Stop hanging around with American reprobates like me. And for Christ's sake, eat your fish or I'll eat it for you. This eel is heaven on a plate.''

''But *why?*'' Jeppe nagged.

Charles shrugged. ''How should I know? Maybe they're trying to warn off some of Reed's friends, whoever they may be. More likely they're putting on a show for the U.S. Intelligence Services. You know what the Soviets are like; they think the Nordic countries are *their* territory. Maybe Reed stuck his nose in a little too far. I mean, if the State Department wanted to put a lid on his killing, you can guarantee that he was a U.S. agent. Maybe he got into something too sensitive for both sides. It happens, you know.''

Jeppe picked at his sole for a moment, then laid his fork down. Charles immediately reached over and lifted the whole fish off his plate, set it down on his own and began to bone it with the dexterity of the very hungry. ''You'll regret this,'' he told Jeppe. ''Tonight when you start feeling ravenous, you'll think about this fish and regret it. In fact, you'll probably hate me forever for having eaten it.''

"Charles," said Jeppe, ignoring this banter, "I want you to do me a favor."

"Official or unofficial?"

"Just between you and me."

"What makes you so eager to carry this business any further? Don't you know when you've been warned off? If they catch me at it, they'll know straightaway who sent me. Everybody from San Francisco to Novosibirsk knows that you and I are drinking partners. Which senior Danish intelligence officer was stopped by the Politi with which retired CIA agent singing 'When Irish Eyes Are Smiling' outside the Tivoli at three o'clock in the morning? Come on, Jeppe, old chum, think about it."

Jeppe said, "I'm serious, Charles. Something is happening; I feel it. Something unusual. The traffic we've been picking up from Moscow has been—what?—too *normal,* if you can understand what I mean. No crises, no problems, even though they're carrying out the biggest summer maneuvers in ten years. And the traffic we've been picking up from Britain and the United States has the same curious quality. Everything's fine, everything's normal. Have you listened to the news lately?"

"Sure. They're starting new disarmament talks next month in Vienna. What's so threatening about that?"

"I don't know," said Jeppe. He sat back, hesitated and then drained his glass of schnapps. "Maybe I'm going bandannas."

"Bananas," Charles corrected him.

"Well, mad in any case," Jeppe agreed. "The whole Soviet Army is mobilized; they've even brought up their reserve divisions into Poland. The Baltic fleet is sailing around like a tiger in a cage. We've had eleven reports from Swedish Intelligence of crawler subs invading Swedish territorial waters; one came within eight hundred yards of the Swedish royal palace in Stockholm; and our own navy has located Soviet submarines passing through Store Baelt, and even through Storstrommen and Stege Bugt. Yet what do we hear from Britain and the United States? 'The Soviet Union is simply overcompensating for having been obliged to come back to the nuclear conference table.' 'They're just showing how concerned they are about peace.' Well, does that make any sense? It doesn't to me. Do you show that you're serious about peace by marching up and down with tanks and missiles and calling up your reserves?''

Charles wiped his mouth with his napkin. ''What are you trying to tell me, Jeppe? I mean, come on, spell it out. What are you trying to say?''

''I don't know,'' said Jeppe unhappily. ''But my bones are aching and nothing seems right.''

''You don't seriously think that if the Russians were considering going to war, America would sit back and smile and say that everything was fine? Or Britain, for that matter? We have hard-line anti-Communist administrations in both countries. Come on, Jeppe; the President would be beating the drum by now if there was any suggestion of war. So would Mrs. Thatcher.''

Jeppe said, ''I hope my feelings are wrong, believe me. But you can check for me, Charles. Just do a little legwork.''

''I don't think so.''

''Charles, you owe me.''

''What for?''

''Lunch, if nothing else.''

Charles took out another cigarette, then decided against it and put it back. ''Let's have another drink,'' he suggested.

Jeppe said, ''It won't be difficult. All you have to do is go to the offices of Klarlund and Christensen and find out whatever you can about Nicholas Reed. You can say that he was a friend of yours, that you've heard about his death and you've just come to see if there's anything you can do to help.''

''You're a very ingenious man, Jeppe,'' Charles told him sarcastically. ''How about some cake?''

Jeppe said, ''Please, Charles. This is important. Something's going on and I can't seem to get a hook on it. Please, Charles, I need to.''

''Well,'' said Charles, rubbing the back of his neck, ''I was hoping I'd given up all that kind of stuff for good.''

"Spoken like a real man," said Jeppe. "Here's the address: Klarlund and Christensen, Six Vesterbrogade, next to Den Permanente."

"I hope I know what I'm doing," said Charles.

SIX

"No," said Hans Klarlund decisively. "We knew nothing about Nicholas at all. We didn't need to. He did his job and went home, and that was all we required. He was an excellent architect."

"That's what his mother always used to say," replied Charles, trying to be friendly and anecdotal. " 'One day, Nick,' she used to say, 'you're going to be another Frank Lloyd Wright.' "

"I see," said Hans Klarlund tightly. He was obviously not a Frank Lloyd Wright enthusiast. He was short-haired, bespectacled, stripe-shirted, sitting behind a desk that was nothing more than a sheet of heavy glass supported by two wooden trestles. His office, to Charles, was forbiddingly neat. The only picture on the walls was a clinical drawing by Jørn Utzon of the Sydney Opera House. Outside the uncurtained windows there was a depressing view of the railway station and the corner of Bernstorffsgade, where Tivoli Gardens lay. A few red and yellow balloons drifted up into the late-afternoon sky. Blowing east, thought Charles, toward the Gulf of Finland and Leningrad. What would the Russians think as they saw them sail by? That we in the West are nothing more than playful innocents, children who release balloons while the bear prowls around our back door?

He remembered the way in which Ivan Yerikalin used to

question him over and over, unable to believe that the West was so unaware of the power and the political intent of the Soviet Union. "You know that we have to invade you one day just to survive. Otherwise our empire will turn in upon itself and collapse. We must always look outward because if we turn our heads inward and look at ourselves, we will be unable to bear what we see. Did you know that in the first few months of this year, over fifteen thousand people fled from Poland, more from East Germany, even more from Hungary? One day those who are unable to flee will turn upon their masters. It almost happened at the end of the Second World War; it can happen again now, at any time. That is why those belligerent geriatrics in the Kremlin must continue to expand their empire. Expand or die. That's what they think, and the rest of the world must tremble every night and every day just to keep them in power."

Charles would ask Ivan why he stayed in the KGB. "I have a family," Ivan would say. "And besides, I am a Russian. Where else would I live except in Russia? They may have dispossessed our bodies but they will never dispossess our spirit."

Charles said to Hans Klarlund, "You don't have any pictures of Nicholas? Anything recent that I could take home to his mother?"

Hans Klarlund shook his head.

"Could I possibly take a look at his desk?"

"Well, I don't know whether that's possible, Mr. Krogh. You have no credentials, after all, nothing from Mr. Reed's family to substantiate who you are."

"I wouldn't dream of touching anything or taking anything," said Charles. He took out a cigarette and ostentatiously lit it, to Hans Klarlund's obvious annoyance. "I just want to make sure he hasn't left anything here of sentimental value. You know, some little token that would make his grieving old mother a more contented woman."

Hans Klarlund stood up, anxious to remove Charles and his swirling gray clouds of cigarette smoke out of his cool, functional, Scandinavian office. "Well, I don't want to seem unsympathetic," he said. "Follow me and I will show you where his office was."

They walked through light and shadow, pastel grays and muted creams, past potted plants and office partitions. Charles, shambling along behind Hans Klarlund with his hands in his pockets and his cigarette sticking up out of the side of his mouth at forty-five degrees, felt that he was walking through a clinic rather than an architect's office. All the architects' offices he'd ever seen were a chaos of paper and drawing pins and curled-up tracing paper, with maybe a desiccated cactus and a dead bluebottle on the windowsill for decoration. You had to say it about the Danes. Their whole life was like *smørrasbørd*: simple, functional, modern, and yet peculiarly unsatisfying.

"Here," said Hans Klarlund. "This was Mr. Reed's office."

Charles stepped inside and looked around. It was quite a big office, with gray-painted walls and black carpet tiles. There was a gray metal desk and a large drawing board on which Nicholas Reed's plans for the old people's retirement village at Roskilde lay still half-finished. Charles leafed through them, nodded and sniffed.

" '*C'est la vie,*' said the old folks," he quoted. "It goes to show, you never can tell."

At that moment a secretary came briskly down the corridor and called Hans Klarlund to the telephone. Hans Klarlund frowned at Charles distrustfully but Charles flapped up both hands like Walter Matthau as if to say, "You can trust me, buddy. I'm innocent, even if I don't look it."

"You'll have to excuse me for a couple of minutes," said Hans Klarlund. "But, please, I must insist that you do not touch anything."

"Do I *look* like a tea leaf?" asked Charles. He reveled in the rhyming slang that John Nelson of Britain's C16 had taught him during his time in London.

"I beg your pardon?" asked Hans Klarlund.

"Thief," Charles explained with a quick, tight grin.

"Oh," said Hans Klarlund in complete perplexity and went off to answer his telephone call.

The second that Hans Klarlund was out of sight, Charles' demeanor completely changed. He propped his cigarette on the windowsill, then quickly checked around the office so that when he reported back to Jeppe, he would be able to tell him exactly where everything was. Desk, drawing board, waste-paper basket and something concealed under a large, gray-plastic cover. Xerox copier maybe? He tugged the cover off and there was a terminal for Klarlund & Christensen's computer, an IBM 2000. Charles looked it over, frowning and wishing he had been trained in computers. Maybe then he could have accessed Klarlund & Christensen's personnel file and found out where Nicholas Reed had come from and who he really was, and why the Soviets had considered it worth-while sending *Krov' iz Nosu* to kill him. Still, it was no use regretting the disadvantages of having been born too early for microchips; he replaced the cover and started on a speedy and systematic search of Reed's office that would have amazed Hans Klarlund if he had seen it.

He opened the drawers of Reed's desk with a lock pick, one after the other, rapidly scanning the packets of tracing paper, the neat rows of pencils, the Mars-Staedtler drawing pens, the Winsor & Newton inks, the French curves and plastic erasers. Later he would be able to note from memory every single drawer and every single item that was in it. In the bottom right-hand drawer, under a copy of T.T. Faber's *History of Danish Art*, there was a copy of *Sex Bizarre*. In the center drawer on the left-hand side there was a half-eaten packet of butterscotch Life Savers.

Charles frowned at the Life Savers. Now who was it he had once known who had always eaten butterscotch Life Savers? There wasn't time to think. He closed all the drawers, relocked them and then quickly checked around the floor of the office for unusual cigarette ends, fragments of wastepaper, anything that might help him identify Nicholas Reed and what he had been doing here. By the time Hans Klarlund came back three and a half minutes later, Charles had gleaned from Nicholas Reed's room all the information that anybody could possibly have found there—apart, of course, from what the computer might reveal. He stood looking out the window at the early evening traffic of Hammrichsgade, whistling softly to himself.

"I am sorry I kept you waiting," said Hans Klarlund.

Charles said, "What? Oh, don't worry."

"I don't really think I can allow you to look at Mr. Reed's

desk," said Hans Klarlund. "Not unless you bring us a letter from one of his relatives. His mother perhaps."

"Well, sure, I understand that," smiled Charles. "I'll probably be phoning her this evening so I'll tell her to drop me a note of authorization; you know, in case there's anything here that she wants. Anything sentimental."

"Yes," said Hans Klarlund. He was clearly waiting for Charles to leave. Charles nodded, smiled, smacked Hans Klarlund on the shoulder and said, "That's it, then. That's fine. Thank you very much. You've been real patient. Patience is a virtue, coveting your neighbor's ox is a sin."

Jesus, he thought, when he was out in the street again, these humorless Danes. It's all that dairy food they eat. The saturated fats clog up their hypothalamus. Probably their bowels too.

It wasn't far for him to walk back home to Larsbjørnstrade. It was a warm evening with a high, clear sky the color of boysenberry jam. The trees were rustling, the bells were ringing from Vor Frue Kirke, the streets were still busy with people going home or going out to eat. The Tivoli lights were sparkling through the leaves. He bought a copy of the *Ekstra Bladet* and glanced at the headlines: "Soviet Minister Hints at New Thaw." He folded the newspaper and tucked it under his arm. He wondered if Jeppe were right and everything they were being fed by the media was false. Too *normal*, Jeppe had said. He found himself silently whistling, "I prefer boysenberry . . . more than any ordinary jam . . . I'm a citizen for boysenberry jam, Sam. . . ." On the corner of Jerbanegade and Hans Christian Andersens Boulevard he stepped out in front of a Volvo and was nearly knocked over. The car's tires squealed, its suspension bounced, people looked around.

"What are you, blind?" Charles demanded in Danish. He sometimes missed New York. At least in New York the driver would have given him the finger or climbed out of his car and started an interminable argument. "Under *my* wheels you want to commit suicide? I've got a family, a business." But this driver did nothing more than give him a milk-and-water scowl and drive on.

Ah, well, fuck it, thought Charles. He needed a drink. The nearest bar was just across the road, the Club Ambassadeur on Rådhuspladsen. He crossed over, dodging more Volvos, and pushed his way through the door into the darkness of the bar. It wasn't open yet; it didn't open until ten, although it stayed open until four, but Anker the manager was already there with Alfred the barman; and a pianist, who sounded as if all his fingers were bandaged, was practicing "Night and Day."

"Mr. Krogh, you know we're not open," said Alfred. He was thin and blond, with a black waistcoat far too tight for him.

"Did I say you were open?" asked Charles. "Lend me a Jack Daniel's, straight up."

"I'm sorry, Mr. Krogh."

"You're sorry? Why should you be sorry? I nearly got run over out there. Some speed-crazed citizen in a Volvo full of dairy produce."

"Lend him the drink, Alfred," said the manager from the far side of the club. He was standing under a red light and all Charles could see of him was a black silhouette and a red gleam shining from his greasy hair.

"You're a pal, Anker. In fact, for a Dane, you're almost human."

"Just drink your drink, Mr. Krogh," said the manager. "We all know how much you love Denmark."

"What do you want, three choruses of '*Kong Christian stod ved højen mast*'?"

"Just drink your drink," the manager repeated.

Charles took the shot glass that Alfred had already filled for him, tossed it back in one gulp and then replaced it on the bar with exaggerated neatness. "You saved my life," he told Alfred.

He stepped out of the club and back on to Rådhuspladsen. It was then that he knew, instantly, that he was being tailed. He couldn't have described his intuition to an amateur. Anybody who hadn't lived for years in Copenhagen and who wasn't used to being followed and watched could have detected the unusual way in which the man in the light-gray double-knit suit suddenly stepped out of the entrance of the Burger King on the west side of the square. It was something about the way in which the man didn't look around him before he started walking, something about the way in which he crossed the pavement diagonally, positioning himself so that he had all the options of following after Charles no matter which direction Charles decided to take.

Charles started walking up Vestergade, staying on the west side of the street in the shadow so he would be more difficult to follow. The man in the double-knit suit came after him, twenty or thirty paces behind, glancing from side to side but patently ignoring the shops and the cafés and the bustle of home-going Copenhagen.

Charles turned down Larsbjørnstrade, where he lived, and immediately quickened his pace. On the far corner of the street, a man in a brown-leather jacket noticeably speeded up too, and Charles realized now that there were two of them. That meant more than a tail; that meant trouble. He jogged heavily down the crowded pavement and crossed Studiegade against the lights. A large Volvo truck blared its horn at him but he was too out of breath to answer back.

He didn't want to lead them toward his apartment; that could be fatal, not only for himself but for Agneta too. They obviously didn't know where he lived or they would have been waiting for him there. They had followed him from Klarlund & Christensen, conceivably on Hans Klarlund's tip-off. There was nothing to say that Klarlund hadn't made an outgoing call as well as receiving an incoming call.

Charles glanced into the shop window next to him; the man in the brown-leather jacket was reflected clearly in it, directly across the street. Charles didn't want to turn around but he could guess that his friend in the double-knit suit was pretty close behind too. And the problem was that he was simply too old and too unfit to be able to shake them off. He wished he hadn't drunk that shot of Jack Daniel's. He was sweating, and that jog along Larsbjørnstrade had shaken up the bourbon with his fishy lunch, along with the added flavor of ashtrays from his last cigarette.

On a sudden inspiration, Charles dodged into a narrow entrance above which a flickering red-neon sign announced that this was the way to "7th Heaven." He found to his relief that the battered, purple-painted door was unlocked and he struggled his way up a flight of dusty, carpeted stairs until he reached the second-floor landing. Through an arch there was a gloomy bar crowded with Formica-topped tables and a stage with drooping, red-velour curtains. Sitting on the edge of the stage, smoking a cigarette and reading a newspaper, was what appeared to be a glamorous blonde in a black-sequinned cocktail dress, pouting-lipped and Bardotesque, with long, sooty eyelashes. At one of the tables a big-busted black girl with a beehive hairstyle was painting her fingernails green and singing Michael Jackson's "Summer Love."

The blonde on the stage looked up, took the cigarette out of her mouth and tapped the ash carefully onto the floor.

"Charlie," enthused the blonde. "Darling, we haven't seen you for centuries."

"How are you doing, Roger?" Charles asked the blonde. "Juanita, how are you?"

"This is a surprise," said Roger, jumping down from the edge of the stage and straightening his dress. "But you look so *hot*. What have you been doing?"

"Running, as a matter of fact."

"Running? That's very rash of you."

"He's in training for the next Olympics, didn't you know?" teased Juanita. "The cardiac dash."

Charles said, "There are two guys." He nodded toward the arch. "They may try to follow me in here."

"Muggers?"

"Unh-hunh. I don't know who they are. But they look as if their intentions are slightly less than charitable."

"Well, well, what have you been up to?" asked Roger. He brushed the shoulders of Charles' jacket with picky, feminine fingers. "I thought you'd retired from all that."

"So did I," said Charles. "I was doing a favor for Jeppe."

"Oh, Jeppe. How is the dear boy? I haven't seen him for ages either. Not since I had my op."

"You haven't—?" Charles asked.

"Oh, no, my dear, not that. I'm not that extreme. It was just a little bit of nip and tuck." He leaned close and whispered, "Hemorrhoids." From this close, Charles could see the grainy creases under his eyes, the powdered shadow of his beard. He had been a merchant seaman once, before coming to Copenhagen and finding his transvestite niche at 7th Heaven.

Charles had seen him naked in his dressing room. He had muscles like bunches of knotted rope. And yet he made a very appealing and elegant-looking girl. "It's coordination," he used to insist. "You have to *move* like a woman and then people will believe you really are a woman, even if you're six foot three and built like a truck."

"Would you like a drink?" Roger asked. "There's some rather nasty wine or some warm schnapps."

"Thanks all the same," said Charles, shaking his head. And at that moment they heard the street door bang and the sound of footsteps clumping up the carpeted stairs. Charles looked meaningfully at Roger and said to Juanita, "I'd go lock myself in my dressing room if I were you. These boys might be rather unpleasant."

"I'll stay," said Juanita, fanning her wet fingernails, but she stood up so that she was facing the door. She was wearing a turquoise leotard cut high on the hip and a pair of high-heeled turquoise boots.

The two men who had been tailing Charles came through the archway and stood side by side. The man with the brown-leather jacket had his hands thrust in his pockets and was chewing gum. The man in the double-knit suit adjusted his skinny little tie even though it was already knotted tight. They were both blond, both Danes by the look of them, although the man in the gray suit had slightly Slavic-looking cheekbones and could have been a Pole or a Russian.

"Mr. Krogh?" he asked in a neutral, Americanized accent, the type of accent heard behind the counter of jewelry boutiques at Hilton hotels.

"What's it to you?" Charles asked.

"You've upset somebody, Mr. Krogh." The two men moved forward through the crowded tables.

"Oh, yes? And who's that?"

"Friends of Mr. Reed's, that's who. People who don't like you sticking your nose in where it isn't wanted."

Charles said, "What movie did you get that line out of? Now get out of here. This is a private club and you're interrupting a conversation."

The man in the double-knit suit said, "What we've got to

say is a lot more interesting, Mr. Krogh. What we've got to say is, back off.''

Charles didn't answer. The two men came over and stood close to him, only four or five feet away, and regarded him with the pale eyes of men who like to think they're frightening.

"We're going to have to work you over, Mr. Krogh. That's our job. Now you can make it easy for yourself, or you can make it difficult.''

Charles glanced at Roger. A silent message passed between them; after years of drinking together, they knew each other's faces well enough, and similar situations had arisen before when Charles was still working for the CIA.

"I think you'd better *vamos*,'' Charles said dryly.

The man in the double-knit suit shook his head. "I'm sorry, Mr. Krogh. A job is a job. If we don't work you over, we don't get paid; you wouldn't like me to go back to my wife and hungry children with no pay envelope, would you? That wouldn't be nice. Now, do you want to tell these ladies to make themselves scarce?''

Roger said in a reedy voice, "All right, all right. We're going.'' And he walked around the man in the double-knit suit with that unerringly accurate Brigitte Bardot sway of his, so convincing that the man didn't even notice that Roger was only an inch shorter than he was and that his shoulders were even wider.

Just as he passed behind him, Roger bunched up his left arm and punched the man in the kidney, a blow so hard that the man was almost lifted off his feet. He cried out and rolled over on one of the tables, crashing to the plastic-tiled floor. Before the man in the leather jacket could grasp what had happened, Roger had brought his knee slamming up between his legs, and as the man jackknifed in shock, Roger hit him a right-handed uppercut that made his jaw crack like a pistol shot.

Charles meanwhile had bent over, seized the first man's tie and dragged him up to a sitting position. The man was boggle-eyed, gasping and scarcely able to breathe.

"Let's talk about that pay envelope, shall we?'' Charles demanded. "Let's talk about who pays it.''

The man said something strangled in Russian.

"What?" Charles snapped, tugging his necktie violently from side to side. "What did you say?"

"Ya nyi panyimayu."

"You don't understand? Do you understand 'punch in the nose'?"

"Oo myinya dornata. Oo myinya bol' v spinyeh."

"Too bad," said Charles. "Serves you right for threatening ladies and old gentlemen."

"What did he say?" asked Juanita. "What's that he's talking, Japanese?"

"Russian," said Charles. "He says his back hurts."

"Is he a spy or something?" asked Roger.

Charles made a face. "Nothing so romantic. A hired thug, and not a very good one at that."

The man in the double-knit suit stared at Roger in horror and disbelief. Roger bared his teeth at him and the man tried to shuffle away crabwise across the floor until Charles tugged him back.

"Who pays you? *Kto?*"

"Ya nyi panyimayu."

"Vi gavarityi pa anglyski?"

"Niet. Ya panyimayu nichyevo."

Charles released the man's tie and said to Roger, "Do you mind breaking his nose for me?"

Roger didn't hesitate. He grasped the man's hair at the back and punched him relentlessly in the nose. Blood sprayed everywhere and the man fell back on the floor, howling and thrashing his legs.

"You're a hard man, Charles," said Roger, fluttering his eyelashes at him.

"So they tell me. Can I use your phone?"

"Did I ever deny you anything?"

Charles gently patted his cheek. "Not that I can remember, Roger."

He stood behind the dusty curtains and phoned Jeppe. "Jeppe, you're right. There's something going down here and it's definitely Russian. I went to see Klarlund and Christensen and was followed on the way back. Two of them, a genuine couple of KGB boneheads. Well, I went to Seventh Heaven and Roger sorted them out for me. Nothing serious. A broken nose and a couple of throbbing nuts. Not including the psychological shock of being beaten up by the prettiest woman this side of Kattegat.'' Roger gave him a little finger wave when he overheard this; Charles finger waved back.

Jeppe said, ''What did you find out at Klarlund's?''

''Not much. But Nicholas Reed had an IBM terminal in his office and it's conceivable that Klarlund's personnel files are stored in their databank. If you can find me a bagman who can access other people's computers, chances are I can get you what you want.''

Jeppe was silent for a while. Charles said, ''Are you still there?''

''Yes, still here. I was just thinking, that's all. It has to be somebody totally reliable. Jens Jørgensen is probably the best but he's got friends in the Ministry. We're better off as far as security is concerned with Otto Glistrup.''

''I remember Otto. The world's most boring man.''

''That's him.''

Charles turned around. The two KGB men were sitting side by side on the floor with Roger standing over them swinging the baseball bat he always had ready in case any of his customers became too enthused by his act. ''Do you want me to hit them again?'' asked Roger. The KGB man in the double-knit suit looked up in horror, his face and shirtfront a dark splash of blood. The man in the brown-leather jacket was still rocking backward and forward in pain.

''What am I going to do with these two apes?'' Charles asked Jeppe.

''I don't think you have any choice,'' Jeppe replied. ''You're going to have to let them go. If you call in the Politi, they're going to want to know why they were following you and what's been going on. Then sooner or later it'll all get back to the Ministry and that'll be the end of me.''

Charles said, ''Okay, if you say so. But you're going to have to get me a gun. I can't come rushing up here looking for Roger every time they start following me around.''

''I'll get you one,'' said Jeppe. ''Anything special?''

''I'll leave it to you. But something big that goes boom when you fire it.''

They arranged to meet at ten o'clock that night by the

Ferris wheel in Tivoli Gardens. Jeppe meanwhile would see if
he could find Otto Glistrup. Charles hung up the phone and
said to Roger, "Let's have some of that warm schnapps. You
two, *ukhadityi*, get lost."

Miserably the two men limped out of the club and made
their way slowly back down the stairs to the street. Roger was
regluing one of his eyelashes while Juanita went to find the
bottle of schnapps. "It's behind all those dirty knickers somewhere," Roger called airily.

"Well," said Charles after Juanita had poured out the
drinks, "how can I thank you?"

"You could take me dancing. How about the Kakadu?"

Charles smiled. "I don't think so. It's not that I *mind* going
dancing with you. It's just that I don't dance so good these
days. How about I buy you dinner next week? I'll call you."

Roger finished fixing his eyelashes and said, "You're an
angel, Charles. You always were."

When Charles got back to his flat, Agneta was waiting for
him and there was a savory aroma of *hönse kasserolle*. She
was wearing a white, low-necked T shirt without a bra and a
pair of Gloria Vanderbilt pedal-pushers in red. As soon as he
unlocked the front door, she came out of the kitchen and said,
"Charles? Why are you so late? I've been worried."

He kissed her forehead. "I met some friends."

"There's blood on your jacket. What's happened?"

"I'm okay. Nothing's happened. It's not my blood. Say,
something smells good."

He went into the kitchen to find himself a beer. Agneta
followed him and said, "You haven't been getting involved
in work again, have you?"

"Me? Work? You've got to be kidding." He tugged the
ring pull on a can of Special Brew and poured it into a tall
glass.

Agneta said, "Don't lie to me, Charles. Not to me. You're
working again. I know it."

"It's nothing. I'm helping Jeppe a little, that's all."

She came up close to him and touched his face with her
fingertips, as gently as if she were touching glass. Her eyes
were very green and he found that he couldn't look at them

without turning away. "So, it's Jeppe," she said. "I always said that man would be the death of you."

Charles didn't know what to tell her. He felt guilty because he had long ago promised Agneta that he would never get involved with intelligence work again. But he also felt a familiar tightening in his heart, an exhilarating, alarming feeling that he was once again a player in that vast, invisible game without rules; that game of deception and bluff and sudden extraordinary danger; that game without which the world could never be safe, never be peaceful, no matter how uneasy the peace might be.

SEVEN

It was a dazzlingly bright afternoon at Moscow's Sheremetyevo Airport when the British Airways 747B taxied into the terminal. John Bishop had slept for most of the flight; he had been up until two o'clock in the morning finishing off the programming for *Tovarish!*, which Michael was planning to unveil for the first time this week.

Michael had been unable to sleep. He had tried to read a copy of *Newsweek*, then the first three pages of the Jeffrey Archer novel that Margaret had bought for him. But he kept thinking about Wallings and the guidance complex out at Central Airport, at which he was supposed to "take a shufti." He looked across at John, lying back in his seat with his mouth open and his horn-rimmed spectacles perched sideways, a twenty-eight-year-old schoolboy with an overwhelming passion for computers and fishing and very little else except occasional forays to the theater with a strident girlfriend called Sonya, who bred golden retrievers and habitually wore Wellington boots, even when she was cooking supper. Michael often wondered whether John was still a virgin. It wouldn't have surprised him. John's conversation was confined almost exclusively to floppy disks and dry flies.

"John," Michael nudged him. "John, we've arrived."

John opened his eyes and stared at him. "By George," he said, "I was having a dream about my old school teacher."

"You are the only person in the entire cosmos who still says 'by George,' " said Michael.

John adjusted his glasses and squinted to peer out the window. "Well, now, look at that. The Soviet Union. Looks modern enough, doesn't it? Quite a few cars around."

They were slowly disembarked by a smiling British Airways stewardess. "Good-bye, sir. Hope you enjoyed your flight."

"Slept," said John. Then they were ushered through to the immigration hall, where they waited half an hour to have their visa books checked by a uniformed soldier with a green band around his cap. The soldier said, "You are coming for the Toys Exhibition? Yes?"

"That's right," said Michael, half-afraid that he would blurt out something about the guidance complex too. "We're toymakers."

"Ha!" said the soldier, handing back their visas and smiling. "Father Christmuss!"

They were directed through to customs. A customs officer with shining brilliantined hair said, *"Sigareti? Sigari? Tabak?"*

"Don't smoke," said John. "Makes you cough and that frightens the fish."

The customs officer stared at him coldly as if he suspected him of trying to smuggle some kind of subversive Western lunacy into the Soviet Union. "Books, papers, political material?" he asked without taking his eyes off John.

It was then that they were approached by a smartly uniformed Intourist girl with cheeks as Slavic as a squirrel's and an energetic stride. She was carrying a clipboard and as she came up, she checked the clipboard and said loudly, "Mr. Bee Shop? Mr. Townce Ent? Welcome to the Soviet Union! All your baggage and your freight will be cleared for you." She said something in Russian to the customs official, who replied, *"Pryikrashna,* fine," and wiped his brilliantined head with the palm of his hand and sniffed.

"You can come with me now," said the Intourist girl, leading the way briskly through Terminal 11, which was echoing and bright. There was a pungent smell of Russian tobacco and disinfectant. On either side there were souvenir shops, their glass shelves crowded with red-and-yellow *matryoshka* dolls and Ukrainian embroidered blouses and enameled Palekh boxes.

"We have a guide arranged for you; her name is Miss Konstantinova," the Intourist girl told them in the same loud, unmodulated voice. "You are booked into the Hotel Rossiya, deluxe class, and Miss Konstantinova will drive you there. She has already arranged all the formalities of your car rental except that you will have to produce your driving license and sign your Ingosstrakh insurance form if you require insurance."

"Well, well," said Michael. "The VIP treatment."

"Yes, correct, VIP," said the Intourist girl without smiling. She took them to the Intourist office, decorated with large, colored posters of the Kremlin and Zagorsk. "Please sit down; we will not keep you waiting for long." She picked up a phone and had a lengthy conversation in Russian that seemed to involve endless repetition of the name "Rufina."

It was twenty minutes before Miss Konstantinova appeared. She came into the office—a small, dark-haired girl in a white blouse and a gray skirt—and said, *"Zdrastvuytye. Kak pozhivayete?"*

"I'm sorry," said Michael, "I'm afraid my Russian is confined to *'da'* and *'nyet'* and *'gde uborniye.'* "

Miss Konstantinova smiled. "I am pulling at your leg," she said. "That is good-day and how are you in Russian. You will have to learn how to say it for yourself. Moscow is a city of manners."

"Oh, well, then. *Kak pozhi*-whatever-it-is to you," Michael replied, inclining his head. "This is Mr. Bishop. I'm Mr. Townsend."

They shook hands. "Your car is waiting," said Miss Konstantinova. "I have had your luggage stowed for you in the trunk. Please follow."

"This is all very efficient of you," Michael remarked as Miss Konstantinova led them through the terminal.

"Well, *Igrushek Two-thousand* is a very important exhibition," Miss Konstantinova replied. "We are trying to make your visit here as comfortable as we can."

She turned and smiled at him, and for the first time, Michael saw how pretty she was. Her hair was drawn back sharply from a classically featured Russian face to accentuate high cheekbones, slanting brown eyes and a short, straight nose, as well as the kind of slightly pouting, provocative lips that looked as if they were on the very edge of blowing a kiss. Her blouse was plain but obviously expensive, and her gray skirt was well-tailored over her narrow hips. Michael was surprised to recognize the perfume: Madame Rochas. Intourist guides must be well-paid, or well-rewarded.

"Can I change some money?" asked John, struggling along behind with two large vinyl bags and an armful of computer magazines.

"You will have no difficulty in doing that at your hotel," Miss Konstantinova told him. "Just be sure to take with you your passport and your currency-control certificate. And please remember, it is illegal to deal privately in currency."

"We're very law-abiding," said Michael.

"Of course," nodded Miss Konstantinova. "I was not suggesting thievery on your part."

She led them outside. The sun was bright although there was a fresh northeastern wind blowing. They crossed the terminal forecourt until they reached a parking lot where a white Volga 22 with blue-nylon upholstery was waiting for them. Miss Konstantinova helped them in and then settled herself in the driver's seat. "You would do well to watch how I drive. The regulations may be unfamiliar to you. But it is only twenty miles to the city center, so please relax."

The transmission whinnied like a tank as Miss Konstantinova drove them away from the airport and headed southeast along the broad, straight highway of Leningradsky Prospekt toward Moscow.

"You didn't bring jeans, did you?" Miss Konstantinova asked Michael.

"Jeans? No. I thought about it but there wasn't room in my suitcase."

Miss Konstantinova nodded. "These days you should bring Adidas running shoes. All of Moscow youth is wild for Adidas. When they want to say something is wonderful, they even have a word for it, *Adidasovsky!*"

"I've got some Hush Puppies," said John from the backseat. "They're rather worn out though."

"*Ushapupis?*" asked Miss Konstantinova frowning, then laughing.

Eventually, through the clear and gilded afternoon, Moscow arose in front of them, far more majestic and strange than Michael had ever imagined. First, the concrete walls of the Dinamo Stadium; then, as they drove toward the center, the gray, Stalinesque spires of the Hotel Ukraina to the south and the towers of Moscow University ("That is where thirty-two thousand young people study," Miss Konstantinova informed them, "and there are more than forty-five thousand halls and rooms and laboratories"); and at last the golden onion domes of the Kremlin Palace; the red-brick heights of Spassky Tower with its famous gilded clock; and the bizarre, turbaned turrets of St. Basil's Cathedral.

Miss Konstantinova drove across the cobbles of Red Square, past the huge GUM department store and to the banks of the Moskva River where it curved around in front of the Hotel Rossiya. Michael was rather disappointed to discover that the Rossiya was a flat-fronted, modern hotel without the towers and spires and revolutionary stars with which the Hotel Ukraina was decorated. But Miss Konstantinova told him they were better off here. "In the Hotel Ukraina, the elevators do not work so well and there are no stairs. You can spend some hours getting in and out." Michael climbed out of the car and looked down toward the river, shining brilliantly now in the four-o'clock sun so that the pleasure boats that plied their way under the concrete bridges were silhouetted black.

Although it was May, there was a keenness to the wind that made Michael shiver. Miss Konstantinova came across, stood next to him and said, "This is your first time here, isn't it?"

He nodded. "I feel far away from home, if you don't think that's rude of me."

"Of course not. I understand."

John came over and accidentally dropped a sheaf of computer magazines on the pavement. "I could do with a cup of tea," he said somewhat dolefully.

"Let me help you register," said Miss Konstantinova. "Come with me, I will show you. You will have to give the desk clerk your passport, also your Intourist vouchers for accommodation. Then he will give you your *propoosk.*"

They entered the hotel. The lobby was as wide as a playing field and carpeted in crimson. Miss Konstantinova led them over to the wide marble-topped desk and helped them fill in their registration forms. The nodding desk clerk gave them each a *propoosk*, which turned out to be a pass with their name and room number on it. Guests were not given keys. Instead, they had to present their *propoosk* to the woman attendant on their floor and she, the *dezhurnaya*, the keeper of the keys, would admit them to their rooms.

Miss Konstantinova said with a detached little smile, "Your *dezhurnaya* will do much for you, Mr. Townsend. She will call taxis, make tea, take messages, but she also has the right to enter your room with force if she believes that you are committing a moral offense."

"You mean like sleeping with no pajamas on?" asked Michael and felt rather flirtatious and sophisticated for having said so.

Miss Konstantinova, however, appeared to take him literally. "Sleeping without pajamas is not considered a moral offense. But having a woman in your room who is not your wife, well, that is a different matter. This will not be the case, I am sure."

"No," said Michael, "this will not be the case."

They reached the third floor and found their *dezhurnaya*, a stout, middle-aged woman in a dark-green jacket and skirt, her hair parted in the dead center of her scalp, and with a baggy, humorless face like Lyndon Johnson's. She noisily opened their rooms for them, throwing the door wide and switching on the *televideniye* as if to make sure they noticed it. Michael went straight to the window of his room and looked out toward the west, toward St. Basil's, Lenin's Tomb, the Hotel Ukraina and far beyond, where factory chimneys and cooling towers smudged the horizon with smoke.

Miss Konstantinova stood in the open doorway watching him, while the *dezhurnaya* stood in the corridor censoriously jangling her keys. On the *televideniye* there was a documentary about the Bratsk hydroelectric power plant. Miss Konstantinova said, "I will wait for two hours while you bathe and change, if you wish to. Then perhaps we will have dinner. I have reserved a table at the Moskva Café; I think you will enjoy it.''

"Can I call my wife?" Michael asked her.

"You can book a call through the hotel desk. But usually it takes two hours or longer.''

"Well, perhaps I'll book a call for the morning.''

Miss Konstantinova said, "You should call me Rufina. In the next few days we shall be together very closely, for six hours of the day every day. We should be *druzyamyi*, friends.''

"Yes, well, I'd like that," said Michael. He began to wonder when he would ever get the opportunity to escape from Miss Konstantinova and inspect the guidance complex out at Central Airport. Perhaps he would find it impossible, in which case he would have a perfect excuse for Mr. Wallings. He said to Miss Konstantinova, "Good. *Pryikrashna*. I'll see you later, then.'' He pressed his fingers into the oatmeal-colored spread over his bed and remarked, "Seems soft enough,'' and then realized that he might have been unwittingly suggestive. Alan Taylor had warned him about how prudish the Russians were. Alan's wife Jill had been stopped by the *militsya* for wearing Bermuda shorts in Gorky Street when she was shopping. Michael added, "I should sleep well,'' and then wished he hadn't said that either. But Miss Konstantinova didn't seem to be embarrassed. She simply nodded her head and said, "I will meet you downstairs in the lobby at seven o'clock if that is acceptable to you.''

"Yes," said Michael. He looked at her and for a second she looked back at him with extraordinary boldness. "Yes, that'll be fine.''

"You should now say good-bye," nodded Rufina Konstantinova. "You should say *do svidanya.*''

Michael hesitated and then pronounced slowly, *"Do svidanya.''*

Rufina Konstantinova said, "That means good-bye, but of course not for ever.''

"Well, I hope not.''

When she had gone, John came wandering into his room, scratching his head. "You haven't seen my toilet bag, have you? It's a Boots' one, with blue flowers on it. I was carrying it separately. I hope I haven't left it on the plane.''

"Knowing you, John, you left it at home."

John went to the window and looked down at the traffic crawling around St. Basil's: Moskviches and Volgas, occasional Saabs and Wartburgs. "Don't think much of the rooms, do you? Not my idea of deluxe. I had a better room at Bournemouth when Sonya and I went down for the dog show."

"John, we're not here for a holiday. This trip could make us if we place enough orders."

"All the same though," John remarked, blinking at Michael through his glasses. "Wouldn't like to arm-wrestle that lady who looks after our landing, would you?"

Michael took a bath and was glad of the universal rubber plug that he had brought with him on Alan Taylor's advice; so many Russian baths and basins had no plugs. The sunlight crossed the pale-green tiles on the walls and danced in reflecting curves. He felt suddenly lonely and afraid and wished he hadn't come. The worst part of it was not being able to call Margaret whenever he wanted to.

He put on his best gray suit and splashed his chin with Christian Dior. John wore the same brown-corduroy jacket he had worn when they met their bank manager in Croydon. Rufina Konstantinova was waiting for them at the far side of the lobby in a white-embroidered dress, and she smiled and waved as soon as she caught sight of them.

"The Moskva isn't far," she said, "but we can take a taxi."

The restaurant was sparkling and heavily luxurious, with crystal chandeliers glinting over two long rows of tables spread with white-linen napery. Michael noticed that most of the diners were Americans and Swedes, although almost all of them seemed to be accompanied by an Intourist guide, polite, obliging, explaining the menu as they went along.

They sat in the corner. Rufina Konstantinova ordered caviar and chilled vodka, which they had with black bread. "In the Soviet Union, we call caviar *ikra*, black for the sturgeon and red for the salmon. It is very expensive these days."

They toasted each other *"Vashe zdorovye!"* and then again *"Vashe zdorovye!"* until their cheeks were pink and they were laughing.

Rufina held Michael's hand and said, "You must be the sort of man who cares very much for people, to make toys. In the Soviet Union everybody loves children and they say that people who love children love the world."

John squinted at her through his glasses and countered, "How can people from the Soviet Union say they love the world when they have the most powerful army, the most threatening navy and more missiles pointed at the rest of the world than anybody can count? Is that love? It's not even friendship."

Rufina smiled, but her smile was not one of amusement; it was more a smile of indulgence. "In the guidebooks to the Soviet Union, Mr. Bee Shop, it says not to involve your guide or interpreter in a political or polemical discussion since this can sometimes spoil the mood of your visit."

"Mood?" said John. The vodka had already gone to his head; that and jet lag. "What kind of mood can anybody be in to position an SS-Twenty?"

"Mr. Bee Shop," Rufina insisted, "please do not mar a potentially memorable evening."

Michael said to John sharply, "Shut up, John, do you mind? This isn't the time or the place."

John shrugged. He knew by Michael's tone of voice that he was serious. Rufina ordered *gribi v smetane*, hot mushrooms with sour cream, and then *tsiplyata tabaka*, chicken flattened out on a buttered skillet and cooked until crisp. They drank Tsinandali white wine and Narzan mineral water. By eleven o'clock, when the Moskva's lights began to dim, Michael felt heady and unreal, and ready for bed.

They took a taxi back to the Rossiya. The evening air was cold. The river curved like a silver snake. Michael closed his eyes for a moment in the back of the taxi and didn't even realize that the hand clasping his was Rufina's. Or perhaps he did realize and didn't care. They walked in through the brightly lit hotel lobby and the doorman returned their *propoosk* slips so they could show them to the *dezhurnaya* upstairs. Michael said to Rufina, "What time shall we see you tomorrow?"

"Let us discuss that upstairs," she said. "Please, you look very tired."

"Yes," said Michael, "I think I am."

John disappeared to his bedroom down the corridor with a back-handed wave. Michael went into his room, stripped off his jacket and loosened his tie. Rufina stood by the window, looking out over the lights of Moscow. On top of the Palace of Congresses, five red stars shone out over the city; street-lights were reflected in the river. Rufina said, "This city has changed so much and yet so little. If you look at the Kremlin today, you know, its skyline is not so different from the way it looked in eighteen hundred."

Michael lay back on his bed and rubbed his eyes. "I don't think I'm used to Russian vodka," he said, smiling at her.

She tugged the curtains closed. "The Soviet Union is not what you think it is, Mr. Townsend."

Michael didn't answer. He knew now that he was being propositioned. He watched Rufina as she crossed the room and closed the door. He said, "Is that what happens to all British businessmen? Courtesy of Intourist?"

Rufina sat down on the bed beside him. She took off his tie and unbuttoned the front of his shirt, laying her hand on his chest. "There are times when even a guide can feel different," she said.

"What about the *dezhurnaya?*" he asked.

"Sometimes the *dezhurnaya* can be persuaded to have a temporary case of deafness," smiled Rufina.

"You've paid her off?"

"A little French perfume goes a very long way."

Michael said, "You know that I'm married. It may be unfashionable, but I'm a faithful husband."

She stroked his hair. "Of course. Can I call you Michael?"

"Yes, of course. Michael."

"Well, Michael, what I am talking about is not immorality but companionship. You have a difficult visit ahead of you. There will be much competition to face. Perhaps if you had a woman beside you who would help you and appreciate your talent, you would be more successful."

Michael said nothing. But Rufina began to unbutton her dress, one button at a time, erotically, deliberately, as if she were daring Michael at each button to say, "Stop." "I am not asking to make love to you," she said. "Only to sleep beside you, to give you a feeling of comfort. You are married; you can understand such things.''

Michael licked his lips. "I'm not sure I can."

She stroked his hair and then leaned forward and kissed his forehead. "If you object to me, I shall go."

"No, I don't object to you. Quite the opposite."

She said nothing but leaned forward once more and gave him another kiss.

"Did they ask you to do this?" Michael said, watching those slanting brown eyes. She was much younger than Margaret, only twenty-four or twenty-five, and there was something flawless and fresh about her that appealed to him. He had never had many girlfriends, none that had been strikingly pretty like Rufina Konstantinova, and he had to admit to himself that he had thoroughly enjoyed going out with her this evening and watching the way men's heads turned.

"Is that what you think?" she asked him. "That the KGB wanted me to sleep with you?"

"I'm sorry. That was a crass thing to say."

"But is that what everybody believes in Great Britain? That our lives are ruled by the KGB?"

"No, of course not."

Rufina Konstantinova stood up and for a moment Michael was afraid she was going to leave, but then she went across to the mirror beside the bathroom door and in a strangely expressionless way, watched herself unbutton her dress all the way down. Then she peeled it back from her shoulders and let it drop softly to the floor.

"We have deep feelings, great passions," she said. "We are a patient people. Do you know how patient? *Pravda* said that last year the Soviet people spent thirty-seven billion hours waiting in queues for basic necessities like food and clothing. Thirty-seven billion! But sometimes we can be very impatient, very hungry for what we want."

She was wearing a small white lacy bra and a pair of lacy bikini briefs through which Michael could detect the dark shadow of her pubic hair. She turned around and faced him, her features lit by the lamplight from beside the bed. "I would not force myself upon you, Michael. But I would wish very much to be with you."

Michael said nothing for a long time. He was thinking of Margaret. But somehow Margaret and the house in Sanderstead seemed to have shrunk away, diminished by time and distance to the size of a tiny dolls' house somewhere far away on the face of the night. Would it really be betrayal to spend the night in the arms of this pretty Russian girl? Or would it be the kind of adventure he deserved and had never experienced? Perhaps it might even make him a better lover, improve his marriage. Alan Taylor had boasted about a fling he had had with a French girl when he was in Zürich and he always swore that it had been the making of his marriage to Jill. "Absolute making of it, old chap."

Michael sat up, then stood up, overbalancing a little. He came over to Rufina and put his arms around her. She was much smaller than Margaret, she came up only to his chest. He suddenly felt very masculine and protective. His first night in Moscow and already he had managed to find himself a girl. It was absurd, but he hadn't felt as confident or as attractive as this in years.

With the practiced hands of a married man, he unfastened her bra. Her breasts were higher and firmer than Margaret's and the nipples were as red as raspberries. He touched them gently and they tightened. He kissed her, the palm of his hand flat against her left breast.

He undressed, letting his shirt and his pants lie where they had fallen. His erection bobbed up like the mast of a dinghy. They stripped back the covers and dived slowly together into the bed, all arms and elbows and kisses. Her hand guided him into her sticky hairiness. The bed made no sound, unlike the bed at home, although halfway through their lovemaking, there was a tremendous rattling and shuddering of hot-water pipes in the room above theirs.

Rufina climaxed with a small gasp, almost polite. Michael ejaculated immediately afterward. They lay side by side for a long time, saying nothing, watching lights traverse the ceiling from the narrow gap in the curtains.

"You are not regretful?" asked Rufina, touching his shoulder.

"Why should I be?"

"Well, you are not thinking of your wife now with guilt?"

He shook his head. "I don't think that what we've done is anything to feel guilty about." He kissed her cheek and wished he could believe himself.

Michael fell asleep quickly and dreamed no dreams that he could remember the following morning. When he woke up, the sun was gleaming on the domes of the Kremlin and the sky was pale and clear. Rufina was in the bathroom, washing her face, naked in front of the basin.

"Ah, *zdrastvuytye,*" she said. "How are you feeling today?"

Michael sat up and rubbed his eyes. "I don't know yet. I think I have a hangover."

Rufina walked unself-consciously through to the bedroom. She was densely hairy between her thighs, a shaggy sexual pelt. She climbed onto the bed and kissed him on the mouth. Then she stayed there on hands and knees, staring at him, so close that he couldn't focus on her face.

"We're not going to be able to behave like this during the day, you know," he told her. "If John realizes what's happened—well, of course he'll be bound to tell Margaret."

"Would Margaret not understand?"

"No," said Michael. Then, "No, I don't think so."

"Well, we must go and find some breakfast," Rufina suggested. "If you have a hangover, the best thing for you is ham and eggs and a glass of vodka."

Michael swung his legs off the side of the bed and stood up. He felt nauseous and his eyes refused to focus on the gilded cityscape outside the window. He was halfway across the room, frowning with his headache, when the door suddenly opened and John was standing there, dressed in an orange-nylon shirt and a pair of green-cotton slacks, his glasses askew, obviously all ready to go downstairs to breakfast. He blinked at Michael, then he blinked at Rufina, and then he abruptly swung the door closed and called out in a muffled voice, "I'm sorry! Beg your pardon."

"Well, that's done it," said Michael. He sat down suddenly on the end of the bed.

Rufina came up close to him. He could feel her bare breasts touching his back. She ruffled his hair and said, "Why should you worry? He is your friend. If you explain everything to him, he will not say anything to your wife, will he?"

"I suppose not," said Michael glumly. He could see himself in the mirror—naked, vulnerable, tousle-haired—and wondered why on earth he had allowed Rufina to stay with him last night. He must have been so drunk that it was a miracle he had been able to perform. In fact, he found it impossible to remember most of what had happened. He could recall the restaurant, the caviar, the crisp white table linen. He could remember Rufina holding his hand in the taxi. But what had happened after that? What had suddenly taken hold of his mind and made him decide to take her to bed?

Rufina said, "Come on, Michael. Let us go and have our breakfast. You must not be worried about John. He will say nothing; I know his kind of man. Perhaps he will disapprove of you but he will not jeopardize your marriage."

"You don't think so?"

She kissed him again. "Do not let anxiety stand in the way of love. And remember what Richard Stern said: 'When love gets to be important, it means that you haven't been able to manage anything else.' You can manage much more than me, Michael, and much more than Margaret. We are nothing more than incidents in your life. There is far more for you in your life than either of us."

Michael went to the bathroom and peered at himself in the mirror. To his surprise, he hadn't changed at all. He didn't even look as tired and as hungover as he felt. He splashed his face, brushed his teeth and then dressed. He went downstairs to the café with Rufina, and the *dezhurnaya* didn't even glance at them.

John was already sitting at one of the tables in the café, drinking milky coffee and eating toast. Michael sat down and said, *"Zdrastvuytye,* John." John didn't say anything but put down his toast and reached for his coffee cup.

"That means good-morning," said Michael.

John wiped his mouth. "Well, you've obviously had some coaching."

"What's that supposed to mean?"

Rufina still hadn't joined them; she was talking to another Intourist courier at the door. John said, "You know what it means. They do it on purpose, don't they? Entrap you. And who's the first person to fall for it? You. The great sophisticated Michael Townsend.''

"Don't be so damned naive," Michael breathed at him.

"Oh, naive, is it? I'd like to hear what Margaret has to say."

"It's nothing. It's none of your business. So forget it."

John waved his toast airily. "None of my business? Well, that's all right. It's just my livelihood we're talking about, that's all."

"John!" snapped Michael. "For Christ's sake! Stop judging me! Stop judging the Russians! Just stop your bloody judging!"

John stared at him through the refracting lenses of his glasses. He said nothing, but it was then that Michael realized how much John had fancied the idea of going to bed with Rufina himself. Rufina came over, smiling at both of them, and said, "You slept well, Mr. Bee Shop? *Kak pozhivayete?*"

John irritably spread his toast with acacia honey. *"Zamyich-yatyil'na."*

Michael looked at Rufina and wished to God he knew enough about this country to understand what he had done, what risks he had already taken and what the day might bring.

EIGHT

That morning, across the shining curve of the world, several crucial messages were sent by satellite link, by telephone and by word of mouth.

The President of the United States was eating breakfast outside on the patio at Camp David when he was handed a message by Colonel Henry Heinz of the Air Force, making it clear that the armed forces of the Soviet Union were now in a position of full strategic readiness.

"The latest satellite pictures show that the Sixteenth Air Army has now divided its forces into two, sir, and that just about completes the picture."

The President smoothed back his hair. On the other side of the patio, his russet spaniel suddenly raised its head and looked at him with sorrowful, inquisitive eyes. The President said, "How soon will General Cordwell be ready to implement *Gringo*?"

"Stuttgart says he's ready now, sir."

The President hesitated for a moment. There was no word for the tiredness and the resignation that Colonel Heinz could see in his eyes. Then he said, "All right, Colonel. Tell Cordwell to issue the first-level instructions. But on no account is he to proceed to second level until I authorize it personally."

Just then the President's National Security Adviser, Morton

Lock, pushed his way out through the sun-flecked screen door, carrying a cup of coffee in one hand and a briefcase in the other. "Ah, Morton," said the President. "It seems that the Soviets are now in the go mode. I've given Cordwell the word to start redeploying the nonessential staff for evacuation."

Morton stood still for a moment and looked at the President seriously. "You know that we haven't yet had the final verification from Copenhagen?"

The President said, "I know. But there isn't any doubt that we will, is there? It's all wrapped up; all they need to do now is to tie the ribbon around it. Gorbachev warned me that it might take a little time to get an agreement from the Cubans. Hot-spirited, that's what he called them. It will probably help them make up their minds if they know for sure that *Gringo* is already underway."

Morton said, "The latest intelligence assessment from Langley says that Castro will almost certainly fall into line. He can't afford not to. He just wants to go down in a blaze of defiant glory, that's all."

"There's nothing glorious about any of this, Morton," the President told him dryly.

"Well, sir, maybe not, sir," Morton replied. "But it's pretty difficult to think of any important event in the history of warfare that *was* glorious, wouldn't you say? The Indian wars? The Civil War? Hiroshima? They seem glorious only when you look back at them, don't they, when all the dead have been tidily buried and everybody's had time to make his excuses."

The President gave Morton a humorless smile. "Nobody could ever accuse you of being an optimist, could they, Morton?"

"That's why you hired me, sir."

Morton sat down, took a quick sip of coffee and opened up his briefcase on his knees. The President watched him for a while and then said, "Tell me, Morton, what do you think the history books are going to say about all this?"

"The American history books or the Russian history books?"

The President's mouth tightened at Morton's cynicism but he said doggedly, "Either. Both." He really wanted to know the answer.

Morton took out the papers he wanted, then closed his briefcase and set it aside. "Well, sir, I think the American history books are going to put you down as the first true realist of the twentieth century."

"That isn't necessarily a compliment," the President remarked.

"Are you looking for compliments, Mr. President? Or are you looking for straightforward recognition that sooner or later *somebody* had to do what you've had to do?"

The President said nothing but picked up a piece of toast and then put it down again.

"Let's be straight about one thing, sir," said Morton. "Every president since Truman has realized just how far the balance of world power has been out of kilter since the end of World War Two. But what have they done about it? What have they done about finding the *natural* political balance between East and West, the *natural* division of territory between communism and capitalism? Well, sir, you know the answer to that as well as I do: they haven't done anything at all except to maintain the same stressful out-of-balance situation year after year and to spend more and more money on weaponry instead of committing it to industrial development and human welfare. You're a realist; you've understood that situation and you've done something about it."

"And the Russian history books?" asked the President, lifting his head.

"You know what *Pravda* has been calling you already. 'The Great American Pragmatist.' "

The President looked out across the lawns of Camp David toward the treeline, where two armed security guards were talking to each other. "Perhaps I should have done things differently," he said.

Morton waited. He had seen the President in moods like this frequently lately. Somber, reflective, relentlessly self-critical. It was difficult for the President to understand that every member of the White House staff felt the same way, that the burden of responsibility for what was about to happen was shared between all of them with just as much agony and soul-searching, and with just as much guilt.

But what choice did they have? The secret report last April from the Defense Advanced Projects Research Agency and its accompanying evaluation by the Joint Chiefs of Staff had finally brought them out of their desperate fantasies that nuclear confrontations were either "winnable" or even "strategically useful." In spite of $5.7 billion already spent on its development, the interception of Soviet missiles in space by the so-called "Star Wars" technology was, in a word, unworkable. What was even more daunting, the weaponry that would now be necessary to maintain the balance of military power into the early part of the twenty-first century would drag the nation into such a catastrophic fiscal deficit that the long-term effect on the Western world would be almost as serious as out-and-out war. Unemployment, poverty, drug addiction, famine and disease. The Cold War had at last priced itself out of the market.

One of the two white telephones on a small table beside the President's elbow gave a discreet, almost apologetic, bleep. He picked it up and said, "What is it, George?"

"Deputy Commander-in-Chief, European Command, sir."

"Very well. Put him on."

It was General John Oliver, speaking from Frankfurt on a scrambled satellite link. The security of *Gringo* was rated so high that part of his voice was bounced off one FLTSATCOM and the other part was bounced off another, the two parts being reconnected through the central defense computer system at the Pentagon before transmission to Camp David on a more conventionally scrambled land line.

Despite the slightly metallic quality caused by the double scrambling, General Oliver's voice was loud and hearty. "Good-morning, Mr. President! I gather that Colonel Heinz has already apprised you of the Soviets' condition of readiness. I thought you ought to know that as far as our ground and satellite surveillance indicates, there have been no major breaches by the Soviets of any of the prearranged tactical or strategic positions. We sent up two extra DSCS Elevens on asymmetric orbits just to make sure. You know how the Soviets tend to freeze all troop activity to coincide with our satellite-overfly timetable. Well, the same way we do with theirs, of course. But as far as we can surmise, no problems."

"Thank you, General," said the President and without further discussion, he put down the phone. As if trying to show that he could be decisive after all, he picked up his piece of toast and ate it, although he didn't taste it. "Well, then, Morton," he said after he had swallowed, "as soon as we get word from Copenhagen, this is it."

Morton said, "We still have time to redefine our position, sir."

The President looked up balefully and shook his head. "We were locked into this situation years ago, Morton. This is the inevitable outcome of Yalta. If you want to blame anybody, blame Churchill and FDR. But there's no turning back."

Colonel Heinz was still waiting, his cap tucked under his arm. "Is there anything further, sir?"

The President frowned at him as if he couldn't remember who he was or why he was here. "Yes, Colonel," he said at length. "You can tell your children one day that when the future of America was finally and completely secured for all time and when the threat of nuclear devastation was at last expunged from the face of the earth, you were there."

"Yes, sir. It's an honor, sir." He didn't have any children but refrained from saying so.

The President picked up his coffee cup, peered into it and realized it was empty. "An honor," he repeated as if it was a long time since he had heard the word.

In London at almost the same moment, the Defense Secretary was just sitting down to lunch at the Savage Club with William Wright, the flamboyant literary agent known as much for his loud suits as for the hefty advances he managed to secure for his authors.

"And Auberon said—" William Wright was declaiming when the bell captain came hurrying through the high-ceilinged dining hall to touch the Defense Secretary's arm and tell him in a low whisper that Mr. Vaudrey wanted to see him, if he could, and that he could use the secretary's private office.

The Defense Secretary took one sip of the chilled Sancerre that had only just been poured into his glass and stood up.

"Excuse me, Bill. It's probably Aldershot complaining that they've been issued fifteen thousand left boots."

He walked across the dining hall, buttoning up his elegant, dark-blue Huntsman suit. He was tall and lean, with fair hair that was a bit too long for a government minister. The bell captain showed him through to the office where Hubert Vaudrey was waiting for him, inspecting the framed cartoons on the wall. Hubert Vaudrey always reminded the minister of a Harley Street psychiatrist, smooth and swarthy, although in fact he was deputy head of liaison between British and NATO intelligence services.

"Sorry to cut into your lunch, sir," he said, shaking the minister's hand. "I've just been given the message *Gringo*."

"Have you indeed?" asked the Defense Secretary. "Any further word from Copenhagen?"

"Nothing yet. But my feeling is that the Yanks are trying to speed up a settlement by preparing to pull out their nonessentials ahead of the agreed-upon schedule. A demonstration of good intent, so to speak. Weisenheimer tells me the Cubans are still proving a little obstreperous."

"I'm having lunch with Bill Wright, as a matter of fact," said the Defense Secretary. "He's trying to persuade me to write a book on rhododendrons."

"Well, we don't *have* to do anything straightaway. In fact, Moxon would rather we didn't."

"What about the PM?"

"Lunching with the Argentinians, of course. God knows how long that's going to take. Some bright spark ordered lamb as the entrée instead of beef."

"As long as they didn't call it *Agneau aux Malvinas*."

"Wait till after lunch, then?" asked Hubert Vaudrey.

The Defense Secretary nodded. "And personally, I think the Americans are being rather premature. I'd rather hold off until we get the absolute final word from Denmark."

"We did of course give Stuttgart the impression that *Cornflower* would be actioned as soon as they actioned *Gringo*."

"Let me take care of that. Drake waited until he'd finished his game of bowls. I'm going to wait until I've had my lunch. Bill says this book could be quite a little winner. Besides, they've got sea bream on the menu and I wouldn't miss that even if the Russians were marching along the Champs-Élysées with snow on their boots.''

"All right, then," said Hubert Vaudrey. "What shall I say if Weisenheimer starts nagging?"

"Be nice, that's all."

"Righty-ho."

In Manchester, one hundred eighty miles to the northwest, the president of the National Union of Mineworkers, Albert Grange, had just arrived at the Great Northern Hotel to meet a delegation of Polish mineworkers for a buffet lunch and a roundtable discussion on cheap coal imports. He paused for a moment or two on the pavement outside the hotel while news photographers took pictures, then went into the hotel lobby, laughing loudly at some remark made by his Scottish deputy, Stuart McLaren.

Albert Grange was short and stocky; not even his tailor-made suits could hide his miner's shoulders. He had a ruddy face, wiry gray hair and a permanent smile. He smiled even when he was angry.

He was on his way through to the conference room when a black-haired woman in a gray suit and a white ruffled blouse made her way through the union officers surrounding him and said, "Mr. Grange?"

"That's me, love."

"I've got a message from Rodney."

"Oh, good old Rodney!" said Mr. Grange in a cheerful voice. He gripped Stuart McLaren's elbow and said, "You go ahead, Stu. I won't be a moment."

The woman in the gray suit led Mr. Grange through to a small private-interview room next to the toilets and firmly closed the door. Mr. Grange offered her a cigarette but she declined with a shake of her head. "Well, well," he said, lighting up with a gold Dunhill lighter. "So Rodney's been in touch, has he? I was wondering when we were going to hear from him."

The woman's face was expressionless. She could have been a librarian or a schoolteacher: gray-faced, middle-aged, spinsterish. In fact, she was a "sleeper" and had been for nearly twenty-one years, all of them spent in preparation for this one assignment: contacting the British trades unions and telling them that at last the proletariat revolution was imminent.

"You must be aware that the military preparations in Europe are now complete," said the woman in a flat South London accent.

"Well, I've been reading the newspapers."

"All we are waiting for now is the final signal. This will be in days rather than weeks. Meanwhile, your own union is to start strike action on May seventeenth."

Albert Grange said, "That won't be difficult. We've already locked horns with the Coal Board over pit closures in Derby."

"The TGWU will be coming out two days before; the railwaymen and footplatemen will be coming out the day after. The following week, the Civil Service unions and the electricians will come out."

"This is really it, then?" said Albert Grange, blinking at her through his cigarette smoke.

"I am allowed to tell you that this is not just a simulation."

"When will I get my full instructions?"

"Not until later. You are cautioned to have patience and to take no action other than normal strike action until you are specifically told to do so. You are particularly advised not to be inflammatory in anything you or your members say or do, but to be creatively obstructive to the mining and movement of coal and to encourage mass peaceful picketing that will absorb as many police resources and as much police time as possible."

Albert Grange listened to this, nodding, and then said, "Supposing they bring in the army?"

"That, of course, is the ultimate aim. If the armed forces are brought in to handle the movement of essential services, they will be wrongly positioned and wrongly deployed when the time for the revolution actually comes."

Albert Grange said nothing more for a while. The woman watched him and at last said, "I must go now. You will not see me again. Any further instructions will come to you by other means."

"Is there anybody I can get in touch with if I have any problems?" Albert Grange asked.

"Talk to Comrade Philips, as you usually do. He will pass on any information you require."

The woman opened the door and left. Albert Grange sat in the interview room and finished his cigarette. So here it was at last. An end to the class struggle, the final defeat of capitalist oppression.

He thought of his father all those years ago, sitting at the kitchen table in their miner's cottage in South Yorkshire, reading aloud from Karl Marx: "From each according to his abilities, to each according to his needs."

He also wondered, in a peculiarly heretical flash of lateral thinking, whether the Russians would allow him to keep his country house and his Jaguar.

About an hour and a half later, while he was working out in his home gymnasium on his Haden Dynavit Aerobiotronic exercise cycle, the junior senator from Connecticut, David Daniels, was interrupted by his housekeeper Cora, the only person allowed to interrupt him when he was exercising: an hour a day of advanced aerobics, cycling and weight training, all on the most advanced and expensive equipment.

"Senator, Miss Modena says she has to speak to you urgently."

David nodded, his forehead glistening with perspiration as he completed his eleventh mile.

"She says it's very urgent, Senator."

David slowed the cycle and stopped. Cora handed him a towel and he buried his face in it, then patted at his underarms. Eventually he dismounted from the cycle, touched his toes four or five times, shook his arms and legs to loosen out the muscles and walked on squeaking Nikes to the door of the gym, Cora following behind.

It was a warm, sunny day in Darien. The patio doors of David's split-level house were wide open and the lace curtains rose and fell in the slightest of inland breezes. Through the white-carpeted living area, out on the red-brick patio, David's personal secretary, Esther Modena, was waiting: a tall, pretty girl with a fashionably tangled mane of dark hair, wearing a white Indian-cotton dress. David walked through the lace curtains and stepped outside into the sunshine, his towel around his neck.

"This has got to be *real* urgent," he remarked. "Do you want a lemonade?"

She shook her head no. She watched him as he went across to the white cast-iron table and poured himself a drink from a big glass jug. Sound of ice cubes clanking in lemonade. She knew he was angry; she could tell by the way he wouldn't look at her directly. Usually he was warm, open and communicative.

"You know my friend Wally, the one I was telling you about?"

"I remember. The guy you wanted a hundred bucks for just to take to lunch."

"I think the hundred bucks may have paid off," said Esther.

David could detect something unusual in the tone of her voice and he turned around and looked at her, sharply focusing his deep-set eyes. He was a well-built, good-looking man, broad-faced, sharp-nosed, strong-jawed, with brown wavy hair. His only physical failing was that he was a little overweight, for all of his workouts, and that had given him a jowly, slightly debauched look, as if Superman had been eating too many cream pies and drinking too much soda pop.

"Wally called me about an hour ago. He said there's a strong rumor going around that Fidel Castro is preparing to stand down in Cuba and institute free elections."

David drank his lemonade and said nothing but carefully watched Esther over the rim of his glass.

"He said he's also seen confidential reports from Nicaragua and Ecuador that Communist guerrillas have ceased all hostile activity and that many of them have already surrendered and handed over their weapons."

David said, "What's his source? On Castro, I mean?"

"He won't say any more, just that it's a rumor."

"Some rumor. Do you think he's really got something, or do you think he's simply trying to earn himself a little extra scratch?"

"Come on, David. I said before that Wally's sincere."

"Even sincere people have to eat."

Esther sat down on a white cast-iron chair next to a brick tub of fluttering red begonias. "He says it's obvious that something really important is happening. Office doors are being closed and there's an incredibly heavy increase in secret communications traffic. He says that somehow the Castro thing and the Nicaraguan thing seem to be connected but he's not at all sure of how, or why."

David sat down, too, and shook his head.

"I can't believe that Castro's contemplating a free election. After twenty-five, twenty-six years? It doesn't make any sense. And if he is, why hasn't Zucker made a huge publicity splash out of it? You know what Zucker's like. Diplomacy by circus."

"I can only tell you what Wally said."

"Can he find out more?"

"I asked him," said Esther. "He said it wasn't going to be easy. C Street's like the Kremlin at the moment."

"Still, ask him to dig."

Esther said, "Can I pay him? Maybe a couple of hundred?"

"Okay. Make it two-fifty. But that has to include some clarification. If I'm going to raise this in the House, I'm going to want to give some facts, maybe some Xerox copies if he can lay hands on them."

"I wouldn't like him to get in trouble."

"He won't get in trouble. I'll make sure of that."

Esther made a couple of quick, scribbled notes on a pad; then she looked up and said, "There's one more thing."

"Hmh?"

"He said he didn't want to mislead you but he keeps picking up odd references to somebody called Gringo."

"Gringo? That doesn't mean anything to me. In connection with what?"

"Well, in connection with all of this Fidel Castro business."

David shrugged. "Maybe Gringo's some kind of go-between. Maybe Zucker's been carrying on secret negotiations with Castro; free elections in exchange for financial aid. I don't know. It doesn't seem to make very much sense. Ask your friend if Cuba's going to be withdrawn from Comecon at the same time."

Esther made another note. "Are you still flying back to Washington on Wednesday?" she asked.

"As far as I know. That's as long as Helen doesn't make any undue fuss over the house."

Helen was David Daniels' second wife. At the age of forty-one, he was about to be divorced for the second time. The official reason was incompatibility; the real reason was that David's career had simply taken up too much time. Helen had begun to feel that David loved the Senate more than her and that she could have cited Capitol Hill for taking him away from her. In fact, she could with greater success have cited Esther; she and David had made love in a ski lodge at Aspen early this year, and again only four or five weeks ago at The Pilgrim's Inn in Salem, Massachusetts. They were not regular lovers, however, and never could have been. Their interests in life were too disparate. Esther was interested in political philosophy and saving whales and making Early American quilts. David was interested in power and how it could be used to change the face of the world. George Roth, the senior senator, called him "The Young Centurion."

David kissed Esther lightly on the lips and then led her to the front door, his arm around her waist. "I'll put out a few exploratory feelers myself. You remember Jimmy Mocarelli down in Phoenix? He's closely tied in with all those rich Cuban exiles there; he may know something that helps to put a frame around this particular painting."

Esther's red Datsun ZX was parked under the shade of the rustling oaks that screened David's house from the road leading north to New Canaan. David opened the door for her and waved as she drove off. Then he went back into the house and through to his library: cool, venetian-blinded, with cubist sculptures standing against bare white walls.

He picked up the phone and punched out the number of *The Washington Post*. When the call was answered, he asked to be put through to Jack Levy on the city desk.

"Jack? David Daniels. Yes. I'm at home in Connecticut. Well, that's right, it's going through next month. Listen, Jack, I want you to do me a small favor, usual terms. I've had a tip-off from C Street that something interesting may be going on in Cuba. That's right. Well, nothing short of a free election. Well, no, I don't have any authentication whatever. It's a heavy-duty rumor at the moment, that's all. But it may be connected with something else that's going on, something better-documented, and that is that Communist insurgents in Central America are beginning to put down their weapons and come on in. Did you hear anything about that? Well, no, me neither. But it's supposed to be true. Then there's one more thing. Just a name: Gringo. You ever heard that name, Gringo? Could be a code name, like Deep Throat. Could be a man, could be an operation, who knows? But start on C Street, then try some of those contacts of yours in the Pentagon. Okay. Well, I'm flying back Wednesday. Well, it depends. Okay, then. Take care."

He put down the phone. As he did so, a fat-bellied man who was sitting on the opposite side of the New Canaan road in a '74 Thunderbird put down the earphones of his telephone equipment too, and the cassette tape deck on the seat beside him automatically clicked to a stop.

David padded back to his gym. He still had twenty minutes to go on the exercise cycle, at the end of which time his efforts, had his bicycle not been stationary, would have taken him at least thirty miles, all the way to Fairfield.

The fat man in the Thunderbird, breathing asthmatically, dialed a mobile number and said, "Hatchet? This is Bird. We were right about our friend. You got it. We have another friend too. Well, we can deal with him later. All right. I'll leave it to you."

The fifth crucial message that morning was received by telephone at a small, pink-washed house in the village of Arendsee in the province of Altmark in East Germany, close to the West German border. The phone rang for almost three minutes before a short, powerfully built man came into the sparsely furnished living room and answered it.

"*Doch?*" he said. He wore a checked shirt and light-green corduroy trousers. He could have been anything from a game-keeper to a farm laborer. Only the pallor of his face gave away the fact that he spent most of his time out of the sun, in dark and shadowy places.

"Is that Arendsee fifty-eight oh-oh forty-three?" said a

muffled voice. It sounded as if the caller had a scarf or a handkerchief over the mouthpiece.

The man drew back the net curtains at the window and looked out over the marshy reaches of Arendsee itself, reflecting the blue-gray sky like polished slate. Two small boys on bicycles rode through the yellowish grass; an army lorry whinnied past.

"Who wishes to know?" the man inquired after a pause. His eyes were as vacant as the lake of slate.

"*Der scheckiger Pfeifer* sent me. He said he had trouble getting rid of a rat."

"What color?"

"White."

The man let the net curtain fall back again. "It isn't so easy this time of year. What's he prepared to pay?"

"Ten."

"Not enough, I'm afraid."

"Twelve, then."

"Twelve-five."

"Very well. When and where?"

The man paused for a while and then asked, "Where is your rat located?"

"Wünsdorf."

"Can you bring it any closer?"

"It's possible. Day after tomorrow I have to be in Haldensleben. I could bring her there."

"You can't manage any closer than that?"

"It's impossible."

Another lengthy pause. Then, "All right. Bring your rat to Haldensleben day after tomorrow. As soon as you arrive, call Magdeburg sixty-seven twenty-three oh one. Tell them again that you were sent by the *scheckiger Pfeifer*. They will give you instructions on what to do. Oh—and make sure you bring the money in cash. What number did the *scheckiger Pfeifer* give you?"

"Nine."

"Very well. We will wait to hear from you."

"*Auf wiederhören*," said the voice on the end of the phone.

The man said nothing but put the phone down, took out a handkerchief and loudly blew his nose.

Another man came into the room, thinner, with near-together eyes.

"Was that him?" he asked.

The stocky man wiped his nose from side to side and nodded. "Marshal of the Soviet Union T.K. Golovanov in person."

NINE

Tivoli Gardens sparkled with lights and music as Charles wove his way through the crowds toward the Ferris wheel. He was already five minutes late. Agneta had insisted he eat a sandwich before he left, wholewheat bread and Danish blue cheese, to soak up some of the alcohol. The sandwich had taken him almost ten minutes to eat because he had no saliva, and it was still working its way painfully down toward his stomach like an unoiled elevator descending a condemned building.

Jeppe was already there, smoking. Standing next to him, dwarfish and hunched over, was Otto Glistrup. Otto was the second-best bagman in Copenhagen. He personally considered that he was the best. Jeppe had rehabilitated him from a life of safe-cracking and bank-computer frauds, and now the Danish intelligence services kept him reasonably busy all year 'round. His only problems were his vanity and his monotonous, endless obsession with his ugly wife and how much she mistreated him.

Charles shook hands with Jeppe and then with Otto. "How are you doing, Mr. Glistrup? I haven't seen you in a long time."

"I've been away," said Otto in a nasal voice. "Hedvig was ill and insisted I take her to stay with her sister in Lolland. Five months we were there, and every time I suggested going back to Copenhagen, she had a relapse. 'Oh, my poor sinuses, I can't go back to Copenhagen, too much dust from the lime trees.' I had to promise her a new winter coat to get her back and still she complains, sneezes and complains."

Charles took Otto's arm and together the three of them walked slowly around the gardens, between the flower beds lit with green-and-white stars of light, and along the tree-lined avenues. Somewhere close by, a promenade orchestra was playing "The Radetzky March," and Jeppe hummed, *"Diddle-dum, diddle-dum, diddle dum-dum-dum!"*

Charles said to Otto, "I want to get into somebody's computer."

"Well," nodded Otto, his face as sharp as a weasel's, "I can do that for you, depending on how cleverly the computer has been protected from outside interference, but you don't need *me* for such a job. A computer can be broken into just as easily from the outside; what do you want with a break-and-entry man? There are far better computer people than me. Try Peder Statfeldt; he's half my age. He can gain access to your computer from his own bedroom."

"The information we require may not be stored in the computer," said Charles. "We want you to go through the files first."

"What kind of an establishment are we talking about?" asked Otto. "I charge double for embassies, you know; three times for Middle Eastern embassies; and I won't do any Libyan building at all."

"It's nothing like that," Charles reassured him, putting his arm confidentially around Otto's twisted shoulder blades. "It's an architect's office, that's all, here in Copenhagen. Klarlund and Christensen, just across the road. No special security, nothing to worry about."

"The last time somebody told me there was nothing to worry about, I had all the fingers in my left hand broken."

"Believe me," said Charles, "all the security problems have already been dealt with."

Otto was silent for a while. Charles and Jeppe glanced at each other over the top of his head. Jeppe gave Charles a wink that obviously meant Otto would agree.

"My wife wouldn't approve," said Otto. "She says I shouldn't work for people like you; it's too dangerous. She says I'm going to kill her one day from blood pressure."

"Well, Otto, we all have to go sometime," said Charles. "You know, life is just like boating on a lake. Sooner or later they call out your number and say, 'Time's up, my friend.' You know that as well as I do."

Otto didn't answer. They came to an ice-cream stand and Charles bought them each a vanilla cone with chocolate chips. They walked underneath the trees licking their cones as if they were three small boys planning a daring prank.

"I can't do it tomorrow," said Otto. "Nor the next day. My wife's brother is coming over from Fyn."

"Is there anything wrong with tonight?" asked Charles.

"Tonight? With no preparation?"

"What do you need?"

"Well, nothing much. Just my tools."

"Where are your tools?"

"In the back of my car."

"And where's your car?"

"In the multistory on Vesterport."

Charles squeezed his shoulder enthusiastically. "In that case, there's no problem, is there? Shall we go take a look at the office?"

"I don't know," said Otto. Then he suddenly stared at his ice cream. "Why am I eating this ice cream? I hate ice cream." He dropped the cone into a litter bin.

They crossed the wide pedestrian bridge that spans the southern end of Tivoli's lake, and the lights from the pleasure park dipped and sparkled in the dark water. Then they made their way back to Vesterbrogade and along to Banegårdspladsen. They stopped opposite the offices of Klarlund & Christensen and Charles said, "There you are. The whole place is in darkness. Standard alarm system as far as I could see. Standard locks. No problems at all. You could be in and out of there in ten minutes flat."

Charles cleared his throat and then smiled at Otto as if he were a real-estate agent showing him a particularly desirable family home in New Rochelle. "Can't you just imagine yourself and Mrs. Glistrup and all the little Glistrups on the lawn in summer? Oh, I beg your pardon, no little Glistrups? Well, never mind; more peaceful for both of you.''

Otto looked the building up and down. "I'll have to get closer. Can I get closer?''

"No reason why not. They don't have any security guards.''

They crossed the street. Jeppe kept a look-out for police patrols while Otto crouched down beside the glass front door of Klarlund & Christensen and examined the lock. After a while, he stood up and frowned at the brushed-steel surround of the entire office facade, sucking at his front teeth from time to time. The lights of Vesterbrogade were reflected in the plate glass, a world within a world.

"Well?" asked Charles impatiently.

"The locks are easy. I'm not so sure about the alarms. They have the usual electromagnetic sensors and I expect they have an infrared beam across the lobby somewhere. But I don't know. I'm not so sure about this. It doesn't feel good.''

Jeppe said, "Are you going to do it or not?''

"I don't know," said Otto. "I need more time. I'd like to see a plan of this building, maybe find out who installed the alarms and see if I can't get hold of a diagram.''

Charles said, "How long will that take?''

"Well, it depends. Six or seven weeks maybe.''

"I don't think we can wait that long," said Charles.

"Jobs like this, you can't hurry.''

Charles said to Jeppe, "What's it going to take to persuade this dwarf that we need to get into this building as soon as possible?''

Jeppe said, "Come on, Otto. This isn't so difficult. How many times have you done a job like this before?''

"I don't know," Otto repeated. "It just seems wrong. I don't know what it is, but something's wrong.''

"Do you think you can get into the building without triggering the alarm?" asked Charles.

Otto shook his head. "I'll tell you what makes me suspicious. They have an adequate alarm system as far as I can make out from a superficial inspection like this, but it's nothing like foolproof. Now who would spend money on an alarm system that isn't foolproof unless he *already* has a back-up alarm that is completely impregnable? You see that box there? Those light-housings over on the floor there? They may be real alarms but they're a decoy. These people have a far better alarm system, something that really keeps people away. They may even have booby traps.''

"In an architect's office?'' asked Jeppe skeptically.

"My dear Jeppe,'' said Otto without turning around, "whatever one man is interested in stealing, another man is interested in keeping safe. I don't know what it is that you expect to find here. You know me, Jeppe, I never ask questions. But if it is valuable enough for you to want it so bad, it must be valuable enough for these people to protect it in the most sophisticated way they can think of. There are visible alarms here, what we call frighteners. An amateur will think twice about breaking in when he sees them. But they are also a warning to the professional like me, for it is obvious that they are not one hundred percent. They are a subtle message that if I *do* try to break in, I shall find myself in deep trouble.''

"So what do we do?'' Charles demanded.

"We don't do anything,'' Otto replied. "Not without weeks of proper investigation and surveillance, not without sending people here in the daytime to check out the controls, not without learning this building's alarm system inside and out.''

Charles said, "The trouble is, Otto, we really would like to know what's going on here *now*. I mean tonight.''

Otto pouted and shook his head. "I'm sorry, Mr. Krogh. I can't do anything for you tonight. It just isn't my way of working. I'm not a burglar anymore. I'm a professional.''

Charles appealed to Jeppe. "Jeppe, tell him he has to.''

"You have to,'' said Jeppe.

Otto stared at Jeppe and then turned around and stared at Charles. "I hope you don't mean that seriously, Jeppe,'' he said at last.

"I mean it seriously, Otto. You have to.''

"If you don't,'' put in Charles, "I'm going to have your lily-livered guts for breakfast with a side order of cottage fries.''

Otto looked up at the Klarlund & Christensen building with deep unhappiness. "I suppose this is some kind of headquarters,'' he said.

"Not that we happen to be aware of,'' said Charles.

"Well, for headquarters, I charge time and a half," said Otto.

"That's all right," said Jeppe. "If it turns out to be some kind of headquarters, any kind, you'll get time and a half. Guaranteed, with the royal seal of Margrethe II."

"In that case," said Otto, "it seems to me that we will have to be as unsubtle as these alarms are subtle. Can you somehow find me an old car? Big and heavy, maybe American. But it must still run."

"I think we can oblige," said Jeppe. "I'll call Birkers on Nørre Farimagsgade. They've usually got a selection of old cars."

"All right, then," said Otto. "While you do that, I'll go collect my tools."

"Don't worry," Charles told Jeppe. "I'll go with him. Every step of the way."

They walked to the multistory garage on Vesterport. Charles rubbed his hands briskly; the May night was growing chilly. The clock on top of the Rådhus proclaimed that it was already eleven o'clock, and a northeasterly wind was blowing from Sweden. Otto said, "I shouldn't do this, you know. It's against my better instincts."

"What, are you chicken?" asked Charles. "Where's your sense of adventure?"

"I lost my sense of adventure about six weeks after I married Hedvig."

Charles followed Otto up the stairs of the car park until they reached the second level. Otto's Saab was parked in a dark corner. He opened up the trunk and took out a blue-nylon sports bag.

"What do you want an old car for?" Charles asked him, leaning against the open trunk.

"The professional always uses psychology," said Otto, rummaging inside the bag to make sure he had all the tools he wanted. "The people who set the alarms in that building used psychology; we have to use it in return. They are devious thinkers and the only problem with devious thinkers is that they tend to assume that everybody else is a devious thinker too. Well, on the first level, you have to be devious to understand what traps they set. But on the second level, you must be straightforward and crude because there is nothing that upsets the devious thinker like crudeness.''

"You still haven't told me what you want the car for.''

Otto slammed the trunk of the car shut and began to walk back toward the exit with the loping gait of a hunchback. Charles followed him, his hands in his pockets.

"We will gain access to the lobby by driving the car into the plate-glass window,'' Otto explained. "This will no doubt set off all the alarms, but so to my mind would any complicated and time-wasting tinkering. So it is better for us to be quick.''

"Then what?'' asked Charles. "Come on, Otto, we're only four blocks from police headquarters. We're going to have every flatfoot in Denmark down on our ears in five minutes.''

They reached the street and began walking back toward Banegårdspladsen. Otto said, "Use your imagination, Mr. Krogh. If you were to come across a car that had crashed into an office window, an abandoned car, what would you think had happened to the driver?''

"I would assume that he had run off,'' said Charles. "Drunk probably; that's what I'd think.''

"Precisely,'' said Otto. "You wouldn't imagine for a moment that he had actually *entered* the building for the purpose of burgling the files.''

"You're a brilliant man, Otto.''

"You too have a reputation for brilliance, Mr. Krogh. At police headquarters they still tell that story about you, about how you caught that Soviet agent trying to smuggle his way back to Murmansk in a cargo of cheese. That *was* true, wasn't it? Not just a yarn?''

Charles made a dismissive face.

They reached the offices of Klarlund & Christensen. Since there was no sign of Jeppe, they went across the road and had a schnapps at a small, crowded bar called, to Charles' perpetual amusement, the Mars Bar. The Danes seemed to have a thing about planets: two of the best hotels in Copenhagen were called the Mercur and the Neptun. Charles kept an eye on the street and after a half-hour he saw a large, black Lincoln draw up outside and park. Its headlight covers closed like sleeping eyes; then Jeppe climbed out and looked around for them, a worried expression on his face.

Charles went outside. "Jeppe! We're here!"

"Not drinking again," said Jeppe testily.

"Something to steady the nerves, that's all, my dear fellow. Come in and have one yourself."

Jeppe shook his head. "Let's get this over with."

They went back into the bar and found Otto. Jeppe said, "Just tell me what you want to do."

Otto wiped his nose and then said, "You must drive the car diagonally across the street, as fast as you dare, and strike the right-hand door frame with maximum force. That is all. Then you must run away from the car that way, across the street, while Mr. Krogh and I make our entry. You must not look back."

"All right," said Jeppe uncertainly.

Charles inspected the huge Lincoln sedan. "What is this, seventy-four, seventy-five?"

"Birker told me seventy-four. Not that it matters. It goes well enough."

"What did he charge you for it?"

"Twenty-seven thousand kroner."

"Robbery."

"Well, it was after hours. He was having his supper. He had to open up the showroom specially. And of course I had to pay him a few extra for keeping his mouth closed."

"Sounds like a friend."

"Let's just do it, shall we?" said Jeppe. "Otto, are you ready?"

"I suppose so."

Otto guided Charles across the street and into the shadow of a doorway in the building next door to Klarlund & Christensen. They watched as Jeppe climbed into the Lincoln, backed it up a little way and then waited by the opposite curb. The car's engine burbled menacingly through a ruptured muffler.

"I hope this is a good idea," said Charles affably.

"Do you have a *better* idea?" Otto asked him, shifting his weight from one foot to the other with a muffled clanking of tools.

"I don't know. It seems kind of violent to me. I always

thought you were the Harry Houdini of bagmen, not the Incredible Hulk.''

"Sometimes, Mr. Krogh, it pays us well to behave out of character."

"Whatever you say."

Otto glanced quickly around the street; for a moment there was a lull in the late-night traffic and it was relatively quiet. He lifted one hand, fingers spread, and then gave a quick, abrupt wave. The Lincoln's tires squittered on the road, its engine roared and it surged diagonally across the street, bouncing up onto the curb and hurtling toward the glass facade of Klarlund & Christensen like a vast black killer whale.

The crash was ear-splitting. The heavy glass doors were wrenched from their hinges and sent shattering across the marble floor of the lobby; then the stainless-steel door frame collapsed, bringing down the huge sheet of plate glass that was supported on the architrave. The glass smashed edgewise onto the pavement and exploded like a bomb, showering Banegårdspladsen with thousands of glittering fragments.

Several passersby turned in shock and surprise. Charles said, "Jesus," but Otto was already shoving him with his elbow and urging him, "Go, go, go. Into the lobby before anyone sees us."

They ducked low behind the Lincoln, their feet crunching on broken glass. At almost the same time, Jeppe opened the driver's door on the opposite side of the car and sprinted across the street toward Reventlowsgade, his tie flapping behind him, his head lifted as if he were running a college 200-meter relay.

Charles and Otto crunched quickly across the lobby and slid behind a pillar to conceal themselves from the street while they looked for the staircase. Already six or seven passersby had gathered around the Lincoln and Charles could hear them saying, "Did you see that? It came out of nowhere." "Just like that, smack into the doorway." "But where's the driver?" "Drunk, most like." "I think I saw him. A kid. He was running off down that way."

Otto touched Charles' arm. "There are the stairs, look. If we keep low behind that desk, we should be able to reach them without being seen."

Charles said, "I don't hear any alarm."

"Ah, you don't hear it but there's an alarm all right. The interesting thing to know would be where it's actually going off. Don't you worry, Mr. Krogh, somebody has been alerted. So we must be quick."

They made their way crab-fashion across the lobby until they reached the door to the staircase. Charles eased the door open while Otto awkwardly made his way through it. Then Charles followed and carefully closed the door behind them. They could stand straight now, but Otto touched his finger to his lips to indicate that they should stay silent.

Charles was beginning to regret his dissolute lifestyle by the time they reached Nicholas' office. While Otto unpacked his tools and laid them out neatly on Nicholas' desk, Charles leaned against the wall, dabbing the sweat from his face and neck with his handkerchief. "I used to be able to run 800 meters without even panting," he said.

"Let's start with the files," Otto suggested. "If the files give us nothing, we can start on the computer."

"You're not even breathing hard," Charles complained.

Otto smiled like a small rat that has just eaten a rather pleasant piece of Gruyère. "If you had a wife like mine, Mr. Krogh, you would keep fit too. Better an hour spent exercising than an hour spent listening to all her complaints. Anyway, my back hurts me less if I exercise."

Charles cleared his throat. "I guess the personnel files will be in Klarlund's office. He seems to be the *Obergruppenführer* around here."

Guided only by Otto's subdued flashlight, they walked through the deserted offices until they reached the door marked *Hans Klarlund, Direktor*. The door was locked but Otto picked it so deftly that he might have had a specially made key. "Nothing special, an Ingersoll five-lever." He zipped up his little black-leather case of picks.

At night Klarlund's office looked even more severe. Charles went over to the window and peered down into the street while Otto inspected the light-gray filing cabinet. There were red-and-blue police lights flashing across Banegårdspladsen, and even through the double-glazed windows, Charles could hear the blare of sirens. Otto said, "This filing cabinet is unmarked. What are you looking for?"

"Anything on office personnel or on somebody called Nicholas Reed."

Otto picked the locks on the filing cabinet one after the other and rolled out the drawers. "There it is. You can take a look for yourself."

Charles squatted down in front of the bottom drawer. He leafed through sheaf after sheaf of architectural plans, building permissions, diagrams, Xerox prints and correspondence. "Look at this," he said. "I didn't know they were thinking of building a new hotel on Nørre Søgade."

Otto was sitting on the windowsill like a crookbacked crow, waiting for Charles to finish. "Who's this fellow Nicholas Reed?"

"That's what we're here to find out," Charles told him.

It took him almost fifteen minutes to go through the whole cabinet, but even though there were detailed personnel files *"Andreas–Wuppe"* in the top drawer, there was no mention of anybody called Nicholas Reed. Charles pushed the drawers back in with a sniff of resignation and dusted his hands together. "Okay," he said, "you can lock it all up again now."

"Do you want me to try the computer?"

"I think we're going to have to. It's an IBM-Two thousand."

"Mr. Rifbjerg told me that. Don't worry about it. I went through the IBM-Two thousand at the *Forenede Danske Motorejere* last year, specially for Mr. Rifbjerg. He was very satisfied."

"Come on, then."

Charles opened the door of Hans Klarlund's office but as he did so, he caught the faintest clicking sound. He waved Otto back and said, "*Ssh.* I think I heard something."

Otto immediately switched off his flashlight. They waited, holding their breath. Charles could hear his Seiko watch ticking away the seconds. He looked back at Otto, who made a questioning face.

"It sounded like a door being closed," whispered Charles.

"Maybe a draft," Otto suggested.

Charles opened the door a little wider. The corridor appeared to be deserted. There was no sound now but the distant swishing of traffic down in the street; the police sirens had been silenced.

"How would anyone know we were up here?" asked Charles.

Otto said, "It's quite possible they have photoelectric beams all over the building. We could have been setting off more alarms just by walking down the corridor."

"All right," said Charles after a while. "Let's get back to that computer terminal. Do you think you're going to need very long?"

"It depends how well they've concealed the information you want, if it's stored in the computer at all."

"Well, let's get to it," Charles told him.

They walked quickly and quietly back to Nicholas Reed's office. When they reached it, however, Charles felt a sudden tingle of alarm. The door, which they had left wide open, was now almost completely closed. He held Otto's wrist and lifted one finger to indicate that he should hold back and stay silent. They listened for a while but then Otto whispered, "It must have been the draft. I must get back in there. My tools."

"Okay, but gently," Charles cautioned him. He wished he had reminded Jeppe to bring him that gun. He used to be quite good at unarmed combat, a rather disorganized combination of karate, kung-fu and bear wrestling, but he hadn't trained for so long that he doubted he could handle anybody meaner than a grade-school kid with glasses. He could have done with Roger right at this moment, blond wig and all, if only for physical reassurance.

Otto approached the door to Nicholas' office and touched it softly with his fingertips. It opened a little way, then struck something and juddered to a stop. Otto turned around and said, "There's something behind it. A chair, or a coatstand. You didn't knock anything over when you came out, did you?"

Charles shook his head. Otto gently pushed the door again, and again it stuck.

"I think we'd better get out of here," said Charles. "Come on, Otto; Jeppe can put in a chit to buy you some more tools."

"It's the police I'm worried about," said Otto. "Inspector Willumsen will have to take only one look at those tools to know who they belong to. That will mean jail for me for certain, and trouble for Jeppe too."

Charles regarded the door with a puckered, indecisive expression. Then at last he said, "Okay. Give it a try. But take it easy."

Otto reached around the door, keeping his eyes on Charles all the time. "It feels like a chair," he whispered. "Yes, it is. Somehow it's fallen against the door and—"

He let out a whoop of pain and surprise. *"Aaaaaahhhhh!"* he screeched, his voice as high as a woman's.

Charles stumbled forward. "Otto? *Otto?* What? What is it?" He seized Otto's left arm and tried to pull him away from the door.

"Don't pull me!" screamed Otto. "Don't pull me!" He was shuddering like an epileptic and staring at Charles wild-eyed, his face contorted. "Don't pull me! *Don't pull me!"*

Charles yelled, "What? What is it?" but Otto was beyond telling him. Charles took two or three quick steps back across the corridor and then charged at the door with his shoulder, colliding with Otto, the door and the chair behind it, and with somebody else who was standing behind the door. Otto let out a piercing shriek so high-pitched that Charles didn't know if he had actually heard it or just felt it cut through his brain.

Charles tumbled into the room, staggering, overbalancing and hitting his shoulder against the side of the desk. He turned around, winded, and saw Otto standing in the open doorway, trembling all over and holding up his right arm in agony and terror. From the elbow up, all the flesh had been stripped off so that he was holding up nothing but glistening bloody bones, radius and ulna, twisted with sinew. His right hand had been shredded into a distorted claw. Blood was splattering everywhere with a noise like a running tap left to splash on a carpet.

Charles stared desperately into the shadows behind the door, gasping from fright and sudden exertion. And slowly the door was eased back again so that he could see who it was who had mutilated Otto so ferociously, and how

It was a huge, bulky figure of a man, and even though

Charles couldn't see his face in the darkness, he knew at once who it was. The man raised both fists in front of him, and between those fists there coiled a gleaming circle of wire, tinged russet with blood. The man said nothing but let out a deep, volcanic growl and moved toward Charles with the terrible inevitability of a dark wall of lava.

Otto made no sound but slowly and carefully sat down on the floor, still holding up his fleshless arm as if it were some kind of grisly trophy. Blood puddled all around him. Charles said, "Otto! Otto, hold on! Everything's under control!" Otto said nothing.

The huge man advanced steadily on Charles, twanging the wire between his fists so it made a tensile, steely sound, all the while grumbling still, deep in his throat.

Charles moved cautiously around behind the desk. The man came after him, twanging the wire. Charles feinted to the left and the man feinted with him. Charles felt within himself that dark surge of total panic he had first experienced in Korea that rainy afternoon when he had been surrounded by enemy troops at Changjin Reservoir in 1952. No way out, not this time. Because now he was faced not with untrained Korean recruits but with *Krov' iz Nosu*, old Nose Bleed himself.

He feinted to the right. The huge man followed him, still flexing his deadly length of wire. *Twing, twing, twing.*

"I might have guessed you'd be here," Charles said loudly in English.

The huge man didn't answer but watched him out of the obscurity of the shadows with emotionless, glittering eyes. Over by the doorway, Otto had started to moan: a low, subdued, agonized moan; a moan that told Charles just how much his injury had begun to hurt him. *Krov' iz Nosu* must have wrapped that wire viciously tight around Otto's arm when he reached inside the room to remove the chair, wrapped it so ferociously that when Charles had at last forced open the door, all the flesh had been suddenly stripped away from Otto's bones like an electric cable stripped of its vinyl jacket. Otto's days as a safecracker were certainly over forever: he would be lucky if he lived. His brachial artery was pumping wildly and he was too shocked to press it so it would close.

Charles couldn't help Otto, not yet. *Krov' iz Nosu* was moving around the desk toward him, his burned face at last illuminated by the streetlights, and there was no question at all but that he intended to kill them both.

Charles warned, "You come any nearer, I'm going to give you a hard time."

Krov' iz Nosu didn't respond; all that Charles could hear was his harsh, uneven breathing. He was more like an automaton than a man: a killing machine of muscle and twisted tissue, a thing that had forgotten how to be human. Somewhere, at some time, *Krov' iz Nosu* had lost the sensitivity that distinguishes a human being from a robot. Perhaps it had happened when his face and body had first been splashed with molten metal. Perhaps it had happened during his endless skin grafts and surgical reconstructions. Perhaps it had happened afterward, when he was trying to build his body into the most powerful physical structure ever known. All Charles knew from his CIA files was that *Krov' iz Nosu* was more powerful than any Olympic weight-lifter, more adept at martial arts than any ninja, and that he had no compunction at all about killing his fellow human beings as bloodily and as mercilessly as possible.

Charles backed his way around the room until he reached the window. He groped behind him, feeling for the latch. *Krov' iz Nosu*'s wire went *twing, twing, twing. Krov' iz Nosu*'s face remained impassive, as burned as a side of beef, merciless. The sort of face to which it would be impossible to appeal for clemency.

Charles said, "I don't know anything about this. Honest. This has nothing to do with me. I'm the janitor. I only work here. Can I carry on with cleaning up, please? *Pozhalusta?*"

The huge, disfigured Russian said nothing but knocked aside a chair and continued to bear down on Charles, his steel wire flexing and an expression on his face that could almost have been interpreted as a smile.

"*Pozhalusta,*" he repeated in a breathy voice. In Russian the word for "please" could also mean "you're welcome."

Charles eased open the window latch. Thank God for Danish efficiency. In an American building, the latch would probably have been locked, seized up or painted over. He hoped to God that he could remember the karate move known as "the diving cormorant."

Krov' iz Nosu paused for a moment, building up power like an electric substation. Then he rushed at Charles, stretching his steel wire out wide just to make certain that if he didn't catch Charles' neck or his chest, he would at least snag it around his arm. Charles thought wildly: diving cormorant, here goes!

Charles dived heavily into the floor as if he were diving into a swimming pool. As he did so, he caught *Krov' iz Nosu*'s left ankle and heaved it up and over as forcefully as he could. *Krov' iz Nosu* tripped, stumbled, reached out to save himself and hit the tilting window. The window, unlatched, swung open and *Krov' iz Nosu* tumbled halfway out of it, grappling at the outside sill to prevent himself from falling into the street three stories below. Charles scrambled immediately to his feet and seized *Krov' iz Nosu*'s ankles, wrenching them upward to force him to lose his balance.

There was a tussle between them of wolflike grunts, high-pitched shouts and cries of anger. Charles gripped both of *Krov' iz Nosu*'s big, hairy ankles and shook them violently. Then he pushed them forward inch by inch until the Russian was on the edge of losing his balance. But *Krov' iz Nosu* kicked at him and began to lever himself back into the room. Charles could see his face, glaring and yellow and burned, staring at him upside down through the windowpane.

With a sudden surge of energy fueled by fear, Charles pushed at *Krov' iz Nosu*'s legs again, and abruptly the Russian was gone. No warning, no cry. Just a rush of air from the street below, a pause and then a faint thud.

Charles stood up straight, his chest bruised from his inelegant "cormorant-dive," sweating in rivulets. He leaned out the open window but it was too dark to see anything. *Krov' iz Nosu* had gone and that was all he cared about. Gone, broken and dead.

Charles knelt down beside Otto, feeling Otto's chilled blood soaking into the knee of his trousers.

"Otto," he said, "I'm calling the ambulance, okay?"

Otto said nothing but Charles could tell that he was still alive. He kept gasping in high, shocked gasps. Charles went to the phone and dialed 0041, the number of Copenhagen's emergency medical service. While he was waiting for an answer, he lit a cigarette.

At last a woman's calm voice said, "Emergency medical service." Charles told her, "Get me an ambulance, please, as quick as you can. Klarlund and Christensen, next door to Den Permanente. You can't miss it; no, there's a crashed car right in front of it. We're up on the third floor."

The woman was about to ask him for more details but he put down the phone, tugged off his tie and crawled on his hands and knees across the floor to rejoin Otto. "Otto, the ambulance is on its way. You're going to be fine." Otto was shaking and whining and Charles could tell from experience that he was going into deep shock. He remembered a nineteen-year-old boy in Korea, a young infantryman with his groin blown open by a Communist grenade. The same shuddering, the same whining. Charles wound his tie around Otto's upper arm and thought to himself, maybe it's the same war too.

He used a steel ruler from Nicholas Reed's desk to tighten a tourniquet around Otto's arm. There was so much blood splattered everywhere that he couldn't tell if he had managed to stanch the pumping artery or not. He wiped his hands on the carpet but his fingers still stuck together. He was shocked himself; he was beginning to feel cold; and the bruises that he had sustained in his struggle with *Krov' iz Nosu* were aching dully.

He went back to the desk and picked up the phone. Coughing, he dialed Jeppe's number. The phone rang for a long time before anybody answered it. "Jeppe?" he said.

A deep, harsh woman's voice answered.

"Nobody of that name here. You must have a wrong number."

"That's sixteen fourteen oh six?"

"That's correct. But there is nobody named Jeppe here."

Charles wiped sweat from his forehead with the back of his arm. "Are you certain about that? Jeppe Rifbjerg?"

"Quite certain. Now, please, good-night."

Charles put down the phone. He drew tightly at the last inch of his cigarette, then crushed it out. He hoped he wasn't beginning to feel frightened. The game hadn't often frightened him in the past, especially when it was nothing more than intelligence gathering, deceptions and feints and bribes. But this was something different. In this he could detect that frozen, dark wind of Communist restlessness that had come before Hungary and before Czechoslovakia. In his mind he could imagine looking east through the night and seeing spread out before him the vast, helmeted armies of the Soviet Union, pale-faced and grim. *Ye shall hear of wars and rumors of wars.*

He heard a door close somewhere else in the building. He heard footsteps, too calm and unhurried for ambulance attendants. He listened and his ear could detect that faintest of sounds that a human body makes as it moves quietly through the night. Cautiously he stepped over Otto and into the corridor. There was no doubt about it. He had done as much as he could for Otto. It was time to leave.

He made his way quickly to the staircase. He heard a sharply accented voice calling, "Lyosha?" He froze with his hand on the staircase door. Lyosha was the Russian diminutive for Aleksei, and *Krov' iz Nosu*'s real name was Aleksei Novikov. Or had been. Now, with any luck, he was dead *baranina*.

"Lyosha?" called the voice again. Charles opened the door to the staircase and cautiously descended. He felt very old and very sweaty; Otto's blood was drying on his hands and on the knees of his trousers. In the distance, he could hear an ambulance siren. He paused for breath at the bottom of the first flight of stairs, listening, but there was no more sound from the third floor.

"Dear God in heaven," he whispered under his breath.

And where in hell was Jeppe?

TEN

She called him at six. He opened his eyes, frowned, reached for the phone and said, "Yes?" Then he twisted around and looked at the bed beside him and realized that at some time during the night, she must have gotten up and left him.

"Michael? This is Rufina."

"Where are you? I thought you were here."

"I am downstairs in the lobby. I have had my breakfast already. I have to go out this morning to BIIHX—*vay day en kha*. We have a large party of French engineers to show around the Blast-furnace Exhibition."

"Will you be long?" Michael picked up his watch and checked the time.

"I will be back by eleven-thirty to take you out to the Toys Exhibition. So you should not worry. You and John could do some shopping, perhaps at TSUM or one of the Beryozka shops. You will not have many more chances to buy souvenirs."

"All right," said Michael. He didn't know what else to say. He certainly didn't want to say "I love you." But it had been a night of slow, concentrated lovemaking during which he had experienced feelings and sensations that for many people would have been the nearest they would ever come to being in love. He was certainly infatuated with her, whatever John had to say about his being naive.

He showered, dressed in a plain-white Van Heusen shirt and gray trousers, and called John. They went down to breakfast together, not saying much. Their *dezhurnaya* grinned at them with one front tooth missing and said, *"Zdrastvuytye,"* and they chorused *"Zdrastvuytye"* in return.

John took off his glasses and polished them with his handkerchief as they went down in the creaking elevator. "Rufina is not joining us?" he asked diffidently.

"She's gone off to *vay day en kha*. The Exhibition of the Economic Achievement of the USSR. Apparently she has some French people to take around."

"Let's hope she doesn't meet some Charles Aznavour type and give you the elbow."

"John, there's no need to be so bloody sour about it."

John put his glasses back on and sniffed.

Michael said, "We've got three hours free. Perhaps we should try out the metro."

"I still have some work to do on that *Tovarish!* game."

"You can do that later. Come on, John, we're here for only nine more days."

The elevator reached the lobby and the doors slid open. John said, "Did you call Margaret?"

"Yes, as a matter of fact."

"All right, is she?"

"Yes, thank you."

John said as they sat down at the breakfast table and the waiter brought them the breakfast menu, "Expect she's looking forward to having you home."

Michael said with a despairing laugh, "Drop it, will you? I want a business partner, not a traveling conscience."

John was silent for a while. Then he said, "All right. I'm sorry. I just like Margaret, that's all. And I like you too."

"You like Rufina, that's your trouble."

John sat back in his chair and looked out over the river. It was a dull, overcast day with clouds like heavy, gray quilts pressing down on the distant spires of Novodevichy Convent and Moscow University. "She reminds me of my music teacher," he said absently, as if that explained everything.

After they had paid for their breakfast with their Intourist vouchers and received a small saucerful of kopeks in change, they went upstairs for their jackets and raincoats and then ventured out. A damp, warm wind was blowing from the southwest; it felt more like early October than May. They crossed Red Square and entered the metro at the Sverdlova Square station. They were nudged forward through the turnstiles by a long line of shuffling Russians. Michael inserted five kopeks, the standard fare for any distance, and at last struggled through. John got the tail of his coat caught in the turnstile and had to be tugged free by a friendly woman twice his size.

The metro station was crowded, echoing and decorated like a glittering palace, with chandeliers and gilded plasterwork on the arched ceilings. The floor gleamed, the bronze handrails were highly polished and there was no litter anywhere. They descended an express escalator that seemed to plunge them down forever into the bowels of Mother Russia. As they waited to reach the platform, a teenage boy with Cliff Richard glasses tapped Michael on the shoulder and asked him, "Any Adidas, man?"

"Sorry," said Michael, shaking his head.

"Rokmusik kazety? T shirt?"

"Sorry."

"Where are you going, man? Want somebody to guide you? I speak excellent translation. You want *perevodchik?"*

"I think we can find our own way, thanks."

"Okay, that's cool," said the boy.

They made their way onto the metro platform. John said, "Where *are* we going, anyway?"

"We're just looking around," said Michael. He frowned at the metro map and was appreciative that the Cyrillic characters for "Airport" were no more daunting than АЗРОПОРТ. The first train rushed into the station, destination Rechnoy Vokzal. Michael nudged John forward and they pushed their way into the car and found a seat. The tall teenage boy stood opposite them and winked when they glanced his way. Michael discreetly looked around at his fellow passengers and thought that he had never seen such a collection of cheap, shapeless clothes in one underground car in his life, although their wearers seemed cheerful enough and one man opposite

was telling a joke that had his two lady companions screaming with laughter.

John said, "Sounds hilarious, whatever it is." As the train
approached Gorkovskaya, he checked his watch and said,
"Come on, I think we've seen enough of this. Let's go do
some shopping. Didn't Rufina say something about Kalinin
Avenue?"

"We're going the opposite way," said Michael.

"Well, I hate to be a nuisance but I'd really like to know
why."

"There's something we have to do."

"What? What do you mean, there's something we have to
do? You're not running errands for Rufina, are you?"

Michael said, "Let's wait until we get where we're going;
then I'll tell you."

John said furiously, "I'm not waiting for anything. I'm
getting out at the next station."

"You can't."

"Do you want to bet?"

Almost as he spoke, the train slammed noisily into
Gorkovskaya. Michael snatched at John's arm but to the
undisguised curiosity of the passengers around them, John
shook himself free and stalked out through the car doors.
"John!" Michael barked. But John ignored him and before
Michael could go after him, he had been absorbed into the
crowds, the train doors had closed with a hiss and the train
began to move away. Michael turned around in a last effort to
see where John had gone and briefly glimpsed the back of his
old corduroy jacket. He also saw the teenage boy in the Cliff
Richard glasses following John toward the exit. As the train
sped along the platform, the boy looked around at Michael,
caught his eye for a second and smiled. A strange, flat,
knowing smile.

Michael found himself jogging through the deep tunnels of
the Moscow metro in a car crowded with staring, Slavic
faces. He didn't know how far down he was: the actual depth
of the metro was a military secret. But he began to feel
claustrophobic with shoulders pressing close against him on
either side and unblinking faces staring at him as if he were
peculiar or mad. He said out loud, "Anglyiski," and smiled

and nodded, but the faces remained unmoved, unsmiling and unrelentingly curious. Every breath Michael took in smelled of sweat, stale Balkan tobacco and some other odor that was distinctively Russian. He had tried to analyze it and had come up time and again with the same possible ingredients: cardboard, pickled herrings and furniture polish.

The metro ran quickly through the stations that only three days before, Wallings had listed on the fingers of one hand. Mayakovskaya, Byelorusskaya, Dinamo and, at last, A3POI-IOPT. Michael stood up and waited for the doors to open. He realized he didn't have to do this, that he could just as easily pretend that Rufina had never left him alone and that he had never had the opportunity to come out here. Yet a strange compulsion made him step out of the train, not the least part of which was a sense of loyalty to his country. The other part, of course, was fear.

The doors closed behind him. There was a rush of noise as the train streamed down the tunnel again, toward Sokol. He was about to make his way toward the exit BbIXOII when a flat-faced man in a short bronze-colored raincoat and a gray, wide-brimmed hat came up and laid a hand on his shoulder.

"Mr. Townsend?"

"What of it?" asked Michael. Another man was approaching him from the far end of the platform, dressed in a brown pinstriped suit with flapping trousers.

"*Izvinite*, Mr. Townsend. Excuse me, but we have been told to take you straightaway to the Toy Exhibition in case you are late. Is Mr. Bishop not with you?"

"I'd like to know what this is all about," Michael retorted. "I only came along here for the metro ride. It's five minutes past nine, if you care to take a look at that clock over there, and I don't have to show up at the Toy Exhibition until eleven o'clock at the very earliest."

"Nevertheless, it seems that you are required there. Would you come along with us, please?"

It didn't seem to Michael that he had much choice. He reluctantly allowed the two men to escort him through the exit, up the escalator and out on to Leningradsky Prospekt. A fine drizzle had begun to fall and Michael was glad of his raincoat. The wide street was slicked with wet.

"Mr. Bishop is back at the Hotel Rossiya?" asked one of the men, wiping rain from his face.

"Mr. Bishop could be anywhere. He came with me on the metro as far as Gorkovskaya, then he got off."

"Do you know where he is now?"

"Of course not, but there was nothing I could do to stop him."

A black Volga 21 drew into the curbside, its engine clattering, and the man in the bronze-colored raincoat opened the rear door for Michael and said, "Please to get in."

"Can you tell me what's going on first?"

"Please. It will be better for all of us if there is no fuss. And the sooner we can drive back to Gorkovskaya, the more chance there is of finding Mr. Bishop."

Michael reluctantly climbed into the car. The man in the bronze-colored raincoat sat down heavily next to him, while the man in the brown pinstriped suit got into the front and buckled his seat belt. The car was being driven by a swarthy man with greasy hair. Michael couldn't see the driver's face but he could see his eyes in the rearview mirror. Hooded, watchful. My God, thought Michael, I've been taken in by the KGB. They probably knew why I was going out to the Kholinka airfield all along.

The Volga sped southeast, back toward the city. The rain grew heavier. The man in the raincoat said, "It is very important we find your friend, you know. In fact, we're sorry we left it until so late. We should have come around for you last night. But there were problems."

"I don't understand any of this," Michael told him.

The man squeezed his arm. "You will, my friend. Please have patience for half an hour."

"*Militsia*," remarked the driver, glancing in his mirror. He slowed down four or five miles an hour as a yellow highway patrol car with a broad blue stripe on it overtook him and carried on toward Gorkogo Ulitsa.

"We had hopes that your friend would be with you," said the man in the brown suit.

"Well, so did I, but we had an argument. Listen—I'm not under arrest, am I?"

"No, no, my friend. Nothing like that. But there is danger."

"What kind of danger?"

None of the three men would answer that question. In any case, they had now reached Gorkogo Ulitsa and were driving slowly along on the right-hand side, obviously looking for John.

"Please keep your eyes wide too," asked the man in the raincoat. "It is very crucial that we find your friend."

The rain meandered down the Volga's windows. Michael lowered his head so he could see out the opposite side of the car, but the pavements seemed to be crowded only with hurrying Russians in plastic raincoats and fur-collared anoraks.

"Any sign of him?" asked the man in the brown suit. "What's he wearing?"

"A raincoat. Blue, with a belt. Nothing special."

The man in the raincoat took out a pack of Russian *papirosi* cigarettes and offered one to Michael without looking around. Michael said, *"Nyet, spasibo."*

The man stuck one of the cardboard-tube cigarettes in his mouth and looked at Michael with interest. "You have been remembering your phrase book?"

Then he smiled and said, "Ah, no. My apology. You have been making friends with Konstantinova."

Michael said, "Listen. I demand to know what's going on. And I certainly demand to talk to the British Embassy."

"My friend, for your own safety, the very worst thing you could do is to speak to the British Embassy. We are saving you from the British, not to mention everybody else."

"Who are you?" Michael demanded.

The man lit his cigarette and filled the car with pungent blue smoke. He wound down the window a little way so the smoke eddied out in fits and starts. "We are friends, Mr. Townsend; that is all we can tell you at present. Please have patience. And do try to see if you can spot your friend."

"We're not going to the Toy Exhibition?"

The man shook his head. "Where do you think they will look for you first?"

"Where do I think *who* will look for me first?"

The man in the brown suit turned around and said, "The KGB, my dear fellow. You thought we were KGB? Well, if you knew the KGB, their typical people, you would know at once that we are not. You see now, Miss Konstantinova, there is your typical KGB officer. Good quality too. We know her very well."

"Rufina Konstantinova is a KGB officer?" asked Michael. "Listen, really, this sounds ridiculous—"

The man in the brown suit smiled. "Of course. You have never been to the Soviet Union before. Security matters of this kind are not within your usual experience. They seem like a play from the theater. Men in raincoats rushing around in strange cars. Mysterious women. Secret rendezvous in the Moscow metro. All this happens in New York and London, of course, but somehow not with the same heavy-handedness."

Michael sat back on the stretch-nylon seat covers. "I think you'd better take me back to my hotel."

The man in the brown suit covered his mouth with his hand. His eyes were thoughtful but amused. There was a wart on the side of his forehead and another on his chin, diagonally balanced. He said, "You have failed to understand, Mr. Townsend. You cannot go back to your hotel and you cannot go to the Toy Exhibition. You have been rescued."

"Rescued? Rescued from what?"

The man in the bronze-colored raincoat tapped his cigarette into the Volga's cheap chrome ashtray. "We have a friend who called Rufina Konstantinova late last night in the guise of her Intourist director on Marksa Prospekt and told her she would have to go early to BИHX. In point of fact, that was a way of removing your chaperone without making too much of a fuss. Our plan was to go to your hotel and explain matters to you so you would have time to leave with us before Rufina Konstantinova returned. But we had difficulty. Our movements are always observed by the KGB and we were delayed. By the time we reached the Rossiya, you were just leaving, and worse, you were being followed by a KGB agent."

Michael said, "Tell me what he looked like, this agent." He was serious now.

"Young, tall, a few spots on his face. He looks like a teenage hoodlum. He always approaches foreign tourists asking for *shutz* and *rokmusik* and Adidas sports bags."

"Shit," said Michael.

"Problem?" asked the man in the raincoat. The Volga

turned left across the rain-slicked intersection with the Moscow Ring Road and drove east past the Hotel Minsk, across the junction with Novoslobadskaya Ulitsa and toward the Moscow Circus. The rain came in pattering waves now, like watery locusts, against the windshield. Because of the Volga's inefficient ventilation system, the windows began to fog and Michael began to feel that he was in a world without sight or sense.

"That boy," he said, "that teenage boy. Well, that KGB agent, if you say that's what he was. He was following John out of the station."

The man in the raincoat squeezed Michael's arm reassuringly. "I regret that in that case, the KGB has probably taken him in. I am sorry. We should have been able to prevent that from happening. But at least we have managed to save you from such a future."

"But what have they taken him in for? What has he done? What do you mean, 'taken him in'?"

"Please, Mr. Townsend, please don't panic. There is danger but no necessity for panic. You will be safe if you are careful and stay with us. It is dangerous for us also, but we everywhere take the best of precautions."

"But why have they taken him in?" Michael insisted.

"They have taken him in because it has been prearranged with the British government that all scientists and lecturers and computer experts, all people like you, should be obliged to remain here in the Soviet Union once you have entered."

"What?" Michael demanded. "What the hell are you talking about?"

The man in the raincoat said calmly, "Where were you going today?"

"Nowhere. Just for a ride on the metro."

"To Aeroport? For a man who is staying in Moscow for twelve days, a metro ride to Aeroport is not logical. Why should a busy man on his one free day take a metro ride to Aeroport? When you have come to a new country, you want to explore new places. The Kremlin, Gorky Street, Arbat Square. But Aeroport?"

"I wasn't going to Sheremetyevo."

"Then where, my friend? To the Kholinka field perhaps, to look at the new guidance installations?"

"How did you know that?" Michael asked hotly.

The man in the raincoat took out another cigarette. The Volga was turning north now, up Mira Prospekt. The man lit his cigarette and blew twin funnels of smoke through his nostrils. He seemed calm but also alert, as if he were quite prepared to die at any moment. Perhaps life in Moscow made everybody a little like that. It wasn't the fear of being caught by the sudden lunacies of New York or Los Angeles; it was the fear of being steadily crushed under the great and ever-present weight of the state.

The man said, "Three English businessmen have now passed through our hands; two out of the three said they had been asked to go to the Kholinka airfield and look at the new guidance installations. There may have been more who declined to come here once they had been asked by your government to undertake this task, and there may be others about whose future we have heard nothing."

Michael was silent. The man smoked and brushed curls of ash from his raincoat. "This coat cost me one-hundred-fifty roubles."

They drove past the Polish Roman Catholic Church. The rain began to clear and the windshield wipers started blurting in protest against the Volga's glass.

The man in the raincoat said, "In the past year, the KGB has taken in scores of businessmen from Great Britain and the United States, and they will remain here to contribute their expertise to Soviet science and Soviet economy until further notice; that is all we know. Somehow and for some reason, Great Britain and the United States are renting or lending out the services of some of their most talented people, but it is done very discreetly. There has been no information about it in the Western press or on television. If there have been any distracted relatives in the West, certainly we have seen no news of them."

Michael cleared his throat. The face of the man in the raincoat was wreathed in smoke so he looked like one of the Gorgons. Michael said, "Who are you?"

The man said, "I don't know what you would call us. Heroes,

villains, cowboys? We have no name, really. Many of us have worked for the KGB before; some of us work for Western intelligence services. Mostly we are agents who have seen the cynical nature of the political structure on both sides of the world. Actually, for want of a better description, we call ourselves Lamprey—that small, parasitic marine creature that attaches itself to larger fish and gradually rasps off their flesh with its teeth. We are an association of professionals dedicated to undermining those intelligence structures for which we once worked; we are doing this in the interests of international harmony and plain humanity. There are many hundreds of us, from lowly clerks to important colonels. We share one mission.''

"Where are you taking me?'' asked Michael. "All my clothes are back at the hotel. My passport too. I can't just—''

"Your clothes and your passport have already been taken care of. Your room at the Hotel Rossiya is empty. Your bed is made, your razor and your toothbrush gone. When the KGB returns to see where you are, it will look as if you have never existed.''

Michael felt a tightening of uncertainty. If these men really had removed all trace of him from the Rossiya, they had cut off his last communication with the real world. As far as Intourist, the British Embassy and Margaret were concerned, he might just as well have stepped through to another dimension, vanished, without any way of being followed.

As if he could hear aloud what Michael was thinking, the man in the raincoat said, "You mustn't be concerned for your safety, Mr. Townsend. You are safer now than you were in the arms of Miss Konstantinova. You must realize that she was specially assigned to make it emotionally easier for you to accept the fact that you would not be returning to England and for a while you would be working for the Soviet Union.''

"What about John?''

"Your friend Mr. Bishop? Well, they would have provided him with a woman if they had considered it worthwhile. But they will already have been sent a dossier on him by M-Fifteen in London, and judging by Mr. Bishop's behavior and appearance, I would guess that his dossier has revealed that he is more turned on by computer hardware than by pretty women, and they will give him plenty of that to play with."

"You mean that M-Fifteen is working in cooperation with the KGB?"

The man in the raincoat nodded. "The international balance of power is changing, my friend, for an ultimate purpose that we have begun to guess at but that may be far greater and far more devastating than we can yet discover. Certainly there have been enormous increases lately in security communications between Moscow, London and Washington, and much of this increased traffic has been in very highly coded form, which makes it almost impossible for anyone without access to their defense-department computers to understand."

Michael said, "What are you going to do? Are you going to try to smuggle me out of Russia? Or what?"

"We will keep you somewhere safe until you can be returned to England. Once you are back there, you should have no problems as long as you make it your business to forget everything that has happened to you. Your government will be too embarrassed to take any action against you. At least, that is our belief."

"Can I call my wife?" asked Michael. "She's going to think I've been killed or abducted or something."

"We will make sure she knows that you are safe and that you will be returning to her shortly."

They reached a small, dull street on the outskirts of Moscow, lined with weather-stained 1960s apartments. The driver pulled the Volga into the curb and the man in the raincoat climbed out and said, *"Bistra,"* which Michael knew to mean "quick." They crossed the pavement in the slanting rain and passed through the smeary glass doors of a concrete housing project. The hallway was lit by a single flickering neon tube and smelled strongly of disinfectant. The man in the raincoat pressed the button for the elevator and after a while it arrived, letting out a groan like a man suffering a severe stomachache in an echoing public toilet.

As they ascended, the man in the bronze-colored raincoat shook Michael's hand and said, "My name for anything you care to say to me is Lev Unishevsky. You can call me Lev if you like. Neither name is real."

The elevator groaned again and stopped at the fifth floor. They walked in silence down a narrow corridor until they reached the last apartment. Lev rapped quickly at the door and said, "Lev." A few moments elapsed and then the door was opened by a young, pale-faced woman in a blue head scarf.

Lev said: "We lost the other one. Vakhmistrov got him, I think."

The girl closed the door behind them and led the way through to a cluttered living room full of stale cigarette smoke, where two men and a girl were sitting on a sagging sofa discussing a large map of Leningrad. They looked up briefly as Lev brought Michael in with him and one of them said, "*Zdrastvuytye,* Lev. You were a long time. Did your shopping as well?"

Lev unbuttoned his raincoat, brushed it briskly with his hand and folded it over the back of an armchair. "We had some difficulty. They were watching the Saratovskaya Street garage. In the end, we had to call Gorovets."

He took out a cigarette and lit it. He was a short man with a middle-aged spread that wasn't flattered by his sleeveless Fair Isle pullover. "We are going to have to run Mr. Townsend back to England very quickly, I think. It seems that we are being watched more and more."

"What about his friend?"

"I don't think there is anything we can do, not at this stage. If Vakhmistrov has got him, they'll probably have him out at Zagorsk by now."

"What happens at Zagorsk?" asked Michael.

Lev called, "Nadia, make some coffee, would you?" Then he looked at Michael through his clouds of cigarette smoke and said, "At Zagorsk there is a KGB center for preparing aliens like your friend Mr. Bishop for work in the Soviet Union, making sure they understand the simple principle that if they decline to cooperate, they will be obliged to stay in the Soviet Union even longer, until they do cooperate."

Michael said, "Really, I think I ought to call the British Embassy about this."

Lev shook his head. "If you do, you will be doing nothing less than signing your friend's death warrant. He will disappear and the KGB will deny they have ever seen him. After all, what evidence do you have that Vakhmistrov actually abducted him? You see, you have none. You are not in England now, my friend, and even if you were, I doubt if you would be able to elicit much sympathy from your authorities.''

Michael said, "I'm very confused. Yes, I will have a cup of coffee.''

He sat down in one of the armchairs. The man on the end of the sofa nearest him leaned forward confidentially and tapped his knee. *"Izvinite,"* he said. "Excusing me.''

"Yes?'' asked Michael.

The man smiled sheepishly and gestured with one hand in the air. "Kenny Dalglish,'' he said. Then, explosively, *"Futbol!"*

"Yes,'' said Michael. *"Futbol."*

It was only then that he saw the AKM automatic rifle propped up against the bookcase and the boxes and boxes of ammunition. He looked at the gun and then he looked at Lev. Lev smoked, keeping one hand in his pocket, and simply shrugged as if to say, *This is the real world, what do you expect?*

ELEVEN

Golovanov said offhandedly, "I wish to take Inge with me when we go to inspect the Twentieth Guard Army. That could be arranged, I imagine, without too much fuss?"

Yeremenko was buttoning his right-hand glove. He looked across at his senior officer through yellow-tinted sunglasses. They were standing on the airfield at Luckenwalder on a gray but glaring afternoon while only a few yards away a huge An-12 transport plane disgorged troops and trucks and clattering rocket launchers. On the far side of the field, twenty-two silvery-white MiG-23 bombers were lined up, their canopies open like the transparent wing cases of exotic beetles, while mechanics and weapons experts prepared them for the moment when Operation *Byliny* would be announced.

Yeremenko replied, "No serious difficulty, Comrade Marshal. Well, not in arranging it. She could travel with Major Grechko. I just wonder if her presence on this inspection would be . . . well, entirely discreet."

Golovanov's smile looked as if it had been cut into clay with a tight length of wire. "She works for the KGB, my dear Yeremenko. How could I possibly be more discreet than that?"

Yeremenko made a halfhearted attempt to register surprise but Golovanov laughed harshly and grasped his arm. "Do you take me for a milk-fed fool? Inge has been passing back

140

to Dzherzhinsky Square every grunt and every groan of every visit I have paid her. You don't seriously think they would allow me a private sex life, do you? No, I take her for what she is: a beautiful woman who has been assigned to keep her eye on me and to make sure I behave myself, ideologically speaking. All this business of having poor Poplavskiy drive me out to her house and collect me again in the morning, when the houses all around must be crammed to the chimneys with KGB. No, *britchik*. I am allowed this little pleasure because I have earned it and because it is a way in which our political masters can keep a watch on me day and night. So Inge will come to Haldensleben with me. You can do that for me, can't you?''

Yeremenko's face was expressionless, although behind his calmness he was enraged by Golovanov's intemperate lust and his bullying nagging about Inge, and insulted by having been called *britchik,* which meant ''little shaver.'' He felt sorely tempted to call Katia, Golovanov's wife, and let her know about her husband's antics with Inge. The trouble was, he suspected that the KGB would not be particularly pleased if he were to do that because they had spent years recruiting Inge for the express purpose of entertaining high-ranking army officers. Through her they could not only check on Golovanov's continuing loyalty to the state and the *Stavka,* they could ensure that his natural pomposity did not inflate into delusions of military grandeur. It was still remembered in the KGB that Golovanov was a protégé of the rebellious Rokossovskiy.

Yeremenko took off his sunglasses, peered across the airfield and told himself to be patient. There was a Siberian saying that the greatest patience brought the biggest bear.

Lieutenant-Colonel I.M. Gudkhov came smartly across the dry concrete of the runway and saluted Golovanov and Yeremenko with a snap as brittle as somebody breaking a piece of ice.

''We are honored to have you here today, Comrade Marshal! You will see that we are in a state of complete readiness. If there were a war tomorrow, I would have only to click my fingers and all of these aircraft would be scrambled and flying in eight minutes exactly.''

Golovanov smiled benignly, as if the idea of a war tomorrow was the farthest thing from his mind. "Very good, Colonel. Tell me something about these airplanes." He sounded utterly disinterested, which he was. As Gudkhov began talking, he said to Yeremenko, "Didn't I see Koshevoy's boy yesterday evening at Wünsdorf? The one with the birthmark on his face?"

Gudkhov had to begin again. "These are all MiG-Twenty-threes, Comrade Marshal. Single-seat, all-weather interceptor. Top speed, over thirteen hundred miles per hour. Range, six hundred and twenty miles. All of them are fitted with a single twenty-three-mm cannon and four air-to-air missiles. The NATO code name for them is 'Flogger B.' "

"NATO code name," sniffed Golovanov. He nodded to Gudkhov and said, "Thank you, Colonel. The Defense Council shall have a good report of you." Then he said to Yeremenko, "Let's eat now, shall we? All this touring around has made me hungry."

They walked back to the car. There was a sudden roar of turboprop engines from the An-12 transport as it began to taxi ponderously across the field. "NATO code name," Golovanov repeated. "Isn't that something to make you laugh? But you won't forget about Inge, will you?"

Yeremenko shook his head. He couldn't bring himself to say anything for fear he would lose his temper. Today his temper was like dry ice, fuming but ineffective.

They ate at a small *rastätte* at Kloster Zinna, in a dark wooden-walled room with a view of a dull backyard and a row of fir trees. Golovanov had a small glass of beer and a plateful of pork and green beans. The beans were strangely bright on his plate, the same color as a distant pasture seen before a thunderstorm. Yeremenko ate veal, which he prodded again and again with his fork until it was punctured all over.

Eventually Yeremenko said, "What is it about Inge?"

"You haven't slept with her?" asked Golovanov, sprinkling pepper on his pork.

Yeremenko shook his head. "No. And it seems very unwise for *you* to sleep with her just at the moment, the way things are."

Golovanov used his knife and fork vigorously to cut a thick chunk of meat. "We may die, you know, in the weeks ahead. We have to think of that."

"That doesn't mean—"

Golovanov leveled his knife at Yeremenko. "It means everything, my dear friend. It means that the things we do today we may never have the opportunity of doing again, ever."

Yeremenko was silent. Golovanov lowered his eyes to his meal and said matter-of-factly, "It is very hard to explain to a man like you what a woman like Inge can do. She can exhilarate the mind as well as the body. She is completely woman, in the way that a cat is completely cat. I have had experiences with Inge that have taken me beyond myself, beyond my years. When she is making love, she is dedicated to nothing but my pleasure and she will do anything I ask in any way, but still with fierce, erotic pride. It is her pride that makes her so magnificent, her coldness; yet she will do whatever you ask of her, no matter how debasing it is."

"Well," said Yeremenko, jabbing at his veal again, "I suppose she has a certain allure."

"You make it sound like a smell."

"Comrade Marshal—"

"Hush," said Golovanov with his mouth full of cabbage. "For once just do what you're told. This is not the time for moral speculation."

Yeremenko sat back and irritably sipped his *apfelsaft.* He knew that he ought to keep his displeasure under control. After all, every general in the army had his luxuries, his expensive *dacha,* his chauffeur-driven automobiles, his caviar, his nubile girls from the army's Central Sports Club. But all these luxuries came at a price: the price of a precarious military existence and the constant threat of purge. The last great purge of generals had been in 1960, when Khrushchev had sacked five hundred of them in one day. Such a purge could always happen again, particularly now that Operation *Byliny* was so close.

Yeremenko eschewed luxury and believed that by so doing, he could eventually rise to the very top of the army and stay there. He told himself that he shouldn't fret at Golovanov's lust for Inge, especially when that lust made Golovanov so vulnerable. But all the same, it crawled into Yeremenko's bones.

That night Golovanov went around to Inge's house early. He was driven this time by Colonel Chuykov. As Colonel Chuykov opened the door of the car for him, he said, "You should be careful, Comrade Marshal. You know how things are."

Golovanov squinted at him out of slitted eyes. "Careful?"

"A word of caution, that's all. There are those who would like to see you retired, at the very least."

Golovanov gripped Chuykov by the lapel. "I have lived for a long time, Colonel. I intend to live for a great deal longer." He stared into Chuykov's face with an expression that could have been irritation or anger, or even murderous hostility. Those tiny, deep-set eyes kept flickering from side to side as if Golovanov couldn't decide whether to slap Chuykov playfully on the cheek or have him liquidated.

"Well, that's just my opinion, Comrade Marshal," said Chuykov cautiously.

"Of course. I didn't expect anything else. Tell me, do me a favor. When I have gone inside, go to each of the houses around here, knock at the door and say that you are lost and want some directions back to headquarters. Find out who answers the doors around here. You know what KGB look like."

"Comrade Marshal, I don't think that—"

Golovanov grasped his shoulder. "Don't worry. I was only trying to frighten you. They are probably *all* KGB. But the point I am trying to make is that there are some things that are worth worrying about and others that aren't. I am not afraid of Siberia, Comrade, nor am I afraid of death. Perhaps I am a little afraid of pain. I gave up political opinions years ago as a deliberate decision. I wanted to survive as long as possible for the sake of myself, for the sake of my family, for the sake of my country. But I will never give up being myself. Once I have done that, I will have surrendered everything and they might as well take me to Lubianka straightaway and shoot me. Whatever it is that inspires you, my friend, you will learn the same thing yourself one day."

Chuykov said nothing. He was embarrassed but at the same time, strangely moved. He watched Golovanov walk stolidly up the driveway toward Inge's door and ring the bell. He decided it would be more discreet if he were to leave, and so he did. He executed a clumsy three-point turn in the Volvo that Yeremenko had arranged for him and drove out of the housing estate too quickly.

Inge opened the door wearing a white-silk robe. Her white hair was wet and curly from the shower; her body was still wet so that her shoulders and breasts clung translucently to the silk. She looked at Golovanov without surprise and said, *"Du bist früh gekommen."*

Golovanov said, "Everything it was necessary for me to inspect has been inspected. And, well, perhaps I found that I couldn't wait any longer."

"Come in," she said. He noticed that she glanced quickly out into the road before she closed the door. "I was washing my hair," she told him. "I didn't have time to dry myself."

He took her hand and kissed her. She smelled of shampoo He said, "You must despise me sometimes."

"Why?" she said, combing out her hair, walking across the room, turning her head as she saw herself in the mirror.

"I am always intruding on your life without any notice, without any explanation."

"You are too soft for a marshal of the Soviet Union," she said.

He shook his head. "Believe me, I am not soft."

She reached the opposite side of the living room and stood in the last slanted light of evening, looking so beautiful that he thought this moment should have been frozen cryogenically, preserved for five thousand years while scholars and archaeologists peered through the frost and wondered what on earth they could do with a tall, perfectly proportioned Rhine maiden and a squat frog of a Russian marshal, solidified forever in the only instant that had any real meaning for either of them.

They drank vodka as the sky grew dark outside. They played *Romeo and Juliet* by Prokofiev. Inge's hair dried in rags of blonde; she sat beside Golovanov on the sofa, wearing nothing but white-patterned stockings, smoking *papirosi*, talking every now and then about her childhood in Bavaria, cross-legged, her large breasts patterned with pale-blue veins, her vulva parted to reveal those inner lips as pale and pink as confectioner's sugar.

"Yeremenko will make the arrangements for you to come with me to Haldensleben tomorrow," said Golovanov.

Her pale eyes flickered. She smoked but said nothing.

"So far I have no instructions except to take you there and then to call a certain number in Magdeburg. I suppose you know that there might be some risk."

"This is a dangerous world, Timofey, for all of us. You are just as much at risk as I am. Supposing they discover what you have done?"

Golovanov pouted in that peculiarly Russian way of his so that he looked like a petulant boxer dog. "Don't you think I have lived with risks of this kind for long enough? I know what I'm doing, and Yeremenko isn't so fierce. I have dealt with his kind before."

"And the KGB?"

He touched her bare thigh, sliding his hand from her knee to the concavity just beside her exposed mound of Venus. He wished that his life had been different, that the world had been different, that he had been born somewhere else, in another time, in another identity. Sometimes the burden of being both a man and a marshal of the Soviet Union was just too much.

Later they went into the bedroom. It was dark, mirrored, modern, hushed. Golovanov knew there were microphones. He tugged off his shirt, then sat down on the edge of the bed and took off his socks and his trousers. Inge waited for him, her white skin gleaming in the darkness like the skin of an ice maiden, or the tooth of a shark. He climbed onto the bed on all fours, approaching her with his head bowed. She kissed his forehead, his cheeks, his chin, his shoulders. Then, as he crouched above her like a bear, she slid downward, kissing his chest and his stomach and running her sharp fingernails lightly down his naked sides so he shivered. At last she reached his hard, corded penis, took it between her lips and gently sucked and licked it. He said something muffled from deep down in his throat. She said, "Shall I bite you?"

They made love, slowly and reflectively, as if this might be the last time. His dark-red penis slid glistening in and out of her pale and swollen vulva. It made a sound like discreet kisses in the dark. Eventually he turned her over on her stomach, her hips lifted up, and he knelt behind her and buried his face between the cheeks of her bottom, his tongue tip exploring first the wrinkled tightness of her anus and then plunging deep into her liquid vagina. It was oddly ritualistic; his face was anointed with her juices. Prokofiev, in the other room, reached a pompous, stalking crescendo.

She brought Golovanov to a climax with her hand. His semen fell through the darkness in loops and splashes, pattering on her breasts. Again he said something indistinct, almost as if he were speaking another language. She held him close to her; they shared his stickiness. She kissed his ear. She said, "Hush, Timofey," as if he might be frightened, either of the dark or of his destiny.

"Russia," he said, in the tone of voice an upright son might have used had he found his father with a prostitute.

Inge lay in the darkness stroking his face, touching those brambly eyebrows of his, feeling his heart pound against his ribs. "All, everything that I understand, I understand only because I love." Golovanov had taught her those words from Tolstoy.

He left her the next morning just after six. It was raining again and he hurried to the car with his coat collar pulled up, neither turning nor waving. He would be taken by Mi-24 helicopter to Haldensleben, where he would have lunch with the divisional commanders of the 20th Guard Army, which consisted of one tank and four motor-rifle divisions. Inge would arrive later by car as unobtrusively as possible. Overcast and wet weather was forecast. There was still no signal from the *Stavka* that any diplomatic progress had been made in Copenhagen, although it was now official that the United States had approved the preparatory stages of *Gringo* and that the British would shortly be mounting *Cornflower*.

Golovanov ate a breakfast of frankfurters and tomatoes at the mess at Zossen-Wünsdorf while Chuykov and Grechko briefed him on the day's schedule. There were messages from the Commander-in-Chief of the Far Eastern Strategic Direction at Khabarovsk, from the Czechoslovakian HQ in Milovice and from the northern group of forces at Legnica. Most of them were irritable queries about how long their forces would have to be kept in a high state of readiness since the psychological tension and the physiological strain were becoming critical. Men needed their sleep; they also needed feeding. Keeping an entire strategic force at fever pitch was an expensive and harrowing business for both the troops and their commanders. If something didn't happen soon, the armies would pass the peak of readiness and rousing them up to it again would be arduous and difficult.

Chuykov said, "It appears that only agreement with Cuba is delaying us now. Otherwise *Byliny* is completely ready to go."

Golovanov spooned four spoonfuls of sugar into his glass of *kyefia* and stirred it. "We must be patient, that's all. The success of *Byliny* depends on complete diplomatic agreement all around. And there is the future to consider once *Byliny* has been successfully accomplished."

Chuykov said, "I understand that we are to be joined in Haldensleben by a personal friend of yours, Comrade Marshal." His voice was wary. Given Golovanov's reputation, he felt it needed to be.

Golovanov wiped *kyefia* from his mouth with his checked napkin. "Who told you that?"

"Comrade Yeremenko, sir."

Golovanov drummed his fat fingers on the table, a disapproving blurt of noise. "I would of course have briefed you later," he said. "But since you know already, yes, Inge is joining me in Haldensleben."

Grechko said, "She is to stay at the Sachsen Hotel, so I believe."

"So," said Golovanov. He was annoyed that Yeremenko had taken his aides into his confidence, although he knew it made administrative sense. "The Sachsen Hotel, hmh?"

He said little more except to dictate a reply to the commander of the central group of forces at Milovice, telling him in explicit military prose to stop whining and wait for further instructions. Then he finished his milk, gathered his briefcase and his baton, and led the way out to the helicopter landing area at the rear of the headquarters building. The rain had eased off but the silver humpbacked Mi-24 helicopter was still beaded with droplets. Its rotors turned lazily and its engine made a noise like a vacuum cleaner run along the corridor of a Russian hotel. Although it was only being used to carry Marshal Golovanov from Zossen-Wünsdorf to Haldensleben, it was fully armed with a four-barreled 12.7-mm machine gun in the nose and two pods under its stubby wings armed with 57-mm rockets. From the moment the preparations for Operation *Byliny* had been announced, the Soviet Army had technically been at war.

Yeremenko was not joining Golovanov on this particular visit; he had too many administrative duties, including the repositioning of the 4th Guard Tank Army and the preparation of the Baltic fleet, which had been giving him some headaches. While it was comparatively easy to pretend that the Soviet ground forces were involved in nothing more threatening than annual exercises, it was more difficult to deploy the fleet without immediately arousing the suspicions of Sweden, Finland, Norway and Denmark, each of whom became instantly clamorous whenever a Soviet submarine ventured into its territorial waters.

Golovanov, puffing a little, was helped aboard the helicopter. Chuykov and Grechko sat facing him. Noisily the aircraft rose over the Zossen-Wünsdorf headquarters and angled away northwest over the trees and marshes and orange-tiled houses of Brandenburg, heading out of the district of Potsdam toward Magdeburg. Rain spattered the windows again but ahead the sky began to clear, patches of watery eau-de-Nil between the gray, lowering clouds.

"Well," said Golovanov, easing himself back in his seat, which was a size too small for him, "what do you think of Comrade Yeremenko?"

"He seems efficient," remarked Chuykov guardedly. He knew what these interrogations by Golovanov could be like.

"And you?" Golovanov asked Grechko.

Grechko shrugged. "That's my impression. Efficient."

"A good leader?" asked Golovanov.

"I think so."

"Faithful to the army? Devoted to the Party? Patriotic? Keen? Aggressive?"

"I think so," said Grechko.

"Then," said Golovanov, "you are a fool. You see nothing, unless of course you are lying about what you think, and if you are doing that, you are even more of a fool. Yeremenko is unscrupulous, self-centered and interested in nothing but his own career. He is patriotic only because he *has* to be patriotic to make his way to the upper echelons of the army; he is superficially efficient but a great deal of his efficiency is nothing more than shouting and screaming and sending out memoranda, all flash and no substance. You mark what I say, Major. Yeremenko is a poor friend, a vicious enemy and a lover of nobody and nothing except himself. Why do you think he told you about Inge meeting me in Haldensleben? To demean me in front of your eyes and to make himself look morally scrupulous and efficient. Well, I shit on his moral scruples, and I shit on his efficiency. You mark what I say, he is no soldier. He is a military shark, without any human compunction. If you are ever tempted to do anything for him in his efforts to dislodge me, just think of what it would be like to work for such a bastard night and day."

It took them twenty-five minutes to reach Haldensleben and then they were circling around the spire of St. Magnus and over the lime trees that lined Magdeburg Strasse. They landed in the grounds of the small gray *schloss* that was the temporary headquarters of the 20th Guard Army: a dismal building with blank attic windows, grime-encrusted statues of deer and walls streaked with green and black from a hundred and seventy years of dampness. There was a weedy lake that dully reflected the row of SO-152 Akatsiya self-propelled howitzers parked nose-to-tail under the trees.

War again, thought Golovanov, climbing out of the helicopter. It never changes; none of us ever learn. There seems to be no way of avoiding it. The commander of the 20th Guard Army was waiting for him on the broken-down veranda of the *schloss*, accompanied by his divisional commanders. All were saluting, serious-faced, proud. Golovanov, as he saluted and shook hands and embraced the commander, wondered for a moment if he were falling to pieces, as if the pressures of the last few months had been too much for him.

"Not a very happy place to make a headquarters," he

remarked. "It seems to have an air of doom about it. Do you know what I mean? It reminds me of nineteen forty-five."

Major-General Zhukilov, a young, broad-faced man with a glossy brown mustache, said, "We shan't be staying here long, Comrade Marshal. As soon as the summer exercises are over, we shall be back in Magdeburg."

"Yes," nodded Golovanov. He walked toward the open door of the *schloss,* the young generals following him, young soldiers who had scarcely been born in 1945. What did they know of bombing, starvation and German flamethrowers incinerating children where they stood? Well, they would soon experience the test of war, although they didn't know it.

"We have something special for lunch today," smiled Zhukilov. "Roast sucking pigs from the farm."

"Let me look at your rosters first," said Golovanov testily.

After lunch he excused himself and went to the private office that General Zhukilov had set aside for him. There wasn't much there: a desk, a map of Western Europe, a glass decanter filled with stale bubbly water. A sharpened pencil and a pad. He went to the window and looked down at the dark, scummy lake. Then he picked up the phone and dialed Magdeburg 67 23 01. It was an outside line so there was little danger of being intercepted. And, after all, why should anyone think of listening in? He was a marshal on a routine inspection. He belched. The roast sucking pig had been too fatty for him.

A voice said, *"Sechs-sieben zwo-drei nul-eins."*

Golovanov cleared his throat and then said, *"Der scheckiger Pfeifer* told me to call."

"Your number?"

"Nine."

"You have the rat with you?"

"The rat will be here later. By four o'clock at the latest."

"Where?"

"The Sachsen Hotel. Suite three-oh-one."

"You have the money?"

"Yes, of course."

There was a pause. "You will be there too?"

"Is that necessary?" asked Golovanov. "It won't be easy for me."

"What you are asking, my friend, will not be easy for us."

"Well, I appreciate that."

"Can you be there at seven?"

Golovanov thought for a moment. He was supposed to be having dinner with the SPETSNAZ commander at seven-thirty, but if he dressed beforehand, he should be able to make it in time without any difficulty. He said, "Very well, then, seven. But please be prompt."

"We will do our best, Number Nine. It is not always easy."

Golovanov put the phone down. He was beginning to wish he had never agreed to smuggle Inge out of the country. He was intoxicated with her, certainly, but what would he get in return? She would go off to the United States and he would never see her again in spite of all her promises of what she would do once everything was over. He had heard about California, of how enticing it was. All those handsome movie actors, all that sun and money and capitalist self-indulgence. Why should she even think of coming back to Europe to an old man whose sole attraction was that he was a marshal in the world's most ruthless army?

Still, he had promised, and perhaps after all, Inge would be true to her word. Perhaps this was really a way in which he could get rid of her at last so she would no longer haunt him. Inge, the German ice lady, thirty years too late, a million miles too far away.

Commander Zhukilov rapped politely at the door. "Your car is here, Marshal."

"Thank you," said Golovanov. Then, "You seem to have done well here, Commander." With a vague wave of his hand, he indicated the *schloss,* the line-up of howitzers, the room.

Commander Zhukilov bowed his head but said nothing.

The Sachsen Hotel was on Potsdam Platz, just to the east of Haldensleben's main square. Rain had glossed the cobbles as Golovanov's staff car creaked to a halt outside. He had already been back to the house where Commander Zhukilov was staying—a large, modern farmhouse on the western out-skirts of Haldensleben—to bathe and change for dinner.

Chuykov and Grechko were to meet him there later, at 7:45. He hoped desperately that there would be no delays.

Outside, the Sachsen Hotel was a flat-fronted, unprepossessing building with a dripping porch. Golovanov pushed his way through the heavy revolving doors into the lobby. There was a violently patterned carpet in red and gold and a row of stags' heads mounted on one wall. He could smell meat and dust. A large, white-haired woman approached him from the opposite side of the lobby. Her face looked as if it had been made by a clever schoolboy out of aging potatoes. She inspected Golovanov's uniform, the red-and-gold shoulder boards, the dark spatters of rain on the khaki coat. *"Guten Tag,"* she said with a distinct lisp. "I cannot believe that you are looking for a room."

"I am looking for somebody who is staying here. A fraulein . . ." his voice trailed off. She obviously knew who he meant. He reached into his pocket and produced a crisp bill, pressing it into her palm as if he expected her to tell his fortune.

"Come this way," she told him. She rattled back the folding gates of the elevator. "There, press three for the third floor. She's in three-oh-one."

"Danke sehr," nodded Golovanov.

The white-haired woman watched him fixedly until he had closed the door. Then he rose into the gloom, and for some reason, he began to feel apprehensive, like a young officer being called up in front of his captain. The elevator whined to a halt and he stepped out.

Room 301 was at the far end of the corridor. From one of the rooms he passed on the way, he could hear music. "Good Vibrations" by the Beach Boys. "I . . . I love the colorful clothes she wears. . . ." He reached 301 and rapped on the yellow varnished wood with his knuckles.

"Komm," said Inge's voice. He turned the handle and found that the door was not locked. Inside, there were no lights. He took off his cap and stepped into the gloom, smiling. Inge was standing by the window wearing a white blouse with padded shoulders and a slim blue skirt. She turned as he came walking across the room and said, "Ah . . . not the best of hotels. I think your friend Yeremenko was trying to make a point."

He held her cool fingers and kissed her. "Yeremenko is mean in his soul. One day he will do something so tight that he will disappear up his own ass."

Inge said, "You're right on time. I was worried they would keep you."

Her shadowy profile was perfect against the blue evening light from the window; that curved forehead, that uptilted nose, those exquisitely bowed lips. He sometimes wondered what it must be like to be as beautiful as she was, to turn heads wherever one went.

Golovanov said, "Well . . . I try to be punctual. Have you heard from anyone yet? The *scheckiger Pfeifer*?"

Inge looked over his shoulder, and the way that she did it warned him that things were not quite as they appeared to be. He had fought in too many battles, ducked his head too often, stepped away too often. He had developed an instinct for danger both in war and in peace: fighting Germans and Chinese, and Afghan rebels, and also fighting the Politburo and its most ambitious minions. He raised his head and was about to turn around to see what Inge was looking at when she said sharply, "*Don't*!" Then, "Don't move!"

Golovanov stayed where he was. "They're here already?" he asked.

She nodded without looking at him. He heard footsteps squeaking on the floorboards behind him.

"Can I look now?" he asked but Inge said, "No."

"Very well," said Golovanov; then, in a louder voice in pidgin German, "Gentlemen, the rat is here. Can you help her? I have the money all ready."

A blond-haired young man in impenetrable dark glasses came around into Golovanov's line of vision. Golovanov would never have recognized him again in an identification line-up, but he would have recognized his gun: an Ingram Model 10, a small black shoebox with a short barrel poking out of it but capable of firing 1100 rounds a minute, one .45-caliber bullet every .05 second. Golovanov, without being bidden to do so, raised his hands.

"Something is wrong?" he asked thickly. "I have all the money here."

The young man shook his head. "Nothing is wrong, Marshal Golovanov. Everything is working according to plan."

"Then you can get Inge out of East Germany for me?"

The young man nodded.

"Well, that is some relief," said Golovanov and lowered his hands. "Would you like your money now? I have to leave. They will be expecting me at seven-thirty."

"Yes," said the young man. "But they will have a very long wait."

"I beg your pardon?"

"You are coming with us," the young man told him.

Golovanov's mouth opened and closed and he laughed. Then he stopped laughing. "I am a marshal of the Soviet Army," he said. "You cannot possibly expect me to come along with you."

"Well," said the young man, "it is either that or this," and he lifted the muzzle of the Ingram and pointed it at Golovanov's head. "Have you ever seen a man hit by one of these? This is the Ten, with the heavier round. I am not averse to decorating this hotel room red."

"What are you talking about?" Golovanov demanded. "Inge?"

Inge raised her finger to her lips. "It was the only way, Timofey. Now please hurry. Your aides will start looking for you soon and we need all the time we can get."

"Where are you taking me?" Golovanov demanded. "This is preposterous!"

"We are going west," the young man told him. "We have a couple of friends on duty at the border post at Helmstedt; they are waiting for us now. You will be in Bonn by nightfall."

Golovanov said in a throaty voice, "You have no idea of what you are doing. If you try to take me away, you will provoke the most serious diplomatic incident in years! You are mad, both of you!"

Inge came up to Golovanov and took his hand. Her eyes were pellucid, unreadable, the eyes of a girl who has decided years ago that she will be on nobody's side but her own. "Timofey," she coaxed.

"You must let me go," said Golovanov.

The young man said, "You have two choices and fifteen seconds in which to make up your mind which one to accept. Either you come with us to Bonn or we kill you now. We have no time to waste. The choice is yours."

Golovanov looked at Inge and smiled soulfully. "Well," he said, "you have me well and truly trapped, haven't you?"

Inge smiled and squeezed his hand. "You will always be my bear, Timofey."

"You think you can get away with this?"

Inge nodded, still smiling. "We would have preferred to take Yeremenko. After all, he knows more about the movements of the Western Strategic Direction than you do, more of the details. But we are not dissatisfied. You know the strategy, don't you? You know the master plan. We can find out the tactical details from some of your junior officers."

Golovanov turned to the young man with the Ingram. "What do you call yourself?" he asked.

"Dichter," said the young man calmly.

"Well, Dichter, you had better shoot me," said Golovanov. "I am a soldier. I am prepared to die at all times; that is a soldier's lot. A life of enforced idleness, qualified only by the knowledge that death may come instantly and violently at the most incongruous of times."

Dichter lifted the Ingram and squinted down its length at Golovanov's head. There was a moment's pause. Golovanov turned to Inge. But Inge backed away, and that was an unequivocal sign to Golovanov that she knew Dichter would pull the trigger. Golovanov had a conscious thought that his whole life was *not* passing in front of him, that he was considering nothing but his own survival. No thoughts of Katia and the children; no merry memories of the military academy, of the night they had nailed their sergeant to the floor. Only calculated panic, the freezing of the nervous system as if he had been drenched in iced vodka.

After a moment Golovanov cautiously raised his hand and said, "Very well. I will come with you. Are you happy now?"

TWELVE

That afternoon the President was napping in his private bedroom when Morton Lock came in and gently shook his shoulder. The President opened one eye and stared at his Security Adviser as if he had been dreaming about instituting the guillotine for minor infringements of the Chief Executive's rest periods. After all, he was three years older than Richard Nixon, and Richard Nixon had long gone back to Saddle River and his new Lanier word processor, opting for peace and relaxation and yet another profitable book on politics, while the President was still burdened with the cares of a nuclear world, and *Gringo*, and nightmares about 1988.

How the hell was he going to explain *Gringo* to the Irish?

Morton said, "Mr. President? We've just had word from Copenhagen."

The President said nothing but continued to watch Morton with one hostile eye.

Morton said, "Fidel Castro has agreed to democratic elections. It's official. The package is complete."

There was a long pause. Then the President slowly sat up in bed and looked at Morton like a man who has been told that his appeal to the Governor has just been turned down and that today he has to die.

"I see," he said flatly. "Then . . . that's it?"

"Yes, sir."

"And General Oliver's still happy?"

"Yes, sir."

"All right. Give me a few minutes to dress and then get the Kremlin on the phone."

"Yes, sir. Do you want to talk to the British as well?"

"Let's find out what kind of time framework we're dealing with first. The British thing is going to be tricky, especially the way the Soviets want to handle it."

Morton suggested, "I don't think we ought to leave it too long, sir."

The President stood up and reached for his robe. "I don't think there's any need for haste, Morton. Sometimes it's easier to turn the world upside down than it is to get a decent cup of coffee."

Morton was unsure of whether that was an instruction to find the President a cup of coffee or nothing more than a philosophical remark. He said, "The strategic side is all tied up anyway. Admiral Truscott was concerned about the British forces in the Falklands. He thought they might decide to hold out on their own, and let's face it, they do have some considerable firepower down there. But the Second Fleet could borrow Task Force Sixty from the Sixth Fleet for a while, at least until *Gringo* is complete, and that should give him sufficient backup."

"All right," the President nodded. "Can you get the Joint Chiefs down here later this evening? I want a complete picture."

"Very good," said Morton. Then, "Would you care for that cup of coffee, sir?"

"Coffee?" said the President. "I think I'd rather have a Jack Daniel's, straight up. But, no, go on; get me some coffee."

It was nine-twenty at night in England. The Defense Secretary was in his office at the House of Commons when the telephone rang and his secretary told him he was wanted at Number 10. He crushed out his Fribourg & Treyer cigarette and said under his breath, "Damn."

He walked up Whitehall accompanied by his PPS, Dick Mallard, and a plainclothes officer from Scotland Yard whom

Dick always called "Old Stoneface." It was a warm May evening, ideal for walking although the streets were unusually quiet. The Defense Secretary remembered that tonight was the first showing on British television of "The Return of the Jedi." He thought there was something rather ironic about a population threatened with real thermonuclear war spending its evening watching a fantasy about war in space. It was rather like sitting at a Beethoven concert listening to a tape of the music on a Sony Walkman.

They were admitted through the glossy black door of Number 10 into the gray-painted entrance hall with its marble fireplace and its black-and-white checked floor. The Prime Minister's private parliamentary secretary came fussing through from the corridor, his hands flapping like a haberdasher's, and said, "She's waiting for you upstairs, sir."

"Old Stoneface" stayed behind. He would probably go into the kitchen for a cup of tea with five sugars. The Defense Secretary ran his hand over his hair to smooth it down as he followed the PPS up the main staircase, which was lined with oil paintings of past prime ministers. Then they went through to the Prime Minister's study, a large room decorated in Adam green, with small eighteenth-century landscape paintings hung between the three tall windows that overlooked the garden.

The lamps were lit; the Prime Minister sat at her green leather-topped desk wearing her reading glasses. Sitting in one of the sagging crimson-velvet chairs, large-faced and rangy and showing a great deal of pale and furry shin, was General Sir Walter Fawkes, chief of the general staff.

"Hallo, Malcolm," the Prime Minister said in a distracted voice as the Defense Secretary came in. He drew one of the Queen Anne armchairs across the carpet so he could sit nearer to her. He didn't know that his habit of moving any piece of furniture before he sat in it was intensely irritating to her and that it was all she could do not to snap at him.

"Prime Minister," said the Defense Secretary formally. Then he nodded to General Fawkes and said, "Sir Walter."

The Prime Minister took off her glasses and laid them on the desk in front of her. "We've received official confirmation of *Gringo*," she said. "So far no specific date has been set but the Americans have promised to let us know within twenty-four hours."

"You can start *Cornflower* then?" the Defense Secretary asked General Fawkes. General Fawkes cleared his throat like a Vickers machine gun and nearly managed to say something in reply.

"Any word from the Russians?" the Defense Secretary wanted to know.

"Not unless your people have heard anything. But it appears that Castro has at last agreed to stand down and hold a free election under United Nations supervision in return for a number of guarantees for his personal protection and increased investment in Cuban agriculture from U.S. federal funds."

"So we're ready to go at last," said the Defense Secretary unnecessarily.

"What mostly concerns me at the moment is the industrial situation here at home," said the Prime Minister. "The miners don't vote until tomorrow but all the indications are that this time, Grange will get a yes. I've just heard from Patrick that the railwaymen are considering strike action starting on Monday and that the dockers are refusing to discuss their pay offer until the middle of next week."

"You're not suggesting that the strikes have anything to do with *Gringo*?"

The Prime Minister lifted her head. In the lamplight, the Defense Secretary could see how tired she looked, how much the events of the past year had aged her. Being an unwilling party to the dismembering of the world had dimmed so much of that political sparkle, worn down so much of that administrative abrasiveness. He thought of all those hours of aggressive negotiation in Brussels when she had argued and fought and browbeaten their EEC partners into lowering Britain's contributions. Now, within the space of a few days, the EEC would be swept away and all of that struggle would be meaningless.

General Fawkes made an explosive noise and swung his furry leg backward and forward. The Prime Minister said,

"AR-Seven has some evidence that the miners' and the dockers' strikes were coordinated and that they were somehow initiated by instruction from outside." AR7 was the code name for the government's anti-union team; last year its members had successfully managed to bring the power workers' strike to an end by exposing corruption within the union committee, and they had infiltrated almost every major left-wing union right up to the executive level.

"I think perhaps I'd better have a chat with Hubert Vaudrey about that," said the Defense Secretary. "The last thing we want is to find out that *Gringo* has some unforeseen effects." He did not have to spell out what he meant by "unforeseen effects." The British government's dependence on the United States during the Copenhagen negotiations was far greater than the Prime Minister would have liked, and at least three of her ministers had protested violently about being excluded from the final discussions. One minister had resigned, citing ill health; a second had found himself involved in a lurid scandal with a pregnant librarian. The third had promised to keep quiet but it had been made abundantly clear to him that his days in the Cabinet were numbered.

"There's one more thing," said the Prime Minister. "Chancellor Kress has called twice today expressing concern at the continued strategic positioning of the Soviet Army and asking again why our administrative staff seems to be doing so much moving around. I think we have managed to satisfy him that our administrative activity is in direct response to the Soviet level of military maneuvering, but I cannot emphasize strongly enough how important it is that not one word about *Gringo* or *Cornflower* reaches any of our allies."

She spoke that last word, "allies," with scarcely any emphasis. It was a bitter word for her to have to use, particularly since she had always believed so deeply in the Western Alliance. She hoped to God that she would have the strength and the clarity of purpose to continue as Prime Minister once *Gringo* was all over.

The Defense Secretary jotted a note on a small, leather-covered Cartier pad, then tucked his fountain pen back in his pocket. "Jolly good," he said at last, then looked up. "We'd better start clearing the decks, hadn't we? Getting ourselves shipshape?''

General Fawkes grumbled, snorted again and let out a fusillade of coughs. The Defense Secretary often thought that General Fawkes had reached his position of eminence in the army by never saying anything with which anyone could either agree or disagree; his entire conversation consisted of inarticulate but military-sounding explosions.

There was a polite knock at the door. It was the house manager. He said, "Excuse me, Prime Minister. Tea?"

Four hours later, just as dusk began to cling around the warehouses and riverside buildings of New York's West Village, Esther Modena alighted from a taxi at the intersection of 13th Street and Ninth Avenue. The cabbie didn't take his eyes off her once as she paid him his fare; he knew what kind of a place it was that she had asked him to take her to. Outside, the triangular building looked shabby and commercial; inside, it was the location of the Hellfire Club, the most notorious of all New York's sex clubs, a sado-masochistic rendezvous that was supposed to make the celebrated Plato's Retreat look like a parent-teacher meeting.

"You wearing anything?" asked the cabbie at last, unable to contain himself as he counted out Esther's change.

Esther looked down at her simple dove-gray dress.

"Underneath, I mean," said the cabbie. "Someone told me you people ride around the city with no underwear, or just chains or something."

Esther gave him a faint smile. "I'm not one of them," she told the cabbie. "I'm just visiting."

"Scares the living shit out of me," said the cabbie and drove off.

Esther crossed the pavement and then cautiously stepped into the club's run-down entrance, watched with unrelenting curiosity by two pale-faced men in T shirts, both of which were printed with the message ONLY AN ANIMAL COULD UNDERSTAND. One of the men said, "Hi," but Esther ignored him. Rock 'n roll throbbed through the door as if the building itself were a lewd and voracious beast and the music the urgent sound of its heart.

She had argued with Wally when he had asked her to meet him here. She had said desperately, "Wally, I just don't *like* those kind of places."

"You've never been in one. How do you know?" he had repeated over and over. And in the end she had agreed simply because he had refused to meet her anywhere else. She had to admit that it made good sense in a perverse kind of way. It was well away from Washington; it was a locale where *she*, at least, was completely unknown; and it was crowded. It was also preeminently the sort of place where nobody asked any questions and nobody wanted to know who you were or where you came from.

On the ground floor there was a crowded leather bar where sulky young men with dyed heads and shaved scalps were sitting on stools, drinking beer and watching themselves with unswerving fascination in the dark-tinted mirror behind the bottles of liquor. One of them glanced at Esther and nodded her wordlessly toward a narrow, brown-carpeted staircase that led to the basement. She stumbled down, almost losing her footing. At the bottom of the stairs there was a huge man with a Mr. T hairstyle and spiked leather gauntlets, his belly bulging over tight, black-leather jeans. Next to him, sitting cross-legged on a gilt chair, was a white-faced woman with bright orange hair, bare-breasted, her waist cinched tight by a red-leather corset. Esther had never seen such high heels on anybody anywhere; they were as long and as red as daggers.

The huge man said, "Fifteen bucks, cash, and sign the waiver."

Esther paid him and scribbled her signature on the Xeroxed form that said she was not a policewoman or an undercover agent and that she would not gamble or take drugs on the premises. Then the man lifted the beaded curtain for her and she stepped apprehensively into the club.

It was dark and sweaty in there, and jostling with people. The cinder-block walls were painted black and the only illumination came from red, green and blue light bulbs. On the opposite side there was a bar behind which a naked man was serving drinks in plastic cups. In the middle of the room, a tall woman wearing nothing but thigh-high vinyl boots was standing in conversation with a middle-aged man in pink stockings and a garter belt. Around the woman's wrist there was a manacle from which a long silver chain ran. On the other end of the chain, collared like a dog, stood a young, naked boy, no more than sixteen or seventeen years old, handsome but vacant-eyed. A muscular black man was standing not far away, his thighs tensed, masturbating, involved in nothing but his own feelings.

Esther's mouth went dry with alarm. Yet what was going on down here in the club was more incongruous than dangerous. A portly, gray-haired man walked past in a green mini-skirt and as he passed, she saw that he had a long cucumber protruding from his backside. The sight was so absurd that she felt strangely relieved, as if she were no longer threatened.

She slowly edged her way around the perimeter of the club. In the far corner, a young blonde girl with a figure as slim as a boy's was kneeling on the floor, persistently sucking at the cock of a thin, vague-looking forty-year-old man. Esther stared at them for a moment, and a short, fat girl whose naked body was trussed up tight in thin, black-leather laces said helpfully, "That's her father. They come down here two or three times a month. Sometimes the mother comes too, and they do it together."

A preppie-looking boy in Nike shorts and track shoes came up to Esther and said, "Are you submissive? Do you smoke? Do you want to see my scrotum ring? I had it specially made in Thailand."

Esther tried to smile and shook her head. She couldn't see Wally anywhere, and she was beginning to feel claustrophobic and panicky. Everywhere she moved there were sweaty bellies and bare buttocks and men and women with rings through their nipples and tattoos on their backs and chains between their legs.

She was just about to give up and leave when someone touched her gently on the shoulder and said, "Don't turn around. It's me. Listen, I have some red-hot information for you. But it has to pay more than two hundred and fifty. It's red hot."

Esther started to turn but Wally moved behind her so she couldn't see him. "How much?" she asked.

"A thousand."

"I can't do it. Not a thousand."

"I drove here; that cost me plenty."

"I could never get you a thousand," Esther told him. "I'm sorry."

Wally said in that odd monotone of his, "This information is *hot*. This is world-class information. I promise you, Esther, this is worth every penny. In fact, it's worth five thousand. I know lots of people would pay me five thousand for this information."

Esther took a breath. She seemed to be able to breathe in nothing but the smell of stale sweat and leather. "Listen," she said, "the two-fifty is guaranteed. I'll see what I can do to get you more."

"I don't know," Wally demurred.

"Wally, it's the best I can do. I'm just not authorized to offer you that kind of money."

She turned around. Wally was standing just behind her wearing nothing but black-leather shorts, black socks and grubby white sneakers. He was a thin-faced man with thinning mousy-brown hair, a bulbous nose and one of those expressions that looks like a watercolor painting left out in the rain: indeterminate and blurry.

"All right," he said at last. "Okay. You win. But see what you can do, right? This trip has put me out of pocket."

"You were coming to New York anyway, weren't you?"

"Yes, but that isn't the point."

Esther waited for a moment. Beside her, she heard the tall woman say, "I have this recurring fantasy of having my breasts nailed to the seat of a wooden chair." The preppie-looking boy was telling a bored girl in red satin all about his scrotum ring. "Do you want to see it? It's real silver."

Wally said, "There's a booth over there with a glory-hole. Go stand in the booth. They'll be starting a show in a minute or two; while it's on, put your ear to the hole and listen. I'm only going to say it once."

Esther would have paid a thousand dollars simply to get out of the Hellfire Club but she nodded and pushed her way through the crush of naked and half-naked bodies until she reached the booth. There was a circular hole in the chipboard wall, halfway down. The idea seemed to be that a man could push his penis through the hole to invite the ministrations of any passing stranger, male or female, who happened to be interested.

She waited for three or four minutes, impatient and afraid. Two or three time she was approached by wandering men who said, "How about it?" in a flippant, half-hopeless way, and when she shook her head, wandered off again, bemused but apparently not angry at being rejected.

Abruptly the rock music was changed to a scratchy tape of Indian drumming and a dazzling white light illuminated the middle of the club's floor. A tall, fierce-looking woman with a black crew cut came dancing out into the light, jut-jawed and broad-shouldered, with big, pendulous breasts that bounced as she danced. She wore black rubber stockings up to the top of her thighs and a silver chain belt that ran tightly around her waist and then down between her legs, cleaving deep into the black bush of her pubic hair. There was whistling and applause as she danced sinuously around the club, snarling and hissing from time to time at the men who were standing watching her, jiggling themselves in submissive delight. Esther lowered her eyes for a moment, scarcely able to believe that any of this was real and that she was really Esther Modena on a Thursday night in New York City.

Now two muscular men in studded belts came out, dragging between them a thinner man, naked and bound, whose head was covered by a tight rubber hood. There was a circular valve in the hood where the man's mouth was, which showed that he had an inflatable rubber gag inside his mouth. He could neither hear, nor see, nor speak.

The man was roughly spread-eagled against the far wall of the club by his two burly guards. The tall crew-cut woman danced across to a side table and danced back again, holding up a heavy carpenter's hammer and four eight-inch-long nails. The preppie-looking man, who was leaning against the side of Esther's booth, said, "You want to watch this; they do it twice a week. It still makes me shudder."

Esther prayed that Wally would hurry. She didn't know how much more of this she could take. She saw the crew-cut woman approach the spread-eagled man and position one of the nails in the palm of his left hand, which was firmly held against the wall by one of his two muscular guards. Esther closed her eyes. There was a brisk knocking noise in time with the Indian drums. An excited moaning rippled around the club. Esther opened her eyes again and saw the crew-cut woman position another nail, this time in the man's right hand. The left hand had been nailed tight against the cinder block. There was no blood but Esther felt a surge of nausea. If Wally didn't come in thirty seconds flat, she was going to leave.

The crew-cut woman squatted down in front of the spread-eagled man. Esther glimpsed the bright chain that cut tight between her big white buttocks. She heard more hammering but she couldn't watch anymore. "His scrotum, right between the balls," whispered the preppie-looking man, licking his lips.

"God," said Esther.

"Oh, it's all right," the man reassured her. "He loves it. He does it over and over."

It was then that the crew-cut woman lifted her fourth and final nail and showed it around to the audience. For some reason, a hush of anticipation fell over the club and there was no sound but the tap-tapping of the drums. The woman stalked up to the spread-eagled man and placed the point of the nail against his rubber-masked forehead.

"Doesn't she just make you *wet* yourself?" panted the preppie-looking man. "She won't really do it, of course, but can you imagine what it's like, being nailed to the wall by your balls, feeling that nail against your forehead."

Without any warning, the crew-cut woman hammered the last nail straight into the spread-eagled man's head. They heard it knock against the skull, then crunch against the cinder block. The spread-eagled man trembled violently and then remained still. There was no blood at first but at last a single crimson line ran down his nose and dripped onto his scrawny, bare rib cage.

The silence and the fear were immense. The crew-cut woman stood there defiantly for a moment, her hands on her hips, and then she pointed directly at Esther and gave her a snarling, toothy grin of triumph.

Oh, God, thought Esther in a surge of sickness. *Oh, God, it's Wally!* Then all the lights went out and the club was a screaming, chaotic tangle of arms and legs and shoving bodies. Esther found herself jammed and shoved against one of the cinder block walls, grazing an arm and a knee. She didn't even realize until she managed to push her way out to the staircase that she was screaming herself.

David Daniels, at that moment, was just stepping out of the shower to answer the phone. Normally he would have let it ring but he was expecting Esther to call him as soon as Wally had passed on his information. He hadn't relished the idea of Esther's going to the Hellfire Club any more than Esther had. He had read an article about it in *Playboy* once and from what the correspondent had written, it had sounded like a halfway house to hell and damnation. Wrapping a dark-blue Turkish towel around himself, he padded through into his dressing room, picked up the phone and said, "Yes?"

"David? This is Jack Levy."

"Sorry I took so long," said David. He bent down slightly so he could see himself in the mirror. He raked his fingers through his wet hair. "These days it's usually some lawyer wanting money. Either that or somebody griping about his taxes."

"David, I'm afraid I'm going to have to beg off."

"Beg off? Beg off what? You mean this Gringo business?"

Jack's voice sounded peculiarly distant, as if he didn't really want to talk about Gringo at all. "I'm real pushed right at the moment, David. I'm all tied up with a big story on the budget deficit. I don't think I'm going to be of much use to you."

"Listen," said David, "you haven't been *warned* off, have you?"

"No, no. It's just that I can't spare the time. I'm sorry. I should have told you when you first called me. I feel guilty about that."

"Jack—"

"I'm sorry, David. That's the way it is."

David blew out his cheeks in resignation. "Okay, if you can't, you can't. But do you know somebody else who might be able to help?"

"David, take my advice," said Jack. "Just leave the whole thing alone. It doesn't amount to anything. Just back off and leave it alone."

"You've been threatened, haven't you?"

There was a sharp crackle on the line. David suddenly realized what was going on. He said to Jack without altering the tone of his voice, "How are things coming along with that new apartment of yours?"

Jack was perplexed at this abrupt change of subject. "Well, fine," he said. "It's coming along fine."

"Tell me about it. What color are you going to paint the den?"

"What?"

"Tell me about it," David persisted. "Go on, I want to know everything. What you're going to do with the kitchen, whether you're going to have blinds or drapes. Come on, Jack, I want to hear it all."

At last Jack realized what David was asking him. Hesitantly he said, "Well . . . we're going to paint the den in eggshell blue. And the hallway . . . well, we're going to leave the hallway white. And the stairs—"

He kept on talking while David carefully set the telephone on the bed and tiptoed across to the window. He peered across the street and saw the Thunderbird straightaway, with the man sitting behind the wheel wearing earphones. If he hadn't been looking for him, of course, he never would have given him a second glance, but there he was, placidly listening in. He was so calm, in fact, that he was eating a sandwich and there was a plastic cup of coffee perched on the dashboard.

David went back to the phone and said, "Go on, Jack, tell me more." Then he quickly struggled into his jeans, pulled a T shirt over his head and went to the bedside table. He took out his .38 Smith & Wesson revolver and swiftly walked out of the bedroom, down the stairs and out the side door of the house. He felt the short grass prickle beneath his bare feet as he ducked low behind a long beech hedge; and then he crossed the street twenty yards behind the Thunderbird so he could come up on it from behind. Those '74 Thunderbirds had a substantial blind spot to the rear quarter and with any luck, he would be right up on it before the driver realized he was there.

Raising the gun in one hand, he made his way quickly along the grass verge until he reached the back of the car. The man was still sitting behind the wheel, munching his sandwich and listening to Jack tell nobody at all that they were going to move that large mahogany bureau into the study. David crouched next to the car, grasped the gun in both hands and shoved it through the open passenger window.

"Freeze," he ordered.

The man stared at him for a moment, then shrugged and laid his half-eaten sandwich on top of the dashboard next to his coffee. "Okay, so I'm frozen."

"Take off those earphones."

The man unhooked the earphones and put them down carefully on the passenger seat.

"Now you have ten seconds to tell me who you are and what the hell this is all about."

The man sniffed and wiped his nose with his finger. "Can I show you my ID?" he asked.

"Don't show me, just tell me."

"My name is Frederick B. Timberland and I am an agent of the Federal Bureau of Investigation."

"And what the hell are you doing listening in to my phone calls?"

"I was told to."

"On whose authority?"

"I don't know. Nobody ever tells me things like that. My instructions are to sit here and listen in. That's all."

"All right, Mr. Timberland," said David. "Show me that ID."

Frederick Timberland lifted his ID wallet out of his shirt pocket and tossed it over. David opened it left-handedly, glanced at it and then tossed it back.

"Right," he said. "I want you to get back to your office and tell whoever it is who sent you that all hell is about to break loose. And I mean all *hell*."

"Yes, sir. I got that."

David stood up, lifting his gun. Frederick Timberland started his engine, poured the remainder of his coffee out on the road, wedged his sandwich into his mouth and drove off. David watched him go, then walked back to the house. Upstairs, Jack was still waiting on the phone.

"Phone tap?" asked Jack hoarsely.

"You got it. Some clown who said he works for the FBI."

Jack was silent. David could almost hear his embarrassment. After a while David said, "Are you still off the case? Or do you want to keep at it? This Gringo must amount to something. And believe me, I'm going to be calling Schachocis at the FBI just as soon as I put the phone down and I'm going to give him *hell*."

Jack said, "I'd sooner forget it, thanks, David. You know how it is."

"I'm not sure I do."

"Well, if you want to know the truth, there were threats against my wife."

"What kind of threats?"

"Mutilation, that kind of thing. She's scared to go out."

David bit his lip. "Have you found out anything at all?"

"Not that I want to tell you. But believe me, David, this is coming down from the highest possible level. If I were you, I'd be careful about stirring up too much of a stink with the FBI."

David paused for a moment, then said, "Okay, Jack I understand. I'll talk to you later. Maybe we can have dinner when I get back to Washington."

"I'd like that," said Jack and hung up.

Almost immediately, as if somebody had been watching and waiting for him to finish his call, the phone rang again. David picked it up, wedged it under his chin and said, "Yes?"

"Senator Daniels?"

"This is he."

"You don't know me, Senator, but my name is Jordan Crane. I work for the National Security Council; you can check my credentials if you wish."

"Well?" asked David sharply.

"Well, sir, I have been requested by Mr. Morton Lock to call you and advise you that the investigations you are currently attempting to instigate are overlapping into an area of national security and that he would very much appreciate it if you would desist for the time being. He says that if you wish to discuss the matter any further, he will be glad to meet with you and talk it over."

David said, "We're talking about something called Gringo?"

"I'm sorry, Senator, I'm not at liberty to say."

"But that's the area of national security I'm supposed to be overlapping?"

"It is related to the area, yes, sir."

"And I'm supposed to keep my nose out even though one of my best friends has had his wife threatened with mutilation and some goon from the FBI has been sitting outside my house illegally tapping my telephone?"

"I'm sorry, sir, I don't know anything about either of those incidents. But I'm sure that Mr. Lock would be more than happy to make everything clear at a personal meeting."

David said tautly, "You can tell Mr. Morton Lock that until he comes around here and explains all this in person and makes sure that Jack Levy's wife gets an apology and a promise that nobody is ever going to threaten her again, I'm going to continue my investigations into Gringo and I'm going to make damn sure I find out what it is and why Mr. Lock is so desperate to keep it under wraps."

There was a short silence; then Jordan Crane said, "I have been authorized to caution you not to do that, Senator."

"Caution me? *Caution* me? What does that mean?"

"It simply means that it would not be in your personal interests to carry your investigations any further."

David said in a low, unsteady voice, "You try and stop me, Mr. Jordan Crane." Then he banged the phone down and sat on the edge of his bed, his cheek muscles working with anger and emotion.

He went downstairs and mixed a dry martini. As he was

stirring it, the phone rang again. He picked it up and said, "Yes?"

"David," sobbed Esther. "David, you have to help me."

THIRTEEN

He rang Jeppe for most of the day, once every twenty minutes, but there was no reply. In the end he took a taxi around to Jeppe's apartment on Halfdansgade, on the other side of Sydhavnen, next to the university, but nobody answered the doorbell, and strangest of all, there was no name on the mailbox. The summer wind blew across the street; the taxi waited for him, engine running, the driver watching him through the reflecting windshield. Charles began to realize that Jeppe had probably gone forever, disappeared into that mirror world where spies and secret servicemen go when their luck and their time run out.

It was mid-afternoon. Charles had been listening to the radio all morning and had bought an early edition of *Ekstra Bladet* to see if there was any news about their break-in at Klarlund & Christensen, but so far there had been nothing at all. He had passed Klarlund & Christensen on his way to Jeppe's apartment; the whole ground-floor facade had been boarded up with plywood but workmen had already been cutting new glass. The Lincoln had been towed away.

Agneta had said to him that morning, "What's wrong? You look worried, the same way you used to look in the old days."

Charles had shrugged. "Something's wrong here. Some-

174

thing's all wrong. The trouble is, I don't understand what it is. I can't get my mind around it."

"Leave it," Agneta had urged him.

He had ruffled her pixie-blonde hair. "No," he had told her in the gentlest of voices.

She had said, "It will lead only to trouble, I know it."

Charles had nodded. "I know. But I think the trouble has happened already. All it's doing now is waiting for somebody to find out what it is."

The taxi crossed Langebro. Beneath the bridge, the waters of Sydhavnen sparkled bright cobalt blue, the color of the sky. Clouds passed over Copenhagen's spires and rooftops, as stately and slow as dreams. Charles lit a cigarette and the driver tapped the sign that told him no smoking. He said, "Forget it, I'll walk."

He paid the cabbie and walked back along Hans Christian Andersen Boulevard smoking ostentatiously, his hands in his pockets. He had known agents and security men to disappear before. One of his earliest mentors in the CIA, Dashley Pope, had completely vanished at the same time as Jimmy Hoffa, and although Charles had spent months trying to pick up a lead on where he might have gone, the result had always been the same. A mirror facing a mirror, a corridor that led to nowhere.

He bought another copy of *Ekstra Bladet* and quickly leafed through it. No news about the Klarlund & Christensen break-in. He tossed the newspaper into a litter bin and continued to walk. Jeppe had been running away from the crash the last time Charles had seen him. So what had happened to him after that? Had someone been watching the Klarlund & Christensen building all along and caught Jeppe as he tried to get away? Or had he been fingered by the used-car dealer he had gone to and picked up later on? That was more likely. The Lincoln could have been identified in minutes by anybody with access to the police computer, and after that it would only have needed a heavyweight visit to the dealer and Jeppe would have been nailed.

The question was: who had the authority to eliminate a senior officer in the Danish security services? *Krov' iz Nosu* was a high-ranking killer, no doubt about it, but he wouldn't

have been able to waste a man like Jeppe without sanction
from higher up. Charles, of course, was a little different.
Charles was retired now, no longer officially attached.
If someone from the KGB or the GRU decided that his presence in Copenhagen was irritating and eliminated him,
not even the slightest of diplomatic ripples would disturb
the dark web of international security. Nobody would seek
to avenge him. There would be nothing but mild relief
that he had gone.

Charles reached Larsbjørnstrade hot and sweating and feeling like a drink. He clumped heavily upstairs and was just
about to push his key into the lock when he stopped, lowered
his arm and stepped back. He had a system with Agneta, a
throwback to the old days when he had never quite known
who might come around to pay him a visit. They kept a tiny
piece of white celluloid, the end piece snipped off a shirt-
collar bone, tucked into the side of the lock. If anyone
unwelcome called and forced his way in, Agneta was to
slip the piece of celluloid out of the side of the lock so
Charles would be warned before he opened the door. Now
the piece was missing; and there was no sign of it on the
floor, so it couldn't have simply dropped out. Charles wished
that Jeppe had been able to get him that gun before he
had disappeared.

He walked quietly along the corridor until he reached the
stripped-pine door at the end. This led out to a small balcony
that had originally been crowded with rubbish, but Agneta
had cleared it and decorated it with clay geranium pots.
Occasionally, on warm evenings, they took a bottle of wine
out there and looked out over the jumble of Studie Strade and
St. Peders Strade, and beyond to St. Jørgens Sø. Now Charles
stepped out there, closed the door cautiously behind him and
hoisted himself up onto the wrought-iron railing.

He could just reach the guttering along the orange-tiled
roof if he stood on the railing on his toes. He didn't dare look
behind him; it was too far down to the cluttered yard below.
He didn't dare think of the age of the railing either, or how
rusted and weak it might be. He could hear traffic in the
streets all around him, and the wind whirring through the
ventilator on top of the chimney. He thought: Jesus, Krogh,

you're too old for this kind of thing. You can't even lift your own weight anymore. But he gripped the guttering and swung, his shoes scrabbling against the wall, and at last, grunting, he managed to lift himself up so that the top half of his body was over the edge of the roof, his arms as rigid as if he were exercising on parallel bars.

Now, he thought to himself, get your leg up now. Because if you don't, you're going to drop down onto the balcony, and if you drop, they're going to hear you. He didn't allow it to enter his mind for a moment that the slip of celluloid might have fallen out of the door by accident and that there was nobody in the apartment apart from Agneta. In the CIA, they taught you to think negatively. Imagine the worst, then double it.

He heaved one foot up onto the gutter, then the other, and at last he was on the roof. He was panting and gasping, and he knew that he wasn't going to be of much use if it came to a fight. God, for a gun!

He eased his way across the tiles. They made a gritty, grating sound beneath his weight. Halfway up the roof there was a skylight that overlooked the kitchen and most of the breakfast area, and he hoped that from there he would be able to see what was happening inside the apartment.

It took him two or three strenuous minutes to reach the edge of the skylight. He pressed himself against the tiles for a moment, listening, but all he could hear was the wind and the chimney ventilator whirring in fits and starts, and the bustling noises of Copenhagen on a busy afternoon. He decided to risk it and take a look into the skylight.

At first he could see nothing but one corner of the kitchen counter. He carefully brushed the grime from the windows, and it was then that a man stepped abruptly into view: a gray-haired man in a gray suit, smoking a cigarette. He was obviously talking because he kept jabbing his cigarette in emphasis toward somebody on the other side of the room but Charles found it impossible to make out what he was saying. No doubt about it though; he was a secret-service type of one persuasion or another, and he was looking for Charles.

The man moved out of sight again. Charles clung to the

roof, wondering what he ought to do next. If he knocked on the front door of the apartment and announced himself openly, the gray-haired man might very well blow him away without even asking what time of day it was. He knew what his old CIA training instructor would have told him (eyes squeezed tight, cigar clenched in the corner of his mouth): "Get the hell out as quickly and as quietly as you can and don't go back there, ever. Once you're a marked man, they won't let you go. They'll systemize you anywhere, any time, without warning, even if you've retired to the country with a plain wife, three children and a secondhand station wagon." "Systemized" had replaced the older euphemism of "terminating with extreme prejudice." It had originated from "SYS 64738," the Basic computer command to wipe everything off the screen.

Charles' old CIA instructor, however, hadn't given his trainees any suggestions for dealing with emotions. It was all very well getting the hell out, but supposing you had to leave behind a girl you happened to be more than extremely fond of, and in the hands of a man you suspected of being a professional tomahawk?

Charles peered down through the skylight again. Since he didn't have a gun, his only weapon was surprise. He had never jumped through a window, although he could remember his instructor's advice on how to do it. Jacket tugged over the head, arms folded tight over the chest; then dive like you're diving into a swimming pool. With any luck, you won't get anything important sliced off. Of course a skylight was something else. After going through the glass, there was still a ten-foot drop to the floor to think about.

"Shit," Charles muttered to himself. It was more out of frustration than anger. A large crow came and perched on the ridge of the roof not far from him and stared at him beadily as if he were some kind of ungainly and obtrusive bird who might have to be pecked out of its territorial airspace.

Cautiously Charles edged his way over the skylight and slid his left leg across until the welt of his shoe was perched on the dry crust of putty at the lower edge of the window frame. Then, gasping, he raised himself up so that he was hunched over, head down low between his shoulders, scarcely keeping his balance. For one teetering second he nearly fell backward off the roof, and he knew that if he did, there wasn't much hope of tumbling onto the balcony. It would be a one-way express trip down to the yard. Cobblestones, broken back, a wheelchair at best.

"God in heaven," he muttered. Then, just as quietly, "Geronimo!"

He fell into the skylight shoulder-first, heard the glass crack squeakily like ice, felt the cold brush of a broken edge across his cheek. Then the whole rotted frame collapsed and he was plummeted into the kitchen in a shower of wood and fragments and sparkling splinters, his right foot landing first so that for one split second he was beautifully balanced with his arms clenched to his chest, his left leg kicking high, and then he rolled over heavily on his hip, knocked his forehead against the door of the china cupboard and ended up flat on his face, winded and bloody.

He picked himself up, whining for breath, and lurched immediately toward the kitchen counter where Agneta kept her carving knives in a wooden block. He snatched out the longest knife and then threw himself backward against the wall beside the door. Instantly, as if he had been given a cue by a stage director, the man in the gray suit walked into the kitchen and Charles unhesitatingly stabbed him straight through the back of his suit, gripping the carving knife with its blade sideways so it sliced with a minimum of resistance between his lower ribs and into his pancreas.

The man turned, surprised, and for a moment stared at Charles as if he were about to say something. Then he collapsed to his knees on the tiled floor and let his head sink between his shoulders. With a sharp clatter, an automatic pistol fell to the floor beside him and Charles lunged forward and snatched it up.

"Na pomasch," the man whispered. He reached around behind him and tried to take out the knife.

Charles said, "Not on your life, chum. Agneta!"

From the living room, there was silence. Charles nudged the gray-haired man and said, "Are you alone? Or what?"

The man dropped sideways to the floor and lay there panting. Charles hefted the pistol in his hand, the good old Tula-Tokarev 1930 7.62 mm. At least he knew now who he was up against. He called again, "Agneta? Are you okay?"

Silence. That meant someone else was here, guarding her. Charles eased his way around the doorjamb, keeping the pistol raised, and made his way along the short, carpeted corridor that led to the living room. He paused and listened. The corridor was lined with prints of the runic decorations found on Jellinge stones in Jutland: ancient, mysterious, elaborate. Charles could feel blood sticking to his collar and hoped his face wasn't too badly cut. It was beginning to sting, all the way from his right eye to the right side of his mouth.

He eased his way into the living room and there she was, sitting on the beige wool chair by the window: white-faced, tense, as upright as a statue. A thin man in a gray suit stood directly behind her, pointing an automatic pistol at her head.

Charles said nothing but carefully took aim at the man's head in the approved CIA manner, one hand steadying the butt.

The man said, "You have cut yourself, Mr. Krogh."

Charles said, "Put down the gun."

"Well, I don't think so, Mr. Krogh. I think that for my own safety, I would prefer to keep the gun aimed exactly where it is."

"You have a count of five to put down the gun. Then I'm going to kill you."

The man smiled tightly. "I don't think so, Mr. Krogh. One flinch from you and this lady will die instantly."

Charles kept his gun raised. "Five," he said in a level voice.

"Now then, Mr. Krogh," said the man calmly, "you are being ridiculous. This is not what I expected from a man of your caliber."

"What did you expect?"

"I expected cooperation. After all, you have not been behaving yourself, have you?"

"What's that supposed to mean?"

"Come now, Mr. Krogh. Are you going to pretend that it

wasn't you who broke into the offices of Klarlund and
Christensen last night and caused such mayhem? Breaking
windows, rifling files; and what did you do to my poor friend
Lyosha? He was quite bruised and battered from falling out
that window. It was lucky for him there was a ledge two
floors down. Lucky for you too, Mr. Krogh. If Lyosha had
died, there would have been a price on your head that
almost every killer in the world would have found irresistible.
Lyosha is special to us, you know. A personal favorite
of the Premier.''

Charles said, "Four."

The man smiled even more broadly. "Please don't make
the situation more fraught with difficulties than it already is,
my dear sir. All we want to do is to ask you some questions.
You are no longer on the staff of the Central Intelligence
Agency; you have no allegiances. What is the harm in answering one or two simple queries? Like, what were you
looking for in an architect's office? What did you expect to
find? Why did you risk so much and fight so hard?''

Charles said, "You know the answers to all those questions, old buddy, even before you ask them. So, you know,
don't bullshit. Just put down the gun and stand back.''

The man shook his head. "That is not possible, I regret.''

Charles said, "Three" and pulled the trigger. There was a
single deafening report and the man's face imploded like a
speeded-up movie of a can of red paint being spilled. He
disappeared behind Agneta's chair, leaving a whiplash of
crimson spatters all the way up the pale-fawn Scandinavian
wall.

Charles and Agneta held each other close, tight with affec-
tion, tight with fear. Agneta touched Charles' cheek with her
fingertips. "You cut yourself. Look, you're bleeding.''

"It's nothing. Jesus, Agneta, it's nothing. What the hell
were these guys doing here?''

"They said they wanted to talk to you, that's all. I told
them you were away in Stockholm but they didn't believe
me. I barely managed to slip the marker out of the lock.''

"Thank God for that. These are Russians, Russian agents.
KGB, I don't know, or worse.'' He lifted the Tula-Tokarev

automatic, turned it this way and that, then slung it aside. "Lousy monkey-made guns. I was lucky to hit him."

Charles didn't know what else to say. There were two dead men in his apartment, Agneta was shuddering with fright, Jeppe was gone, and Otto was probably dead too, and he still didn't know what in hell was supposed to be happening. This wasn't the game the way he used to play it back in the days when he was on active service. This was a different game, far more confusing, far more violent. In the old days they wouldn't have sent a killer like *Krov' iz Nosu* after small fry like him. Something had changed, something fundamental. There was a big secret around somewhere and it was being guarded with maniacal ferocity.

"Listen," he told Agneta, "I want you to go stay with Roger for a while. You don't mind that, do you? Roger will take care of you. Apart from that, he won't give you any trouble, if you know what I mean."

"But what about these men? What about you?"

"Just leave this to me, okay? Everything's under control. It's just that I want you to go stay with Roger. Maybe for a week or two, not more."

"And what will you do?"

"I have to find Jeppe. Or at least find out what happened to Jeppe. I also have to find out why these goons broke in here today. I also have to have a drink."

Agneta clutched him close. God, he thought, I love you. I don't know why, I don't *care* why, but I do. She smelled of Chanel No. 19 and clean hair and Danishness. Who could tell what that was? A kind of mixture of ozone, *smørrasbørd* and pine. He kissed the top of her head and thought: I'm far too old for any of this. I should have retired by now to Whispering Palms in Southern California. I should be playing golf in checked pants and blue sports shirts with little crocodiles on them. Instead, I'm dipping my arm into the jaws of hell and risking the lives of everybody around me, including the lady I love the most.

Agneta said in Danish, "Do you want to go back to America? Do you think you should? Charles, I don't mind coming with you. Please, if you want to go."

"No," he told her. He kissed her again. "Honey, I'd love

to, but it doesn't end there. Many are called, you know, but only a few are chosen, and for some reason, I happen to be one of the chosen, and that means I've got to do my duty here and find out what the hell is going on. I mean, for Jeppe's sake, if nobody else's.''

He went to the phone and dialed the Politigården. When the receptionist answered, he said, ''Give me *Politidirektor* Isen.''

There was a silence. Agneta said, ''Oh, God, Charles, I wish you would give this up, let this go. I will come to America with you, I promise.''

Charles said, ''Povl? How are you doing? This is Charles. Charles Krogh, of course. Krogh with a K. Yes, that's right. Povl, I have a problem here. I mean I have a problem at home. Well, it's to do with the KGB. Well, yes. I have two KGB personalities here who seem to be disinclined to leave.''

God help the Danish sense of humor, he thought, as Povl Isen asked him, ''You want somebody to tell them to go? I have patrolmen who can do that.''

''Not exactly, Povl. The problem is, they couldn't go if they wanted to. They are ex-KGB. Systemized, you get me? Program deleted.''

''Charles, I thought you were retired.''

''I am, Povl, but something's come up.''

''KGB? You can establish that beyond question?''

''Are you kidding? They have gray suits from Daells and Tula-Tokarev automatics.''

There was a long silence. Povl Isen was a serious, reputable policeman who had never taken kindly to intelligence antics in Copenhagen. It was arguable which organization he disliked the most: the KGB or the CIA. Both treated Copenhagen as if it belonged to them; both regularly incurred the wrath of the Copenhagen police headquarters. Povl Isen had spoken to both the U.S. and Soviet embassies twice this year and warned them that they were guests, no matter how strategically Denmark might be placed. ''You are forbidden from practicing your wars in my city,'' he had told them. Both ambassadors had expressed surprise and concern that Povl Isen should imagine for a moment that they were doing such a

thing. The Russian ambassador had sent him a case of
mukuzani, which Povl Isen had promptly sent back.

"I shall have to have you questioned," Povl told Charles.
"Whenever there are dead bodies, there must be an investigation."

"I understand," said Charles. "I'll wait. You know where
I live, don't you, on Larsbjørnstrade?"

"I know where you live, Mr. Krogh with a K."

Charles put down the phone and then sat for a moment
smiling at Agneta. "God, it's a hard life," he told her. She
came over, knelt beside him and touched the friendly creases
of his face. "I think I'm crazy," he told her.

"Yes," she said, "I think so too. But I love you."

Of course he didn't wait for the police. He cleaned up the
cut on his face, which was long rather than deep, and changed
out of his bloody clothes. He packed a bag with soap, razor,
towel, shirts and his second-best suit while Agneta packed
herself a larger suitcase with three dresses, a pair of jeans,
half a dozen T shirts, some bras and cosmetics. No panties;
she never wore any. They locked the apartment door behind
them and held hands in the back of the taxi as they drove
around to Roger's apartment in Peder Skrams Gade; then they
kissed fleetingly before Charles went on to the Københavner
bar on Gothergade.

Agneta said, "Call me tonight, Charles, even if it's only
quickly."

He blew her a kiss. "I love you, you dummy."

Charles walked into the Københavner bar and left his bag in
the cloakroom. He approached the bar, rubbing his hands
while the barkeep regarded him balefully. "Hallo, Mr. Krogh.
What happened to you?"

"Hand slipped shaving."

"I'll believe you. What do you want to drink?"

"Jack Daniel's on the rocks. What else?"

"Maybe Suntory?" asked the barkeep, bending down to
find a glass, his blond hair shining in the unexpected gleam of
a spotlight.

"Suntory," Charles intoned. "Do they make *smørrasbørd*
in Peru?"

"No, sir."

"You're right, Frederik. Neither do they make whiskey in Japan."

Frederik poured him a straight measure of Jack Daniel's on the rocks. Charles drank it as quickly as if it were soda pop, then held out his glass for another. Frederik filled him up and watched as he took the first sip.

"You look tired, Mr. Krogh, if you don't mind my saying so."

"I don't mind."

"You had some calls."

"Calls? How many?"

"Six or seven. All from the same lady."

"I had calls from a lady and you didn't tell me?"

"Peder thought it better not to call you at home in case of upsetting the cart of apples."

"Is that right?" said Charles a little irritably. "So who called?"

"The lady said . . . just a minute, I should have a note of it here. Here it is. The lady said she worked for the Hvidsten Inn in Jutland."

Charles felt the coldness of terrible and inevitable destiny run through his veins like mercury. Hvidsten: that was where *Krov' iz Nosu* had killed Nicholas Reed. And nothing in the world could persuade Charles that he could hear the name of a boondock village like Hvidsten twice in one week without there being some threatening connection.

He shook out a cigarette and lit it one-handedly. "Did she leave a number?"

"No, sir. She just said the Hvidsten Inn and something about 'the old code.' And one thing more; I didn't understand it but she said you'd probably know. Lamb prix. I kept saying, 'Don't you mean Grand Prix,' but she said no, lamb prix."

"Lamb prix?" frowned Charles through a tangle of smoke. But then he realized what he had just said. "*Lamprey.* That's what she meant. Lamprey."

"I still don't understand it, Mr. Krogh."

Charles said, "I know you don't, my friend, but I do. Pass me your phone."

The barman put the phone in front of him. "You're not calling long distance?"

Charles was sorting through his untidy pigskin wallet. At last he found a dry-cleaning ticket with a telephone number written on the back in neat Continental numerals, all the sevens crossed. "Long distance?" he asked the barkeep as he dialed. "It depends what you mean by long distance. Is Bonn long distance?"

"Bonn?" queried the barman. "Bonn where?"

Charles cheerfully patted his cheek. "Are there two Bonns?"

The phone rang for two or three minutes before somebody answered it. A girl's voice said, "What number are you calling, please?"

Charles repeated the number with exaggerated care. "And the password is Mentionable. At least that's the only password I've been given."

"I hope you're going to pay for this call," said the barkeep.

"Give me another drink," Charles told him.

There was a clicking on the line and then a man's deep voice said, "Give your name, please."

"Charles Krogh. I'm calling from Copenhagen, Denmark."

"Yes, from the Københavner bar on Gothergade."

Charles said, "Fast trace. I'm impressed. At least you take care of yourselves."

"What's on your mind, Mr. Krogh?"

"I've just received a message that was left for me here by Nicholas Reed when he was at the Hvidsten Inn in Jutland."

"What was the message?"

"Lamprey, that's all."

"You know something about Nicholas?"

Charles blew out smoke. "I know who systemized him. I was checking up on his background with Jeppe Rifbjerg. Now Rifbjerg's gone vacant and the same guys who systemized Nicholas are trying to do the same to me."

There was a pause. The long-distance wire sang a mournful, warbling song. At length the man said, "It was you who tried that bag job on Klarlund and Christensen?"

"I'm afraid so."

"Well, we need to have a word with you, Mr. Krogh. Stay where you are for a short while; I'll send somebody to contact you."

"Just answer one question," said Charles.

"If I can."

"Just tell me how heavy this is, on a scale of one to ten."

"We're not sure. We have our suspicions. We may be receiving some valuable new information very shortly."

"But heavy?"

"Yes, Mr. Krogh. Heavy."

Charles put down the phone, took DKr 25 out of his pocket and tossed them on the bar. The barkeep scooped them up and nodded in appreciation.

"I always pay my way," said Charles. "Now, what about another drink, on the house?"

FOURTEEN

Michael was dozing on the sofa when Lev shook him by the shoulder and said, "Mr. Townsend? We have news of your friend."

Michael opened his eyes. For a split second he couldn't imagine where he was. His mouth felt dry and the rough fabric of the sofa had imprinted a red pattern across his cheek. He sat up slowly and coughed. The apartment was stale with cigarette smoke and sweat. Underarm deodorant was not considered an essential in the Soviet Union and it was usually impossible to buy it at the local *aptyeka*.

Lev said, "One of our people has just called us to say that your friend is at the KGB office on Kazakova Ulitsa and that apparently he is being questioned. Miss Konstantinova is there too." He checked his cheap steel wristwatch. "They are to be driven at four o'clock to Zagorsk, just as we expected."

Michael said, "You're still sure there's nothing I can do?"

Lev sat down beside him and laid a hand on his arm. He had short, stubby fingers with broad, close-cut nails. "Mr. Townsend, there may be, but there is always an element of danger. The safest thing for you to do is to stay in hiding, at least as long as it takes us to get you out of Russia."

"It's just that I feel responsible," said Michael. "It was my idea for us to come and exhibit here in Moscow. Now the whole thing's gone wrong. John's been virtually kidnapped,

I'm stuck here, not to mention all the stock and prototypes we've lost.''

Lev said, "We have been considering the possibility of rescuing your friend before he reaches Zagorsk.''

"Rescuing him? How?''

"Well, there is some considerable risk involved, for all of us. But he will be driven there in a KGB car, probably with one or two *militsia* outriders but no more protection than that. After all, what would be the point?''

"You're not suggesting an ambush?'' asked Michael.

"We have discussed it.''

"Can you do such a thing in the Soviet Union? I mean, could you possibly get away with it?''

"My dear Mr. Townsend, the Soviet Union is vast. There are miles of roads on which you can drive for hours without seeing anybody. The road to Zagorsk, in places, is no exception. We were discussing the possibility of attacking your friend's car just south of Tekstil'sciki and then making our escape not west, as the KGB and the *militsia* would expect us to do, but east to Scolkovo, and then doubling back during the night.''

Michael said, "Do you think I could have a cup of coffee?''

"There's some tea in the samovar in the kitchen. I think you will find it quite fresh.''

Michael eased himself up from the sofa and walked through to the cluttered kitchen. A blonde-haired girl in baggy jeans and a checked shirt was spooning *tvorog* cheese out of a dish and a man was leaning against the door smoking and talking to her earnestly, as if he were trying to persuade her to go to bed with him, or hoping to change her political opinions.

Michael rinsed a glass under the tap and poured a cup of tea. It was tepid but all he needed was something to freshen his mouth with.

"You could get us both out of the country?'' he asked Lev.

"If you are both prepared to assume the risks.''

"And what about the risks to *you*?''

Lev shrugged. "We accept those risks as a part of being members of Lamprey. Also, we would very much like to talk to Rufina Konstantinova.''

"I see,'' said Michael. He walked back into the living room. "And after you've talked to her, what then?''

"Does that really concern you?"

"Yes," said Michael. "As a matter of fact, it does."

Lev looked at him with pale, penetrating eyes. "You're not in love with her, are you?"

"I don't think that's any of your business."

"Well, perhaps not. As long as your holiday romance doesn't jeopardize you or any of my people."

Lev said something in Russian to the girl in the kitchen, something long and involved that seemed to include endless repetition of the word *avtomobilya*. The girl nodded and nodded, although when Lev had finished, she came back with an equally lengthy and involved reply that sounded frankly argumentative.

At last Lev said, "We think the risks may be pretty favorable. In other words, if we ambush the KGB car quickly and unexpectedly and leave them no time for consideration, we may get away with it. But of course you will have to come with us since we will take you straight to the Finnish border as soon as we have retrieved your friend, or even if we fail to retrieve him."

"Supposing the police track you down?"

"My dear Mr. Townsend, you talk as if this kind of thing is not happening in the USSR all the time. There have been scores of attacks on KGB agents in the past twenty or thirty years, sometimes by foreign hit men, quite often by Soviet dissident movements. You don't seriously believe that a regime as repressive as that of the Politburo could have survived for so long unscathed?"

"I suppose not," said Michael. He sipped more tea. Then he said to Lev, "Do you have any idea of what's going on, of why the British are allowing the Russians to keep people like John?"

"Well, we have some theories," Lev told him. "The least-provocative theory is that the British are anxious to improve trade links with the USSR because of the gradual breakup of the Common Market and that they are offering some of their best scientific talent as bait."

"Do you believe that?" asked Michael.

"Not myself, no. I believe that something far more serious is happening. I believe that we are witnessing the first moves

in a major realignment of world politics, the first major realignment since the Russian Revolution. You see, priorities
change, international economic needs flow like great currents
beneath the surface of diplomacy. Nations alter and grow in
the same way that people do. The old East-West confrontation has been outdated since the late nineteen fifties and a
radical change is long overdue. Dulles and Khrushchev have
been buried for years, my friend. We are now living in an age
of computers; politicians are almost irrelevant. So here is the
world. How would a computer divide up the world for the
maximum benefit of all? Not the way in which the French and
the English tried to divide it in the nineteenth century, not the
way in which Hitler and Stalin tried to divide it, not the way
in which it was divided at Yalta. A computer would divide it
according to today's practical needs, according to today's
anxieties and today's fears. Differently, you see, from the
way it was done in years gone by. And that is what I believe
is happening; the redivision of the world, the changing of
international boundaries and alignments. The world can no
longer bear the pressure of the Cold War. It has become too
expensive, too burdensome on both men and resources, to
carry on for the sake of protecting political systems that are
decades out of date. At what period in world history have two
opposing regimes remained so statically and so unbendingly
at loggerheads with each other, building up great arsenals of
weapons and yet never actually fighting each other face-to-
face? So much has changed, so many things have altered.
Morals, technology, world events. No, my friend, a major
change is about to take place, something that will shake the
very earth, and the taking of your friend is part of it.''

Michael said nothing. He went to the window and looked
down on the narrow gap between this block of apartments and
the next. Old postwar apartment blocks, gray and unprepossessing, Moscow at its saddest. You could see the same kind
of buildings in London and New York. Blocks put up in a
time of optimism and determination, when the memory of the
war was still fresh and everybody was convinced it would
never happen again. Michael thought: they might just as well
have tried to wish away cancer. Was it for this that I went
every day to my primary school in South Croydon, in my

cropped haircut and gray-flannel shorts? Was it for this that I studied and played and cried and religiously read every copy of the *Eagle* and never missed a single episode of *Journey Into Space* on the radio? He suddenly missed Margaret and Duncan and wished bitterly that he had never thought of coming to Russia.

Lev laid a hand on his shoulder as if he understood through mental osmosis what Michael was thinking.

"We have no choice, my friend. We are like grains of sand in the hourglass, you and me." He pronounced it with a hard "h"—"howerglass." "When the hourglass is turned upside down, we have no alternative but to tumble through with all the other grains of sand."

Michael nodded. "Can you show me how to use one of those guns?"

"The AKM?" Lev asked him, surprised. "Such a thing is not for you, my friend."

"Can you show me how to use it?"

"Of course; it is simple enough. It was designed for use by amateurs."

Lev said something in Russian to the young man who was sitting on the sofa smoking a filter-tipped cigarette. The young man reached behind him and hefted the automatic rifle in his hand, tossing it over to Lev, who caught it and then handed it to Michael. The rifle was unexpectedly heavy; it weighed over nine pounds, and it smelled of grease.

"The lever on the side controls the rate of fire," said Lev. "Up, and it won't fire at all. In the center, and it fires automatic. Down, and it fires single-shot. This catch here, at the front of the trigger guard, releases the magazine. All you have to know apart from that is that the barrel points toward the enemy and the wooden end points toward us."

The young man on the sofa laughed, his cigarette dangling between his lips.

There seemed to be endless complicated arrangements to be made that morning; Lev was almost an hour on the telephone. But Michael had learned from the short time he had spent with the dissident intelligence group calling themselves Lamprey that not one of them ventured out of the apartment for any reason without elaborate checks first being made that the street was empty of suspicious observers, that their drivers were going to turn up on time, and that every possible contingency had been covered, from the sudden appearance of tails to the nonappearance of friendly agents. They lived in constant expectation of discovery and sudden death. To Michael, who had never had to worry about anything worse than an overdraft at the bank, their attitude was astonishingly pragmatic, and yet understandable too. He hadn't been in Moscow for more than a few days but already he had become conscious of the oppressive restrictions of the state: the absence of Western newspapers from the newsstands, the interminable waiting at stores and restaurants, the requirement that every foreign visitor who drove out of Moscow file a route plan with Intourist lest he be sent back to the city, the law that forbade foreign visitors from spending the night in the home of a Soviet citizen. In itself, each prohibition seemed petty. Taken together, they amounted to a massive and suffocating infringement of personal rights.

By two o'clock, Lev and his companions were ready to leave. Their driver would pick them up outside the apartment at 2:07 precisely. The girl in the checked shirt was coming with them, as well as the young man who had been sprawling on the sofa smoking cigarettes. Their firepower amounted to two AKMs, one of them carried by Michael, two revolvers, and an RPG7 antitank gun, which the young man carried into the street wrapped in a blanket with the head of a floor mop protruding from its muzzle so it looked as if he were carrying an invalid child in his arms. A Moskvich sedan drew over to the side of the road as they emerged from the apartment building and in a matter of seconds they had all climbed in, slammed the doors and stowed their weapons in the backs of the two front seats, which had been sliced open and then sealed up with Velcro. The car was small and cramped but Michael recognized the suppressed burble of an engine that has been successfully souped up. He had once done the same with an old Morris Minor, and until it had finally shaken itself to pieces on the Reigate bypass, it had bellowed around the roads of Surrey like a BRM.

He suddenly realized that he was tremendously excited and that he enjoyed sitting here with Lev and his companions, driving through Moscow in a revved-up car loaded with guns. It was conspiratorial and boyishly thrilling.

"We have to be careful of the state police," said Lev. "They have patrol posts all the way along the major highways and if they see us, they are likely to stop us. If that happens, we must ask you to say nothing. Leave everything to us. They will only have to suspect that you are a foreigner and we will be in serious trouble."

They drove north along Mira Prospekt and out through Moscow's suburbs. It was a dazzling, gilded afternoon. Off to the west, Michael could see the silvery needles of planes arriving and taking off from Sheremetyevo Airport and for a moment his adventure lost some of its luster. He thought of Margaret. She was probably worried sick by now. He just hoped she didn't get any trouble from British intelligence. He was beginning to understand that all that *Smiley's People* stuff was no exaggeration; in fact, if anything, it was underplayed. Intelligence services served governments, and governments had no thought for the well-being of hapless individuals. Intelligence services were the unacceptable face of bureaucracy.

The Mira Prospekt took them past Sokol'niki Park and then close to BIIHX, the huge Exhibition of Soviet Economic Achievements, to which Rufina had been diverted by Lamprey's false telephone call. From the avenue they could see the *Monument Kosmosa*, the sweeping concrete spire that commemorates Soviet triumphs in space. Then the highway turned northeast toward Zagorsk and their rendezvous with the KGB at Tekstil'sciki. "Now you are having your guided tour at last," Lev remarked wryly. "It's a pity you won't get to see Zagorsk. The Cathedral of the Assumption is quite spectacular, and they make wonderful toys in Zagorsk. You have a son, don't you? He would have liked a toy from Zagorsk."

"As long as he gets his father back, I don't think he's going to be too concerned about toys," said Michael.

The girl checked her watch. "We should be well ahead of the KGB car. As long as we don't have any trouble, we should have plenty of time to prepare an ambush."

They crossed the Jauza river. The countryside reminded Michael of parts of Worcestershire. Crows rose in a speckled storm from a distant field and circled around and around in the sunlight. The sky was almost white.

"Police," said the driver, glancing in the rearview mirror.

Michael was about to turn around to look but the girl clutched his thigh and said, "Act normal, please. Say nothing. Smile."

The yellow-and-blue highway patrol car overtook them and flagged them over to the side of the road. The driver obediently pulled in and switched off the engine. They sat in the car expectantly as two armed officers climbed out of the patrol car and came walking back toward them. The driver wound down his window.

"Zdrastvuytye," the driver smiled as the officer bent down to see who was in the car. *"Mi pravil'no yedem v Zagorsk?"*

The officer's face was expressionless, mealy textured like a loaf of wholewheat bread, with raisins for eyes.

"Mahi prava? Tekhpasport avtomobilya?" demanded the officer dryly.

The driver opened the glove compartment, which banged down flat on a broken hinge, and rummaged around for his driver's license and his registration documents.

In Russian, the officer said, "I want to see all of your identity papers."

As Lev handed his papers through the open window, the officer said, "What is the purpose of your journey?"

"We're visiting my mother," said Lev. "She's been sick lately. *Ryevmatyizm.*"

"All of these people are visiting your mother with you?" asked the officer. He kept Lev's papers and held out his hand for the young man's documents.

"They are my friends. They love my mother, almost as much as I do."

"What is your mother's name?"

"Yevdokia Safanova. She lives at Nine, Rubleva Andreia Ulitsa. Second floor at the back, next to Mrs. Rotmistrova." Lev had a way of speaking to officials as if he were a harmless Russian idiot. The police officer sniffed and wiped at his nose with the back of his glove.

"And you?" he asked Michael. "Where are your papers?"

Michael didn't understand him, although he had a fair idea

of what he was being asked for. He simply smiled and shrugged. The police officer flicked his fingers impatiently and said, "Come on, show me your papers."

Michael shrugged again. The police officer immediately stepped back and took out his pistol. He said something in Russian and pointed to the road beside the car.

Lev said, "He's telling us all to get out and stand against the side of the car."

"What are we going to do?" Michael asked him, his throat tight.

"You'll see."

They climbed stiffly out of the small car and stood beside it. The police officer waved his pistol at them and said, "Hands up. That's right. And keep them up."

Lev turned around and said, "I don't suppose you'd be interested in a green ticket?" A "green ticket" was a three-rouble note that Russian motorists habitually slipped into their licenses for those times when they were stopped by the highway patrol for a road check. A "red ticket" was a five-rouble note, which occasionally took care of speeding or parking problems.

The officer ignored him and called to his colleague, "Get me a check on this vehicle and all of these people. You—" he said sharply to Michael—"what's your name?"

Michael smiled and shook his head.

"He's not too well," put in Lev and then, confidentially, "*Galava* problems." He meant that Michael was not quite right in the head.

The officer said, "Wait," as if he were undecided about what to do next.

"A red ticket?" Lev asked.

The officer said to his colleague, "Hurry up. And don't forget to ask them what time Khomyakov's meeting us tonight."

Michael kept his hands above his head. He glanced at Lev for reassurance but Lev didn't seem to be concerned over their predicament. He was looking out across the nearby field and whistling. Crickets chirruped in the rough grass beside the highway; there wasn't another car to be seen. Michael was about to say, "There isn't—" when the early afternoon tranquility was punctuated by two light pneumatic sneezes, like somebody pumping up a bicycle tire. Michael turned around in perplexity just in time to see both highway patrolmen buckle at the knees and collapse to the pavement.

The girl in the checked shirt was already tucking a silenced Beretta automatic back into a light nylon holster under her arm. Lev said, "Quickly, now," and he and the young man ran across to the patrolmen, gathered them up under their arms and dragged them, their boot heels scraping on the concrete, back to their patrol car. Both dead men were heaved into the front seats of the car and their seat belts fastened to keep them in place. Lev deftly reholstered the first officer's revolver and straightened his jacket.

Michael was fascinated by the speed and silent efficiency with which Lev and his colleagues worked. They might have rehearsed it, like *Swan Lake* at the Kirov ballet. They started up the patrol car's engine, then released the hand brake and steered it off the edge of the road into a narrow ditch, where it came to rest with a grinding crunch and its engine stalled. The girl handed Lev her scarf, which he deftly fed into the patrol car's gas tank until only a corner of it was protruding. He lit the corner of the scarf with his cigarette lighter and then came running back to the Moskvich.

"That's it, let's go. Sorry for the inconvenience."

The Moskvich's tuned-up engine let out a blaring roar as they squealed away from the side of the road and sped northeast again. Lev lit a cigarette and sneezed. Behind them there was a sudden *pumf*! and Michael turned around to see the highway patrol car blazing fiercely in the ditch and a column of oily smoke already rising into the white afternoon.

"That won't put off the KGB, will it?" asked Michael. "I mean, they won't change their route if they see that wreck by the side of the road?"

Lev shook his head. "The highway patrol are notoriously bad drivers, my friend. Crashed police cars are quite commonplace. A few glasses of vodka for lunch, a boring afternoon with no motorists to harass, a race along the highway just for the hell of it, a hundred miles an hour. All of a sudden they lose control and—what do English people say?—they have had their ships."

"Chips," Michael corrected him.

"Chips," Lev repeated with dogmatic relish. He was proud of his English.

The girl smiled at Michael but Michael couldn't think of any Russian phrase that might be appropriate to the occasion, even though Rufina Konstantinova had taught him many words of love. What was the Russian for "Do you enjoy shooting policemen?" Or "Your gun has a splendid silencer; where did you get it?"

The smoke from the burning patrol car had scarcely disappeared behind them when Lev said, "Here, this will do. Pull off the road and park behind those trees."

Without reducing speed, the driver turned the Moskvich off the highway and they jounced over pebbles and ruts and rocks, their suspension banging loudly, until they were completely out of sight of the road behind a scraggly stand of firs. Without hesitation, Lev and his companions tore away the Velcro that kept the backs of the seats in place and took out their weapons. Lev handed Michael his AKM and two magazines of ammunition. He made no comment except, "Don't shoot unless I tell you, and don't shoot unless you have to." Michael nodded and swallowed.

They waited for a long time, lying flat in the grass with the sky gradually darkening over their heads as a May storm came in from the west. The grass rustled and stirred; the crickets sang; Michael sneezed two or three times because of his hay fever. They watched a few private cars whirr north and south, and a convoy of army trucks. Otherwise the afternoon was peaceful, with butterflies blowing through the trees and the wind singing songs of Poland and Scandinavia.

Lev, watching the highway with binoculars, at last said, "Here they come."

"You're sure?" asked Michael. Without a word, Lev passed him the glasses and he squinted southwest until the wavering horizon of the road came into view, and on the road there were two motorcycle *militsia* with glaring headlights, a black Volga-22 following close behind.

"KGB, no doubt about it," said Lev. "Anton, are you ready?"

Anton had already shouldered the RPG7 antitank launcher and loaded it with a 40-mm bomb. The bomb weighed five pounds and could penetrate armor to a depth of over a foot. Lev said to Michael, "Switch your gun to rapid fire. Even if you don't hit anything, you should frighten them."

The KGB car with its motorcycle escort came closer and closer until Michael was sweating. They must fire soon; otherwise the car would pass them by. But just as Michael began to think that the ambush hadn't worked, Lev raised his hand, paused, and then dropped it again, and there was a sudden, teeming rattle of automatic gunfire.

Both motorcycle policemen went down instantly as if they had ridden straight into an outstretched wire. They tumbled over and over like acrobats, their arms and legs flailing, while their bikes slid roaring across the road on either side of them in showers of sparks. The Volga-22 tried to swerve between them but then there was the sharp *whoompphh* of the RPG7 launcher and the front of the car exploded in a strangely surrealistic arrangement of twisted metal and broken glass. The car lurched and slithered to a stop and the two KGB agents sitting in the front immediately clambered out with their hands on top of their heads. "Don't shoot!" But there was another quick burst of machine-gun fire and they dropped to the road beside their motorcycle escort. The whole attack took fewer than fifteen seconds and then there was silence. Lev stood up and walked toward the wrecked car, his AKM held high in front of him. Michael followed, his own gun raised although he hadn't fired a single shot.

"You see, it simply takes organization," said Lev, turning over one of the KGB men with the toe of his shoe.

Michael looked down at the puffy, staring face. A young man of twenty-eight or twenty-nine, he guessed, with a scrap of toilet paper stuck to his cheek where he had cut himself shaving that morning. His blood ran across the road to join that of the others, a crimson jigsaw.

Michael said, "You astonish me. I never could have used this gun at all, not once."

"There was no need. A gun should never be used unless necessity demands it."

"No," said Michael. He looked across at the Volga. Under his breath he said, "Shit."

The young girl opened the rear door of the car. "Get out,"

she said in English. Awkwardly, John climbed out of the
backseat. He was handcuffed by his right wrist to Rufina,
who climbed out just as awkwardly after him. "Michael?"
blinked John. He seemed to have lost his glasses. Perhaps the
KGB had taken them away from him. "Michael, is that
you?"

Michael touched Lev's arm as a gesture of thanks and
reassurance. Then he slung the AKM over his left shoulder
and walked forward quickly so John could see that he was
there. John squinted at him myopically and then reached out
to clasp his hand. Rufina seemed completely dazed. She
stared at Michael, then at Lev, and then across the road at the
sprawling bodies of the *militsia* and the KGB men.

"What's this?" asked John. "Michael Townsend's private
army? I can't believe it. Did you actually fire that thing?"

Michael shook his head. "These people are friends. They
tried to stop the KGB from laying their hands on us yesterday
morning but they didn't quite make it in time. Lev, this is
John Bishop. John, this is Lev."

"We must be quick now," said Lev. To Rufina he said,
"Where is the key to these handcuffs? Do you have it?"

Rufina, still pale, whispered, "No," and then pointed to
one of the KGB men lying on the road. Lev's two companions had already dragged the bodies of the motorcyclists into
the bushes and were now wheeling the damaged bikes across
the verge.

Lev rummaged through the KGB man's pockets and at last
found a bunch of keys.

"Which one?" he demanded but Rufina could only shake
her head.

"Damn it," said Lev. "Come on, we don't have any more
time."

They hurried back to the Moskvich. John said, "I can't
believe this is real."

"It's real," Michael told him. He glanced at Rufina but
Rufina said nothing.

All the weapons were dismantled and stowed in the car.
The young man and the girl were going to leave them here and
walk two miles cross-country to a small collective, where a
motorcycle would be waiting for them. Lev sat in the front

with the driver, John and Michael sat in the back with Rufina
between them. They swerved out of the bushes, bounced back
onto the road, skidding around the wreck of the KGB car and
heading southwest, the way they had first come. They would
drive only a few miles down the highway, however, before
they turned off east toward Scolkovo.

"I never thought this kind of thing could happen in Russia," said John. "In fact, I never thought it could happen at
all."

"Lev will tell you," said Michael.

Lev turned around in his seat and nodded toward Rufina.
"Not in front of madam here."

A truck roared past in the opposite direction, toward Zagorsk,
the first vehicle they had seen in ten minutes. Up ahead the
smoke from the highway patrol car still smudged the sky and
Michael could make out a cluster of police cars and fire
trucks.

"It was you who burned that car?" Rufina asked.

"We were short of logs, my dear," Lev told her sarcastically.

"Well, they will catch you," said Rufina.

"Maybe," said Lev. "We didn't come out here on a
picnic."

"Michael," said Rufina, "you don't know how *dangerous*
this is! If you don't give yourself up straightaway, the authorities will have you shot! Being an accessory to murder is a
capital offense in the Soviet Union. But if you persuade these
people to surrender to the police, I promise you that I will
testify on your behalf."

Michael looked at Lev. Lev made a face and said, "Per-
suasive, isn't she?"

"Michael—" Rufina repeated but Lev snapped, "That's
enough from you, thank you, *devushka*."

John said, "Perhaps we can get these handcuffs off now."
Lev tossed the keys over to Michael, who sorted through
them, trying out anything that looked as if it were small
enough.

"They took me to an office somewhere and made me sit in
a waiting room for about three hours," said John. "Then
some chap came in and told me I was under arrest for
bringing subversive literature into the Soviet Union and that

they were going to have to question me. I asked to speak to the British ambassador but they said I couldn't. They said he knew about me already and had agreed that I had to be interrogated. I asked to call you but they said they had no record of anybody called Townsend and that I'd better start getting used to the idea that I was going to have to stay in the Soviet Union for a long time.''

"You see?" Lev nodded.

They turned on to the Scolkovo road and began to speed east. Behind them, a Mi-4 helicopter clattered to the north, following the Zagorsk highway, and was quickly followed by another copter.

"They've found out about the ambush," said Lev. "Any minute now we're going to have to turn off the road and hide for a while."

"This is insane," said Rufina.

"We are known for our insanity," Lev told her. "You will find out just how insane we can be when we come to question you."

Rufina said nothing more but sat back and waited while Michael tried yet another key for the handcuffs. At last the lock clicked and the hasp sprang up. John lifted his wrist and rubbed it.

Lev said, "Lock Miss Konstantinova's hands together. I don't want her to get any ideas in her head about getting away." He smiled at Rufina with tobacco-stained teeth. Then he said, "I should congratulate you, Michael. She is a very pretty girl. Not like the usual dragons who work for the KGB."

John said, so quietly they could scarcely hear him, "They broke my glasses. That was one of the first things they did." Then he sat with his chin in his hand, staring out the car window at a landscape that was blurred by both shortsightedness and tears.

FIFTEEN

Yeremenko was about to go to the mess to meet B.Y. Serpuchov, Commissar of the Western Strategic Direction, when Colonel Chuykov came running along the corridor, his polished boots clattering like a horse at the gallop.

"Well, Comrade Colonel, you're in a hurry," he remarked.

"I have to see you confidentially," Chuykov panted. He was sweating and he had obviously run a long way. It suddenly occurred to Yeremenko that Chuykov was supposed to be in Haldensleben with Golovanov and that only a few minutes earlier, he had looked up from his desk as a Mi-14 had come roaring over headquarters in an unusually low pass.

"Something's wrong?" asked Yeremenko.

"Please, sir. I was specifically told that I should pass this intelligence on to you personally, and in private."

"Very well," said Yeremenko. He looked at his watch. He was already five minutes late for his meeting and he knew that by now Serpuchov would be growing irritable. Serpuchov considered that anyone who treated him discourteously was ipso facto discourteous to the Party. Yeremenko opened the door of the office marked "Duty Officer," and waved Chuykov inside. "Well," he said, switching on the fluorescent lights, "is something wrong with Marshal Golovanov? His heart?"

Chuykov said breathlessly, "No, sir, not his heart, sir."

"Then . . . ?" asked Yeremenko encouragingly.

"He's disappeared, sir. The GRU officers at Haldensleben think he may have been abducted."

Yeremenko stared at him. "Golovanov? Abducted? Golovanov is a marshal! Golovanov is a Hero of the Soviet Union! How could he possibly have been abducted? Nobody abducts men like Golovanov! This is preposterous! I refuse to believe it. He's probably—I don't know—shacked up somewhere with that girl of his."

"I'm afraid it's true, sir. I flew straight back from Haldensleben as soon as I could. Major Grechko is helping to coordinate the search with the KGB and the GRU, as well as with the German police."

Yeremenko sat on the edge of the desk. "Damn," he said. But then he almost smiled. "It was that Inge, wasn't it? I suppose there's no sign of her."

Chuykov unhappily shook his head.

"Well, in that case," said Yeremenko, "I imagine we are all to blame for the marshal's disappearance, every one of us who was prepared to see Marshal Golovanov make a fool of himself with a girl like Inge. Oh, what a tremendous laugh, hm, Colonel?—to see him go bugeyed for a girl who wouldn't have looked twice at him if he hadn't been a marshal and she hadn't been an intelligence officer for the KGB! And now of course we have to eat our laughter. She doesn't work for the KGB at all, unless she tried to protect Marshal Golovanov and was killed, and I very much doubt *that*."

"But if she's not working for the KGB, sir—?"

"I don't know. She's not working for the Americans, at least I wouldn't have thought so. She certainly doesn't belong to the usual espionage community. They are like an exclusive club that won't let anybody in unless he has all the right credentials. I don't know, Colonel. But of course we must find out."

Colonel Chuykov said hoarsely, "What about Operation *Byliny*, sir?"

"What about it?"

"Well, sir, if he has been abducted . . . the people who abducted him are very likely going to try to make him talk. That's if they haven't killed him already."

"You're trying to suggest that Operation *Byliny* may no longer be secure?"

Chuykov said, "It would be unfair of me to suggest that, sir. After all, I am sure that Marshal Golovanov has a very strong will and can manage to resist most methods of interrogation. His father did, although he died from his injuries."

Yeremenko bit at his thumbnail. "No, no, Colonel. You may have been right. I'm not denying for one moment that Marshal Golovanov comes from strong stock, and it's nothing to do with disloyalty. But these days, methods of interrogation are far more effective than they were in the days of the Great Purge. We cannot entrust the lives of hundreds of thousands of soldiers to the questionable ability of one old man to withstand torture . . . not with a campaign like Operation *Byliny* about to commence. Tell me, do you know if Marshal Kutakov has been informed?"

"He was informed by special messenger, sir."

"Very well; I think we'd better call him. Come back to my office with me."

Chuykov followed Yeremenko back to his office. While Yeremenko picked up his scrambler phone and asked to be connected with the Supreme Commander, Chuykov took out a folded handkerchief and dabbed at his forehead. So far, the whole evening had been like something out of a nightmare. Everybody at Haldensleben had assumed that Golovanov was with somebody else. Major Grechko, who had been late for dinner, had assumed that Golovanov was with Chuykov; Chuykov, who had arrived at Commander Zhukilov's farmhouse punctually at 7:45, had assumed that Golovanov was with Grechko. Golovanov's driver had assumed that he was fornicating with Inge before dinner. The landlady of the Sachsen Hotel, who had seen Golovanov leave in the company of Inge and a young man in dark glasses, had assumed that Golovanov had been driven back to headquarters.

It wasn't until nine o'clock that frantic messages began to fly around the base at Haldensleben and Golovanov's driver had gone up to Inge's room at the Sachsen Hotel to find all trace of Golovanov and Inge meticulously eradicated. Whoever had cleared out the hotel room had been superbly professional: he had even removed the U bend from the washbasin drain and cleaned it out in case there were any incriminating hairs or stubble trapped in it. Golovanov was utterly gone.

Even while Chuykov was being flown back to Zossen-Wünsdorf to tell Yeremenko what had happened, security along the East German border had been clamped down tight. The sudden alert, right on the brink of Operation *Byliny*, was a major source of concern not only to the local front commander, but to the *Stavka* too. The very last thing they wanted at this eleventh hour was to arouse the suspicions of the West Germans, who were already jittery enough because of the Soviet Army's prolonged summer maneuvers and because of persistent rumors that "something unusual" was happening at NATO headquarters and throughout the American and British armed services.

Yeremenko at last got through to Marshal Kutakov. The Supreme Commander sounded weary and dyspeptic and Yeremenko suspected that the disappearance of Comrade Golovanov had interrupted his dinner, which he ate with difficulty at the best of times. Marshal Kutakov suffered from chronic ulcers but hated soup, especially borscht and *ukah*. He had once been served *ukah* at the home of one of his favored subordinate officers and in the next month had posted him off to the Transbaykal in disgrace.

"Well, Ivan," Marshal Kutakov said to Yeremenko.

"I've just received the news, sir, from Colonel Chuykov."

"Do you have any idea of what might have happened to him? I was told that he disappeared in the company of a young German lady, a prostitute."

"Not exactly a prostitute, sir. She was working, as far as I understood it, for the KGB. Personal intelligence duties."

"Well, yes, that is what I was told too. But it seems that she has been playing some other game, doesn't it? Unless Timofey has suffered a brainstorm and taken her off somewhere."

Yeremenko said, "No question of that, Comrade Marshal. Not in my estimation. He was temperamental on occasion, but always wise."

"Will he talk if pressed?" asked Marshal Kutakov.

"I don't know. It depends on how, and on how hard."

"This is a serious crisis, Ivan. I have a report from General

Glinka that the West Germans are growing increasingly suspicious and that they have already started to mobilize some of their reserves." General Glinka was the head of the Chief Intelligence Directorate, the GRU. "The whole planning behind Operation *Byliny* depends on utmost secrecy right up to the very last moment."

"Of course, sir. Do you think it might be expedient to bring the date of *Byliny* forward by one week?"

There was a pause at the other end of the line. Then Marshal Kutakov said, "The Defense Council has of course discussed it."

"I didn't mean to be impertinent, sir."

"No, of course you didn't. But the question of bringing forward the timing *has* been considered, and . . . well, it is still under consideration."

"Yes, sir," said Yeremenko courteously.

Marshal Kutakov cleared his throat and paused again. Then he said, "Find out what's being done to track down Timofey and call me later."

"Yes, sir," said Yeremenko. "Thank you very much, sir."

He put down the phone with a smile. Colonel Chuykov looked at him questioningly but was not senior enough to be able to ask him directly why he seemed so pleased. After a while Yeremenko stood up, clasped his hands behind his back and paced across the office. When he reached the window, he bent forward and peered into the darkness, although all he could see was his own reflection, a pale ghost on the face of the night.

"Who do you think did this?" he asked Colonel Chuykov. "Who has the gall to kidnap a marshal of the Soviet Army and risk arousing the gravest international incident in a quarter of a century?"

Chuykov shook his head. "There are so many dissident groups. So many terrorists. Perhaps the CIA took him as a guarantee that our own army should keep within its agreed-upon limits. A political hostage."

"I don't think Fraulein Inge Schültz had anything to do with the CIA," said Yeremenko. "Nor do I think she is a terrorist. She is a highly trained intelligence agent rather than a saboteuse or a thrower of bombs."

Chuykov said nothing but waited for Yeremenko to continue. He was used to listening to high-ranking officers, familiar with their speech patterns. They all liked to pause for dramatic effect and walk up and down the room. Perhaps it was something they were taught when they were first promoted to general. Speak. Pause. Walk. Turn. Speak again.

Yeremenko said, "Whoever took Marshal Golovanov suspects that something important is about to happen on the Western strategic front. They must have some inkling of what it is because otherwise they never would have risked the turmoil that his kidnapping would normally cause. They probably intend to interrogate him until either he cracks or he dies. Obviously we would prefer it if he were to manage the latter alternative first."

"Failing rescue, of course, Comrade General," put in Colonel Chuykov as hopefully as possible.

"Well, of course," said Yeremenko as if the idea of mounting a rescue operation to retrieve Golovanov had already occurred to him. In fact, it hadn't. The only search he had considered setting up was to find out where Golovanov was being held and to kill him before he could reveal anything to his captors about Operation *Byliny*.

The truth was that Yeremenko was indecently delighted by Golovanov's abduction. Not only would Yeremenko's influence with the *Stavka* now be greatly enhanced, but he would have the opportunity to control *Byliny* in the Western Strategic Direction without Golovanov's interference and to claim all the glory for himself when it succeeded, which it inevitably must. As far as his career was concerned, it was one of the greatest pieces of luck he had ever had. And what was more, it would all happen much more quickly because he bet five roubles to a bent pfennig that Kutakov would decide to bring *Byliny* forward in case Golovanov talked. Today was Thursday. If *Byliny* was brought forward by a week, they would be ready to roll across the West German border at three o'clock in the morning on Sunday, two days from now.

The scrambler phone bleeped. Yeremenko turned quickly toward it but checked himself. Colonel Chuykov picked it up for him and said, "Yes, sir, he's here." He passed the telephone to Yeremenko and stood watching him with expressionless eyes. He decided that he disliked Yeremenko. There was something about the nakedness of Yeremenko's ambitions that was disgusting, like a man showing his erect penis in company.

Yeremenko said, "Yes, sir. Yes, sir. I understand, Marshal. Yes. Everything will be ready, sir. Have no doubt. Yes, sir, I shall make sure that all the inspections are completed. Yes, sir. I understand."

He put down the phone and paused. He rapped his fingers on the receiver. Then he said, "Operation *Byliny* has been brought forward by seven days, to Sunday morning. Marshal Kutakov has already talked to the White House in Washington and to Number Ten Downing Street in London."

He took a breath and his eyes shone glittering black like the muzzles of two rifles. "The great day is with us at last, Colonel. The beginning of the world is at hand!"

To Chuykov's astonishment, he folded his arms and began to kick a slow Cossack dance around the office, his head thrown back, his back straight, singing and humming as he went. It was an old village song, the sort of song that grandfathers would teach to the children on days when they were picking fruit and the skies were warm. "My father's tree is bearing plums! Plums, plums, plums, plums! I cannot wait till summer comes! *Odin, dva, tri, chetire,* plums for everyone!"

As Yeremenko sang, Marshal Golovanov, Hero of the Soviet Union, was lying on a sagging cot in a farmhouse in Mariental, a village only thirty miles from Haldensleben but on the Western side of the border. He was snoring peacefully, drugged by paraldehyde, dreaming dreams of sliding through tunnels and floating out over strange Arctic landscapes. He was watched by a young girl of about twenty-two with blonde, plaited hair, Aryan blue eyes and a red spot on one cheek (too much chocolate). She sat cross-legged in a gray track suit, an Ingram machine gun resting in her lap. The night wind ruffled the red-gingham curtains; somewhere a farmer's dog was barking at the warm European darkness.

Inge had gone over the border first, in a ten-year-old BMW driven by a bald-headed, bespectacled man whose papers had described him as Herman Ebinger, a pottery salesman for Heidenau's in Dresden, and Inge as his wife, Anna-Lise Ebinger. The sixth or seventh vehicle behind the "Ebingers" was a huge white tractor trailer with the name *Zwickau-Tapeten* emblazoned in red on the side beneath a large picture of a smiling baby sitting on a red rug. The picture had been ironic: inside the trailer, under thirty rolls of nylon carpet, Marshal Golovanov had been sleeping like a baby inside a ventilated cylinder that from the outside looked like nothing but a roll of green-speckled sculptured carpet.

Security at the border crossing had been noticeably relaxed. It was all part of the *Stavka's* policy of lulling the West Germans into believing that their "May maneuvers" were quite harmless. Inge had been waved through with her "husband" without any delay; she even got a friendly wink from the East German guard. The carpet truck had been opened up and briefly examined, but the young man called Dichter had leaned against it smoking a cigarette, sharing jokes with the border guards, and after only fifteen minutes, he had been allowed to drive through into the Federal Republic.

Seventeen minutes later the border post had received an urgent coded message that there was to be a complete security clampdown, all the way from Potenitz to Gefell Juchhöh, and all vehicles searched "intensively." The guards were not told what they were supposed to be looking for; as it turned out, the first contraband they came across was a young family from Karl-Marxstadt that was trying to escape to the West inside the empty tank of a milk truck.

Shortly after midnight Golovanov opened his eyes and said, *"Katushka?"*

The girl with the machine gun said nothing but watched him attentively as he tried to lift himself on one elbow.

He stared at her. Then he looked around the room. *"Katory chyas?"* he asked. Then, realizing that she didn't understand, he said more slowly in German, "What time is it? How long have I been sleeping?"

"I'm sorry, I'm not allowed to tell you," the girl replied mildly as if he were a visiting uncle. She called over her shoulder, "Dichter! Your friend's woken up!"

Golovanov rubbed the heel of his hand against his forehead. He felt dizzy and nauseous; his tongue seemed to be three times its normal size and covered by a woolen sock. "Perhaps some water," he said. "Can you tell me where I am or is that a secret too, as well as the time of day?"

"I'm sorry," she said.

"Well," he told her, "at least you obey your orders. There are plenty who don't."

Just then the latch on the door clicked open and Dichter walked in, closely followed by Inge. Dichter had discarded his sunglasses; Inge had changed into a soft-textured, blue-and-yellow-checked cowgirl blouse and a pair of tight blue Vanderbilt jeans. Dichter squatted on the floor next to Golovanov's cot and stared at him closely as if he were an explorer examining for the first time a rare specimen of lizard he had brought back from the rain forests.

"Well, a real live Soviet marshal," he said.

"I suppose you know what a risk you are taking," Golovanov replied. In actual fact, for the first time in his life, he began to feel genuinely frightened. Being a marshal of the Soviet Army was one thing; at least one had one's army. But here in this farmhouse bedroom, God knew where, he was completely helpless. And he knew better than to try to bluster; by their weapons alone, he recognized these people as professionals.

"Actually, old friend, we want to talk to you, that's all," said Dichter. "We would like to discuss the weather and the prevailing wind, and we would also like to talk about your summer maneuvers. So many tanks, so many rocket launchers, just for summer maneuvers?"

"Please, some water," said Golovanov. He was feeling genuinely distressed.

"First we would like to talk about the summer maneuvers."

"You know better than to ask me anything like that. I am Golovanov."

Dichter said, "You were very careless. Perhaps you wanted us to take you?"

Golovanov looked toward Inge and said, *"Digtyi mnye vodi, pozhalusta."*

Inge put her head on one side and smiled at him, that cold, angelic smile that always disturbed him so much. The smile of a seraphim on a marble tombstone. And yet, beneath her checked blouse, her huge, soft breasts moved as warm as rising dough. She shook her head and said, *"Nyet."*

"I can't tell you anything," said Golovanov. "It's impossible. If you don't get me back to Commander Zhukilov's house soon, they will start to miss me and then there will be hell to pay."

"That is impossible, I regret," said Dichter.

"Come, come. I haven't been unconscious for very long. Look, it is still evening! There is no drug that could have kept me asleep for a night and a day. Now let's be sensible."

Inge came forward, touched Golovanov's cheek and stroked his bushy eyebrows. "You are talking like a commissar," she told him. "This is not you! What do you care for the Party? You are a soldier of Russia. Did you not always tell me that? 'My darling Inge, I am a soldier of Russia, first and last!' You care nothing for the Politburo, all those belligerent old men in the Kremlin. Don't pretend that you do. I know you better. I know you in those moments when no politics matter, when nothing matters."

Golovanov said hoarsely, "Inge, listen. Believe me, I am thinking only of you. You set me up, didn't you? All this time. But that is unimportant. I can save your life. All you have to do is take me back to Commander Zhukilov's and I will simply say that I lost my way, that I came across somebody I knew in the war and I had to buy him a drink. Come on, this is ridiculous. I am not a divisional commander or a corps captain. I am the First Deputy of the Ministry of Defense. I am one of the most powerful and important men in the Soviet Union. If it is discovered that I have been abducted, all pandemonium will break loose. You will all be executed instantly! No arguments, no trials, no nothing. Just a post, a blindfold and a bullet. Now, please, have sense. I have loved you, I love you now, and I always will. I have always thought of you as the one woman for whom I could have lived without the army. But this is madness."

Inge sat down on the cot beside Golovanov and turned around to the girl with the machine gun. "Please," she said gently, "bring me some water."

Golovanov nodded. "Thank you," he said. "I knew you would see some sense."

"Of course," Inge told him. "We are rational people. But we cannot take you back to Commander Zhukilov's."

"What time is it?" asked Golovanov.

"The time is unimportant. If you really want to know, it's twenty-five minutes after twelve."

"Well, then, there could still be time for you to return me to the farm. Why risk your life, my dear? I am of no use to anybody. What can I tell you that you do not know already? I am an administrator, nothing else. The Defense Council tells me nothing about its long-term strategy. All I ever do is push pieces of paper from one side of my desk to the other, from the In tray to the Out tray, and salute young officers who salute me first. General Yeremenko thinks I am a military ignoramus and I regret that he is right."

Inge said, "We cannot take you back to Commander Zhukilov's. The simple reason is that we are on the wrong side of the border."

Golovanov stared at her. "We are in *West* Germany?" he asked in the whitest ghost of a voice.

Inge nodded.

"We are in *West* Germany? Are you serious? You have taken me to *West* Germany?"

He heaved himself up from the cot and tugged aside the gingham curtains. Outside there was nothing but darkness and a few sparkling streetlights. "This is West Germany? How could you do such a thing? How did you get me across the border? Inge, this is insanity! I thought you were KGB!"

Inge said nothing but watched him stare wildly out at the night and then swivel around like Long John Silver on the deck of the *Hispaniola,* huffing with perplexity and fear, stamping his foot and then staring out at the night again.

"*West* Germany!"

Inge said quietly, "I was KGB for five years, Timofey. Then the man I loved was found guilty of treason. He was KGB too. He disappeared. I think they probably killed him. That was when I decided I would try to work for liberty instead of fear. But I was wise enough to keep my decision to myself. I kept on working for the KGB, and in the meantime

I made contact with the people you probably know as Lamprey.''

Golovanov jabbed a stubby finger at her. His eyebrows shot up and then crowded closely together. "You—and you—" he said, pointing at Dichter—"*you* are Lamprey?''

"We are part of Lamprey. Lamprey is made up of intelligence agents from all countries, of all persuasions.''

"'And now you have taken me? Well, my friends, that is your mistake! Your great mistake! Now Lamprey will be hunted by the KGB and torn out by its roots!'' Golovanov shook his wrist as if he were shaking radishes.

Inge smiled at him. "Too many KGB belong to Lamprey, Timofey. Too many CIA. Too many M-Fifteen. No government intelligence agency will ever truly discover what Lamprey is, how it works and who belongs. It exists without territory, without files, without offices, without borders, without anything but the constant inspiration that there must be a better way for nations to live together.''

Golovanov sat down on the edge of his cot. The young girl with the plaited hair came back and handed him a child's ABC mug brimming with water. She was carrying the Ingram in her other hand. Before drinking, Golovanov said, "A great ideal, my darling Inge. But then, think, both the United States and the Soviet Union were founded on ideals.''

Inge said, "The people of Lamprey are not idealists, Timofey. They are realists. They will accept anything provided it is better and it works.''

Dichter was growing tired of this conversation. He looked at his watch and said, "Now then, Marshal, what about these summer maneuvers? What about these rumors of war?''

"War?'' asked Golovanov, wiping his mouth with his handkerchief. "What kind of nonsense is this?''

"There are rumors of war,'' said Dichter flatly.

"Well, you should not pay attention to rumors, especially in your business,'' Golovanov told him.

Dichter slowly stroked his hair as if he were thinking about something else altogether. "You realize we shall have to torture you.''

Golovanov lifted his head pugnaciously. "My father was

tortured by far more expert torturers than you. You do not frighten me with talk of torture."

"Tell me about these summer maneuvers," Dichter repeated. "When are your divisions going to stand down?"

"In the normal course of events, when the maneuvers are over."

"The maneuvers have been going on for an unconscionably long time."

"We have a large army, Herr Dichter," said Golovanov. "It takes us considerable time to move it around. Of course, if the Western powers were not so warlike, we would need only a token army and our maneuvers would be over much more quickly."

Dichter said coldly, "I asked for an explanation of your military movements, Marshal, not a line out of an *Izvestia* editorial."

"My dear young man, you expect too much. But then the young always do, don't they?"

Dichter was silent for a while as if he were waiting for Golovanov to say something else. But then he said in a decisive voice, "We are going to move you to another place, farther away from the border. There we are going to ask you these questions once again, and this time we shall expect some sensible and constructive answers. Inge will be going with you."

"Well, that is one compensation," smiled Golovanov.

"I don't think that you will find it so, Marshal. Besides being an expert in giving pleasure, Inge is an expert in inflicting pain. She is to be your torturer."

SIXTEEN

"It's Kress again," said Morton Lock, holding up the phone.

"Oh, damn," said the President. "All right."

It was eleven o'clock in the evening, Eastern Standard Time, and for the third time that day, the Chancellor of the Federal German Republic, Otto Kress, was calling Camp David to demand an explanation for all the chaotic military movements throughout southern Germany. Twice the President had been "asleep" or "unavailable." Now he was going to have to talk to him.

"Otto!" he said with feigned enthusiasm.

"Good-evening, Mr. President." The Chancellor's voice was flat and unimpressed. "I am glad that you are now available and awake."

"What's on your mind, Otto?"

"It is your troop movements that are on my mind, Mr. President," said Otto Kress. "Yesterday I asked my Defense Minister to speak to General Oliver, but General Oliver replied that he could say nothing and that any questions on the matter should be referred directly to you."

"So they should, Otto, so they should. I'm always here to help."

Otto Kress launched into a long and technical complaint. The President listened patiently. Yes, said Otto Kress, there had been agreement that U.S. forces would be able to carry out a "general redeployment" in order to make way for new arms and vehicles from the United States. Yes, he was pleased that updated arms and fresh *matériel* were arriving in Western Germany. Yes, all the proper arrangements had been made with the police, the Bundeswehr, the highway authorities, Deutsches Bundesbahn, Lufthansa and everyone else who was concerned. "Mr. President, I am not disputing any of this."

But southern Germany was already in "pandemonium . . . like the hour before the Flood."

The roads between the U.S. bases at Ansbach, Würzburg and Frankfurt were congested with endless convoys of military trucks, tank transports and self-propelled howitzers; the depot at Illisheim was crowded with hundreds of M1 Abrams battle tanks. The skies over Mannheim and Darmstadt were thunderous with Hercules, Starlifters and Galaxies, and whatever the official paperwork said about "general redeployment," it appeared that the bulk of the U.S. military movement was west, away from the East German border and toward the 8th Infantry Division base at Bad Kreuznach.

And where would they go from there?

This afternoon Chancellor Kress had himself talked to General Oliver at U.S. Army headquarters at Heidelberg, but General Oliver had begged ignorance of anything other than "military musical chairs" and had again suggested, "with immense respect, sir," that the Chancellor talk to the President.

Kress sounded strained. "Mr. President, I believe I deserve an explanation for all these movements, don't you?"

The President beckoned Morton Lock to pick up the other phone. "General Oliver did make sure that your people had all the necessary paperwork, didn't he?" the President asked Chancellor Kress.

"Mr. President, the actual movements appear to far exceed the paperwork."

The President sniffed. "Well, now, that sometimes happens as I understand it, but it's nothing to get steamed up about. You know General Oliver. Remember that dinner in Brussels? Well, he's something of an opportunist when it comes to regulations. But well-intentioned, you understand, and a fine officer. I don't know what to tell you, Otto. If the

Seventh Army has overstepped the mark, let me tell you here and now that I'll get to hear about it, and let me tell you here and now that all the appropriate steps will be taken to admonish those responsible. But you have to remember that we're preparing to ship something in the order of—''

"Six billion dollars," Morton Lock mouthed from across the room.

"—that's right, something in the order of six billion dollars' worth of advanced military hardware, tanks, missiles, infantry equipment—right into Western Germany in the next few weeks—all for the purpose of enhancing *your* security. So we have to make room for it somehow. And if it's noisy and causing difficulties, I'm sorry."

The President was aware of the fragility of this excuse but what else could he say? That West Germany as Chancellor Kress knew it was about to come to a sudden end?

Chancellor Kress said, "I regret that your explanation sounds a little thin, Mr. President, under the circumstances. Let me say this: I am relying on all the treaties and understandings that exist between us. I have to. For if I did not, I would look at the activity taking place in your military bases throughout southern Germany and I would have to say that your movements of men and ordnance are beginning to take on the appearance of a full-scale withdrawal."

"Listen, Otto," the President replied, "all I can tell you now is that the United States is as committed as ever to the political and military integrity of the Federal German Republic. I understand your anxieties. The Soviets have been particularly threatening of late. And let me say this: if General Oliver has been insensitive enough to unnerve your people by moving his equipment too boisterously, if he's shipped even one can of beans more than the paperwork allows, well, let me assure you of this, Otto, he's going to be reprimanded by me personally."

Otto Kress said edgily, "I think that some kind of public statement would be of material assistance." His voice was trembling and Morton Lock could tell how angry he was. Even as Chancellor of West Germany, he was in no position to challenge the validity of the President's personal reassurance, but all the same, he wanted the President to commit himself as openly and as positively as possible in *Time* and *Die Welt* and the *Herald-Tribune*.

The President replied, "Let me tell you, Otto, I'll look into this whole business straightaway. You'll have a full report in the morning. Yes, that's a promise. And meanwhile, I'll have Morton Lock speak directly to General Oliver and see what's going on. I'm sure it's going to turn out to be nothing more than a little bureaucratic mix-up, something of that kind. Well, very good. Yes. And you too."

The President put down the phone and said, "Damn it. He's as jumpy as a jackrabbit. I knew this would happen. Didn't I tell Gorbachev that? I told him this would happen if we had to pull out any quicker than scheduled."

Morton Lock said, "There are only two days left to go, sir. We should be able to baby Chancellor Kress along until then."

"Oh, damn it all," protested the President. He was less irritated by the anxious nagging of Chancellor Kress than he was by the way in which the Soviets had forced him to bring the whole operation forward.

This morning, in a blustering five-minute phone call, the Soviet premier had advised the President that word of *Gringo* had somehow leaked through to West German intelligence and that the source of the leak was undoubtedly an American double agent. Of course! For how could an agent of the KGB have done such a thing with the whole future of the Soviet Union at stake?

It was therefore imperative that Operation *Byliny* be started as soon as possible, and as soon as possible was Sunday morning, only two days away. The President had argued but Gorbachev had been adamant.

Afterward the President had yelled for ten solid minutes at the director of the CIA. The director of the CIA for most of the time had remained red-faced and silent. He had no knowledge of any U.S. agents who might have any acquaintance with the meaning of *Gringo* or *Byliny*. No CIA agents were missing; security as far as he was concerned was tight. That morning a note had been left on his desk to the effect that Marshal T.K. Golovanov had not attended a dinner given for him the previous evening by Commander Zhukilov—it was one of those tidbits of information for which the CIA paid anything between $25 and $50—but the director had not made any connection. He was too concerned with the wrath of a president who hated having America blamed for anything and who, more than anything, hated to be hustled.

Morton Lock sensed what was annoying his chief and held up his clipboard. "Boggsley has one or two names that might lead us to something on that security leak, sir."

"Oh, yes?"

Morton lifted the top sheet of his board. "A guy called Wallace T. Greenbaum, a clerk who worked for the State Department. He was dealt with yesterday though, and we don't have any reason to suspect that he managed to pass on any specific information about *Gringo*. Then there was Jack Levy, a correspondent for—"

"Wallace Greenbaum?" interrupted the President, frowning. "Don't I know that name?"

Morton quickly scanned the sheet of biographical background on Wallace Greenbaum. "No, sir," he said, pursing his lips. "Greenbaum was a left-of-center type of character, came from KC originally, graduated in law from Kansas State U. at Manhattan. Thirty-one years old, white, Baptist, unmarried but had some pretty bizarre sexual predilections apparently, including rubber fetishism and sado-masochism. Often frequented way-out clubs in New York and Baltimore."

"In that case," said the President seriously, "I don't think I *do* know the name. What happened to him? When you say 'dealt with,' what do you mean?"

"It seems that he had a calculated misadventure, sir. He was attempting to pass a classified State Department memorandum to some unidentified woman at a sex club in lower Manhattan. What he didn't know was that he had been under surveillance for some months by a CIA plant called Heidi van Cruyf. According to Boggsley, Heidi van Cruyf is some tough lady, recruited by the CIA from the Doma Club in Amsterdam with a view to keeping an intimate eye on all those government and United Nations officials who like to dress in raincoats and garter belts and get themselves whipped. Boggsley says that sado-masochism and high security clearances are a volatile combination. Anyhow, Miss van Cruyf managed to dispose of Mr. Greenbaum during a sexual performance. Quite common at this type of club, so Boggsley remarks here. Clients are always strangling or choking or sitting on the wrong end of a stiletto heel. The local police are used to it.''

"Any lead on the woman?" asked the President with obvious distaste.

"I'm sorry?"

"The woman he was supposed to be passing the information to."

"Oh. Oh, no. No trace so far, at least none recorded."

"All right," said the President. "I'm going to get to bed. I'm just about beat."

"What do you want me to do about General Oliver, sir?"

"General Oliver?"

"Well, do you think he ought to be asked to keep *Gringo* a little more low-profile?"

The President thought for a moment, then shook his head. "I think the safest option is to leave Kress guessing. He has only forty-eight hours, as you say. If he calls again though, don't put him on to me. Just tell him that everything's fine and that he'll get his report by the weekend."

"Yes, sir."

The President retired, closing the door. Morton Lock sat back for a while, looking through the papers on his clipboard. He wondered if he ought to have told the President that the FBI had already identified Wallace Greenbaum's contact at the Hellfire Club as Esther Modena, secretary and occasional lover of the junior senator from Connecticut, David Daniels.

But no, not yet. The time would come when he would be able to use the information to its maximum potential. For he was one of the very few people who happened to know that the President's daughter Janie had been "close" with Senator Daniels on and off. And he could think of no two more lucrative pieces of intelligence in the world today than that Senator Daniels had been associating with a sado-masochistic spy and that Janie had been associating with Senator Daniels. Morton Lock saw an assured career for himself in high places. He smiled and put down the clipboard.

In London, the 4:00 A.M. edition of the *Daily Telegraph*, which had just arrived at the Department of Trade and Industry in Victoria Street, carried for the first time in two years a banner headline that ran all the way across the top of its eight columns: *TUC Threatens General Strike on May 30*. Underneath there was a subhead that read: *Troops Will Maintain Essential Services, PM Declares*.

The *Daily Mirror* trumpeted, *All Out on May 30,* and carried a front-page editorial in heavy black type that spoke of "the day of reckoning" for "this repressive, uncaring government."

The Secretary of Trade hung his crumpled jacket over the back of his chair, unbuttoned his vest with one hand and shuffled through the early newspapers with the other. The news was uniformly serious. In an unexpected display of solidarity and industrial intransigence, every major union had called for "indefinite" strike action against the government's social and economic policies. Arthur Grange, president of the National Union of Mineworkers, had spoken of "complete victory for the working classes."

The door of the minister's office quietly opened and his secretary, Miss Forbes, stood just outside the circle of lamplight, her glasses reflecting the dull, orange shade. The minister looked up. He was overweight, with thinning gray hair and the large, sad face of a downtrodden public-school boy.

"I've put the kettle on," said Miss Forbes.

"You should have gone home, Nan," the minister told her. "Don't you know what time it is?"

"I saw the papers, sir. I thought you might like a nice cup of tea."

The minister thrust his hands into the capacious pockets of his trousers. "I don't know, Nan. Tea was good enough for the blitz but I'm not sure it's going to be good enough for this."

"You'll pull through, sir. Remember the dock strike?"

"Only too clearly, thank you."

He pressed the intercom on his desk. The nasal voice of the night operator said, "Yes, sir?"

"Get me the Secretary of Defense, would you, Sheila? Oh, and Sheila, scrambled, if you please."

"Yes, sir."

Miss Forbes kept hovering beyond the range of the lamplight. "Would you care for a drink, sir? We've still got some of the brandy we bought for that Nigerian delegation."

The minister nodded. "Very well. Yes, I think I would. Just a small one, mind."

The Secretary of Defense came through on the red scrambler telephone, and he obviously hadn't been to bed either.

"What do you think, Francis?" he asked.

The Trade Minister reached down between his legs to draw up his chair and sat down heavily. "I'm beginning to think that your suspicions are probably well-founded, old man. The timing is far too neat. The date of the strike wasn't announced until *after* the Yanks made their final decision on *Gringo*."

"Well, I've had some more bad news," said the Secretary of Defense. "One of our AR-Seven chaps was found dead about three hours ago in Leeds. According to his control, he was on the track of two women who have been traveling around the country talking to various union representatives about coordinating a nationwide stoppage. He was beaten so badly he couldn't be recognized at first. Well, it was made to look like a mugging but the inspector told me the beating was too professional."

"That's very nasty. What does the PM have to say?"

"She doesn't want to jump to any conclusions, not at this stage, but I think she took the point I was making. We're going to be faced with the choice on May thirtieth of either maximizing our defense or keeping most of our essential public services running. Of course we've got the nineteen seventy-seven Contingency Plan to fall back on, not to mention all the emergency powers, in the event things in Europe go farther than they're meant to. But I can't say it makes me a happy man, Francis."

The Trade Minister glanced up. Miss Forbes was bringing him a small glass of neat brandy on a polished silver tray. He whispered, "Ice," and when she frowned and said, "Pardon, sir?" he repeated more loudly, *"Ice."*

"What was that?" asked the Defense Minister. "These phones are getting worse if you ask me. Like trying to talk with your mouth full of lavatory paper."

The Trade Minister picked up the *Daily Telegraph* and dolefully scanned its front-page story. "Well," he said, "I

don't propose to do anything just now, not until morning.
You've been advised of the PM's briefing, I suppose? Eleven
o'clock sharp. I don't think there's much more we can do
until then.''

Friday was beginning to dawn across Victoria; out of his
window the minister could see the red-and-white-striped brick-
work of Westminster Cathedral, piled up against a sky the
color of a cheap tin of salmon, watery orange with flecks of
gray. He swallowed his brandy and knew it would still be
pooled in the bottom of his stomach when he went to Downing Street, giving off the fumes of confusion and despair.

Three thousand miles away, it was still dark in White Plains,
New York, as David Daniels drew up in his red Eldorado
outside a block of apartments just south of Mamaroneck Avenue. The night was warm and windy as he climbed out of his
car, locked it and then crossed the pavement and opened the
squeaking iron gate. Far away to the north, a siren warbled
through the darkness.

Standing on the concrete porch, David pressed the buzzer
next to the label that said ''R. Cameron.'' He waited impatiently for a moment and then pressed it again. A girl's voice
said, ''Who is it?'' with undisguised anxiety.

''It's David. I just got here.''

There was a second's hesitation, then the buzzer sounded
and the door unlocked. David went inside, quickly closing the
door behind him, and hurried across the dimly lit hallway
toward the elevator. He could just about make out his blurred
and worried face in the smeary mirror on the opposite side of
the cage. He rode up to the fourth floor.

Esther was waiting for him, the apartment door ajar but the
security chain still fastened. She unlocked it for him, let him
in and hugged him tight. ''Oh, thank God you've got here.
I've been so scared, I haven't slept a wink. Every time I
heard the elevator, my stomach tightened up and I started to
shake.''

David tugged off his jacket and tossed it across the back of
the sofa. The apartment was plain, plainly decorated and
modest. Department-store furniture upholstered in beige wool,
light-teak cupboards, beige-and-yellow lithographs of forests

and oceans. A pottery vase of dried flowers stood in the middle of the dining table. Ron Cameron was an insurance broker, a one-time college buddy of David's, now divorced and frequently abroad. He allowed David to use his apartment whenever he was away, although David rarely did. He just liked to think that in case of emergency, he had somewhere to disappear to.

"It was awful," said Esther. "That terrible sex club. And she actually nailed his head to the wall. I couldn't stop looking at it, and yet I couldn't bear to either."

"It's okay," David reassured her. "Come on, sit down now. Is there anything to drink around here?"

"That's about *all* there is, except for some stale Fritos."

David went through to the kitchen, opened the refrigerator and took out a bottle of Miller. "What time did you get here?" he called to Esther. "Did you find it all right?"

"Oh, finding it wasn't any trouble. I got here around seven."

"And you didn't see anybody following you up from the city?"

"I kept checking my rearview mirror and once or twice I stopped just to see if anybody slowed down."

David came back into the living room, pouring his beer into a glass tankard emblazoned with the crest of the 1984 Olympics. "I did some checking of my own. The man who called me and *cautioned* me, well, that's what he called it, Jordan Crane, he's a deputy department chief at the National Security Agency. He's quite legitimate. Therefore I was being warned off officially. I also had my old police buddy down on the lower West Side look into the matter of a slight homicide at the Hellfire Club. The police held two people in connection with the death of Wallace Greenbaum; one of them was a well-known sado-masochistic heavy called Winford Ellis, if you can believe it, and the other was a Dutch immigrant alien called Heidi van Cruyf, who came to live in the United States about five years ago."

Esther said wanly, "She must have been the woman who—"

David laid a hand on her shoulder. "You bet she was the woman who. My old buddy down on the lower West Side said he wouldn't go two rounds with her even if his gloves were full of lead. He wouldn't even lay money on it. The interesting thing is, though, that she was released on thirty-five-thousand-dollars' bail only two hours after she was arrested. And who arranged the bail? A midtown law firm called Fuller, Simons and Halperin.''

Esther shook her head uncomprehendingly. But David said, ''It just so happens that I know all about Fuller, Simons and Halperin. You remember that congressional inquiry into FBI payments to Mafia informers? Maybe three years ago? Well, Fuller, Simons and Halperin was set up for the sole purpose of laundering FBI payments to what they liked to describe as 'helpful undesirables.' In other words, mobsters, stoolies and spies.''

''Do you mean that Wally was killed by the FBI?''

''I don't have what you might call trial evidence. But Wally was passing State Department information on to you, or at least trying to, and he was killed before he could manage to do it by a woman whose interests seem to be taken care of by the FBI. I mean, does that lead your mind along certain paths or doesn't it?''

David walked across the room and purred his finger over the spines of a shelf of books. He turned his head sideways to read the title of *The City at the End of the Rainbow*. Then he said, ''Wally came across something real big. Somehow it's connected with Fidel Castro's agreeing to democratic elections and the withdrawal of Communist insurgents from Central America. Somehow it's big enough for the FBI to kill somebody in order to keep it quiet and big enough for Jordan Crane from the National Security Agency to take the chance of calling me up and making what I can only interpret as a straight threat: 'Keepa you noss outa dis business, or else.' ''

David paused and then said, ''They'll kill you, too, if they can find you, and I don't have much doubt that if I don't show them I've well and truly backed off, they'll put me on the list. Jesus, Jack Levy was frightened for his life. When did you ever know Jack Levy frightened for his life? He busted open that huge story about corruption in the Pentagon last year and was he worried? But now it's all, 'Sorry, David, no can do! Sorry, I've been threatened!' Well, what we have to find out is, what goes on here? What frightens a man like Jack Levy?

What frightens a man like me? I mean, I'm not usually frightened, but I am now.''

"Don't say that," said Esther.

"What, that I'm frightened? Why should I pretend?"

They said nothing for a while. David finished his beer. Esther glanced up at him from time to time, wondering if she ought to ask him what she should do next. She couldn't live in a fourth-floor apartment in White Plains for the rest of her life, could she? Or could she? She began to understand for the first time in her short career the meaning of political tyranny.

David swallowed and said, "I managed to call Jack at his favorite watering hole. Sayward's, on M Street. I gave him the number here and told him to call me when he could. He knows a whole lot more than he told me."

"You don't think that's a risk? Jack Levy knowing this number?"

"My love, everything's a risk. But we have to find out what's going on."

"Yes," said Esther gently. "I'm sorry. It's just that I can hardly believe any of this is real."

David put an arm around her. "You hungry?" he asked.

"I don't know. I don't think so."

"How about a hamburger? There's a twenty-four-hour hamburger place back on Mamaroneck. Guppy's or Wuppy's, something like that."

"I don't think so."

David tugged his necktie loose. "Okay, then," he said. "What do you say we get some sleep? Something tells me we've got ourselves a long day in front of us tomorrow."

They went into the bedroom. Esther had been watching a late-night movie, *The Rose Tattoo*. She took off her nightgown with her back to David and then climbed quickly into bed. There was no light in the room but the flickering blue glow of the television. She kept the sheet drawn up to her neck and watched him with careful eyes. He unbuttoned his shirt and said, "I'm going to take a shower."

Later, at dawn, they made love. He kissed her and found her cheeks inexplicably wet with tears. He touched her nipples and they stiffened, but perhaps it was only because of the cool morning air. Her thighs parted, however, and he felt the slipperiness of a woman who was more than ready for him. He pushed into her slowly, trying to be graceful, trying to be stylish, so that she would always remember him as having been the very best. He didn't know that he never could be; not for her, not for any woman. The only place he could be the best was inside his own head.

At six the phone rang. He was still awake, his eyes gritty. He snatched up the phone quickly in case it woke Esther, who was sleeping with her face against the pillow in a blur of hair. He said in a low voice, "Cameron."

"David?" said Jack Levy's voice, very distant.

"Jack! I was expecting to hear from you earlier."

"I had to drive around for a while. I wanted to make sure nobody was following me."

"Where are you now?"

"St. Elizabeth's Hospital, on a pay phone."

"You're not sick?"

"No, nothing like that. It just seemed like a good place to lose myself while I made a call."

"Have you had any more threats?"

Jack coughed. "Nothing direct. But there's been a black Mercury waiting outside my house for most of the night and I've seen it around the office a couple of times."

"Jack, I'm warning you. These people really mean business."

"I know that, David. But with what's going on down here—well, it's bigger than anything I've ever come across before—I can see why they want to keep it to themselves."

David said, "Did you talk to that friend of yours on the general staff?"

"Unh-hunh. He wouldn't say a word. All he kept telling me was, 'Jack, forget it. It isn't real.' But in the end I managed to get through to some young communications officer who works for the assistant secretary in charge of installations and logistics. Well, we did a story about him two or three years ago when he was involved in a court-martial concerning some homosexual incidents up at Fort Dix in New Jersey, and you could say that he owes me a favor or two."

"Well?" asked David.

"Well, at first he didn't want to play. He didn't know very

much, but he did know that something big was going down. That something is called *Gringo*. It's not somebody's name; it's not a thing; it's a military acronym for some kind of large-scale operation.''

''An attack? You don't think we're planning on attacking the Soviet Union, something like that?''

Jack cleared his throat. ''No, I don't think so. The indications are that we may be reducing our military presence in Western Europe, presumably to save money on the defense budget; but we may be doing it kind of sneakily so we don't shake anybody's confidence or appear to be welching on any of our commitments to NATO.''

David thought for a while. Then he said, ''Do you really think that kind of secret is worth killing for?''

''People have been killed for less. Remember the Charleston grocery case last month? Three guys murdered just because they discovered their supermarket was rigging broccoli prices?''

''Are you going to print anything?'' David asked.

''Not me, pal. I want my family to stay alive.''

''In that case, do you mind if I raise it with your publisher?''

''You can do what you want as long as you leave my name out of it.''

''Okay, Jack,'' said David. ''I understand.''

''Listen,'' said Jack, ''before you hang up, can I ask you a favor?''

''Sure.''

''If anything does happen to me or to any of my family, make sure the bastards get what they deserve, won't you?''

David told him, ''That's what I'm in business for.''

He hung up. Then he went across the room and found his small black Bijan telephone book, one of the last gifts his second wife Helen had given him before they split up. He found the number of the publisher of *The Washington Post* and quickly punched it out on the telephone.

''Mr. Lewis? This is Senator David Daniels from Connecticut.''

''Good morning, Senator. Always good to hear from our representatives. But it's kind of early, isn't it, for business?''

''I think I have a story for you,'' said David.

As he was talking to Cal Lewis, the affable new publisher

of *The Washington Post,* Jack Levy was leaving St. Elizabeth's Hospital on the east side of the Potomac, next to the U.S. Naval Station, and climbing into his metallic-green Chrysler Cordoba. He sat in the driver's seat, tired and haggard, and brushed back a long strand of thinning brown hair. He was only forty-eight, yet he was beginning to feel that he was far too old for this kind of story, far too worn-out for this kind of physical and political pressure. You can open up only so many cans of political maggots. After the fifth or sixth can, you begin to realize that corruption is everywhere, that honesty is the exception. You begin to think, what's the point? Take the money, keep quiet. It's safer and it makes more sense.

He turned the key in the ignition and for some inexplicable reason, he knew at once that he shouldn't have. He whipped his left hand to the door handle and yanked at it, but then the five pounds of cyclonite planted under his seat detonated with a high, cracking bang and he was blown into ticker-tape shreds of liver and bone and sinew. The Cordoba caught fire immediately and stood in the center of the parking lot with black smoke rolling up from every window, its paint blistering and its tires blazing like wreaths at an Indian funeral, until at last it sagged and collapsed on its suspension and its windows splintered.

The fire department arrived too late to do anything but extinguish the flames and mask the grisly ruins with foam. They were still standing around the wreck when David finished his conversation with Cal Lewis and put down the phone.

Esther stirred and lifted her head from the pillow.

"David?" she asked him.

"Ssh," he told her. "Everything's fine. Everything's absolutely fine."

SEVENTEEN

"You knew Nicholas Reed, of course," the man told Charles quietly as they walked slowly through the gardens of Rosenborg Castle in the center of Copenhagen.

Charles looked at him sharply but said nothing.

The man paused at the end of one of the pathways between the flowers and stood with his hands on his hips, admiring the view of the castle and the placid summer sky. It was Friday, almost lunchtime. Charles was beginning to feel like one of Fiskehusets' turbot specials, or even a Burger King if Lamprey's budget didn't stretch to haute cuisine. He had stayed last night with a Danish friend, an insurance-company executive who lived on Ved Stadsgraven. His friend was relentlessly mean and had given him only one glass of schnapps with his supper (three slices of salami, and salad) and only skimmed milk and *muesli* for breakfast. Charles had long ago passed the age where he could function equally effectively with or without eating, and right now, in the gardens of Rosenborg Castle, he was beginning to feel as if his empty stomach was more important than almost anything else, including the fate of the Western world.

"Listen," he said, "do you think we could go find something to nourish ourselves with? I'm starved."

The man looked at him for a moment, then smiled and

nodded. "Yes. I'm sorry. My wife always prepares me a very substantial breakfast. Meat, fish, muffins."

"I could use a drink too," said Charles. The man had irritated him even more by reciting his breakfast menu.

"I'll treat you," said the man, taking Charles' elbow. Charles didn't particularly like being held this way by another man but allowed himself to be escorted out of the gardens of Rosenborg, across Kronprinsessegade to Dronningens Tvaergade, where the man politely propelled him into Hos Jan Hurtigkart's restaurant.

"I don't think I'm dressed for this," said Charles. He saw himself in the mirror behind the reception desk and realized how shabby and crumpled he looked. His shirt was clean but he had never been a good packer.

The man appeared to have a regular table. In any case, they were discreetly escorted through to the back of the restaurant; fresh napkins were cracked over their laps and Charles had a large Jack Daniel's in his hand before he knew it. All around there was the happy burble of people eating and laughing and enjoying one of Copenhagen's more expensive restaurants. Charles said, "Lamprey has an entertainment budget?"

The man smiled. He was short, stocky, with cropped blond hair and one of those open, fatherly faces that invite trust. He wore a green-twill hunting jacket and a brown-checked shirt with a tightly knotted brown tie. He could have been any one of a million Danes; he could even have been a Swede or a German or an American. He was nondescript to the point of invisibility, and yet Charles felt instinctively that he liked him, especially since he was going to buy him his lunch.

"Lamprey is financed by those intelligence services for whom its members work," said the man. "The United States unwittingly contributes most of Lamprey's budget, followed by the USSR, then Britain, then Germany. Even Denmark pays its tithe. There is such waste, you see, in intelligence budgets, and such secrecy that it is difficult for governments to keep track of where their money has gone. Appropriating a few hundred thousand dollars for our activities is not so very difficult."

Charles swallowed his drink and set the glass back on the table. "Do you have a name?" he asked.

The man continued to smile. "You could call me Hans if you like. Will that do?"

"What are your other two names? Christian Andersen?"

"Now, now, my friend." The man called Hans smiled and laid his hand on Charles' wrist.

Charles had made the arrangement to meet Hans in the grounds of Rosenborg Palace through a thin-faced young messenger who had arrived yesterday evening, as promised, at the bar, wearing a motorcycle helmet. The messenger had simply said that a senior representative of Lamprey would see him tomorrow at eleven-thirty opposite the bridge that crossed the moat. And so it was that Hans had arrived, bland and genial, and shaken Charles' hand even before Charles had identified himself.

"Something very dangerous is happening," Charles had said. He had called Agneta at Roger's place twice during the night to make sure she was all right.

"Well, my friend, you are quite correct," Hans had agreed. "There has been a disturbance throughout the world's intelligence communities for some months now, a strange kind of ripple. These men, of course, are chosen for their sensitivity to political fear, just as you were once chosen. Well, the feeling is very strong. You can lift your nose to the wind and smell it! Somewhere deep down, the ground is moving!"

Charles had said, "Tell me about Nicholas Reed. What went on at the Hvidsten Inn?"

"You knew Nicholas Reed, of course," Hans had told him.

Now he said, his hands resting in repose on the linen tablecloth like the hands of a priest or a doctor, "Nicholas Reed was a CIA agent called Peter Secker. He had previously been working in the Philippines but he was posted here after the assassination of Benigno Aquino."

Charles felt an empty pang. Of course, the butterscotch candies at Klarlund & Christensen in "Nicholas Reed's" desk. Peter had always had a weakness for butterscotch candies; he had once told Charles that his mother used to make them at home when he was a kid back in—where was it?—Mankato, Minnesota, someplace like that.

Hans saw that Charles was affected by what he had said. He looked at him for a moment and then asked, "Are you all right?"

"Oh, sure. I didn't know him that well. We worked on a couple of things together, nothing spectacular. The Bomlafjorden business in Norway. That was one. But he was very good at undercover work. He could even make *me* believe he was somebody else. Good at plain old systematic detective work too."

"That's why he was chosen to infiltrate Klarlund and Christensen."

"Do you have any idea of what goes on there?" asked Charles.

"Well, some. But of course Peter was killed before we found out everything we wanted to know."

The waiter came up, a napkin over his arm, to take their order. Hans said, "The escalope of veal will do for me."

Charles said, "The turbot, plain-broiled, no butter. You got that? No butter."

"Kosher, sir?" the waiter asked him politely.

"No," Charles retorted. "I simply don't care to have one of the finest fish that swims the world's waters tainted with some rancid juice that was squirted out by cows."

"Yes, sir. I'm sorry, sir."

Hans pointed to Charles' drink. "Another one?" he asked quietly.

"What the hell," Charles agreed.

When the waiter had gone, Hans said, "We first began to suspect that something unusual was happening at Klarlund and Christensen about seven months ago. One of our clerks noticed a British intelligence agent called Jaggs coming out of the Klarlund and Christensen building one morning and of course he notified his senior officer. We kept the building under observation for five weeks, and we saw not only intelligence staff but senior diplomatic staff from the United States, from the Soviet Union, from Great Britain, from Cuba, from Ecuador, from China. From almost everywhere, in fact, except Western Europe. No Germans, for instance. No French, no Italians, no Swiss, no Dutch."

Charles watched without speaking while the waiter brought him another drink. He felt like knocking it back straightaway but decided he could wait. He said to Hans, "It sounds like some kind of high-powered conference."

"Exactly, and the indications were that some kind of major agreement was being reached about Western Europe without the participation of those nations most deeply affected. Peter at first believed that it was economic, that Britain would agree to pull out of the Common Market and forge closer ties with Comecon. He had access to one of Klarlund and Christensen's computer terminals but he was unable to break into their databanks. That, presumably, was what you and Jeppe Rifbjerg were trying to do the night you crashed into their lobby."

Charles nodded. "I'm sorry. If either of us had realized that you people were already on the case . . . well, the least we would have done was to ask you for some protection."

Hans hesitated for a moment. Then he said, "You know that Jeppe Rifbjerg was found?"

"Found? No, I didn't. I spent most of yesterday trying to call him on the telephone."

"Beyond the reach of telephones, I regret, Mr. Krogh."

Charles' lips suddenly felt dry. "When was this?" he asked.

"This morning. They gave me the news shortly before I came out to meet you."

"What did they do to him?"

Hans shook his head. "You don't want to know that."

"I'm asking you. What did they do to him?"

Hans looked down at the table and carefully adjusted his knife and fork. "He was found in a garage on St. Annae Gade. They had cut off his arms and legs while he was still alive."

Charles felt the liquor rise up in his throat. He sat there for a long time with watering eyes before it consented to sink down again. Then he reached inside his jacket and took out a pack of cigarettes. "You don't mind if I smoke?"

"They're bringing your fish."

Charles stared at Hans for two or three seconds, then returned the cigarette pack unopened to his jacket pocket. "I ought to work with you. I think you'd help me to quit. You've got those eyes. What is it? Hypnosis?"

Hans said, "Our suspicions so far are that the United States and Great Britain have forged new agreements with the Soviet Union that in the long term may have a beneficial effect on world peace. Britain will almost certainly withdraw from the Common Market and trade independently, with an increasing bias toward the Communist bloc, while the United States may well agree to withdraw substantial numbers of troops and missiles from West Germany."

Charles broke up his turbot with the edge of his fork. He didn't need to be told what a dramatic effect it would have on the world if Britain were to pull out of the EEC and the United States were to withdraw even a fraction of its military forces from Germany. His political instructor at the CIA had always told him, "The world is like one of those mobiles you hang from your child's bedroom ceiling. Only one small piece of that mobile has to be out of balance and the whole world starts trembling."

He couldn't eat very much even though he was hungry. He kept thinking of Jeppe lying on the floor of that garage, limbless, bloody, like something out of Tod Browning's *Freaks*. Halfway through lunch he excused himself and went to the men's room and was violently and painfully sick. He stood for a long time with his head bowed over the washbasin until Hans came in, stood watching him and said, "You can help us, you know. In Lamprey we need everyone we can get. Especially now."

Charles raised his head. The window of the men's room was open and looked out over copper rooftops, dreaming sky. Pieces of green and gold and endless blue; the world of the Little Mermaid. "Why is it," he asked, "that poor bastards like you and me become responsible for the whole fucking world?"

Hans laid a hand on his shoulder. "My friend," he said, "you and I are the engineers of international politics, the ones with the greasy rags who have to duck under the pistons while the machine is in motion to keep it running smoothly, the ones who risk their lives in order that governments may make their decisions and bureaucracies may continue to survive. Don't ask me why such responsibility falls on such ordinary people as us; in every walk of life there are people who ask themselves the same question. We do this job because nobody else will do it and because we cannot bear to see it left undone."

Charles lit a cigarette. His hand was shaking. He blew smoke out the side of his mouth. "Whatever this conference decided, you think that it's stored in Klarlund and Christensen's computer?"

"Certainly there will be clues."

"Otto Glistrup said that the computer could be accessed from outside, on the telephone lines."

"Hm," smiled Hans. "Don't think we haven't tried. But the computer is completely secure. There are too many codes to penetrate."

"Perhaps we should take another crack at breaking into the building."

Hans shook his head. "I don't think so, my friend. The security has been increased tenfold. And you know, of course, that Novikov is in Copenhagen, the one the Russians call *Krov' iz Nosu.*"

Charles nodded. "I had the dubious pleasure of throwing him out a window. Unfortunately, there was a ledge underneath. As far as I can gather, he's alive, kicking and dying to cut me into several hundred small pieces."

He paused and then said, "Was it Novikov who killed Jeppe?"

Hans glanced away, shrugged. "Of course it looks that way."

"Bastard," Charles breathed.

Hans said, "We need a computer expert desperately, a real expert, somebody who can penetrate Klarlund and Christensen's memory banks and not leave a trace that he has been there. Well, I don't know where we could find such a person, but perhaps it could be possible."

"I'll keep my eyes open," said Charles half sarcastically.

Hans thought for a long while and then said, "There is one other possibility. This you must keep in the very strictest confidence. Last night some of our people in West Germany managed to abduct a senior Soviet Army officer, a man close to the *Stavka* itself.''

"You're kidding," Charles said. Then, "You're kidding?"

"Well, of course it was risky," Hans admitted. "It remains risky too. But we feel that these are critical times and that extreme measures are called for.''

"You've kidnapped a Soviet Army officer? What is he, a colonel or something?''

"Higher than colonel.''

"General?'' asked Charles in disbelief.

"You probably know him. T.K. Golovanov, the First Deputy of the Ministry of Defense.''

Charles stared at Hans incredulously. "Holy shit! The Kremlin must be going ape.''

"Well, of course,'' smiled Hans. "But they cannot admit anything publicly because of the loss of face. As yet, you see, they are not sure of whether he was kidnapped or whether he defected. If he defected, which he regrettably did not, they will think he will tell the West everything he knows. At this moment of military tension, it must be crucial for the Defense Council to find out where he is, whether he was abducted or went of his own free will, whether he is dead or alive, whether he will talk.''

"You can guarantee that he won't talk,'' said Charles. He crushed out his cigarette, took out his handkerchief and wiped his nose.

"We can try.''

"Golovanov? He's one of the old toughies. Hide like leather, balls like hard-boiled eggs. He was at Kursk, wasn't he, and Stalingrad?''

"I repeat,'' said Hans, "we can try.''

"Well, good luck, that's all I can say. Meanwhile, is there anything you can do to help me get Novikov off my back?''

Hans beckoned to the waiter. "Do you want anything else?'' he asked Charles. "Coffee? Tart?''

Charles shook his head. "I want to get over to visit my lady in a half-hour. Those Soviet creeps gave her the fright of her life.''

Hans leaned forward on the table. "We have been trying to

keep Novikov under surveillance. So far it has been very difficult because the Soviets have been keeping him well hidden and letting him loose only when there is a job to be done, like killing poor Peter Secker or attempting to dispose of you. Whatever information Peter had, it must have been vitally important to make them send Novikov to kill him. Novikov, as you know, is their only killer with a hundred-percent success rate.''

"That gives me a feeling of overwhelming cheerfulness,'' said Charles.

"Ah, but you can help us, my friend. If you allow one of our people to follow you, inevitably Novikov will show himself and then perhaps we can get a lead on him.''

Charles shrugged, looked down and drummed his fingers on the table. "I didn't think the time would ever come when I got myself used as the Judas goat.''

"My friend, life is a succession of reverses.''

Charles glanced up again and said, "Maybe.''

"In the meantime,'' said Hans, "we will continue to look for somebody who can break into Klarlund and Christensen's computer, and we will continue to try to persuade Comrade Golovanov to tell us what it is that is disturbing Europe's intelligence communities so much.''

Charles walked to Peder Skrams Gade to see Agneta. It wasn't too far and the afternoon was sharp and bright. He turned down Store Kongens Gade to Kongens Nytorv, then went along by the water at Nyhavn, where the heavy cumulus clouds were reflected in the slate gray of the dock and trees flickered on either side with warm and whispering gentility.

Roger lived on the second floor, over a ceramics shop. The polished window was sparsely arranged with Flora Danica dinnerware and underglazed statuettes. The shiny brass plate by the side door said "R. Strong,'' which was a joke since Roger's real name was Rubins. The door was open, an inch or two ajar. Charles cautiously pushed it wider with the toe of his shoe.

There was nobody there. He mounted the bare wooden stairs, his footsteps clattering. In one of the rooms upstairs, somebody was playing old Jimi Hendrix records loudly on a cheap record player. A small part of Charles' mind was instantly transported back twenty years to summer days in Copenhagen and Stockholm, to young blonde girls in miniskirts, to flowers and sunshine and grass, and to those hair-raising days when intelligence agents had actually come to believe for a while that they were James Bond or the man from UNCLE. Some of them had learned karate and came leaping out at you like idiots when you least suspected it, usually to crash flat on their back on the floor and qualify for three months' sick leave.

Charles reached Roger's door and knocked. He waited with his hands in his pockets. He knocked again and this time the door swung open. It stopped, shuddered, squeaked. Charles listened for a moment, slowly removing his hands from his pockets. No sound, not even the everyday noise of somebody vacuuming or listening to Radio Denmark or taking a shower. Charles called, "Hallo?" and waited, and then, "Agneta?" but there was no reply.

He stepped into the narrow hallway. The floor was of waxed pine and the hall smelled of forests and garlic. On the wall there was a drawing by Malcolm Luber that showed an arrogant and ugly young man brandishing his penis. At the far end of the hall sat a white Danish ceramic planter containing a fern. *Athyrium filix-femina,* the lady fern. Highly appropriate, thought Charles, and he called again, "Agneta!"

He walked into the sitting room, orange brick and pine and bright windows overlooking Inderhavn, where the ships from Malmo tied up. Chimneys, ferry funnels, green-copper roof-tops, dancing trees and a sky that stretched all the way to Russia. He paused and listened. Nothing at all, and that was what was wrong. Agneta had promised to stay in all day and wait for him. He found himself saying under his breath, "Our Father . . . which art in Heaven," and wishing for the second time in two days that he had a gun.

He stepped into the middle of the sitting room, listening, waiting.

"Agneta?" he called again and then shouted out "Hah!" in shock and surprise as the kitchen door opened and Agneta stepped out, her short blonde hair tousled and a kitchen knife held up in front of her, in both hands.

"Charles," she said with relief.

"Are you crazy?" he asked. "The door was wide open. I could have been anybody."

"I didn't realize it was you, my love," she said and came forward and hugged him and kissed him on both cheeks and then on the mouth. He put his arm protectively around her and gave her a squeeze. "It might not have *been* me, for Christ's sake. It might have been one of those goddam Russians. Where's Roger?"

"Roger stepped out to buy groceries. He isn't used to feeding two people. All he had in the refrigerator was orange juice and strawberry-flavored yogurt. Oh, and thousands of sacks of sunflower seeds. Roger believes that sunflower seeds, if you eat enough of them, give you gloss."

"Gloss? That makes you sound like a horse, or a piece of antique furniture."

Agneta was wearing a plain blue-and-white smock, very Danish, and short, knitted socks from the island of Aerø. There were dark smudges under her eyes as if she hadn't slept well. She stroked Charles' arm and then kissed him again. "Did you meet that man? Did you find out what was going on?"

"Kind of. But I'm still not sure. We have to break into their computer first; that's if we can find someone clever enough to do it. Otherwise, well . . . there isn't any otherwise, not as far as I can see."

"But these Russians—" Agneta protested.

Charles shrugged. "They think we know more than we do. Either that or they believe we're more curious than we ought to be. Whichever, they seem intent on killing us."

They heard the front door open. "That'll be Roger," said Agneta and turned toward the hall. "Roger!" she called. "Charles is back!"

There was no reply. Agneta said, "Roger, is that you?" and stepped out into the hallway before Charles realized that it couldn't be Roger. Roger would have answered straightaway, without hesitation, because Roger knew they were being hunted down and the last thing Roger wanted was a knife blade between the ribs before he even had the chance to say, "It's all right, it's me."

"*Agneta!*" roared Charles.

But even as Agneta hesitated, a huge arm swung around the side of the doorway and caught her around the neck, tumbling her off her feet. And then Novikov came into view, the terrible *Krov' iz Nosu,* with his scarred, nightmare face. He held Agneta clear off the floor, her head caught in the crook of his right arm, his biceps tight against her throat. She clawed at his arm with frantic nails and kicked wildly at his shins, but she might just as well have been a kitten, or a small child. He stood motionless and unyielding, squeezing her neck with little flinches of his muscle until she was crimson-faced and hoarse with suffocation.

Novikov said nothing. His twisted, scar-tissued face was expressionless, trapped forever in a meaningless grimace of burned muscle and fire-tightened skin. He said nothing, not even a grunt. Charles backed off, knowing with unappeasable dread that he was up against the fiercest and most relentless killer of modern times, a human machine without fear, without conscience and without any morality except a dogged devotion to the men who had saved his life and sent him to kill others as an exorcism of his own agony and his own fear.

God. He must have been following him all the way from the restaurant. "Novikov," said Charles, "I'm warning you now. Put down the girl and back off."

Novikov did nothing but squeeze Agneta's throat even tighter. Agneta was speechless. Already she was so starved for oxygen that she could do nothing but kick her legs feebly and cling to Novikov's arm.

"*Back off!*" Charles screamed at the killer. He picked up a wooden armchair and advanced on Novikov with it raised over his head. The killer watched him with watery, Mongoloid eyes, not blinking, not flinching, not retreating. Agneta let out a tortured gurgle and Novikov squeezed his arm even more viciously around her neck.

"*You son of a bitch!*" Charles bellowed. "*You goddam half-human son of a bitch!*"

He arched back and swung the chair around sideways as hard as he could so that it cracked against Novikov's hip. Then he hit the huge Russian again and again on the back, on the legs, on the ribs, wherever he could lash out at him without hitting Agneta.

With the last blow, the chair's elm seat split in half but Charles wrenched off one of the legs and brandished it at Novikov's face.

"You let her go, you bastard, or I'll put your eyes out!"

The creature called *Krov' iz Nosu* gripped Agneta's head in both scarred hands and slowly twisted it around. He watched Charles intently with those Frankenstein's monster eyes as if he wanted to relish every second of pain Charles suffered watching Agneta killed in front of him.

Charles heard Agneta's spinal column crack, atlas vertebra dislocated from axis. He heard her muscles tear, the sterno-cleidomastoid and the splenius capitis. Then her carotid arteries popped, and for one moment Agneta was staring at him with bulging eyes, already dead but open-mouthed as if she were about to say something; the next moment her mouth fountained blood.

Charles, for a split second, went berserk. He launched himself at Novikov with a screech of fury and began to batter him around the head with the chair leg, a cracking blow to the side of the face, a sharp blow to the shoulder. Agneta's body dropped sideways to the carpet, her knees buckling as if she were fainting. Blood sprayed across the wall of the sitting room like a brilliant red horse's mane.

Charles lashed at *Krov' iz Nosu* again and again. Any one of the blows with the chair leg would have knocked a normal man to the floor. But *Krov' iz Nosu* accepted them unflinchingly, as if they were as light as kisses, and then grabbed hold of the shoulder of Charles' jacket, shook him violently and hurled him across the room. Charles stumbled against a glass-and-stainless-steel coffee table and then plunged backward into it with a shattering crash. Novikov came after him, his eyes as bland and cruel and relentless as before. There was no excitement in them, not even blood lust. Novikov killed because that was what he did, and that was all.

Terror surged up in Charles' throat. He rolled himself sideways out of the shattered remains of the coffee table and threw himself over the back of the sofa. Novikov circled around, his breath rasping like a tenon saw cutting against slate.

"You bastard," Charles choked. He felt a sharp pain in his ribs and thought it would serve Novikov right if he suffered a heart attack right now and dropped dead on the spot, before the Russian could touch him. Novikov said nothing but tossed aside a brass Italian lamp, which smashed on the floor, and advanced on Charles with both of his burned claws raised as if he were promising in grotesque sign language that he would twist Charles' head off too.

Charles circled around the room, never taking his eyes off Novikov's masklike face. *"You bastard!"* he repeated in an inaudible whisper again and again. *"You bastard!"*

It was then, unexpectedly, that Roger stepped into the room, his arms full of groceries. He stared first at Charles and was about to say something when he saw the splatters of blood and Agneta lying on the carpet, her head twisted around the wrong way. Then he saw the broken table and the smashed lamp, and at last he looked over toward the far side of the room and caught sight of Novikov.

"Charles?" he asked quietly.

Charles couldn't do anything but shake his head.

Roger put down his two brown-paper bags of groceries very carefully, one after the other. There was so much blood on the carpet that the bottom of one of the bags was immediately soaked in crimson. Roger eased off his cream-linen jacket, flexed his fingers and said to Charles, "Anything I ought to know?"

"Yes," said Charles thickly. "This thing's a killer. Do yourself a favor. Put your coat back on and walk out the door. Call Povl Isen at police headquarters; I mean right away. Tell him you know where to find me and tell him to bring a busload of armed men."

Roger nodded toward Novikov. *"This* is a killer? This lump of overdone hamburger?"

"Roger, please, listen to me. This is not just a killer. This is a *killer*. The most dangerous man in the KGB."

Roger hesitated for a moment or two, then smiled. "Quite a challenge, then. Not like those two meatheads who tried to attack you the other day. I could quite enjoy a run-in with a *real* killer.''

"Roger," Charles pleaded, "listen to me. Call Povl Isen. Please.''

But Roger didn't seem to be listening anymore. He took up the crouching stance of the *kungfu* adept and stood facing Novikov for almost ten seconds without moving. Charles was desperate to call him off but anxious at the same time not to break his concentration. Roger's nostrils flared, his neck arched back and he eyed Novikov narrowly, his open hands circling and circling as if he were winding silk out of the air.

Suddenly Roger shrieked, "*Banzai!*" and leaped at Novikov, kicking him hard in the chest. To Charles' amazement, Novikov dropped heavily to the floor. Roger immediately sat down on Novikov's stomach, seized his right leg and began to twist it around.

"All right, you goddam meatloaf!" Roger screeched at him. "Let's see what you think of this!"

But Roger reckoned without Novikov's inhuman lack of concern for pain. Novikov had been splashed in the face with white-hot metal; he had endured years of surgery, years of agonizing therapy and years of the fiercest physical training. Roger was strong; if he had twisted anybody else's leg, even the leg of a professional wrestler, he would have brought shouts of submission. But Novikov was unimpressed by pain. He had suffered so much that it no longer had any effect on him. He could be knocked over, as Roger had proved. But he could not be hurt.

Novikov snatched out with his clawlike hands and dug them into Roger's face. Roger shook his head and snarled happily, but then he suddenly realized that *Krov' iz Nosu* could not be thrown off with such humorous abandon. The Russian's horny talons dug into the sides of his mouth, into his cheeks and into the sockets of his eyes.

Roger's triumphant barking suddenly turned into a scream. Like a man tearing the flesh of a peach stone, *Krov' iz Nosu* tugged the skin and the muscle away from the bones of Roger's face so that for one second Roger looked startled and rubbery, his eyes popping, and the next second his face was nothing but a clawed mass of meat. His eyeballs dropped out,

dangling on their optic nerves, his lips were ripped away,
baring his naked skeletal jaw, and the sound that came out of
his mouth was like nothing Charles had ever heard from a
human before. A chilling, high-pitched gargle.

Charles dived for the doorway. He collided with a young
man who was just coming into the sitting room—brown-
suited, probably KGB—and sent him sprawling across the
corridor and into the large, potted fern. Then Charles was out
the door and bounding down the stairs three at a time. He
reached the street and kept on running, dodging between
startled passersby, crossing Peder Skrams Gade and Holbergs-
gade and limping into Herluf Trolles Gade.

He rested at last at Nyhavn, overlooking the water, sweating and gasping in the summer heat. The stark, bloody image
of Roger's torn-apart face was imprinted on his mind so
vividly that he could scarcely see the boats and the trees
and the children with balloons. A wandering musician
with a piano accordion was playing "Happy Days Are
Here Again."

He lit a cigarette with wildly erratic hands. Then he started
walking again. He would have to hide somewhere, and quickly.
There was no doubt that the Russians were out to kill him the
way they had killed Jeppe and they didn't care who happened
to get hurt in the process. He had already cost Agneta her
life, and Roger too. The shock and the pain of seeing them
killed hadn't begun to sink in, but he knew in a strangely
detached way that it soon would and that it would be better
for him to be hidden away when it happened. Alone, with a
couple of bottles of Jack Daniel's.

He could think of only one place to go. He hailed a taxi,
climbed in and said, "How do you fancy a long trip?"

"American?" asked the driver.

"Do you want the job or don't you?" Charles snapped at
him, already beginning to burst out into the gray sweat of
total shock.

"Sure. Where do you want to go?"

"Drive north on Nineteen until I tell you to stop."

"I'm going to want some money in advance."

Charles reached into his shirt pocket, crammed as usual

with crumpled notes, and sorted out five hundred Danish kroner. "Here. Now let's go."

The driver took the money, shrugged and switched off his FRI light. He turned up Gothergade, passed the spires of Rosenborg Palace and the Botanical Gardens, and drove alongside Sortedams Sø, its waters glittering like necklaces. In the backseat, Charles closed his eyes and tried to convince himself that nothing had happened, that he was on his way somewhere else, that he had never heard of Novikov, or Roger for that matter, or Agneta.

He opened his eyes. They were just crossing Fredens Bro. "Agneta," he whispered, and knew he would never want to speak her name again.

EIGHTEEN

Their driver spoke no English but he told Michael that his name was Yakov. Lev, translating, explained that Yakov was a Lithuanian whose grandfather had hated the Communists, whose father had hated the Communists, and who therefore considered it his family duty to hate the Communists too. His grandfather had owned a garage in Siauliai in the 1920s and had owned and run one of the first Buick Sixes ever seen in Lithuania. His father had taken over the garage in 1935 and even though he had been bombed out during the war, he had taught Yakov everything anyone could ever want to know about cars. Michael believed him: the Moskvich growled along the long, empty roads at nearly a hundred miles an hour, dark forests flashing past like fairy tales, swamps and lakes gleaming between the trees in quick, half-seen instances like words that were thought but never spoken.

It was their high speed that had saved them; that and their devious route east, making sure they created a ridiculous commotion as they sped through Scolkovo, blowing their horn and revving their engine and skidding their way through every traffic signal they came across, only to U-turn back northwest once they reached the eastern outskirts and then drive flat-out to Puskino.

They had turned due west at last where the highway crosses the Vor'a River, and they had seen no highway patrol cars until they reached Dmitrov. There, in a back street overlooking the Imeni Moskviy canal, they had driven their Moskvich into a tatty lock-up garage and abandoned it. A newish Volga-22 was waiting for them in the next street. Lev explained nothing to them, nothing about their route, nothing about how this new getaway car was ready for them. Rufina Konstantinova was still with them after all, but Lev had relented and she was no longer handcuffed, although he knew very well that if they happened to be caught, she would probably tell the KGB everything it needed to know.

Probably but not certainly, for as they sped minute by minute toward the West, as the day went by and they still remained at large, they noticed that Rufina began to change. She talked more freely, with more vivacity. She stopped criticizing Lev and demeaning their chances of escape. It occurred to Michael that possibly Rufina wanted to get out of the Soviet Union almost as much as they did. If she had to go, she might as well enjoy it. Beyond that Western frontier there was a world of cosmetics and perfume and fashion and food. There were books and films and uncensored newspapers and sex and shoes and rock music.

They crossed the bridge over the Volga at Novozavidoskij at three in the afternoon on Friday. The land was flat and swampy, interspersed with low-lying forests. The ruffled surface of the river bobbed with ducks. John, on the other side of the car, was sleeping with his head against the window. Rufina was sitting silently, her hands in her lap. In the front, Lev was whistling softly between his teeth: tension and boredom. Yakov had long ago stopped talking about his father and his grandfather and his Buick Six.

"No roadblocks," Rufina remarked. Michael had been wondering whether it would be wrong of him to reach over and take her hand. They had, after all, been lovers. But real lovers? Or just pretend lovers? Had she felt anything for him or not? She had made love to him in ways that Margaret never had; he could still picture Rufina with her eyes closed, her lipsticked mouth a perfect crimson O around the shaft of his penis. And now he felt apprehensive about holding her hand.

Lev turned around in his seat and remarked, "They still

think we're heading east. But give them time. At least we've managed to cross the Volga without being intercepted.''

Rufina said, ''Are you going to let me go when you reach wherever it is you are headed for?''

''You know where we're headed for?'' asked Lev.

''I presume the West. In this direction. Finland.''

Lev nodded. ''But we can't let you go. Already you know far too much about us. We're going to have to kill you.''

Michael looked at Lev in surprise and concern but there was something in Lev's eyes that warned him to hold his tongue.

Rufina said, ''If you're going to kill me, why don't you kill me now? Why waste *benzin* taking me all the way across Russia? Why didn't you kill me before?''

Lev looked at her coldly. ''The reason for that, my dear, is that some friends of mine in Helsinki would very much like to ask you some questions before you die. Who knows, if you answer them well, they may even allow you to live.''

''Lev—'' began Michael but Lev abruptly shook his head. ''This mistress of yours, Michael, knows exactly why the Soviet Union is abducting British and American scientists and engineers and why she is being allowed to do so not only without protest from London and Washington, but with their active encouragement. You two are experts in computers; scores of other Western experts are now working against their will for the Soviet Union: chemists, aeronautical engineers, physicists, industrialists. And yet when their families attempt to find out what has happened to them, they are met by their own governments with silence and excuses. 'Perhaps he has run off with a Russian woman, Mrs. Whatever-your-name-is.' 'Perhaps he has decided to stay and work in the Soviet Union.' And have you noticed? Not a word in the newspapers, not a word in Parliament or on Capitol Hill. The most complete and utter blackout on news and political criticism there has ever been, *ever*; even more severe than it was before World War Two.''

Lev pointed a finger at Rufina. ''This young lady knows the answer to this strange problem. Perhaps not all of the answer. The KGB is not in the habit of telling its operatives more than they need to know. Well, the same with MI-Fifteen of course, and the CIA. But she knows enough to put us on the right scent."

They were approaching the city of Kalinin now, the Volga winding darkly on their right. The afternoon was windy and the slipstream whistled dolefully around the Volga's badly fitting windows.

Michael said in a tight voice, "Then—after she's put you on the right scent—you're going to kill her?"

"Maybe," said Lev.

"No," replied Michael. "I can't have it."

John woke up and blinked at Michael through unfocused eyes. "What's going on?" he wanted to know.

Lev had turned his back on Michael. There was an awkward pause. But then as a concession, Lev said, "We shall see. I shall do my best to keep her alive. But that is all I can promise. These things are out of my hands."

John frowned at Michael in concern. Rufina, to Michael's sudden gratification, squeezed his hand.

They sped along the Leningradskoje Sosse at ninety miles an hour, the Volga's engine rumbling in protest. In Russian, Yakov said, "I could really tune this car up if I had the time. I could make her fly like a bird, but all I can do now is keep my foot on the floor." They flashed past timber trucks, occasional private cars, and vans from the cotton factories at Kalinin.

Kalinin itself came into view on the far side of the Volga: chimneys and eighteenth-century rooftops and a jumble of flat, uninspiring concrete blocks. The pale sun sparked from distant windows like warning messages from strategically placed heliographs.

Lev touched Yakov's arm and said, "Slow down; there's a highway-patrol post just along here." Yakov eased off the gas but even as he did so, a police patrol car pulled out of a tree-lined side street just behind them and came in clamorous pursuit, its lights flashing and its siren shrieking. Michael turned around to look but Lev snapped, "Ignore them."

"You're not going to stop?"

"Yakov knows what to do. Just ignore them."

They sped over the Volga bridge at Kalinin with the highway patrol car close behind. As they reached the other side of the river, the patrol car came up beside them and the policeman in the front-passenger seat flagged them down with a white-gloved hand.

Yakov obediently slowed and began to draw the Volga into the side of the highway beside a long wire fence and a clump of unkempt pines. The highway patrol car pulled over in front of them and the driver switched off its siren. Yakov came to a stop although he left the engine running.

"What do they want?" asked John worriedly.

"Oh, nothing special," said Lev. "We were speeding a little. The limit along that stretch is seventy miles an hour. Also, they were probably bored."

The patrol officers approached the Volga and one of them indicated with a twirling finger that Yakov should wind down the window. The other officer walked around the car, peering at it suspiciously as if he could tell where it had been and who owned it by the condition of its paint.

"Your speed was checked over the past three miles, Comrade, and it was at all times well over the permitted limit. I want you to produce all of your papers, hand them to me and then step out of the car."

Yakov shook his head. *"Ya nyi panyimayu,"* he said in a clumsy pretense at an American accent. "I don't understand."

"American?" asked the officer. He peered into the car. Michael could see his clear-blue eyes, his wispy blond mustache, his bright-red cheeks. He couldn't be very much older than twenty-five, and Michael prayed in sweaty silence that Lev wouldn't shoot him.

"We're all American," Michael spoke out. "We're on a tour to Leningrad."

"Ah," said the officer. "Then I must ask you to show me your papers from Intourist. I will need your international driver's license, your *pamyatka avturista*, your Motoring Tourist's Memorandum and also your passports."

"Do you think we can make it to Novgorod before dark?" Lev asked the policeman in an accent that sounded more like Jose Ferrer playing Toulouse-Lautrec than an East Coast American on a cultural tour of the Soviet Union.

"You have arrangements to stay in Novgorod?" the policeman asked. His companion had completed his circuit of the car and now came to join him, his thumbs tucked into his belt. The first policeman's hand was still held out for Yakov's papers.

Lev said, "Do you like Adidas shoes?" and beckoned the policemen forward.

The word "Adidas" acted on both men instantly. They stepped forward, smiling, toward the car and Lev lifted his 8-mm T-T automatic and shot them both, very loudly and very accurately, between the eyes. In the space of two seconds, red spots appeared as if by magic in the center of each of their two pale foreheads and they fell over backward onto the road, their legs flopping heavily into the air.

"*Go,*" said Lev, slapping Yakov's shoulder. Yakov crashed the Volga into second and they howled away from the side of the highway, leaving four black snakes of rubber behind them and two sprawled bodies. Lev fired at the police car in a wild attempt to hit the gas tank but all he succeeded in doing was puncturing the rear bodywork and smashing one of the side windows.

"Now we're going to have to go at top speed," said Lev happily. Michael was beginning to understand that Lev actually enjoyed this mayhem and that he had been bored and testy until now only because the dull-witted Soviet police had believed (as they were supposed to) that the fugitives were heading east. Where was the chase? Where was the gunfire? Lev had lived on his nerves for so long that nothing could excite him but hair-raising danger; nothing could gratify his spirit but killing and burning and ferocious destruction.

Fifteen miles northwest of Kalinin, close to Mednoje, they came across a roadblock. They could see it ahead: four highway patrol cars drawn across the road, their headlights glaring. Lev glanced behind to confirm that four more cars had appeared out of the woods by the side of the highway to box them in from the rear.

Lev looked steadily at Michael and said, "Are you afraid, my friend? What do you prefer? Years of enforced work for the Soviet Union or a few moments of real danger?"

Michael said nothing, although he could feel that his face was drained of blood.

"I ask you this because we all could die," said Lev.

"They have the smell of us now, and of course our chances of escaping from the Soviet Union are almost nil. Well, let's say five percent. But I am not a fortune teller. We may be lucky, we may not."

Rufina said, "If you stop now, they will kill us all."

She said it with such earnestness and such conviction that John reached forward, tapped Lev on the shoulder and said, "Go on. Let's take the five percent."

Michael hesitated for a moment and then said with a dry mouth, "All right, let's go on."

"By George, Michael!" said John, suddenly excited.

Yakov twisted the Volga's wheel and flung the car off the highway into the woods. The suspension banged and crashed on the ground and all that Michael could see through the windshield was a jumble of trees, branches, fragments of late-afternoon sunlight, fractions of sky. The trees whipped at the car as if they wanted to catch it and punish its occupants, but Yakov drove like an angel, drove like a bird, so that the car slithered and roared between the trees, flew across gullies, bounced over rocks. Michael had the breath knocked out of him and his hand bruised against the old-fashioned, curved-metal door handle, but Rufina was clinging to him tightly and for a moment that was all he cared about.

John said, "Christ!" and that was the first time Michael had ever heard him take the Lord's name in vain.

Yakov steered the Volga along the precipitous edge of a long gully that overhung a tributary of the Tverca river. Michael peered down into the shadows; he could just about make out the white splashes of foam seventy feet below. At times the Volga's tires seemed to explode against clods of earth, sending them tumbling down into the depths; but Yakov never once lost his control, never once lost his skill, and the next thing Michael knew, they were hurtling down through a long, dark avenue of pines, branches whistling and sizzling against the windows, the car's suspension walloping hard against protruding roots.

They slithered through a dank, muddy valley, then roared up the other side, smoke pouring out of the Volga's exhaust. At the very top of the hill, the back tires lost their

grip and the heavy car hesitated, groaned and began to slide
backward.

Yakov screamed something in Russian that Lev didn't even
have to translate. He rammed the car into first gear, gunned
the engine until it was screaming as loudly as he was, then
popped out the clutch so that the Volga bounded forward as
if it had been hit up the backside by a steam engine. The car
stalled and Yakov had to restart it, but he had got it over the
hilltop. Lev silently crossed himself and said, "Mother of
God."

Now they curved to the west, back toward the highway.
They made slow progress through a boggy field of long grass
and pink swamp-mallow flowers, spattering their windows
with black mud; but then they drove faster across a dry,
diagonal slope of grass that ascended gradually toward the
main Leningrad highway. Soon, through the trees, they could
see trucks and cars running parallel to them, their parking
lights already glowing. They had avoided the roadblock completely and Lev said as he lit up a *papirosi*, "They will still
be searching those woods at Christmas."

Yakov jammed his foot down even though they were now
driving across a slithery field of graded pebbles. The Volga
hurtled toward the highway at nearly eighty miles an hour,
ran up the side of the concrete pavement and catapulted onto
the road with a jarring screech and a shower of sparks. Yakov
almost lost control of the car as it skidded across the highway
but he managed to wrestle it around just as the tires scrabbled
against the median strip. Then they were roaring northeast
again, toward Leningrad, without lights, under a sky that was
still pale and bright but strangely gave little illumination to
the land that lay beneath it.

"They will catch us, you know," said Rufina with unusually passive certainty.

"They haven't caught us yet," Lev retorted. "And as far
as I'm concerned, that's all that matters."

Yakov's energy appeared to be limitless. Sustained by cigarettes and vodka, he drove at top speed into the night, saying
nothing, his eyes fixed somewhere up ahead on a road that
only he could discern. Michael was exhausted; his eyes felt as
if they had been rubbed with fine-grain sand, but for hours he

couldn't sleep. John occasionally nodded off, yelped and opened his eyes again. Rufina remained sitting between them, close, warm, fearful. They stopped a few times to pee by the side of the road and those were the only times they heard the hush of rural Russia, the singing of summer crickets, the wind blowing through the grass.

It was a mad adventure. Michael was certain they were doomed, that they would never be able to pass through Leningrad and that even if they did, they would never be able to escape across the Finnish border.

He never knew which route they took. Yakov drove without consulting any of his passengers, not even Lev. Sometime in the small hours of the morning they must have stopped for *benzin* because Michael remembered lights, people talking in low voices and the sharp smell of low-grade gasoline. He opened his eyes once and saw a sign that said Pelusna but he had no idea of where that was and so he went back to sleep.

They drove through Leningrad at dawn: quietly and slowly, using back streets, approaching Litenyiy Prospekt along Saltikova-Schedrina Ulitsa, and then, once they had crossed the broad, gray expanse of the Neva with the sharp, gilded spire of the Peter and Paul Cathedral shining at them from the west, driving at less than twenty-five miles an hour up Lyesnoy Prospekt. Lev laconically jerked a thumb as they passed under a railroad bridge. "That's the line to Finland. It leads straight into the Finland station."

Michael said, "Why haven't they caught us yet? They must have a description by now."

Lev shook a last cigarette from his packet of *papirosi*. "My guess is that they don't want to catch us. They want to watch us, see which way we go, what we're up to. Maybe they think we're going to lead them to somebody bigger."

John rubbed his stubbly chin. "Perhaps that was why they kidnapped me in the first place, to flush you people out."

Lev laughed abruptly. "We can never be 'flushed out,' as you put it. This is because we are not an organization in the conventional sense. So, yes, they may catch some of us and kill us, but they will never be able to flush us out. How can you flush out something that is inside your soul, just as we are deep inside the soul of every country in which we work?"

They were less than an hour from the Finnish border, driving at almost eighty miles an hour when they saw the first helicopter. It came from the east, probably from the helicopter base at Vsevolosk, traveling low and fast. It overtook them and then circled around to the northwest as if it were waiting for them. Soon after, another helicopter appeared from the same direction, and then a third from the southeast, from Leningrad. The three helicopters formed a triangle between them and followed the Volga-22 along the highway, keeping four or five hundred yards distant but obviously tracking and watching.

"What do we do now?" asked Michael tightly.

"We keep going," said Lev. "I was right, you see; they left us alone after we managed to avoid that roadblock because they wanted to see where we were going. They probably had a succession of unmarked cars following us all the way through Leningrad and all the way out here. Except that here, of course, we are going far too fast for anybody to follow us without arousing our suspicions."

"They could hardly arouse our suspicions any less with those helicopters," John remarked.

"Ah, you miss the point, Mr. Bishop," Lev explained. "They are not concerned about our knowing they are there; they are simply concerned that if we do, we might retaliate in the same way we have from the beginning. That is why they are keeping well out of our way. They are going to have to explain this affair to the KGB and when they do, they would obviously prefer not to have to account for more dead bodies and burned-out police cars than they can possibly help."

"They will stop us though," said Rufina emphatically.

"They will try," said Lev.

They drove through Vyborg and the helicopters clattered after them, still keeping their distance. Then they turned west along the windswept road that runs north of the ragged inlet called Vyborgski Zaliv, on the last stretch of their journey before they reached the border with Finland. Michael, in spite of his anxiety, in spite of his tension, kept nodding off and dreaming that he was hurtling through strange black woods and whispering in unfamiliar streets to hooded strangers.

"You see," said Lev in some other existence, "any event

that takes place in the Soviet Union always generates for some unfortunate official a strangling snake pit of red tape. That is why so much of Soviet life takes place 'under the counter.' Policemen, highway patrolmen, court clerks, they will do anything to avoid paperwork.''

Michael woke up. Rufina had touched his hand. Lev said, ''We have only a few minutes now before we reach the border.''

Michael squinted up at the sky. The three helicopters were still there, closer now so that he could see their pilots and the white of their helmets.

Rufina said, ''We will never be able to get across the border. There are too many guards.''

''Frightened?'' smiled Lev. ''You can always disembark here if you want to and tell your masters that you were unwillingly kidnapped. Which of course you were.''

Rufina glanced away. For some reason—whether she genuinely wanted to escape from the Soviet Union or whether she considered it her duty to stay with the fugitives as long as possible so she could discover more about Lamprey—she stayed silent. Michael looked at her but her expression gave nothing away. High, placid cheekbones, eyes as impenetrable as ink.

They were in sight of the border post now; Michael could see the concrete buildings, and the barriers across the highway. On either side of the road there were thick stands of fir, the kind of trees in which wolves prowled in Russian fairy tales. Yakov slowed the car down to fifty, then to forty, then almost to a crawl. The helicopters had been forced by the height of the trees to remain high above them in the gray morning sky, and for a moment they sped obliviously on toward the frontier, not realizing that the Volga was now far behind.

Lev said, ''There it is, the marker,'' and for the first time, Michael understood the extraordinary planning and organization that had gone into their escape, the careful understanding of the Soviet police and of how they would react. A single white splash marked one of the firs on the opposite side of the road. Yakov swung left across the highway and plunged the Volga into the trees, along an improvised track that once must have been used by woodcutters. Now Yakov pushed his foot down hard on the accelerator and the battered car hurtled through the woods, out of sight of the helicopters, occasionally knocking loudly against tree trunks, skidding on banks of moss and fir cones, heading southeast, away from the border but directly toward the Russian coast of the Gulf of Finland.

They emerged into open countryside, into balding grasslands strewn with large gray boulders. There was no sign of the helicopters, no sign of any pursuit. Yakov drove like a madman; they were bounced and jostled and several times Michael hit his head on the roof. Then as they were about to plunge into another stretch of forest, the helicopters appeared behind them, widely spread out, traveling fast.

Lev wound down the Volga's window and tussled his AKM out from between the front seats. He leaned out as far as he could and fired a wild burst up at the leading helicopter, which veered away from the Volga but quickly returned as Lev struggled back inside the car.

"Bistra!" he yelled at Yakov.

In the next second, a shower of bullets rattled across the grasslands all around them, sending up clods of dirt and chips of rock. One bullet banged through the roof of the car and buried itself in the headrest of Yakov's seat in a blizzard of plastic and foam.

Then they were back in the woods again and Yakov veered sharply left so the helicopters wouldn't be able to fire blind into the trees and hit them on their original course. None of them spoke; they were too winded and tense, and nobody wanted to interrupt Yakov's manic concentration.

At last, after a bruising, jolting half-mile, they reached the rocky shore of the Gulf of Finland. Michael could see the surf breaking on the gray granite beach, the distant reaches of the Suomenlahti Finskij Zaliv, and two large yachts bending toward the strong west wind.

The three Soviet helicopters came roaring up from behind to overtake them and then circle around over the sea to attack them from the front.

"Where are they?" Lev demanded. "They promised they'd be here!"

"Who promised?" Michael wanted to know.

But Lev didn't have time to answer. One of the helicopters came clattering overhead, hovered, and suddenly an amplified voice boomed at them: *"Americans! You have no chance of escape! Abandon your car! Step out with your hands above your heads and you will be spared!"*

Lev tugged out the second AKM and hefted it over to Michael. "When I give you the word, jump out of the car and let that helicopter have it. No hesitation. Full automatic fire; you know how."

John said, "This is absurd."

"Of course it's absurd!" Lev roared at him, the veins in his neck swelling in anger. "Now shut up and let your friend do what he has to."

Michael, dry-mouthed, clicked the AKM's lever to automatic. Then, before he was ready, Lev had opened the door of the car and rolled out, over and over, his gun huddled against his chest.

"Go!" shouted Rufina, and Michael yanked open his door and rolled out too. A sharp rock hit him in the kneecap and he yelled out in pain; but then suddenly he was on his feet, his hair standing on end in the buffeting down-draft from the helicopter's rotors, and firing his AKM.

He was conscious of nothing but the noise of the helicopter and the jumping, chattering gun. He wasn't even aiming; it was all he could do to hold the AKM steady. But then the helicopter suddenly lurched to the left, staggered drunkenly and exploded in a hot and silent ball of orange flame. He watched in dread and astonishment as it whirled around and around with a fierce, crackling noise and nose-dived into the sea. Spray rose up like a fountain, then gradually settled.

Lev screamed, "Your first kill! By God, you'll make a fighter yet! Your first kill!"

But now the other two helicopters were circling around toward them and it was obvious that they were not prepared to take the risk of negotiating. Michael heard the rapid *brrrp brrrp* of four-barreled, 12.7-mm machine guns, and a stream of bullets hosed across the beach and up the rocky shore, suddenly blinding him with dust and dirt and flying fragments of granite. He fired back but knew he had missed. The helicopters roared overhead and climbed above the woods to attack again.

It was then that "they" appeared, the people for whom Lev had been waiting. They came out of the glare of the sea and the sky in two twin-engined Bell UH-IN helicopters, advanced versions of the famous Hueys that had served with such success in Viet Nam. They were painted olive drab without markings, and they came in extremely fast, almost at sea level. Michael saw smoke blurting from their open cabin doors, saw their machine guns, but he heard nothing; the morning was too windy. The next thing he knew, however, was that the two Russian helicopters were lurching away, one of them shedding pieces of fuselage, the other already on fire.

The burning helicopter disappeared behind the trees that lined the shore. There was a distant bang and a black cloud of oily smoke roiled up into the sky. The second helicopter limped and burped away to the east, rising and falling as if its controls had been shot away.

The two UH-INs waltzed around the beach looking for a clear place to land, then noisily settled down.

Michael said to Lev, "Who are they?"

"Friends," said Lev as John and Rufina climbed out of the car. "That is all you have to know. Come on; we must be quick."

Michael took Rufina's arm and began to stumble toward the nearer of the two helicopters, which was silhouetted against the sparkling sea, its rotors still slowly turning. Rufina said, "Yakov? Is Yakov coming?"

They turned around. Lev was leaning against the Volga, staring into the driver's window. Michael whispered, "Oh, no," and ran back across the rocky shore toward the car. Lev came forward and intercepted him, grasping his arm.

"Hurry," he said.

"But Yakov?"

"He knew what the risks were, just as we all do. He has served us well."

Michael twisted free from Lev's grip and walked slowly toward the car. One 12.7-mm bullet had pierced the car's windshield without even smashing it, leaving nothing but a small round hole. There was a matching hole in Yakov's shirt, stained with blood that was already black.

"A lucky shot, huh?" asked Lev.

Michael said nothing but turned away. He was beginning to understand that his experiences here in Russia had already aged him, quickly and remarkably. He was beginning to understand why Lev was so cynical. He took Rufina's hand, not gently but simply because he had to, and led her down the boulder-jagged shore to the waiting helicopters.

John said, "Michael?"

But Michael knew that he had outgrown John, outgrown toys, outgrown everything that had ever happened to him before. He made his way down the beach with his head lowered and wouldn't speak, although he had learned at last what courage really was, why men and women risk their lives for the countries they live in, and why people cry when anthems are played, as they always should.

NINETEEN

Golovanov said, "I should like a drink, please, Inge."

Inge was standing by the window, her arms folded over her breasts, staring out at the garden. She had changed into a white short-sleeved blouse and a tight pair of black-leather trousers; with her white-blonde hair braided into two loops, she looked more Germanic than ever.

"You know what the rule is," she said. "You may drink when you decide to talk. Otherwise no drink, no food, nothing."

"You know I have nothing to say. How can I tell you anything? A marshal in the Soviet Army? I have dedicated my whole life to my country. I could not possibly betray her now."

"Perhaps this *is* the time to betray her," Inge replied. "You have given her your very best years; why give her your soul as well?"

Golovanov made a face. "You, what do you know of souls?"

Inge walked slowly toward him across the white-tiled kitchen floor. Her stiletto heels clicked rhythmically. "My love, I know a great deal about souls. All women do. And wasn't it your own writer, Dostoyevsky, who said that once people ceased to believe in their immortal souls, every living force in the world would dry up, including love?"

263

"Yes, he said that."

Inge leaned forward and kissed Golovanov on the forehead. A cool kiss like being touched by ice.

"What lovers we have been," she said, "and still might be."

Golovanov accepted her kiss but didn't reply. He was handcuffed with his arms behind his back to a heavy kitchen chair. He knew that he had been taken much farther west than Mariental, where his kidnappers had first imprisoned him, but he had no idea of where. They had driven him here in a windowless van and all he had seen of the house in which he was imprisoned was the hallway and this modern, white-tiled kitchen. At the far end of the kitchen there was a window overlooking a red-and-white paved yard and beyond that, a wooden fence. On the horizon there was a row of poplars swaying in the warm afternoon wind, but they were all that Golovanov could see and they might have been anywhere, from Minden to Münster.

Inge said, "I don't want to cause you any pain but you must talk to me soon or my friends will insist that I do something more positive."

"You should shoot me," said Golovanov gruffly.

"Perhaps I should," she replied, stroking his shoulders. He flinched his head away from her; she was beginning to irritate and upset him, and he was feeling desperately thirsty. "But if I shoot you, you will not be able to tell me anything, will you? And that is the only reason you are here. To talk to us, to tell us what you know."

"Don't play with me, Inge," Golovanov told her.

She smiled. "I shall do what I like. Do you remember my telling you about my mother? About what a dancer she was, how she could have been the very best? But she was always too aloof; her dance instructors would shout at her to dance an entrechat this way or that way but she always said, 'No, no, no, my way is the best way.' So she never became a legendary dancer even though she was far better than Krista Müller or Hedwig Brandt. I am the same. I will never do anything but what I like, and that is why you should talk to me, my dearest Timofey, because I will do to you whatever amuses me and it will hurt you more than you can even begin to imagine.

You were in the war, weren't you? You saw men hurt. How
did you feel about it? Pleased, it wouldn't surprise me, that it
wasn't you. Well, now it *is* you; now it's your turn, and you
should be very frightened.''

Golovanov tried to smile. "Obviously," he said, "I can
tell you nothing.''

"In my life, nothing is obvious," said Inge. She stared at
him for a long time, saying nothing, and he found the coldness and paleness of her eyes disconcerting, as if she were an
android, without emotions and without a conscience. He was
frightened, there was no question about that. And she was
right: it was one thing to watch other men screaming in pain;
it was one thing to see your friend's skull blown apart or
watch him trying to heap his intestines back into his gaping
stomach. He had seen all those things and turned away. But it
was quite different to know that you were going to suffer that
agony yourself.

Inge caressed Golovanov's cheek, outlined the curves of
his ears. Then, with one hand, she began to unbutton her
blouse, tugging it loose from the waistband of her black-
leather trousers. One breast was bared, then the other.
Golovanov watched her fixedly, licking his lips from time to
time because he was so thirsty.

"Do you think there should be music?" Inge asked him.

Golovanov shook his head. "I don't know what you're
going to do to me, but do it, do it, don't keep me waiting.''

She unfastened the cuffs of her blouse and then took it off,
hanging it on a hook next to the aprons. Golovanov thought
that she looked extraordinary, like a woman out of a maso-
chist's wildest fantasy. Huge milk-white breasts, gleaming black-
leather trousers, high, spiky heels, and an expression on her
face that could have frozen a river.

"You have to think, always, of what will frighten people
the most," she said. "I have been thinking about you for a
long time.''

"My child, nothing frightens me, not anymore.''

Inge smiled faintly. Then she knelt down and opened one
of the kitchen cupboards. Golovanov looked at the swelling
curves of her bottom beneath the shining black leather, at the
white, wide-shouldered triangle of her back. He thought: even

if she kills me, I will go to whatever purgatory is reserved for Communists and soldiers with her perfume still in my nostrils, the smell of leather, sex and Cartier cologne.

From the cupboard Inge took the motor of a Moulinex blender. Then she searched through one of the drawers and produced other pieces, an orange-plastic collar, a cast-iron screw, and fitted them together.

"What are you going to do?" joked Golovanov. "Blend me into tomato juice? Perhaps if you gave me a glass of vodka first, I could be a Bloody Mary."

Inge finished assembling the blender and plugged it in. She didn't smile. "I'm surprised that you can laugh," she said. She held up the Moulinex and Golovanov saw that she had put together the pieces that made it into a meat grinder. He stared at her and she stared back. The air between them almost crackled.

"Not my hands," he said in a hoarse whisper.

"I wasn't thinking of your hands," she said.

"You had better kill me," he told her.

She shook her head. "I have to have some answers to my questions first."

Golovanov swallowed dryly. "You know that this kind of torture is in direct contravention of the United Nations Declaration of nineteen seventy-five."

"Is that what they tell you when you visit Lubianka?"

Golovanov said nothing. Inge stepped forward until she was standing over him and their knees were touching. Black leather against uniform khaki. He closed his eyes.

While his eyes were closed, she leaned toward him and with her hands pressed her breasts against his face. Her stiffened nipples were pushed against his eyelids, against his cheeks, and brushed his lips. Then she leaned forward more heavily and almost suffocated him in the soft, perfumed depths of her cleavage. He felt her hand unbuttoning his trousers; he felt her fingers prize his penis free and stroke it over and over until it hardened.

"Now," she whispered, drawing back, "all you have to do is tell me why the Soviet Army is still on full alert and what you plan to do."

"You know that I can tell you nothing," Golovanov repeated without opening his eyes.

"But, Timofey, my darling, you must. . . ."

Abruptly he opened his eyes. Inge was gripping his erect penis in one hand and the Moulinex meat grinder in the other. As he stared at her, she switched on the grinder and held it up so he could see the spiral screw turning around and around inside it and the rotating blades that would shred anything caught in the grinder into raw mincemeat.

"You're bluffing," he told her in a tight voice.

Inge shook her head and brought the meat grinder closer to the crimson crest of Golovanov's erection. "Timofey, you should know me by now. Have I ever deceived you, even once?"

The Moulinex was whirring loudly, so loudly that Golovanov could hardly think. If I tell her about Operation *Byliny*, that will be treachery, treason, and the utter betrayal of everything for which my father suffered and died, as well as disgrace to my whole career in the army. My father endured, even when his hands were smashed; why shouldn't I? Yet the thought of being emasculated, the thought of having his manhood ground off—that was more than he could bear. To die as a man was one thing; to die as a neutered eunuch was something else altogether. He had seen men in battle with their sexual organs torn away, bleeding to death; there had been such a terrible indignity about their fate, such a hideous hopelessness

"I can't tell you anything," Golovanov heard himself repeating. Sweat was sliding down the back of his shirt and he knew he was shaking like a man in a fever.

Inge held the grinder closer. He could feel the draft of its motor against his bare skin. "Perhaps I should give you a count of five," she told him. "Five more seconds of manhood, then castration. Do you think that would be a good idea?"

"Inge!" he shouted at her.

She shook her head again and lowered the meat grinder so close that the head of Golovanov's penis disappeared inside the white-plastic funnel. His erection had shrunk now, as if he had been swimming in a cold sea. The cold sea was his own terror, his own confusion, and it was a sea in which even stronger and more determined men than he had drowned.

"Five," Inge counted.

"*Inge!*" Golovanov shouted again. "I can tell you nothing! I know nothing! I am a marshal in the Soviet Army! I am forbidden to tell you anything at all!"

"Four," said Inge. "You are small now, you see, Timofey. You will be ground up in one good turn of the screw. What do you think it will be like to watch it wriggle out the other end as hamburger meat? Do you think that will be frightening? And exciting too! Why do you think I took off my blouse? There will be plenty of blood; I want to feel it on my bare skin!"

"This is nonsense," Golovanov told her, trying to be authoritative. "What kind of torture is this, with a meat grinder? I have never seen anything so absurd in my whole life! Now turn it off and let's talk some sense!"

"Three," said Inge.

Golovanov said nothing. Inge said, "Two."

"Inge, listen to me. You know that I am a very powerful man. Very wealthy. If you behave yourself, I will show you my appreciation. I will give you money, a car perhaps, if you want it. A fur coat. But let us for a moment talk sense."

Inge slowly shook her head, smiling all the time. "Russians never talk sense, Timofey, you know that. They are the masters of double-talk. I don't want sense. I simply want the truth."

"Inge—"

But then Inge said, "One," and lowered the meat grinder just a little more so that Golovanov suddenly felt the edges of the rotating screw against the sensitive flesh of his flaccid penis.

"This is your last chance," Inge told him. Her voice was so neutral and serious that the sweat on Golovanov's back was chilled, as if somebody had suddenly opened a door behind him. He knew without question that if he didn't agree to tell her about Operation *Byliny*, he would never again be able to call himself a man.

"Well," said Inge. "*Es tut mir leid.* We had some good

times together, you and I, Timofey, and they will be times
that can never happen again.''

She reached out and stroked his forehead, and when she
did that, he was completely convinced both logically and
emotionally that she would do it, that she would grind his
genitals up and kiss him and caress him while she did so. He
said, *"Stop!"* in the roughest of whispers, and she frowned at
him kindly and said, ''Are you sure? Do you really want me
to?''

''Stop,'' he said again, a word of aspirate shame.

''First, tell me,'' she insisted without taking the Moulinex
away.

''It is . . . an arrangement—'' he said, although he could
scarcely believe that the sound he heard was his own voice.
Was that really him, Marshal T. K. Golovanov, telling this
half-naked woman all about Operation *Byliny* in some unfamiliar kitchen in West Germany? It didn't seem real, and
perhaps that was how he was able to do it. He must have been
dreaming. He must have drunk too much *moskovskaya*. That
was it, he was drunk. He was spending the evening with
Commander Zhulikov and he had drunk too much vodka.

But Inge said, ''Tell me,'' and when he opened his eyes
again, she was still there and the meat grinder was still poised
over his penis.

''There has been an arrangement made,'' he said. ''An
arrangement.''

''What arrangement? By whom?''

''Between the Soviet Union and the United States, with the
active participation of the United Kingdom.''

''Tell me. Quick, before I get impatient.''

''It was done with the best of intentions. You must understand that. It has probably saved the world from nuclear war.
We were right on the brink, you know. Right on the edge.
The intolerable pressures that had built up over the years
were too much for the old system. The world was like an
antiquated steam boiler about to burst open its casing.''

Inge said nothing but switched off the meat grinder. In the
silence that followed, Golovanov spoke slowly and dully, like
a tired scholar reciting his history books for the umpteenth
time.

"It was intolerable for the Soviet Union to live with American cruise missiles on the same continental soil. The threat was too great, the danger too close. It gave those old men in the Kremlin a terrible black neurosis, a persecution complex. Imagine if you lived in a house and every time you opened the door, there was a hostile stranger waiting for you outside in your garden with a loaded gun. You would naturally keep a gun yourself, to protect yourself from whatever he might do, but your gun would never diminish your fear. It is hard for those in the West to understand the historical anxiety that causes the Russian people to be so belligerent. But if you had been standing beside me at Stalingrad, you would know. The Germans invaded us; the Germans destroyed our homes and slaughtered us in thousands. The war for us was more terrible than you can ever imagine."

Inge said insistently, "I want to know about this arrangement."

"Very well, you shall," agreed Golovanov. "Just as the Kremlin feels neurotic about American forces on European soil, so the White House feels neurotic about Communist insurgents in Central America. It was therefore suggested two or maybe three years ago at a series of secret meetings that the world should be redivided, that Communist expansionism in the Americas should stop in return for which all British and American forces should be withdrawn from Western Europe."

"I don't understand," said Inge.

"It's really very simple," Golovanov told her. "The Soviet Union is to be allowed to take over administrative control of West Germany, Scandinavia, Holland, Belgium, France and parts of Austria without any opposition from British or American forces. In return, Communist guerrillas are to withdraw from Central America and cease their insurgent activities in the Third World; Fidel Castro is to resign and hold free elections; and the Soviet Army is to withdraw over a nine-month period from Afghanistan. Further containment of both capitalism and Communism will be arranged later, once the initial stages of the operation have been successfully completed. But the basic principle is that there should be no Americans in Europe and no Russians in America. The map of the world will be redrawn."

Inge was silent. She set the meat grinder on the floor and stood up. Unconsciously she covered her bare breasts with her hands.

Golovanov said, "Would you . . . ?" and nodded toward his exposed penis. Inge hesitated for a moment and then buttoned him up as if he were an aging invalid.

"It is all for the best, you see," Golovanov told her. "It will end for all time the fear in which young people like you have grown up. At last the world will be stable."

"And oppressed," Inge replied flatly. "Are you planning to administer Germany in the same way you administer Estonia? No national flags allowed, the national language forbidden, the very roots of culture torn out?"

Golovanov smiled. "You have such fervor. You are so cold and yet you have such fervor."

Inge said, "When does this operation begin?"

"It has begun already. At least, all the preliminary preparations have been completed."

"What is its code name?"

"*Byliny.*"

"And who knows about the details of the political agreement? Who negotiated it for the Soviet Union?"

"Well, there were several negotiators," said Golovanov. "We had a team of five. The leader was Marshal Tolubko. On the American side there were six or seven negotiators, I believe, including the Deputy Secretary of State and the Under Secretary of Defense. The British sent three."

Inge said, "Where did these negotiations take place? If they were so high-powered, why did we not get to hear of them?"

Golovanov made a face. "Why you did not get to hear of them, I cannot say. You must look to your own efficiency for that. But I know they were carried out secretly in Copenhagen. Even our own security people were kept in the dark. Even now, even though our army is ready to occupy Western Europe, only the most senior officers are aware of what is happening, and even they believe that we will be taking West Germany only. They do not yet know that we will stop only when we have reached the sea."

Inge walked across the kitchen and picked up the telephone. She did not put her blouse back on yet; that would have been a signal to Golovanov that he was no longer under threat of torture. She said quickly, "The old bear has come out with some kind of story. If it is true, Fredrik must know about it at once. No, I have no verification."

She listened for a moment and then said, "Who do we have in Copenhagen? Do you have a number? All right, very good."

Inge hung up the phone and stood looking at Golovanov without saying anything.

"May I have a drink now?" he asked her.

"You must tell me more. You must tell me when the Soviet Army intends to cross the frontier."

"I have told you all I know. And you must realize that much of what I have told you could be changed now that you have abducted me. Certainly the *Stavka* will have changed the date."

Inge drew up a kitchen chair and straddled it. "You must tell me more. Very much more."

Golovanov shook his head.

"Do you want the meat grinder again?"

He shook his head. His throat was crowded with emotion so that he could scarcely speak. "I want only to die with whatever honor is remaining to me."

Inge touched his cheek. "My poor love," she said.

Tears rolled down Golovanov's face and dropped to his shirt.

"Kill me," he begged.

"No," she whispered. "Never."

TWENTY

Morton Lock was about to leave his office for a lunch appointment with the Secretary of the Army when his intercom flashed. He pressed the switch and said, "I've gone to lunch. I'm already drinking my soup."

The flat Harvard tones of his assistant, Frank Jones, said, "It's Mr. Lewis, sir, from *The Washington Post*."

"In that case, not only am I having lunch, I'm having lunch in Hawaii."

"He's not on the telephone, sir. He's here in person."

Morton breathed, "Damn it," in exasperation. The trouble was, it had always been the President's policy that his administration should be "warm and constructive" to the media, from the White House press office right down to the Minority Business Development Agency. If Cal Lewis had taken it upon himself to visit Morton in person, there was no way Morton could decline to talk to him, not without incurring the President's annoyance, which could be considerable for all his public talk of fair play and tolerance and Christian forgiveness.

Frank Jones said, "Mr. Lewis says he's pretty sure you'll want to talk to him, sir."

"Oh, really?"

"He says it's something to do with *Gringo*, whatever that means."

273

Morton frowned at the intercom as if it had unexpectedly relayed a message from another planet. "What does he know about *Gringo*?" he demanded.

"That's what he's come here to talk to you about, sir." He could hear Frank confirming it with Cal Lewis out in the reception area.

"Very well," said Morton. "You'd better show him in. And call the Montpellier; tell them I'm going to be late."

"Yes, sir."

Cal Lewis appeared, smiling broadly. He was heavily built, fiftyish, with curly gray hair and a crumpled but expensive gray suit. "Good of you to see me, Morton," he said, looking around unimpressed at Morton's wood-paneled office with its photographs of Florida sunsets. Morton had always fancied himself a photographer and all the prints were his. They betrayed an incurable taste for the exotic and the lurid, a visual and emotional obviousness that characterized more than one member of the President's administration.

"Have a seat," Morton offered. Still smiling, Cal Lewis sat down and crossed his legs. He smelled of cigars but he didn't ask if he could smoke.

"Where did you get to hear about *Gringo*?" asked Morton, coming straight to the point.

"Oh, here and there," said Cal. "You know, sources."

"Have you talked to Ken Maxwell?" Ken Maxwell was the White House press secretary.

Cal nodded. "Ken Maxwell was not at all helpful. In fact, Ken Maxwell denied any knowledge of *Gringo*. He asked me if it was a remake of *Pancho Villa*."

"So why come to me?"

"Because somebody knows about *Gringo*, and considering the kind of operation *Gringo* happens to be, that somebody would seem to me to be you."

Morton slowly and overprecisely rearranged the papers on his desk. He didn't look Cal Lewis in the eyes, not once, and Cal Lewis noticed it.

"It's very difficult for me to make any comment unless I know who told you about *Gringo* and how much you already know," said Morton without expression.

"I can't reveal sources," Cal told him. "All I can tell you

is that my information has come from somebody very reputable, somebody whose word is normally taken as reliable."

"If you're talking about a certain junior senator, he may not be as reputable as you think."

Cal kept on smiling. "I didn't say anything about a certain junior senator."

"I know that, but if you are." Morton paused and then demanded, still without raising his eyes, "Are you?"

Cal shrugged. "I guess if you know already, there's no harm in admitting it."

"Well, I thought so," said Morton. "Our security people have had a tag on this certain junior senator for some weeks now. He's been involved in some pretty unpleasant vice business as well as the leaking of highly classified information. You can take it from me that what he says is very rarely trustworthy."

"So *Gringo* isn't what he says it is?"

Morton brushed imaginary dust from his desk, nervously, fastidiously. "That depends on what he says it is."

"We're fencing here, Morton," said Cal.

"Of course we're fencing. You believe you have some important classified information, albeit from a dubious source, and you want to know whether it's true or not. Well, I don't have to tell you anything, I don't have to tell you if *Gringo* exists or not, or what it is, or even what it *isn't*. I am the President's National Security Adviser and my task is to protect the interests of this nation, not to comment on unreliable gossip. But I can't even begin to comment on any gossip at all unless I know what that gossip amounts to. It's up to you, Cal. You can tell me or not tell me. I don't give a damn which."

Cal Lewis said, "Supposing I run a 'What Is *Gringo?*' story . . . along with an editorial about the evasiveness of this administration on matters of national security?"

Morton replied, "Supposing you don't?"

"I hope that doesn't amount to some kind of threat?" Cal asked Morton gently.

"That's not a threat, that's a request," Morton told him.

"A polite request or a forceful request?"

"A *request*, damn it, that's all. Supposing you don't say

anything about *Gringo* to anybody. Do any of your staff know anything about it?''

Cal shook his head. ''I wanted to confirm it for myself before I started discussing it with anybody else. Contrary to what you seem to think, I do care about this country's security, just as much as you do.''

''But you care about your exclusive story first.''

''*Gringo*, from what I can gather, involves the withdrawal of some of our forces from West Germany. Now that's a big story. You can't very well ask me to sit on it. Come on, Morton, it affects the future of the world. The electorate has a right to know about it.''

''The electorate has a right to know squat,'' snapped Morton.

''Can I quote you on that?'' Cal asked him smoothly, still smiling.

Morton stood up, thrust his hands in his pockets and walked across the room to admire ''Dawn Over the Doral, 1977.'' More quietly he said, ''Let me tell you this, Cal; what you've heard about *Gringo* is partly true but not entirely true. It's a theory rather than an actual exercise. A way of rearranging the military budget that may or may not be brought into operation. We won't really have any firm news about it until the Secretary of Defense presents his budget next November. So what I'm suggesting is, why don't you wait until then?''

Cal Lewis thought for a moment or two, then suddenly stood up and extended his hand. ''Thank you for your time,'' he said.

''We're agreed, then?'' asked Morton.

''No, sir,'' said Cal. ''In Monday's *Post* I'm going to run a substantial piece about *Gringo*, as much as I can dig up, and I'm going to run a publisher's comment alongside it. I'm going to say that the manner in which this whole issue has been kept under wraps is further incontrovertible evidence of the way in which this administration is becoming increasingly dictatorial.''

''Cal—'' Morton began but Cal lifted both hands.

''Don't even begin to say it, Morton. That's what I'm going to do. That's unless you feel the urge to issue a full statement about *Gringo* right now.''

Morton hesitated and then said, ''Okay, Cal, you run what

you want to. It's a free country. But don't blame me if this boomerangs on you. You can't start picking up hot potatoes without burning your fingers."

Cal clapped Morton's shoulder. "Do they send you people to a special school to learn how to mix metaphors?"

After Cal had gone, Morton called Frank Jones and asked to have his limousine brought around to the front of the building. Then he picked up his private line and dialed the Federal Bureau of Investigation on 9th Street. When the switchboard answered, he said, "Ten seventy-five," and waited until the extension was picked up.

"D'Annunzio," said a harsh voice like cold water washing over gravel.

"Ernest?" asked Morton. "It's Morton Lock."

"Good-morning," said D'Annunzio. "How are your shin splints today?"

Morton wasted no time on amenities.

"Ernest, we have a serious difficulty with the matter in hand. Yes. It seems that Daniels spoke to Cal Lewis sometime this week about our business in Europe. That's right. Well, Lewis was around here a few minutes ago and he's threatening to run a major news story about it. He says Monday. Yes. But I'm concerned that he's going to go straight back to his office and discuss it with his editorial staff. No, they don't know yet; at least he says they don't. Well, no guarantees, of course."

D'Annunzio said, "Leave it to me, Morton. I'll get Sienkiewicz on it right away."

"Will you do that? And what are you doing about tracking down Daniels? If he's been talking to Cal Lewis, he could have been talking to every damned newspaper and television outfit in America."

D'Annunzio said, "We've made a little progress in that direction. One of our people has located Esther Modena's mother in Indianapolis, and we've put a tap on her phone. So far she's had three calls from Miss Modena in two days, none of them long enough to trace. But don't worry, if she's calling Mom that frequently, we'll get her pretty soon."

"I want Daniels as a matter of total urgency. You know that."

"Yes, sir, I know that. We won't let you down. It's not in our nature."

Morton put down the phone. Almost immediately the intercom buzzed to tell him that his car was waiting. He straightened his necktie and brushed the dandruff off the shoulders of his dark suit. He trusted Ernest D'Annunzio as far as he trusted anybody. In the past, D'Annunzio had arranged for the systemizing of both Jimmy Hoffa and Karen Silkwood. Perhaps his only notable failure had been Ralph Nader during the Corvair days. Nader had changed an appointment and missed one of D'Annunzio's ambushes by a matter of minutes. But Cal Lewis shouldn't be any trouble. Cal Lewis was predictable, unwary and trusting.

And there was no question about it: this was no longer a world for the predictable, the unwary and the trusting.

During Saturday afternoon an extraordinary silence fell over London. Apart from a few private cars, the streets were almost deserted. There were no buses, no subways, no heavy trucks. Drivers and the maintenance staff of the London Regional Transport had walked out on strike at midnight on Friday; the two rail unions, ASLEF and the NUR, had called out their members two hours later. The National Union of Public Employees had withdrawn all but emergency services from hospitals, ambulance stations and fire houses. The giant Transport and General Workers' Union had called an official strike of drivers, loaders and service people.

The Defense Secretary, who had returned to his home in Cheyne Walk, Chelsea, for a bite of lunch and a quick bath, found it possible at three o'clock that afternoon to walk along the middle of the road on his way back to Westminster, without fear of being knocked over. All the way along the embankment, as far as he could see, there was no traffic whatever. It reminded him strangely of *The War of the Worlds* by H. G. Wells, which he had read as a boy. "It was curiously like Sunday in the City, with the closed shops, the houses locked up and the blinds drawn, the desertion, and the stillness." In fact, he was so struck by the feeling of already having been invaded, as London had been invaded by the Martians in *The War of the Worlds*, that he hurried along by the river, unhappy now that he had chosen to walk, hot and uncomfortable and feeling suddenly vulnerable in the bright May sunshine.

The Thames sparkled brightly beside him; on the far bank of the river, the Battersea Power Station stood with its four tall chimneys surrounded by scaffolding, halfway through its twenty-five-million-dollar conversion into a recreation center. On the pavement, a gaggle of scruffy pigeons strutted around a discarded McDonald's bag and pecked at a half-eaten cheeseburger.

The modern *Marie Celeste*, he thought, a city found abandoned, still littered with unfinished cheeseburgers.

It took him twenty minutes to get back to Whitehall. He had often walked before because he had always loved the river and because it was the only exercise he ever got, but today the walk seemed threatening and arduous. He stood over his desk when he arrived, his clean handkerchief pressed to his forehead to cool himself down, and kept his first visitor waiting for nearly ten minutes.

At last, however, Lieutenant-Colonel Lilley knocked on his door and said, "I'm sorry to barge in, sir, but General Fawkes did want me to speak to you as soon as you got in."

"Yes, yes, jolly good," said the Defense Secretary. "Do take a seat. I'm afraid I rather wore myself out walking back from Chelsea."

Colonel Lilley perched on the edge of a large leather armchair, balancing his folders on his bony knees. "We've been trying to keep all the essential services going, sir— power and sewage—but as you instructed, we haven't made any moves to take over road transport or mines. The situation with the fire services seems a little parlous at the moment but unless we get a real crisis, we'd really rather leave it as it is."

The Defense Secretary nodded. His orders today had been clear: the British Army should remain on full combat alert and as few soldiers as possible should be diverted to civilian activities. All British forces returning from Germany in Operation *Cornflower* were also to be kept in a state of combat readiness.

The Prime Minister had not been convinced of the need for the Defense Secretary to be so alarmist about the Soviet

Union; she would have preferred to keep the trains running and the docks open. But he was a favorite of hers and at this morning's meeting of the Inner Cabinet, he had spoken very persuasively in support of continued vigilance. At last she had agreed that the army could be kept up to the highest possible strength, at least until public services had deteriorated below "an acceptable level."

Of course there had been prolonged disagreement about what constituted "an acceptable level." The Home Secretary remarked that what was acceptable to the family of an unemployed docker in Hartlepool would completely horrify the family of a moderately successful stockbroker living in St. George's Hill, Weybridge. The Health Minister considered that matters would be out of hand "when we can no longer bury our dead and rats run freely along Pall Mall." Lord Westley had remarked, not entirely seriously, that life would become intolerable "when they no longer serve fresh crab sandwiches at Green's Champagne Bar."

Public opinion at large seemed to be that Britain would be finished if the taverns closed and television was blacked out.

Colonel Lilley said diffidently, "A couple of extra factors seem to have come up, sir. Well, three or four actually, and they all seem to bear out your suspicions that these strikes might have been deliberately orchestrated. I had a report this morning from some of our intelligence chaps in Belfast and it appears that both the IRA and the INLA are planning a huge bombing offensive in northern Ireland to coincide with the general strike on May thirtieth. Apart from that, CND is going to organize massive demonstrations at all active RAF stations and U.S. cruise-missile bases. The object seems to be to tie up the military as much as possible on nonmilitary duties."

The Defense Secretary listened intently to this, repeatedly smoothing back his hair. "What's your opinion, Colonel? Off the record? You had to deal with this kind of thing in Aden, didn't you?"

Colonel Lilley gave one of his famous self-deprecating smirks. "Difficult to interpret it exactly, sir. But it does seem to me that what the Russians *could* be doing is making sure we keep our side of the bargain. Even if we do change our minds about *Cornflower*, we won't be in much of a position to do anything about it if we're completely snarled up with industrial and political chaos, will we?"

"Or to dictate any revised terms," the Defense Secretary put in. "*Or* to ensure that all or any of the agreed-upon terms are properly complied with."

"Perhaps the Russians intend to vary the agreement, sir," said Colonel Lilley. "Unilaterally, I mean, without any discussion."

The Defense Secretary nodded. "I felt dishonest about thinking them, I must admit, but those were my thoughts too. If you ask me, the Russians probably plan to sweep through Europe flat-out, disregarding the safeguards and guarantees that were written into the agreement, like the preservation of ancient buildings and the taking of proper census statistics. Did you read that translation from *Pravda* yesterday? In spite of all our talks, in spite of everything we've given away, they *still* think of West Germany as another Third Reich, guilty of oppression and hostility and—what did they call it?—'incurable revanchism.' They believe that if they don't crush the West Germans first, the West Germans will roll in and crush them. They seriously believe it and no matter what you say, you can't persuade them otherwise. 'Remember Barbarossa!'—that's all they ever tell you. That's like saying, 'Remember Hastings,' and refusing to speak to the French."

Colonel Lilley was quiet for a moment and then remarked, "I must say, sir, that I didn't think I'd ever see the day."

The Defense Secretary closed his eyes for a moment to show that he understood. "I know how the general staff feels about this, Colonel. But one has to change with the times; one has to adapt oneself to completely new concepts of international security. The political tension in Europe is dangerously high, insanely high. The military balance is close to critical. At the same time, we're finding it far too expensive to keep up our commitments to NATO. All we could see ahead of us on our present path was nuclear confrontation, either sooner or later but inevitably. What is about to happen now will suddenly release that tension, and I think all of us will breathe more easily."

"All of us who remain on the Western side of the fence,"

said Colonel Lilley, trying without success not to sound impertinent or too aggrieved.

"Don't let the Iron Lady hear you say that, Colonel," said the Defense Secretary. "She's put her heart into this. The final solution for the nuclear problem. I've heard her practicing her speech for next week."

"Yes, sir," said Colonel Lilley.

The Defense Secretary said, "It's a victory speech, Colonel. And quite rightly so. She's managed to achieve in four years what most men never manage to achieve in their whole lifetime."

Colonel Lilley put his files together and straightened them. "My father was killed in action in Normandy, sir. So were quite a few of our family friends. It just rather appears to me that—"

The Defense Secretary silenced him with a sharp lift of his eyebrow. This was not the time for sentiment or for scoring easy political points. Outside the window, where the sun fell through the balustrades, making curved patterns like faces and candlesticks, London lay dusty and silent. Pigeons wheeled over an empty Trafalgar Square, where the fountains had been switched off to save power and water.

"Could you give General Fawkes my compliments?" asked the Defense Secretary. "Oh, and could you tell him something interesting?"

"Yes, sir?"

"I found out this afternoon that my Aunt Beatrice and he had the same nanny. At different times, of course."

Lieutenant-Colonel Lilley stood up, a jackdaw in army uniform. "Yes, sir, I'll tell him that. What a coincidence, sir."

At almost the same moment, in his gray-painted office in Bonn, the West German Chancellor received a scrambled telephone call from the Commander-in-Chief of the Bundeswehr, General Heinz Escher. The Chancellor was sitting at his desk with a white towel draped around his shoulders while he was being shaved by his personal barber. Apart from a hunting lodge in the Breisgau, which badly needed redecorating, being shaved by a barber was the only luxury he allowed himself.

General Escher's voice was choked and tense. "Herr Chancellor? I have just received unofficial intelligence that the Soviet Army is planning an imminent advance into the Federal Republic."

The Chancellor was silent for a moment. The razor scraped at his left cheek, cutting swaths of pink skin into the white shaving soap. "What does 'unofficial' mean?" he asked at last.

"The source was apparently the rebel intelligence network known as Lamprey," said General Escher. "A coded message was received about twenty minutes ago at Paderborn. It had all the necessary authenticating codes that the Lamprey usually use to identify themselves. It said simply that they have reliable information that the Soviet Army intends to advance into West Germany at any moment."

"Are we in touch with Lamprey?" the Chancellor wanted to know. "Can we contact them again, ask them more questions?"

"They say they will call again at sixteen hundred hours."

"What do our own intelligence people have to say?"

General Escher said, "They say they have no evidence to support Lamprey's claim, sir."

"Lamprey includes both Western and Communist agents, doesn't it, General?"

"So we are led to believe, sir."

"Then this intelligence could well have been sent to us by a Russian?"

"Yes, sir. I suppose so."

The Chancellor raised his chin so his barber could shave underneath it. He said nothing while the razor scraped its way around his Adam's apple. At last, however, he wiped his face with the towel and waved the barber away. "I want the Bundeswehr on full alert," he told General Escher. "This could be nothing more than a provocative piece of counterintelligence, or a plot by the opposition to make us look ridiculous. On the other hand, it could be true, and what with the British and the Americans moving their troops around like some ridiculous party game, this would be the worst possible time for us to have to face up to any kind of military confrontation."

He opened his desk and took out a bottle of Johnnie Walker. "When Lamprey calls back at sixteen hundred hours, I want to have them connected through to me. If for any reason they refuse to allow this, make sure they are asked where they acquired their information and how they can authenticate it."

He banged down the phone, then jabbed the button on his desk that called his private secretary. "Ella? I want the Soviet ambassador around here at once. I want General Oliver on the telephone. I want the Cabinet convened for an emergency meeting. I also want to speak to Brigadier Smith-Hartley. That will do for a start. Ask Marta for some coffee, and don't think of going home."

He sat for a while watching his barber clean and put away his razors and brushes. He didn't open his bottle of whiskey.

"Willi," he said at length, "if you were drinking in your favorite tavern with your friends and all of a sudden you were faced with a large and angry fellow who wanted to hit you on the nose, what would you think if you looked around to your friends for help and found that they had conveniently left you on your own?"

Willi was an old man. He looked up with eyes as black and glittering as a crow's. "Well, sir, I would think that my friends were cowards perhaps, or else I would think that they were quite pleased to see me beaten."

"Yes, Willi," said the Chancellor. "That is what I would think too."

David Daniels, about ten minutes later, was returning from the Safeway market just north of White Plains with two bags of groceries. He balanced one of the bags on his upraised knee as he fumbled his keys out of his coat pocket and opened the door of the apartment.

"Esther? It's only me."

He closed the door behind him and walked through to the kitchen, setting the bags on the Formica-topped table. "I got us a couple of Cornish rock hens," he called. "I thought they'd make us a good dinner tonight. And a bottle of Zinfandel too, how about that?"

He took out a bag of tomatoes, a head of iceberg lettuce

and a Sara Lee pecan pie. "It's good to cook at home for a change," he said. "I got so darn sick of eating in restaurants."

He searched through three or four kitchen drawers before he found the corkscrew. Then he opened the bottle of Zinfandel and collected two glasses from the cupboard over the sink. Carrying the glasses and the bottle in one hand, he walked through to the living room.

"Do you know something?" he said. "I haven't shopped in a supermarket in years. I felt like a—"

He stopped. A freezing shock went through him from the crown of his head to the soles of his feet, turning every one of his nerves into dry ice. The bottle fell, splashing wine. The glasses fell, snapping their stems. David found himself unable to move, as if his brain couldn't connect with any of his muscles.

Esther had been ritually slain. Her naked body was bound with wire, lying on the rug by the fireplace. She had been cut open from her breastbone down to her pubic hair, and her insides had been dragged out and arranged on the floor in a glistening anatomy display. Lungs, stomach, liver. David was horrified that he could recognize them. Two small bronze statuettes had been forced up between her legs; the agony of that alone must have been crucifying.

"Oh, God," was all he could manage to say. He turned around and walked with dragging feet back to the kitchen. He stood there shaking all over, trying to keep his sanity together. He knew they had killed her so horribly not to punish her, but to warn him. Whatever *Gringo* was, somebody wanted it kept deathly silent, and this was what would happen to anybody who showed an interest.

He looked at the shopping, at the salad that would never be made, at the Cornish rock hens that would never be eaten. All the time he had been walking up and down the aisles of the supermarket, feeling like a husband again, Esther had been tortured and bound up and then disemboweled. He had no doubt but that she had still been alive when they had cut her open. They had probably spread her insides around in front of her as she lay dying. He had seen photographs of that kind of killing when he was sitting on congressional committees on organized crime.

Deliberately he went to the sink and vomited. Then, with tears in his eyes, he drank a large glass of water, wiped his mouth and went to the telephone. He picked it up and dialed his own answering service at home in Connecticut. *"This is David Daniels . . . when you hear the tone, please leave your name and your number and I'll call you back as soon as I can. . . ."*

After the beep, David said, "I know you're listening. I've been here and I've seen what you've done to Esther. Let me tell you that you don't frighten me. You're animals, and I'm not frightened of animals. You can look for me wherever you like; you won't find me, not now. I'm going to disappear right off the face of the earth, but I'm going to make sure that everybody gets to know what you've done. Press, television, everybody. You're going to regret this. You're going to regret this so damned much. Because one day, my friends, I'm going to come after you, just the same way you came after Esther, and I'm going to spread your guts for public display. You hear me? I'm going to put you through hell!"

He was still shaking when he put down the receiver. He knew it was time to go. There was nothing he could do for Esther, they had butchered her too savagely. He couldn't even make her look as if she were at peace. He could only hope there really was a life after death and that she was enjoying it. The trouble was, he didn't believe there was, and as he went down in the elevator, he couldn't stop the tears that started to roll down his cheeks.

He was still wiping his eyes with his handkerchief when the elevator reached the lobby. He left the building as quickly as he could and walked north to the middle of town, leaving his car parked where it was. He crossed the street and walked east to Macy's. There were pay phones there, on the first floor, that nobody would be able to tap or trace. He realized as he walked that his life was going to be like this every day and every night from now on: talking to his friends from obscure telephones, staying in untraceable motels. His only hope was to break the story of *Gringo* in the media; and even then, he knew he would remain a target.

He went to the first pay phone and pushed in his coin. He dialed and as he waited for an answer, he glanced around apprehensively. He didn't even know who was after him. It could be that mild-looking man with the bald head trying on a pair of gloves that were still tied together or that black woman in the flowery dress and upswept glasses. He knew that if he were organizing a hit, he would choose the most unlikely killer imaginable.

The phone was answered. A suspicious-sounding voice said, "Yeah? Who is this?"

"Ray? This is David Daniels."

"Oh, well, hi, David. How are you doing?" Ray Molloy was the only CIA executive that David knew at all well. They had met in Paris three years ago during David's investigation into intelligence-service budgets, and when Ray had returned to Langley, Virginia, as senior finance officer, he and David had kept in touch. Occasional drinks together, one or two fishing trips and a couple of dinner parties.

David said, "I'm in trouble, Ray."

"Oh, really?"

"Well, I seem to have upset somebody heavy, that's all I can say."

"In connection with what?"

"Ray, I'm in trouble, that's all I can say. I don't even know for sure *why* I'm in trouble. I just want one favor."

"Boy, you *are* in trouble, aren't you?"

"Yes, Ray, I'm in trouble. Now, please, could you do this one thing for me? Do you remember we were talking a few months ago about those people in Canada, the ones who went across the border to hide from the FBI? That's right. Well, do you think you could tell me how to get in touch with them?"

"Well, that could be tricky. It might take some money too."

"Listen, I've got plenty of money. Just tell me how to get in touch."

"Okay, then. Hold on for a moment. I'll look it up in my notebook."

Tense, shivering, sweating, David waited while Ray went to check the number. What if Ray was in with the people who were looking for him? What if he was only making him hold on so they could get a trace on his number? He kept thinking about Esther, about the way they had ripped her open, and he knew without any doubt that they would do the same to him. It was a warning to anybody else who might be interested in *Gringo*.

At last, however, Ray came back to the phone. "It's a Vancouver number. That's where they hang out as far as I know. You call this number and they tell you to meet them someplace. That's all I know." He gave David a ten-digit number. "And don't ever tell anybody I told you, you got it? And until you're clean, please don't call me again. That's nothing personal. It's just that I'm engaged to be married now and I'd like to make it through to my wedding day."

David said, "Thanks, Ray. I'll be in touch."

There was no reply. Ray Molloy had hung up with a loud click.

David used two more coins: one to call and instruct his accountant, Lenny Stein, to have $50,000 transferred to Barclays Bank in Vancouver under the name of Walter Ross; the other to call his housekeeper Cora and ask her to close up the Connecticut house for the rest of the summer, drawing the drapes so the furnishings wouldn't fade. Cora said, "You *are* all right, Senator?"

"I'm okay," he told her. He wished he didn't have to lie.

He left Macy's and crossed the street to the Avis office. He used his Master card to rent an LTD and asked the girl behind the desk if he could leave the car in Orlando, Florida. If anybody checked his rental, which they certainly would, they would be waiting for him at the Avis office in Orlando; he hoped they enjoyed their suntan.

He drove northwest, crossing the Hudson shortly after two o'clock that afternoon and heading for Binghamton on Route 17. His plan was to cross into Canada at Niagara as quickly as possible since he guessed that his pursuers would find it more difficult to operate quite so openly north of the border. It was possible that he was wrong, in which case he might be getting himself into even deeper trouble because his route through Canada from Niagara would take him on a wide, northern circuit of Georgian Bay and Lake Superior, through Barrie and Sault Sainte-Marie and all the way through Wawa and Marathon to Thunder Bay. He would lose well over half a day driving around that way, but he preferred to get out of the United States by nightfall.

On the car radio, as he turned onto Route 17 into the glare of the late-afternoon sun, he heard that Cal Lewis, the new publisher of *The Washington Post*, had been found by the police floating in the Potomac close to the Thompson Water Sport Center. He had been shot in the back of the head. The news reporter said, "This follows the bombing yesterday of a car belonging to *Post* reporter Jack Levy, which killed him instantly. Police are treating the two deaths as a possible vendetta against the newspaper, possibly sparked off by its recent campaign against organized crime."

David had to pull over to the side of the highway for a while. He gripped the car's steering wheel tight and twisted it in guilt and frustration. If he hadn't sent Esther in search of the secret of *Gringo*, if he hadn't talked to Jack Levy or Cal Lewis, most likely they would all be alive today. And he himself wouldn't be driving toward Niagara Falls in a cheap rented car with no luggage, no possessions, no friends and nowhere to turn but to some hideaway community of exiles in Vancouver.

At last he started up the engine and pulled away. On the radio, they were playing "Days of Grace":

> *We lived like friends*
> *Through all those days*
> *We lived like earthbound angels dancing through*
>   *that summer haze*
> *And even now, I see your face*
> *And I recall, with smiling tears, those days of grace.*

It was dark by the time he reached Niagara. In Europe it was already one o'clock on Sunday morning. There were only two hours and ten minutes to go before the launch of Operation *Byliny*.

TWENTY-ONE

He called Hans for the fifth time and at last got through. He was sitting in a little wooden beach house not far north of Rundsted, overlooking Øre Sund. The house was hidden from the main road by rows of pines and from the nearest neighboring beach house by a tangle of bushes, undergrowth and flowering shrubs. Beyond the shrubs, the ground dropped sharply to the shoreline, and there in the evening dusk was the sea, speaking in a stage whisper to the grayish sand. The beach house belonged to some old friends of Agneta's, the Holmens. It hadn't taken Charles long to knock open the padlock on the front door with a heavy stone.

Hans said, "Where are you calling from? You sound far away."

"I'm in hiding," Charles told him. He blew out smoke. "That Russian bastard, Novikov, was waiting for me when I went around to Peder Skrams Gade to see Agneta. He—"

Charles found to his surprise that he couldn't speak. His throat was snarled up with emotion. He took a deep breath and said, "Hah," and then at last he was able to say, "He killed her, Hans. And my friend Roger. It was a miracle that he didn't manage to kill me too."

Hans said, "I'm sorry. Is there anything I can do?"

"No. Well, I'm going to have to come to terms with it, aren't I? Other people have lost their friends; I'm no different. I just wish to hell that the people who own this place had left a bottle of Jack Daniel's around.''

"Don't get drunk,'' said Hans. "We're going to need you.''

"I don't think I'm much good to anybody at the moment.''

"Listen to me, Charles. Things are starting to happen. We have had a call from our colleagues in Germany. Where are you speaking from? Not from a hotel or anything like that? Not through a switchboard?''

"Unh-hunh. Private line.''

"Well, that's good. Because our colleagues in Germany have managed to persuade Marshal Golovanov to talk.''

"They have? Well, if it isn't all lies, I congratulate them. What did he have to say for himself?''

Hans spoke slowly and seriously. "He said that the recent Russian maneuvers were only a prelude, a way of bringing the Soviet Army up to full strength and combat preparedness without alarming the West Germans. He said that the Soviet Army is about to invade the Federal Republic of Germany. He couldn't clearly say when. Perhaps the date has not yet been finally fixed. But he did say that it will be done with the agreement and the assistance of Great Britain and the United States. In other words, as the Soviet Army advances, the British and the Americans will systematically withdraw. For the sake of stability in the world as a whole, West Germany will be offered to the Soviet Union as a sacrifice.''

"I don't believe what I'm hearing.''

"Well, it came from Marshal T.K. Golovanov himself, a man not given to fantasy. And he was interrogated by Inge Schültz, one of the most skillful agents when it comes to questioning.''

"I'd like to meet her. Anybody who can get Golovanov to talk must be quite something.''

"You probably will,'' said Hans. "She is bringing Marshal Golovanov to Copenhagen with her, mainly to get him out of West Germany in the event a Russian invasion actually takes place but also to help us interpret whatever we manage to elicit from the computer at Klarlund and Christensen.''

Charles reached over and coaxed another cigarette out of the pack. Only three left. He was going to have to get some more soon, and a bottle of whiskey. He wasn't going to be able to survive the night on *apfelsaft* and milk, which was all the Holmens had left in their tiny refrigerator.

"This is the other good news," Hans explained. "One of our Russian agents has brought out of Russia two Englishmen, both computer experts. They are in Helsinki at the moment but he is going to have them flown to Copenhagen in about an hour, as soon as the necessary formalities have been completed."

"He got them out of *Russia?* What were they doing in Russia in the first place?"

"They were showing some of their computers at the Toy Fair apparently. But the Russians were attempting to coerce them into staying and working in the Soviet Union. It appears that several computer experts and well-qualified engineers have been lent to the Soviet Union recently by Britain and the United States, against their individual will. All of which tends to confirm Marshal Golovanov's story that there is a conspiracy here to sacrifice Germany."

"Listen," said Charles, "I'll come back to Copenhagen but for God's sake, let me have a bodyguard this time, and get me a gun. Can you get me a gun?"

"Of course. What do you want?"

"Nothing stupid. Novikov's a two-hundred-pound berserker and that's putting it mildly."

"We have one or two UZIs here if you're interested."

"I'll take two. I'll take three if you've got them. Where do you want me to meet you?"

Hans said, "Come to Sct. Hans Gade, Number Seventeen, down at the Sortedams end. Ring the bell marked Rasmussen and wait. How long will it take you to get here?"

"I'm at Rundsted. Give me an hour."

Hans said, "Okay," then paused for a moment and said, "Agneta was your girlfriend, wasn't she?"

"That's right."

"Are you sure you can manage after what's happened?"

Charles said, "I can manage. If I get drunk, all I'll be able to do is forget about it for an hour or two. If I come and help you, well, maybe I'll be able to do something about it.

Maybe I'll be able to catch up with that Novikov bastard and twist *his* head off.''

"Would you like us to have somebody clean up your friend's apartment?" asked Hans soberly. "We have an undertaker we use, Blower, he's very discreet."

"Will it cost much?"

"I think this is one service we can let you have for free."

"All right, then," said Charles. "I appreciate it. But do you think she could possibly be buried? She didn't want to be cremated, I don't know why."

"Blower does very tasteful burials. I'm sorry to say that we've had to use him quite a few times."

"Okay," Charles told him dryly. He felt as if his brain had been sandblasted

Charles pressed the telephone cradle, waited for a dial tone, then called Taxa-Ringbilen. "I'm at Rundsted. Yes. Can you send a car up to get me? Listen, I don't care what it costs. Sure. Okay, as soon as you can."

Then he sat on the floral-cushioned bamboo sofa in the middle of the sitting room and smoked and waited, watching himself in the dark glass of the French windows. After a while, tired of waiting, he switched on the radio. He had always known, somehow, that he would never be free of this business. Once you were involved, you could never escape. Because what could you do? Turn your back on the political connivance you had been specially taught to recognize? Ignore the men in the gray suits when you saw them walking through the cities of the world, armed, lethal and prepared to kill anybody who didn't abide by their masters' political ethics?

Lamprey had evolved because so many intelligence agents had at last refused to believe there was any difference between one side and another, not a difference worth dying for. The enemy as far as Lamprey was concerned were the bureaucrats whose political and financial survival depended on international hostility and the great machineries of unfought war. The enemy was human aggression, and human fear.

Since 1945, sufficient conventional arms had been produced by both East and West to fight four hundred wars of the size and scale of World War Two, and that wasn't counting the immense nuclear arsenals produced on both sides. Only Lamprey had seen the true absurdity of it and the full scale of the tragedy it represented. Security was nothing but another word for fright, and hundreds of billions had been spent by Washington and Moscow in guarding themselves against shadows and illusions.

Charles was not idealistic about arms control, nor hopeful about it either. And Hans seemed to be equally cynical. But what could you do? Pretend it didn't matter? Pretend it had nothing to do with you and carry on working in intelligence with no more conscience about it than a white rat running a laboratory maze?

He didn't allow himself the luxury of thinking about his life very often but he thought about it tonight, and the more he thought about it, the more certain he was that he had to go back to Copenhagen and try to stay sober.

Almost forty-five minutes had passed before a faint triangle of light swiveled across the ceiling of the beach house, signifying the approach of a car. Charles switched off the radio and went through to the bathroom to wash his face in cold water. He stared at himself in the mirror over the basin. Gray, exhausted, emotionally beaten, but with eyes that still retained that old professional hardness. Not too bad, he supposed, not for my age.

He suddenly realized that he hadn't heard the car approach the beach house. The driver hadn't come to knock at the door either. He stood up straight, listening and watching himself listening in the mirror. There was no sound at all except for the fussing of the sea and the occasional rattling of one of the kitchen shutters.

He glanced toward the bathroom window. To his horror, through the frosted glass he could see the distorted shape of a huge, dark figure and a face like raw meat.

He wrenched off the bathroom light, snapping the cord out of its socket. Then he lunged out into the sitting room and hit the light switches there too, plunging the beach house into darkness. His mind raced: weapon, what can I use as a weapon? He thought of the Russian automatic he had so contemptuously left behind at Agneta's apartment and wished to God he hadn't been so ridiculously arrogant about it.

Bending low, he made his way crabwise across the thin, rumpled tapestry rug until he reached the stove. He felt among the logs, tumbling two or three of them over until his hand closed on what he was searching for: a hooked fire poker, used for picking up firewood and raking the ashes. It was heavy, with a large brass knob at the end of the handle.

Still crouching, he waited. He heard footsteps slowly circling the beach house; the measured steps of a man who believes that he is invulnerable, a man who is frightened of nobody and nothing. Charles desperately wanted to pee; it was a nervous reaction that most of his CIA and counter-intelligence friends attested to in times of fear. It was no use applying for a job as a field agent if you had a weak bladder.

There was a moment of utter stillness. Even the sea seemed to be holding its breath. Then, like a controlled explosion, the veranda doors of the beach house came bursting in—a blizzard of shattered glass and splinters of timber—and the red-and-white gingham curtains blew apart as if they had been caught in an instant hundred-mile-an-hour hurricane.

"Jesus!" roared Charles. A prayer, a war cry, a scream of fright.

Krov' iz Nosu raged into the room, hurling chairs and tables aside and uttering a noise that turned Charles' stomach upside down. It was a strangled, babylike mewling, a high-pitched ululation of anger from a throat stretched tight by fire, from lips that had once been burned right back to the teeth.

Charles stood up and swung the poker at Novikov in a sharp, sweeping, suddenly remembered motion, the motion of the college star baseball batter. Charles Krogh, class of '53. The blunt, sooty hook of the poker caught Novikov in the side of the neck, snagged a web of skin, tore scar tissue and muscle, and suddenly it was raining blood. Novikov turned, swayed as menacingly as Frankenstein's monster and then flailed his arms at Charles like a torrent of Indian clubs. One blow caught Charles on the side of the face and he was knocked flat on his back onto the floor, hitting his head on the side of the stove. He rolled over the way his CIA instructor had taught him: "Never lie there like a dummy, waiting for the next punch.'' He was still clutching the poker, and in a second he was struggling back to his feet, turning over a wicker chair and a magazine rack and smashing some unseen china ornament, but whipping the poker from side to side and howling his war cry at the top of his voice, scared, angry and vengeful.

He struck Novikov on the shoulder, lashed him across the neck, beat him mercilessly around his upraised arms. It was then that he knew the only thing that would ever stop Novikov was a gun, and a heavy-caliber gun at that. Because the disfigured giant suddenly lowered his arms as if none of Charles' blows had hurt him at all and glowered with such malevolence that all Charles could do was to toss the poker to the floor, scoop up a stool and hurl it at Novikov's head, not particularly caring whether he hit him or not, and then tug open the door that led to the outside patio and run.

He ran into a darkness that smelled of wind and sea. Øre Sund at night, the white houses gray and mysterious, the grass whipping at his shins. He scaled a slanting slope, panting, crested the slope and headed toward the trees. Off to his right he saw a Saab Turbo, black, undoubtedly the car in which Novikov had been driven here. Gasping, stumbling forward on a slide of loose stones and sandy soil, he looked over his shoulder. Novikov had followed him; for a moment he could see one of the gray breakers blotted out by a dark, bobbing shape. It could be only a matter of minutes before the Russian's superior stamina began to tell, and Charles knew then that he was dead. He was already exhausted, trembling with exertion. Novikov would tear him into hamburger meat.

Although it lost him vital ground, Charles lurched sharply right and began to run toward the Saab. It took Novikov a few seconds to understand that Charles had changed direction but when he did, he immediately turned after him and came loping up the shoreline, his feet crashing on the shingle. He whooped in cruel triumph as he ran. He was sure that Charles would never get away from him now.

The Saab was parked farther away than Charles had estimated. His chest was bursting as if somebody heavy was sitting on it, and his legs felt as if they no longer belonged to

him. But then suddenly he was there, colliding with the side
of the car and rolling himself around the back of it on the
ground.

The driver must have been half-asleep, convinced that
Novikov would go into the beach house, finish the job and
come back with the bits. But when Charles banged into the
car, the driver instantly opened his door and began to climb
out, reaching as he did so into his windbreaker to tug out a
gun.

Charles hit him straight in the belly with the Chinese blow
known as *shui-mu*, named after the demon who had been
persuaded to eat noodles that then turned magically into
chains and wound themselves around his entrails. The blow
was advanced unarmed combat and didn't always work. At
least, it had worked for Charles only once before, and that
was in the gym.

Tonight, however, the driver gagged, coughed and collapsed heavily on the ground, his abdominal muscles locked
tight in a reactive spasm. Charles ducked down to pick up his
gun and then twisted himself into the Saab's front seat. At the
same instant Novikov came running up to the car, snatched at
the passenger door and with a grating crunch of protesting
metal and springs, tore it halfway off its hinges.

There was no time to shoot. Charles turned the key, gunned
the Saab's engine, released the brake and slammed his foot on
the accelerator. The car bounded forward, bouncing and jostling over the rough beach, with Novikov running beside it
and the partially wrenched-off door clattering along like the
tin cans on a wedding car.

Charles slued the car around, its tires frantically spinning
for grip on the loose, dry sand. Then he was heading back
toward the highway through the trees, and even though Novikov
was running hard, there was no possibility that he would be
able to catch up now. Charles switched on the headlights and
narrowly managed to avoid a deep gully and a half-hidden
tree stump.

He glanced up at the rearview mirror. Novikov was still
pursuing him, dark and heavy, like a marathon runner out of
a nightmare. Charles had almost reached the highway now; he
could see the red taillights of a passing truck. He groped

beside him for the gun he had picked up from the driver and lifted it quickly so he could see what it was. An FN GP35 automatic, the Belgian version of the Browning high-power. It should be powerful enough to stop Novikov providing the Russian wasn't wearing body armor. He checked the rearview mirror again and then jabbed his foot on the brake so the Saab skidded to a halt beside the shoulder of the highway.

Now be calm, he told himself. If you panic, you're going to miss. He climbed out of the car, leaving the engine running, and hurried around to the far side of it. He cocked the automatic, rested his forearms on the roof of the car and took careful aim at Novikov's silhouette as he came jogging up from the beach. Exhale, he told himself. Steady. Squeeze.

One shot cracked off into the night. Charles stood with both hands raised, holding the smoking automatic, peering into the shadowy treeline to see if he could make out Novikov's fallen body. But there was nothing now, only the darkness. He waited a moment longer and then walked back around the car.

A Volvo sedan drew up beside him just as he was about to start off again. The light on the roof proclaimed that it had come from Taxa-Ringbilen. The young driver got out and walked across to Charles with a piece of paper in his hand.

"I'm looking for Mr. Krogh," he said. "He's supposed to be waiting for me down on the beach somewhere. Are there beach houses down there?"

Charles, with relief, turned off the Saab's engine. "I'm Mr. Krogh."

"What happened to your car?"

Charles frowned across at the nearly torn-off door.

"Oh, that. That's always happening. I guess I just don't know my own strength."

Charles took the keys of the Saab and walked with the driver over to the Volvo. The driver U-turned and headed back along the forest-lined highway to Copenhagen.

"You like music?" he asked Charles.

"What have you got?"

"Beethoven's Fifth."

"Sure, that sounds appropriate."

"Are you okay?" the driver asked him after a while.

"What's the matter, don't I look okay?"

"You look like somebody who's seen a ghost."

Charles stared at his curved, distorted reflection in the Volvo's window. Lights passed in the night like speeding satellites. "I never believed in ghosts," he said more to himself than to the driver. Then, "Can you spare a cigarette?"

TWENTY-TWO

"General Abramov is here, Comrade General."

Yeremenko looked up from his strategic map of Western Germany. He was sipping a scalding demitasse of Eastern black coffee, the Russian equivalent of Turkish coffee, and the steam from the tiny cup had slightly fogged the edges of his tinted glasses.

"General Abramov? What is the commander of the Kiev Military District doing here?"

Colonel Khleschev shrugged uneasily. Yeremenko hesitated for a moment, his cup still raised; then he set it carefully in its saucer. "Very well, Colonel, you'd better show him through."

It was 0127 hours and all the way along the East German border, the Soviet Army was massed like one of the great hordes of Genghis Khan for the launching of Operation *Byliny*. The 16th Air Army, over two thousand aircraft, had been divided into two separate air armies in preparation for the massive advance. Under their cover, twelve tank divisions and sixteen mechanized infantry divisions would be advancing in two powerful fronts, one in the north and one in the south. With more than ten thousand tanks, five hundred helicopters, six thousand infantry combat vehicles, five thousand armored personnel carriers and over five thousand artillery guns, mortars and salvo-firing rocket launchers, they would pour into West Germany: along the Baltic coast into Hamburg, along the Berlin autobahn into Hanover, through the Fulda Gap toward Frankfurt and into Bavaria from Czechoslovakia.

It was the greatest army of invasion ever assembled; the lines of T-72 and T-64 tanks were so long that civilian traffic in East Germany was at a standstill sixteen miles back from the border. Behind the tanks came self-propelled *Akatsiya* howitzers, BMD personnel carriers armed with rockets and 73-mm cannon, and hundreds of trucks of infantry.

The two fronts could have been built up to even greater strength if it had been necessary. Had it not been for *Gringo* and Operation *Cornflower*, the Soviet Army would have been able to call up thousands of reserves from Poland and Byelorussia. As it was, they expected to be able to roll through West Germany with little or no serious resistance. Any localized guerrilla attacks could swiftly be dealt with by special groups of SPETSNAZ commandos.

Gringo and *Cornflower* in themselves were just as impressive. The withdrawal from West Germany of the U.S. and British Forces stationed there since the end of World War Two were the two largest and most complicated exercises in military-movement control ever undertaken by either country. The paperwork was mountainous; the computer programs looked like encyclopedias. Arrangements for the speedy removal of hundreds of tanks, trucks, missile launchers, artillery and other equipment were supervised by military specialists who could be numbered in the hundreds. The Allied forces would run one hour ahead of the advancing Russians; that was the agreement. Any vehicles or equipment left behind would be dealt with later by special negotiation.

The Americans alone had to drive or airlift out of their thirty-six West German bases more than two hundred fifty thousand men and women in uniform as well as all their tanks, vehicles and equipment. There was strict instruction from the Pentagon that not one of their new M1 Abrams tanks and not one of their Black Hawk helicopters and not one of their computerized multiple-launch rocket systems should be allowed to fall into Soviet hands, while the British Army was particularly anxious not to let the Russians seize any of its Chobham laminated armor.

General Oliver had remarked, "It might be a bloodless invasion, but it's still an invasion."

Yeremenko, as Commander-in-Chief of the Western Strategic Direction, was holding the reins of the most powerful single fighting force in human history, and he was poised to single-handedly direct the most momentous political territorial event in forty years.

General Abramov saluted him and then shook his hand. "Well, Comrade Commander," he said respectfully, "it seems that the hour has come at last."

Yeremenko slowly rubbed his hands together. General Abramov's unexpected appearance here made him ill at ease. The commander of the Kiev Military District was in times of war the commander of the Southwestern Strategic Direction, with direct responsibility for taking over the armies of Sub-Carpathia, Hungary, Romania, Bulgaria and the Black Sea fleet. Although the armies of the Southwestern Strategic Direction were not actively involved in Operation *Byliny*, they were all on standby at full operational strength; at the very moment when *Byliny* was going to be launched, Yeremenko would have expected Abramov to be waiting at his headquarters in case he was needed. The Kremlin still did not entirely trust the Americans in spite of the Copenhagen Agreement. Supposing the Pentagon suddenly decided to hit back? The old men of the Defense Council retained a terrible fear of cruise missiles and of sudden capitalist treachery. Remember Barbarossa!

"Who is in charge now at Kiev?" asked Yeremenko.

"General Pokryshkin. He was promoted today from Byelorussia."

"Well, Pokryshkin's a good man. A very sound young officer. He was at the Military-Political Academy, wasn't he, once upon a time?"

Abramov nodded. Yeremenko had never liked Abramov. He was very dark; although he shaved twice a day, his chin was always blue, and there were dark, curly hairs peeking out of his nostrils. His eyes always seemed to Yeremenko to be too closely set, as if he were slightly mad. He was overwhelmingly ambitious too, as far as Yeremenko was concerned, and what made this ambition worse was that Abramov was a particular favorite of the Kremlin hierarchy.

"I came from Kiev by helicopter," said Abramov.

"Ah," replied Yeremenko with an exaggerated lack of interest. "For, ah . . . any particular reason?"

Abramov suddenly smiled and then laughed. "The army has never once sent me anywhere for no reason."

"Then you are here to assist me, is that it?"

"Not exactly," said Abramov. He looked around the room, at the lights and the smoke and the groups of officers who were following the progress of the assembling Soviet tank forces. A large clock on the far wall, its face dimly illuminated, announced with a juddering second hand that Operation *Byliny* was one hour and ten minutes away.

"Is there somewhere we can talk for a minute or two?" asked Abramov.

Yeremenko looked at him intently. Abramov seemed almost embarrassed. "Comrade Kutakov wished me to have a word with you," he said.

Yeremenko lifted his left arm mechanically and focused on his wristwatch. "I'm very pushed for time, Comrade General. But . . . well, a minute or two. No longer."

They went through to a small, brown-painted anteroom. There was a row of cheap varnished chairs, a table stacked with files and a portrait of Lenin. Yeremenko stood with his hands clasped in front of him and said, "Well? How can I help you?"

"Normally, of course, this would be done differently," said General Abramov. "But this is a critical moment and the *Stavka* is anxious to cause as little disruption as possible. I am here, Comrade General, to relieve you of your command of the Western Strategic Direction and to request you to return to Moscow immediately for further instructions."

Yeremenko stared at Abramov as if he were unable to believe he existed, as if he were an apparition from some long-forgotten dream.

"I think there must be some mistake," he said flatly.

"I'm sorry, Comrade General. No mistake. I have my written orders. They were brought here by helicopter to meet me when I arrived."

"But . . . I am the Commander-in-Chief of the Western Strategic Direction. I am the architect and chief executive of

Operation *Byliny*. They are ready, Comrade! The tanks! The infantry! Thousands upon thousands! They are out there now, in the night! They are all under my command!''

General Abramov lifted his hands and then dropped them again. "This is none of my doing, Comrade General. You can take my helicopter back to Moscow. They are refueling it now."

"*Why?*" demanded Yeremenko in a fierce whisper.

"I was told to say nothing further, Comrade General. Please . . . you have my regrets. I can give you no more."

"*Why?*" Yeremenko roared. "*Why?*"

Abramov looked unhappy. "If I tell you . . . well, don't repeat it. But it is all because of Marshal Golovanov."

"Golovanov? That old has-been? And anyway, he's gone now; probably murdered, and serve him right."

Abramov shook his dark-blue jowls emphatically. "No, no, Comrade General, not murdered. He was interrogated, so we understand, and we also understand that he talked. The Federal German government has been told about Operation *Byliny* and the Bundeswehr is apparently preparing to defend West Germany to the last, even if the British and Americans withdraw."

"Well?" Yeremenko demanded with extraordinary petulance. "What fault is it of mine if Golovanov could not be loyal to his country? And as for the Bundeswehr, we can crush it like an egg. I am not afraid to fight! I am a soldier!"

General Abramov laid a hand on Yeremenko's shoulder. "Nobody has cast any doubts on your bravery or your capability, Comrade General. That you must understand. But the *Stavka* sees it as an error of judgment to have allowed Marshal Golovanov to consort with that German prostitute. She was a double agent working against the KGB."

"And I was supposed to know that? All I was doing was catering to the old hog's animal appetites! What else could I do? If it was anybody's fault, it was the fault of the KGB for not briefing me."

Abramov said soberly, "The KGB did not know that she was a double agent either. There have also been some demotions at Dzerzhinsky Square. I am afraid, however, that Marshal Golovanov's kidnapping has caused serious embarrassment in the Defense Council and that you have been perceived as the scapegoat.''

Yeremenko was white. He walked across the room diagonally and then walked back again. He took off his tinted glasses. "Operation *Byliny*," he said. "Without my direction, it could never have happened."

"I repeat, Comrade General, that nobody has doubted your ability or your patriotism."

"Well," said Yeremenko, "it seems that I have no choice."

"I'm afraid not," said Abramov, trying to be solicitous but secretly relieved.

Yeremenko walked to the door that opened into the corridor and beckoned to one of his guards. The youth came clumping into the anteroom and stood there with his machine gun in his hand, looking bewildered.

"What is your name, boy?" Yeremenko asked him.

"Gorshkov, sir."

Yeremenko turned to General Abramov and smiled. "Comrade General, Private Gorshkov is to be your keeper for a while."

"I don't understand."

"You are not to leave this room. Private Gorshkov will stand guard over you. If you attempt to escape, Private Gorshkov will shoot you. Do you understand that, Private Gorshkov?"

The unhappy soldier nodded. "Yes, sir."

Yeremenko jabbed a finger at Abramov and said, "Just because he looks like a general, Private Gorshkov, just because he has scarlet and gold on his uniform, that does not make him any less a traitor. So don't let him frighten you with threats of what he will do to you. Don't let him sweet-talk you either. Your duty is to guard him and guard him well, and if he tries to escape, to kill him."

"Yes, sir," said Gorshkov, swallowing.

Abramov called clearly, "Ivan!"

Yeremenko turned.

Abramov said, "This will be the death of you, Ivan, if you try to carry it any further."

"*Byliny* is mine, Comrade," Yeremenko told him in an expressionless voice.

"Not any longer. And the *Stavka* has made substantial changes in tactics now that the Bundeswehr is ready for us. They are all contained in my orders. Airborne drops of SPETSNAZ diversionary troops, new routes of attack. If you attempt to carry out the original maneuvers, you will cause a disaster both politically and strategically."

Yeremenko stood for a while holding the door handle, his lips pursed tight in thought. Then, without a word, he nodded and walked back to the bustling, crowded strategy room, where his coffee was still hot.

Colonel Khleschev looked around in surprise. "I understood that General Abramov was staying here, sir."

Yeremenko waved a dismissive hand. "He has just . . . gone to relieve himself. A long journey from Kiev."

He studied the map of the German border. Then he said, "He brought me the order that Operation *Byliny* was to start right away."

"Have the British and Americans been informed of this, sir?"

"What?"

"I said, have the—"

"Yes, yes. I heard you. Of course they have. But we must start right away. At oh-two-ten hours precisely. I want both front commanders connected through to headquarters for final orders. I also want to speak right away to General Lavochkin."

Yeremenko finished his coffee in quick, nervous gulps while telephones jangled and intelligence officers with sheaves of paper hurried in and out the doors of the strategy room like leaf-cutting ants scurrying in and out of their nest. His immediate staff hovered not too far away, always ready to advise and assist; but earlier in the evening, Yeremenko had made it clear to them that *Byliny* was *his* night of glory and that he was going to direct the launching of the great invasion single-handedly.

He half-realized in a strange way that the size and the scale of the invasion had gone to his head. He was aware now that what he was doing was both insubordinate and dangerous. He could only hope that the British and Americans would speed up their withdrawal and not interpret the early start of *Byliny* as an act of treachery and aggression and try to fight back. Yeremenko's armies would still prevail, of course, even if they did. Both British and American forces were packed up and ready to evacuate Europe and were in no position to mount an organized retaliation. He cracked each of his knuckles in turn. In a way, he would relish a real battle. And he would make sure that he was ready for one by ordering General Lavochkin to prepare his rocket armies with low-yield nuclear weapons.

Any sign of retaliation from the Western forces and he would lay a nuclear carpet across West Germany, from north to south, and devastate any attempt at opposition.

The Defense Council had appointed him Commander-in-Chief of the Western Strategic Direction because he was efficient, because he was ruthless, because he would take Western Europe for them in less than a week. Well, whether they had changed their minds about his appointment or not, that was the result they were going to get.

The alternative was too bleak to consider. If he meekly returned to Moscow to face investigation into the disappearance of Marshal Golovanov, he knew exactly what would happen. Disgrace, demotion and dismissal to Carpathia or Trans-Baykal. Even possible execution. The Defense Council was not kind to generals who fell from grace. When a general was in favor, his life in the Soviet Army was a rich one, with private *dachas*, plenty to drink, limousines and scores of pretty girls. But when he was out of favor, he might just as well kill himself, and many did. The suicide rate among Soviet generals was one of the highest in the world for any occupation, in any country.

To take Europe was Yeremenko's only chance of survival.

It was 0158. Colonel Khleschev came up to Yeremenko and said, "Both front commanders are patched through to your telephone, sir."

Yeremenko picked up his phone but all he could hear was static. "What's this?" he demanded.

Khleschev looked unsettled. "Oh, we've been having trouble with that line all night, sir. Perhaps you'd better take the call in your private office."

Impatiently Yeremenko stalked out of the strategy room.

Junior officers stepped back and allowed him through like the parting of the Red Sea. Colonel Khleschev opened the swinging doors for him and then followed him with clattering shoes as he made his way back along the corridor to his own office.

"I want that telephone repaired immediately!" Yeremenko snapped.

As he pushed open his office door, he realized that of course he should have known that the "faulty" telephone was all a deceit just to get him out of the strategy room. There, waiting for him in the lamplight, under the portrait of Marshal Kulik, was General Abramov with two guards, colonels unknown to Yeremenko, as well as Private Gorshkov with his machine gun and Major Grechko, Marshal Golovanov's secretary.

"Please, Comrade Commander-in-Chief, come in," said General Abramov.

Yeremenko walked slowly to the center of the room. He took off his glasses. Behind him, Colonel Khleschev closed the door.

Major Grechko stepped forward and saluted. "I have to tell you, sir, that you are relieved of your command of the Western Strategic Direction and that you are under military arrest. I have instructions to take you back to Moscow immediately."

"Well, well," said Yeremenko. "Whom can one trust?"

Major Grechko didn't attempt to answer. "I am an officer of the KGB, sir."

"It seems that I have failed, then, doesn't it?" said Yeremenko. "It seems as if the old bear caught up with me at last. Well, well."

"The interests of the Soviet Union and the interests of the Party must always come before personal ambition," Major Grechko recited. He was behaving like the perfect KGB officer, correct and smart and always ready with an ideological admonition. But also, in a way, he was behaving like the sheriff at the end of one of his favorite Westerns, summing up ninety minutes of gunplay with a well-honed moral.

Privately, Grechko was deeply relieved that General Yeremenko had become so deranged. Grechko had been appointed to accompany Marshal Golovanov in order to double-check the surveillance that KGB field agents kept on high-ranking army officers. His failure to identify Inge Schültz as a double agent was going to land him in serious trouble, particularly since it had led to Marshal Golovanov's abduction. With any luck, his rescue of General Abramov and his arrest of General Yeremenko would redeem him.

"Time is short," said General Abramov. "Colonel, will you show me through to the strategy room so we can get Operation *Byliny* started on schedule?"

Yeremenko said nothing as General Abramov and his entourage left his office. Major Grechko stood in the lamplight, watching and waiting. "I understand that the helicopter is fueled and ready, Comrade General," he said at last.

Yeremenko looked up. "It's trust, isn't it? It's trust that's lacking. I could never trust you and you could never trust me. What kind of an army is it that spies on its own officers? If Golovanov had been allowed to indulge himself with whatever woman he wished instead of with a KGB agent, perhaps none of this would have happened. We bring it on ourselves. We are twisted with suspicion. We see *dybbuks* under every bed."

He walked around his desk and opened one drawer after another. There was nothing there he needed to keep. He had no souvenirs, no sentimental reminders, not so much as a pen-and-pencil set.

"Suspicion is a disease," he said without looking up. "A disease from which the Soviet Union has been suffering since the Revolution and which will one day prove fatal."

Major Grechko said, "We'd better go, Comrade General, before the air-traffic embargo is imposed."

"Very well," said Yeremenko.

They left the office and walked along the corridor. At the far end, the large window that overlooked the front courtyard was just beginning to show the gray paleness of dawn. The building bristled with activity: doors swung open and shut; officers hurried from one room to another; computers whirred and clicked. Hardly anyone gave Grechko and Yeremenko a second glance; everyone was too busy with the last few minutes of Operation *Byliny*.

Yeremenko said, "If I tried to escape, what would you do?"

"Escape?" asked Major Grechko.

"Yes. If I knocked you down and ran, what would you do?"

"I would chase after you, I suppose."

Yeremenko looked at him narrowly. "Would you shoot me?"

Major Grechko said, "You're not asking me to shoot you, are you? Because I won't. I have instructions to take you back to Moscow alive, and that's what I intend to do."

Yeremenko said, "Watch me."

He tossed aside his glasses and began to run. Major Grechko, startled, immediately began to run after him. But Yeremenko was fit and athletic and, more than anything else, determined. He ran down the corridor in his general's uniform like an Olympic sprinter, arms pounding, and there was nothing that Grechko could do to keep up with him.

"General!" shouted Grechko and slowed to a trot. Because what could Yeremenko possibly do? They had passed the stairs and there was no way down except by elevator. Yeremenko would have to wait for the elevator to arrive, and that would be the end of it.

It was only when Yeremenko obliviously pelted past the elevator doors that Grechko understood. His stomach lurched and he started running again, but he knew he was far too late. Yeremenko was sprinting toward the huge window at the front of the building and it was obvious that he didn't intend to stop.

There was a railing along the bottom of the window but Yeremenko dived at the glass headfirst, his arms by his sides, clearing the railing by nearly a foot.

The whole window burst, four hundred square feet of plate glass shattering into jagged stars and curving scimitars. Yeremenko, with blood spraying around him in a fireworks spiral of crimson droplets, fell through the sparkling fragments. He hit the shiny black hood of a Volga parked outside and lay spreadeagled across it, dying, his blood running from two severed arteries, neatly channeled into the car's drainage system and flowing onto the pavement.

Major Grechko stood in the corridor staring at the shattered window. His mouth hung open, gaping like an unhinged puppet. He stood there for almost thirty seconds; then the elevator arrived and the doors opened just beside him. The cab was empty. Mechanically he stepped into it and pressed the button for the lobby.

He had only two alternatives now as far as he could see: either to shoot himself to get it over with, or to run. He stared at his pale, ghostly face in the smeary metal sides of the cab.

The elevator reached the lobby. He had decided: he would try to make a run for it. The borders would be open tonight as Operation *Byliny* got underway. There would be darkness, confusion and plenty of opportunities to get ahead of the main body of tanks and troops and ask for political asylum in the West. He didn't even consider going back to KGB headquarters. What could he report? That he had not only been primarily responsible for the abduction of Marshal Golovanov but that he had allowed General Yeremenko to commit suicide right in front of his eyes? Failures as serious as that meant the wall and a firing squad.

The elevator doors opened. Grechko was just about to step out when Colonel Chuykov appeared and said, "Grechko! Just the man!" and grasped his shoulder.

Grechko said, "Haven't you seen? General Yeremenko—"

"What?" frowned Chuykov.

"Outside," said Grechko. Chuykov looked around and saw a military ambulance speeding past the window.

It was too late. Grechko knew there was no chance of escape now. Chuykov would expect him to stay until everything was cleared up. He leaned against the wall beside the elevator and pressed his hand against his forehead.

"What's happened?" asked Chuykov. "What's the matter?"

"It's a disease," said Grechko under his breath.

"A disease? Are you sick?"

Grechko shook his head. "We're all sick, all of us. What are we trying to do? And now we're going to infect the rest of Europe."

TWENTY-THREE

The President was back at the White House eating a late supper of smoked-turkey salad when Chancellor Kress called him from Bonn for the last time. The call was later to become known as the "Turkey Talk" and to cause the President considerable political embarrassment. But on the night of *Gringo* and Operation *Byliny*, the forces at work in the world were enormous. All the accumulated powers of the past forty years were at last being exercised on both sides, and the dangers were extreme.

Chancellor Kress said baldly, "You can deceive us no longer, Mr. President. We understand completely what you have done. You have sacrificed a free Europe in exchange for a secure America."

The President pushed aside his plate. "With respect, I think you've misunderstood our motives here, Herr Chancellor."

"I don't think so, Mr. President. I am not a fool even if I *am* reliant on the United States for much of my protection against the Soviet Union."

"Well," said the President, trying to be conciliatory, "you have to consider the greater forces of history, the push and the pull, as well as your own particular problems."

"All I want to know is whether you are really going to

312

withdraw your forces in the face of a Soviet invasion. All I want to know is the truth.''

The President said, "Try to look at it this way, Herr Chancellor. For every action, you get a reaction, agreed? Now that happens in politics as well as in science. So, during World War Two, the Germans invaded Russia and killed millions of Russians. Millions! Can you imagine their reaction to that? Can you imagine how they feel today? Oh, sure, they took over Eastern Europe, but that wasn't enough to take the fear and the anger out of their system. Imagine if somebody knocked you down and beat up on you and all you got in return was ten dollars and the promise that it wouldn't happen again. Well, you'd be pretty dissatisfied with that, wouldn't you, after all you'd suffered, and you'd still be afraid that one day somebody was going to come back and beat up on you again. That's exactly how the Soviets feel."

Chancellor Kress could scarcely control his frustration and wrath. "Mr. President! I didn't call you for childish lectures on European politics, about which you seem to understand nothing. Nor did I call you to be reassured or patronized. I called you because huge Soviet armies are now massed on our borders, because American forces appear to be on the point of withdrawing from the Federal Republic without any sensible explanation and in direct contravention of all NATO concordances, and because I have been given intelligence information from a highly placed Soviet source that confirms what is already obvious. You have sold us down the river, Mr. President. I believe that is the American expression for it.''

The President was silent for a long time. Then he said, "Could you wait for just a moment, Herr Chancellor?'' and pressed the button that held his end of the call. He beckoned to Morton Lock, who was sitting on the opposite side of the Oval Office leafing through intelligence reports.

"Morton, how long before the Soviets start to roll?"

"Fifty-eight minutes, sir.''

The President released the hold button and said, "Herr Chancellor? I'm sorry I kept you waiting. Listen, I've just been talking to my Joint Chiefs of Staff. Yes, of course. But what we're trying to work out here is a question of balance. Balancing the world *globally*, do you see, rather than continuing with the present system, which is unbalanced and unfair and creates all kinds of tensions, not just between the West and the East, but in the Third World too.''

He took a sip of grapefruit juice and then said, ''I have to admit to you that we have been having secret talks with the Soviet Union over the question of reducing our military presence in Europe. Well, yes, you know that already. But what that will do is to increase security in Asia, South America, Latin America, Australia and Japan. The Soviets needed to feel that they were no longer directly threatened from Western Europe, and that is precisely what we have conceded to them in return for guarantees that *they* will no longer directly threaten the Western Hemisphere.''

Chancellor Kress said tautly, ''Mr. President, the Russians are going to invade us. The very minute your forces have gone, we will become a subject nation.''

''Now, please,'' the President told him. ''Just because the Soviet Army happens to be exercising its divisions close to the East German border—well, they do that quite often, don't they?—I can't see how that amounts to any specific threat.''

Chancellor Kress barked, ''You are lying to me through your teeth. I find it impossible to believe anything you say. You are abandoning us to the most oppressive regime in the history of the Western world. You are a hypocrite and a deceiver!''

''You listen to me, Herr Chancellor,'' the President shouted back. ''Times have changed and the world has changed, and any politician with the least sense of responsibility toward the human race has to change along with them. How much longer do you people in West Germany want to go on living under the shadow of nuclear annihilation? Tell me that! How much longer are ordinary men and women going to be frightened to have children in case they get incinerated before they grow up?''

Chancellor Kress retorted, ''You think we are frightened of nuclear bombs? That is how much you misjudge us! We are far more frightened of the oppression of the Soviet Union! At least with the bomb you are killed and that is the end of your suffering! Have you ever been to Estonia? Have you seen what the Soviets have done there? The old national flag is forbidden, the language is forbidden, the folk songs and the culture are forbidden! Everywhere you go, you are greeted by the huge number 'Forty,' which reminds you that this country has been oppressed by the Soviets for forty years and that they intend to continue their oppression for another forty, and yet another forty.''

"Herr Chancellor, please,'' said the President wearily.

"No, Mr. President. I now see you Americans for what you are. You have become deluded by your own movies. You believe it is enough to be sentimental, to forgo the substance of real loyalty and love. You believe it is right to be ambitious without counting the cost of your ambition to other people. You believe in freedom without responsibility, and in success without guilt. You cannot see the squalor that surrounds you in your own country; how can I expect you to care about us?''

"Now, listen—'' the President tried to interrupt.

"No, Mr. President, no. I do not wish to listen to any more of your cotton-candy cant. History will assess you best for what you are and what you have done. But I have to say this. I am a pragmatic man. I know that the Bundeswehr cannot hold back the Soviet Army on its own. They want to, believe me. My generals are all ready to fight. But the result of unilateral retaliation would be the pointless massacre of many thousands of excellent young Germans and many civilians, besides the risk of inviting nuclear attack from the Russians. You say that I am concerned only with my own small affairs but I am not. For it would take only one nuclear bomb to be dropped for others to follow. So perhaps to that extent you are right and it is better for the German people to be oppressed than for the whole world to be destroyed. But I will ask you one question and if you answer this question with 'no,' I shall order the Bundeswehr to put down their weapons, abandon their tanks, remove their uniforms and go home to dress themselves in civilian clothes. I shall order the Bundeswehr to melt away as if it had never existed. If you answer 'yes,' however, I will order them to stand firm and to fight bravely and hard alongside the men they always believed were their allies.''

The President said nothing, not because he didn't have

anything to say, but because this conversation hurt him and upset him more than he could have explained to anybody, even to the First Lady. He knew what he was doing to Chancellor Kress; he knew what he was doing to the Germans. But he was the President of the United States of America and as such, he had a prime duty to protect the interests of the United States. *Gringo* had been discussed over two years ago, and ever since then he had agonized over it and suffered sleepless nights for the first time in his life. Tonight he was having to face up at last to the consequences of his decision, and so were the West Germans.

Chancellor Kress said, "The question is, will you abrogate your agreement with Moscow and protect us from the Soviet Army? Or not?"

The President paused thoughtfully. Then he said, "Otto— come on, I *can* still call you Otto, can't I?—let me think about this. Give me a break, hm? An hour, that's all I ask. Maybe I can work something out."

On the other side of the office, Morton closed his thumb and his forefinger in a circle of approval. "Fifty-two minutes," he whispered. "Then we're clear."

Chancellor Kress said, "Very well, Mr. President. One hour, and one hour only. Then I disband the Bundeswehr and announce to the rest of the world what has happened."

The President said, "I hope you're being equally strict with Britain."

"Oh, yes," said Chancellor Kress. "The Prime Minister is next on my list of calls."

"Otto," said the President, "I hope you understand what happened here and why it had to happen."

"Yes," said Chancellor Kress. His voice was as bitter as burned Arabica coffee. "I believe I do."

At Number 10 Downing Street the lights had been burning all night. It was nearly two o'clock in the morning, which meant that Operation *Byliny* was due to commence in fewer than twelve minutes. The Defense Minister was in constant touch with the Department of Defense, and the Department of Defense in turn was in close touch with the British forces in Germany and also with the Defense Council in Moscow, who had appointed an incongruously cheerful, English-speaking general called Nikolai Glinka to liaise with the British.

It was a strange and nervous night. The Prime Minister sat at her desk, her supper tray untouched; the Defense Secretary glanced several times at her chicken-breast sandwiches and her congealing Scotch broth and wished he had the nerve to ask her if he could have them. General Fawkes had made occasional appearances but each time he had seemed to be increasingly befuddled by lack of sleep and eventually Brigadier Mount-Avery had taken his place, all beams and smooth shaven chin, pleading that General Fawkes had been "summoned elsewhere," meaning, of course, to bed in Shepperton.

British intelligence had reported just before midnight that Bonn had somehow received advance warning of Operation *Byliny*. This was hardly any surprise since modern communications were so sophisticated and *Byliny* was such a massive military maneuver. If there was anything unexpected about it, it was that it had taken the Germans so long to understand that they were being sacrificed to the greater cause of global peace. But Whitehall's assessment seemed to be that the leak to Bonn had come too late for the Bundeswehr to take any effective retaliatory action. Faced with nineteen divisions of fast-moving Russian armor and artillery, it was unlikely that Bonn would consider it prudent to put up a fight.

The Prime Minister was agitated. She had always known that this would be the worst moment both politically and strategically, not to mention emotionally. This was the moment when the Federal German Republic would realize how completely it had been betrayed. But what choice had there been? Britain had been forced to decide between allegiance to Europe and allegiance to the United States; in the end, there had been no serious contest. The United States was richer; the United States was far more powerful; the United States spoke English. When Britain had first entered the Common Market, there had been talk about "going into Europe" as if Britain was somehow not part of Europe already.

There would be moments in the coming week that would be just as traumatic: when the Dutch and the Belgians and the French began to realize that they had been sacrificed too. By next weekend, the coastline across the English Channel would be Soviet territory, the Autonomous Oblast of Western Europe, and France would be flying the Red Flag at Boulogne instead of the Tricouleur.

The Prime Minister thought: if only it weren't too late. If only there had been some other way. But the enormous build-up of nuclear weaponry in Europe and the huge enlargement of the Soviet Navy had made it impossible for the political map of Europe to remain as it was. Something had had to give; something had had to be surrendered; otherwise Europe would almost inevitably have been devastated. Only the Prime Minister and her closest advisers knew how close it had come to that, and how frequently. There had almost been out-and-out war with the Soviet Union when cruise missiles were first aimed at British soil, and there had been scores of hair-raising incidents when Soviet reconnaissance aircraft had overflown NATO territory.

Ultimately, of course, it had been all those weeks of relentless pressure from the United States that had obliged the Prime Minister to agree to the talks in Copenhagen. With his mid-term elections due, the President had badly needed to be able to boast to a disillusioned electorate that he had achieved total security in the Western Hemisphere and the end of the Communist regime in Cuba. He had also insisted on no further Communist expansion in Asia and no more guerrilla activity in the Third World. In return, he was prepared to give up the military protection of Western Europe, which also happened to be the single most expensive item in his defense budget.

The President had reminded the Prime Minister in a fierce conversation (later described by Downing Street as a "frank discussion") that Britain still owed the United States $12,083,291,413 from World War One and that that was one of her smaller liabilities.

It had been made quite clear to the Prime Minister that if she was not positively in favor of the Copenhagen Agreement, she would be deemed to be against it, with all the unpleasant political consequences this would bring down upon her.

Tonight she remarked to her ministers, "I must say that I would feel a great deal easier about the Russians advancing into Europe if we didn't have all these strikes. How seriously do you think they might have affected our ability to defend ourselves?"

The Defense Secretary took off his spectacles. "Hard to be exact, Prime Minister. I mean, if Britain actually were to be attacked, it's quite conceivable that the unions would do their patriotic duty and call the strikes off at once. But things have changed since World War Two. There are some very strong links between the unions and the Soviet Communist Party. In the last miners' strike, the Russians collected fifty thousand roubles to support them and the miners won't forget that in a hurry. Our nuclear-strike capability won't be seriously affected. Trident will remain just as effective, but as far as beating off any kind of conventional attack is concerned, well . . . we would be very much weaker."

The Home Secretary noisily cleared his throat and threw out one hand as if it were a cricket glove he was trying to toss back into his bag. "It all seems fairly quiet tonight, Prime Minister, on the industrial front. No new walkouts, pickets docile enough. And even Albert Grange is keeping his mouth shut. I wouldn't say the chances are all that hopeful. But, well, we may be seeing the reflection of the light at the end of the tunnel, if not the actual light."

The Prime Minister didn't seem to be amused or reassured. "What if the Kremlin doesn't keep its word? What if the Russians continue to threaten us even after they've taken over Europe?"

"That rather depends on the continued support of the United States," said the Foreign Secretary, breathing on his glasses and polishing them briskly with his handkerchief. He looked across at the Prime Minister with weary eyes. "Come on, Prime Minister, we've discussed this a thousand times. We were caught between Scylla and Charybdis. This is the only way through, and we do have the Copenhagen Agreement."

"An agreement to which Britain was only a secondary party."

"But an agreement nonetheless."

"The Potsdam Agreement was an agreement. In the Potsdam Agreement, the Soviet Union promised to honor the nationality of Latvia and Estonia and Lithuania."

"With respect, Prime Minister, that's history."

The Prime Minister turned away sharply. "Not to the people who live there."

The Home Secretary sighed. He wished he were at home in Buckinghamshire, asleep. He missed his dogs, and his wife. He wouldn't even get his usual Sunday breakfast, with the newspapers and home-cured bacon.

"I really think we have to make the best of a rotten situation," he said. "Perhaps the greatest problem has always been that Britain ought to have been located off the American coast rather than the European."

"I know we're talking about changing the map," replied the Defense Secretary, "but that's rather an extreme sort of alteration, don't you think?"

The Prime Minister said, "I can't believe that it's come to this." She could sense for herself the authority she had lost over her Cabinet since she had been forced to agree to Operation *Byliny*. The ministers behaved like mischievous public-school boys these days, tossing metaphorical paper darts around the Common Room and chalking up insults on the blackboard. Her own political spirit, although she didn't yet dare admit it, had been broken forever. All she could see ahead of her now was a caretaker's job, making sure that Britain remained reasonably free and reasonably profitable. After all, the United Kingdom would now be the only buffer—politically, economically and geographically—between the Soviet Union and the United States. All of her time would be spent in resisting the bullying and the cajoling of both.

It was dangerous, unpleasant and hideously frightening, but perhaps she would be able to save the lives of the fifty-six million people for whom she was personally responsible.

The intercom buzzed. "Brigadier Mount-Avery," said the Prime Minister's secretary tersely.

Brigadier Mount-Avery came in with his swagger stick under his arm, his chestnut mustache gleaming, dressed as immaculately as if he were on his way to salute a visiting head of state.

"Prime Minister," he said, inclining his head, his words clipping out like metal staples. "We've just had the code message from Stuttgart that everything's ready to go. Apparently the Bundeswehr has been kicking up all kinds of fusses, talking about suicide missions and so forth, but the last I heard, they've been ordered to stand down.''

"Thank you, Brigadier," said the Prime Minister. "I've heard the same thing from Bonn."

"They don't seem to know yet how close we are to zero hour," the Brigadier remarked.

"No," said the Prime Minister soberly. Chancellor Kress had called her twice tonight already, appealing for information and for military support against the Soviet Union. Each time she had been obliged to stall him and to lie. She hoped there would never be a more ignominious moment in her career than this. She was glad that her husband was so understanding. He was as frightened of the future as she was.

The Defense Secretary glanced across the Prime Minister's desk at the carriage clock, which was chiming two. "I'd better be getting back," he said, uncrossing his legs. "In about ten minutes, all bloody hell is going to be let loose."

The Prime Minister said, "Wait," and pressed the button on her intercom to call her resident house manager. After a moment or two, he appeared at the door with a silver tray on which there was arranged a ship's decanter of whiskey and a dozen crystal glasses. Number 10's old skewbald cat, Wilberforce, rubbed around his ankles.

"A drink, please, Thomas," the Prime Minister asked the house manager. With infinitesimally trembling hands, he poured one out for each of the ministers present.

When he had done so, the Prime Minister raised her glass and proposed a toast. "Her Majesty," she said in a throaty voice. "May God protect her and all of us."

"Her Majesty," growled the ministers and drank.

There were eight minutes and fifteen seconds left to go before *Byliny*.

During the night, the Federal German government made urgent representations to the UN Secretary-General, Murtala Obasiki; and Chancellor Kress spoke in turn to the prime ministers of Denmark, Sweden, France and Belgium. Each head of government was as powerless and as confused as he was. The key to what was happening lay in the secret Copenhagen Agreement between the United States and the Soviet Union, with the United Kingdom as a cosignatory, and none of them was prepared to discuss the matter "except if it is tabled at the next regular meeting of the United Nations Security Council."

The British and American news media carried scarcely any mention of the European crisis except for a puzzled lead in *The Sunday Times* entitled "What Crisis?" By 3:00 A.M. European time, almost all the British Sunday newspapers had finished printing and the Prime Minister's press secretary was deftly fending off inquiries from BBC and Independent Television News with expressions of urbane surprise that the West Germans should be so concerned about the Soviet maneuvers, which, after all, were "nothing out of the ordinary."

He put down the telephone on the last call only thirty-five seconds before General Abramov gave the order for the East German border posts to be opened and the first Soviet tanks to advance into Western Germany. His order was simple: "Advance—and *pobyeda!*" Victory!

It was raining; scatterings of rain, like raisins. David Daniels was asleep in a side street in Oakville, Ontario, a few miles short of Toronto. He hadn't wanted to sleep; he had wanted to press on and put as much distance between himself and the United States as he possibly could. But it was a good two-and-a-half-hour trip from Niagara to Toronto and despite his determination to drive through the night, the shock and exhaustion of the past day began to tell on him, and at last he turned off Highway 5 into the lakeside suburb of Oakville— population 4,327, climate wet—drove down a neat, dead-end street and closed his eyes.

He dreamed of blood. He woke up two or three times, trembling and muttering to himself. There was blood everywhere, all over his face, all over his clothes, congealing between his fingers. He woke up and the blood was gone, but he was still sitting cramped in his rented car and it was still nighttime and raining, and he was still a fugitive from his own guilt and from the U.S. government's hounds of hell.

At three o'clock in the morning, when Operation *Byliny* had already been underway for nearly six hours, he turned on the car radio but all he could get was Bruce Springsteen singing "The River," and crackly country-and-western. He wished to God that he had been blessed with the foresight to buy himself a few sandwiches and a bottle of whiskey. He didn't even have a razor, and he was beginning to feel very prickly and disheveled.

He decided to move on. Maybe when he reached Toronto, he would be able to find an all-night diner and somewhere to shave. Out here in Oakville in the middle of the night, there was nothing but the stars and the lake and the pattering rain, and the huddle of tidy, suburban houses.

He was about to start the LTD's engine when he noticed a black Ford Tempo parked under the single streetlight at the corner of the dead-end. He leaned forward in his seat so he could examine it more closely in the rearview mirror. He was sure it hadn't been there earlier when he had first parked. It must have arrived sometime within the past two hours, quietly; and now it was waiting for him.

He started the engine and switched on the lights. Still watching the Tempo, he backed slowly into the nearest driveway, turned around and made his way toward the main road again. The windshield wipers squeaked against the glass, leaving smears of reflected streetlights. He paused as long as he dared but he couldn't see anybody sitting in the Tempo. Maybe his imagination was investing the world with ghostly pursuers. Maybe his guilty conscience was creating fantasies of fear. He turned toward Highway 5 again and kept an eye on the Tempo as he drove away. He took a sharp left across Mississauga Drive and still the Tempo remained where it was.

As he approached Highway 5, however, driving alone on the wet, wide street, he saw headlights turning out of the dead-end and following him. He couldn't make out if it was the Tempo or not, but what other car could it be? He pressed his foot harder on the gas and the headlights speeded up to keep close behind him.

He felt cold, sticky sweat on his back. He drove toward Highway 5 at nearly sixty miles an hour, raindrops hovering on the side windows of the car, the windshield wipers groaning, hesitating and groaning. The Tempo was so close behind him now that he was dazzled and he knocked the rearview mirror askew so he could see where he was going.

Instead of taking the ramp that was signposted to Toronto, he sped under the overpass until he was fifty yards out on the other side of it. The Tempo was right behind him. Without warning, he spun the steering wheel and yanked on the parking brake; the LTD slid sideways and U-turned across the slick, wet street, its tires screaming like runover cats, its tail almost breaking out of David's control and spinning around for a second time. But at the last moment he caught it, straightened it up and then released the brake and slammed his foot back down on the gas so that the LTD screeched back under the main highway in a cloud of rubber smoke and steam.

The Tempo hesitated, skidded, stopped, and then more cautiously crossed the median strip and came after him. David accelerated straight down Mississauga Drive and the Tempo accelerated after him until the two cars were streaking through the wet at over eighty miles an hour, sending up high fountains of spray, hurtling over intersections and crossroads, bouncing over dips and bumps in the pavement, telegraph poles slashing past them one after the other, *slash, slash, slash*, careering over wet, shiny railroad tracks, lights rocketing past them on either side, and then taking a wide left-hand curve, almost unmanageable at this speed, their tires on the edge of losing their grip.

David yanked the LTD's brake again and the car spun around and skidded backward across the highway. He saw headlights, streetlights, a chain-link fence. It was no good turning the steering wheel; the car was aquaplaning, its wheels locked, out of control. It banged into the curb on the opposite side of the road, spun around again and then stopped. David saw the Tempo flash past him, traveling too fast, and released the brake again, heading back toward the main highway. He had almost reached the ramp when he saw the Tempo's headlights flashing and dipping in his rearview mirror.

He jammed his foot on the gas pedal and the LTD screamed protestingly up the ramp. When he reached the main highway, however, he slowed down and took a sharp left turn so that he was driving southwest on the wrong side of the road.

It was early in the morning but the highway was already busy. Trucks came roaring toward him through the rain and the darkness, their lights blazing, their horns moaning like wounded dinosaurs. David continued to drive south, gripping the steering wheel tight, straining his eyes ahead to pick out the first glimmer of headlights coming toward him. He was driving at well over seventy miles an hour and if anything came toward him at even half his speed, the closing impact would be over a hundred miles an hour. Most of the trucks were traveling at well over fifty, which meant that if he hit one head on, he would be plastered over the front of it like a smashed can of Chef Boy-ar-dee bolognese sauce. Instantly.

He almost lost his nerve. But then he glanced up at the mirror again and could see the Tempo coming after him, its headlights glaring as a warning to oncoming traffic. He pressed his foot down as far as it would go and the LTD's engine strained to take him up to ninety. The car just wouldn't travel any faster, but then what could he expect from an untuned six-cylinder rental?

Gradually the Tempo began to overtake him. The rain drove even harder, and every now and then a truck or a car would come hurtling out of the spray, its lights flashing, its horn screaming, and David would have to swerve or change lanes. Soon the Tempo was almost alongside him, and the two cars drove at ninety miles an hour neck-and-neck the wrong way along Highway 5, passing signs for Appleby and Burlington, gradually approaching Hamilton. David was so tense that his ankles began to cramp and his shirt was chilly with sweat.

Now the Tempo was alongside him, but he didn't dare take his attention off the road for even one second to see who was driving it. It began to edge in closer until the spray from its front wheels washed over the side of his windshield; then, suddenly, he felt the first jarring shock of a collision. The LTD slued and skidded but David managed to keep control. They wanted to kill him, whoever they were, the same way they had killed Esther and the same way they would kill anybody who showed too close an interest in *Gringo*, whatever *Gringo* happened to be.

David looked up ahead. To his horror, he saw that two

massive trucks were approaching them side by side. Only the passing lane was clear and that was occupied by the speeding Tempo, which was now hugging close beside him like a hungry shark. The Tempo swerved again and there was a shriek of metal as their hubcaps grated against each other. David twisted the wheel around, first left, then right, but he couldn't stop the LTD from skidding madly from one side to the other. His windshield was blurred with truck headlights and rain; he could hear the truck horns blasting at him, but the LTD had completely lost its grip on the highway now and was spinning at ninety miles an hour.

He thought: God this is it, I'm going to die!

It happened like a well-choreographed ballet. The LTD, as it spun, struck the rear of the Tempo. The Tempo, deflected, skidded out of the passing lane and straight into the path of the oncoming trucks. David's LTD skidded the other way, into the median strip, into gravel and grass and scrubby bushes and at last, with a spine-jolting collision, into the steel crash barrier, crushing the front fender and shattering the windshield, dumping fragments of broken glass into David's lap as if they were bucketfuls of crushed ice.

He didn't even have time to turn around to see what happened to the Tempo. There was a noise beside him like a thousand agonized monks shouting out the *Kyrie Eleison*, and that was the noise of a Kenworth TransOrient's airbrakes clutching desperately at eighteen hurtling wheels and twenty-two tons of tractor and trailer and canned salmon. Then there was a bang as loud as a bomb going off, and there were pieces of car flying through the rain, curved segments of fender and wheel housing, and a sudden drenching of blood-red rain.

David shakily forced open the LTD's door. He stood in the wet next to his shattered car and knew with some relief that all he had to do now was to wait for the police to come and get him. The Tempo had been smashed open; only its seats and its rear wheels clung to the front of the truck that had hit it, crushed and black like fragments of insects. The dead bodies of the driver and his passenger lay sprawled on the pavement more than fifty yards away, with that blotchy, butchered look common to all victims of accident and assassination.

The truck driver came over to David. He was six feet three inches tall with a big mustache and a face as white as a wedding cake. "You crazy bastard," he told David in a tight, high voice. "You crazy bastard, I saw what you done."

David looked up at him, the rain dribbling down his chin. "I did what I had to," he said tiredly.

"You did what you *had* to? Those guys are dead. Those guys are stone-cold dead."

"Yes," said David. He closed his eyes and let the rain soak his hair and his face as if it might cleanse him. A long way away, he heard the *whip-whip-whip* of a police siren.

"You crazy bastard," the truck driver repeated. "They ought to lock you up."

TWENTY-FOUR

At dawn on Sunday, Soviet reconnaissance helicopters flying over West Germany were witness to the greatest motorized exodus in modern history. The bright summer sun rose gradually over the woods and fields of Lüneberg and Hanover and sparkled as it glinted off the rear windows of thousands and thousands of cars, all heading west along the autobahns and trunk roads. Every road was jammed solid. E-8 was a glittering river of Mercedes, BMWs and Volkswagens all the way from Braunschweig in the east to Osnabrück in the west, a distance of more than a hundred miles. E-63 was solid from the Eder to the Ruhr.

When they had planned Operation *Byliny*, the Soviet general staff had taken into account the fact that the West Germans owned more private cars than any other nation on earth, and they had expected heavy congestion on the roads. But they had never anticipated anything like this. One Mi-4 pilot flying over the south Teutoburger Wald east of Paderborn said, "Every road is crammed . . . I have never seen so many cars . . . they are pouring through the forests like lava."

To General Abramov, who had left Zossen-Wünsdorf shortly after five o'clock that morning and moved to a forward headquarters at Helmstedt, still on the eastern side of the border, the traffic was a serious tactical setback. A fast-moving blitzkrieg had suddenly become bogged down in a logistical situation that could only be compared with the Long Island Expressway on a holiday weekend. Abramov sent as many tanks as he could cross-country, but West Germany's thick afforestation made progress difficult and slow—added to which, every minor road the tanks attempted to cross was blocked solid with cars.

On E-3 between Hamburg and Bremen, T-72 tanks of the 3rd Shock Tank Army were completely halted by private cars. Their divisional commanders first attempted to clear the autobahn by ordering the West German drivers off the road but this took so long, partly because of the language difficulty and partly because of the Germans' extreme hostility and stubbornness, that eventually the infuriated Russians tried to simply push the cars onto the verge with their tanks. This only made matters worse: the highway was so congested that they succeeded only in blocking it even more effectively, locking together scores of damaged and immovable cars in rafts of tangled metal. By mid-morning they had to bring up huge tracked vehicles to pick up the wrecks by crane and dump them at the side of the road.

Under the terms of the Copenhagen Agreement, no shots were to be fired by the Soviet Army except in self-defense and so the tanks were unable to blast their way through with missiles or armor-piercing shells. Somehow the Germans sensed that the invading troops were under considerable restrictions and did everything they could to make the advance more difficult. Farmers blocked open fields with lines of combine harvesters and immobilized tractors; tank after tank was brought to a halt with broken or damaged tracks, the casualties of spades and paving stones thrust into their wheels as they ground their way almost at stalling speed through villages and suburbs.

Chancellor Kress had decided that without the Americans and the British, any attempt by the Bundeswehr at fighting back would be catastrophic. "It is a bitter decision," he said on morning television, "but I am not prepared to preside over the third massacre of German youth in a single century."

He had lodged a formal complaint with the United Nations and would try by "every means available to me" to oblige the Soviet Army to withdraw.

At the same time, France, Belgium, Holland, Switzerland, Italy and the Scandinavian countries had expressed "shock and disgust" at the British and American withdrawal from West Germany. All had called for urgent meetings but the President and the Prime Minister had responded with nothing more than a one-line reply that had been prearranged between them: "The joint decision of the United States and the United Kingdom to withdraw their military forces from West Germany is irreversible and not open to discussion."

Much previously unflexed strength was applied by both governments during the first day of Operation *Byliny*. Anybody who had imagined that Britain and the United States had a free press was rapidly disillusioned by the earliest reports from Europe. "Peace At Last!" was the headline chosen by the *Daily Express* for its 2:00 A.M. Monday-morning edition. The *Daily Telegraph* said, "Soviets Take Over West Germany—'Permanent Peace' Promised After Benign Invasion." The *Daily Mirror* proclaimed "Comrade!" and printed a large picture of a Russian soldier shaking hands with an old German pensioner in a Tyrolean hat.

On both sides of the Atlantic the tone of television reports was equally cheerful and approving. In the United States, a network editorial from CBS spoke of "a new era in world peace . . . a masterly and deeply responsible redivision of the world's land masses . . . to relieve the pressures of the past and meet the demands of the future. . . ." The President appeared smiling on television and said, "I want you all to know that today is the first day of a happy and secure tomorrow. To those of you who have relatives and friends in West Germany, I want to say that I have received from the Kremlin this morning a written assurance . . . and here it is . . ." holding up a piece of paper "that the rights and property of all citizens of the Federal German Republic will be respected."

The President paused for a moment and then said, more seriously, "In political terms, all that has taken place in West Germany today has been a change of management. One security force has been replaced by another, but the implications in terms of world peace are of course far greater than that. At last we can sleep easy at night . . . at last we can look ahead with complete confidence to the prospect of bringing up our children, our grandchildren and our great-grandchildren. My fellow Americans, today a great shadow has been lifted from the face of the world. The curse of the twentieth century, the nuclear bomb, has at last been lifted.''

The President finished his address by promising that fresh nuclear-disarmament talks had already been arranged with the Soviet Union and were expected to start "momentarily."

In northern Europe, Sunday afternoon was warm but overcast. Gradually the Soviet Army pressed forward and by seven o'clock it had managed to advance as far as the Weser. In the south, it had managed to clear most of the civilian traffic off E-4 and push through the Fulda Gap as far as Hanau, on the eastern outskirts of Frankfurt. General Abramov decided not to enter any major cities until daybreak of the following day because of the risk of sniping and vandalism.

He reported back to the *Stavka* that the day's progress had been "disappointingly slow because of unforeseen traffic conditions and because of the political restrictions placed upon the army" but that it had been comparatively uneventful, with few casualties. In all, seventy-two Russian soldiers had died and a hundred and nine had been injured, almost all of them in traffic accidents.

As the sun began to sink, the fleets of Russian tanks and BMP infantry fighting vehicles came to rest: on heathland, in wide fields of spring wheat, in silent villages and darkened towns. The evening air was heavy with dust and the sharp smell of burned diesel and gasoline fumes. There were more than six thousand DMPs in the Group of Soviet Forces Germany and their high-output engines had been blaring all day. There had also been hundreds of tanks, hundreds of trucks and scores of self-propelled howitzers as well as literally millions of private cars. More fuel had been consumed in West Germany in a single day than was normally used throughout the whole of Europe in two weeks: a hundred and forty billion barrels.

Refugees flowed west all through the night, although the departing British and American forces had done everything they could to persuade German civilians to stay in their homes. The refugee problem had been discussed at length in

Copenhagen and it had been agreed that a huge disruption of the civilian population would be unavoidable, especially since the Russians would not be permitted to land SPETSNAZ parachute commandos ahead of their principal line of advance. However, once the refugees had realized that the Soviet Army was going to occupy the whole of western Europe, it was expected that the majority of them would return home. There would be nowhere else for them to go, except to Britain. And Britain had already showed her indifference to the refugees by forbidding the landing in the United Kingdom of any Lufthansa aircraft, apart from the fact that all of her air-traffic controllers were out on strike.

It was a day of little bloodshed but enormous fear. The fear crossed the European continent like a dark wave across the ocean, and that evening, as the Soviet tanks at last came to a standstill, everybody prayed.

In Scandinavia, lights burned in government buildings all through the night. The Swedes had no doubt that the Russians would also try to take over Sweden, Denmark and Norway. The Finns had already conceded defeat and opened their borders to the Soviet Army so that a representative tank force could drive into the center of Helsinki and park in serried ranks along Mannerheimintie, the main shopping street.

The Finnish correspondent for *The New York Times*, Aaro Haanpää, wrote in his private diary. ''I understand *rationally* why the government has allowed the Soviet Army to drive without resistance into Helsinki; it could not face the prospect of another war of attrition with the Russians. Not another Viipurii, not another Lake Ladoga, not another bombing of Helsinki. There are times when you look back into your mind and you have to say, 'Not again.'

''But walking this evening all the way from Museigatan to Erottaja Skillnaden beside rows and rows of Russian tanks, I felt an emotional fury so great that I could scarcely prevent myself from pounding with my fists on the armor of each one of them and crying out, '*Mitä te olette tehneet maalleni? Mitä sinä olet tehnyt sydämelleni?*' What have you done to my country? What have you done to my heart?''

TWENTY-FIVE

In Copenhagen, on the fourth floor of a gray office block on Thorvaldsensvej, just across from the Landbohøjskolen, an extraordinary meeting was taking place, an extraordinary meeting that would have extraordinary consequences. The office had been borrowed from the Frederiksberg Paper Company, whose managing director was a long-time friend of the man who called himself Hans. It was quiet, air-conditioned, decorated in dark blue. On the walls hung rows of shiny abstract lithographs by young Danish artists. The furniture was made of white leather and curved beechwood.

Michael and John and Lev had been the first to arrive. Rufina was being kept in a house in the suburb of Brønshøj, west of Copenhagen, for questioning by two of Lamprey's Danish agents, one of whom had been a double KGB agent for nearly nine years.

Michael and John were exhausted; even Lev was red-eyed. After they had been picked up from the beach at Vyborgskij Zaliv, the two Bell Jetranger helicopters had flown them first to Karhula, fifty miles farther west along the coast and well into Finland. Then, after refueling from a parked tank, they had been taken to a small, private airfield at Kirkkonumini. From there they had been flown through the night in a LearJet belonging to Suomi Cardboards and had landed in the early hours of the morning at Ledøje in Denmark, an hour's drive by rented car from Copenhagen.

The Finnish helicopter pilots who had rescued them from the Soviet Union were friendly and amusing. During the winter months, they said, they flew food and mail up into Lapland. During the summer, they took any work they could get, and that included "rescue missions" for Lamprey. At Kirkkonumini, while they were waiting for their plane, Michael had talked to the younger of the two, whose face under his huge multicolored knitted hat was humorously troll-like. He had asked him whether the risks of flying illegally into the Soviet Union were worth taking.

The young man had grinned and laughed. *"Meidän ystävämme aina maksavat meille hyvin. Sinä unohdat, heillä on rahaa kuin roskaa! He ottavat mitähe haluavat valtiolta, heillä on varaa olla antelioita. Sitäpaitsi, ystäväni ja minä teemme kaikkemme etta Ryssa näyttäisivat nauretivilta. Ystäväni taistell Viipurissa."*

Lev had briefly translated. Lamprey always paid the pilots well because Lamprey had almost unlimited financial resources: the intelligence budgets of nearly a dozen different countries. What was more, the pilots would do anything to cock a snoot at the Russians.

Michael and John had showered in the green-tiled executive bathroom at the Frederiksberg Paper Company, and a blonde girl called Krysta had brought them clean blue shirts, tailored slacks and new pairs of nylon socks. Then they were taken through to the main office where Hans was sitting on the edge of the desk reading through sheets of computer printouts.

Hans smiled and offered his hand. "Mr. Townsend, Mr. Bishop. You may call me Hans if you wish. It is not my real name but it is better than people saying 'Hey, you' every time they want to speak to me."

"Do we have you to thank for our escape?" asked Michael. Then suddenly feeling weak, he said, "Would you mind if I sat down? I think I've just about had it."

"Please," said Hans and offered them chairs. He walked around the desk, picked up the telephone and said, "Krysta, bring us some coffee, please. Yes, you know where they keep it." Then he walked around the desk again and sat down, rhythmically swinging his leg.

"Your escape was not the first. So far—as Lev might have told you—we have brought seven British specialists out of Russia, not because we were particularly interested in saving them from a lifetime of hard work in some distant and uncomfortable part of the Soviet Union. We are not so philanthropic! No, the reason was that we were interested in depriving the Soviet Union of expertise in several crucial areas of defense. Weapons systems, radar, all kinds of aeronautics, missile-proof armor, computers . . . they were being sent experts of all descriptions. Most of the experts are still imprisoned in the Soviet Union of course, but we did manage to snatch back quite a respectable percentage."

Hans smiled and stood up again. "Now, of course, we know *why* they were being sent these experts and under what kind of arrangement."

Michael said, "You mean that it was all a prelude to what happened today?"

"Of course. The sharing of high-tech information was unquestionably part of a package deal the Americans and the British came to with the Kremlin. It seems to us that the deal has many ramifications, some of which have been obvious, like the withdrawal of American and British forces in the face of the Soviet incursion. Others have not been so obvious, like the very careful protection of ancient monuments. I had word today from one of our people in Bremen that a special detachment of the Soviet Army was protecting the Schütting guildhouse, and presumably they are protecting the *rathaus* too. So you see, this military operation has been very carefully worked out, down to the last details, and it was plainly a major part of the agreement that there should be a minimum of bloodshed and damage to property. The ultimate war, my friends! Far more sophisticated than nuclear attack. Far more frightening in a way. A war in which the outcome has been decided before any of the armies even begin to move."

Michael wearily rubbed his eyes. "Can you still get telephone lines to England?" he asked. "I would very much like to call my wife."

"Of course," said Hans. "But please understand why we have deployed a considerable amount of our resources to bring you here to Copenhagen. You are computer experts, yes? That was fortuitous for us. It would have been even more fortuitous if you had fallen into our hands a week ago. We believe, you see, that some of the details of the agreement reached between the Western allies and the Kremlin may be stored in the databank of a computer here in Copenhagen, and we would appreciate it if one of you could attempt to log onto that computer and extract as many of the details as possible.''

John slowly shook his head and sniffed. ''Can't see much hope of that. Sorry.''

''You are an expert, yes?'' Hans asked him.

''Well, yes, and I can log onto most run-of-the-mill computers, but if any of this agreement is stored in a databank here in Copenhagen, in a country basically hostile to the Soviet Union, you can bet your life that it's totally secure. Protected by prime-number codes, special security passwords, you name it.''

''You can't get in?''

John looked across at Michael, blew out his cheeks and shrugged.

Michael said, ''You could give it a try.''

''Won't get very far,'' said John pessimistically. ''And besides, there's always the danger that the computer's owner may track back and discover where we're coming from. And knowing what *these* customers are like—well. . . .''

Hans said calmly, ''The computer is an IBM-Two thousand located in the offices of a firm of Danish architects, Klarlund and Christensen. There is an IBM-Two thousand here in this office, which is partly why I chose this place to bring you. One of our own people has already had a try at logging onto the Klarlund and Christensen database but without success. What we are particularly looking for is any information stored by an agent of ours called Nicholas Reed. Well, that was the name under which he was working. We think he may have left us some information that will be helpful.''

John looked unhappy. ''I'm very tired,'' he said. ''I'm not at all sure I could do it. Not without codes. Not without half an inkling of what the codes might be.''

Hans looked at his fingernails. ''We are questioning the Russian lady you brought with you from Finland, Miss

Konstantinova. It is possible that she may know something helpful. Not likely, but possible.''

John said abruptly, ''You're not going to hurt her?''

Michael was embarrassed, mostly for himself. He knew now that from the moment they had been met by Rufina at the Sheremetyevo airport, John had taken a fancy to her. Well, they both had. But whereas Michael had been reasonably good-looking and confident, John had been tongue-tied, bespectacled and clumsy, unable to compete. Yet he still cared for her, and he showed it without shame.

Hans smiled. His smile was like the slow-burning fuse of a stick of dynamite. ''We never hurt anybody,'' he said. Then, still smiling, ''You believe that, don't you?''

''I want to call my wife,'' said Michael. Anything to change the subject.

John took off his glasses, an extra pair that had been lent him by Yakov, and wiped his eyes. ''Well, if you're going to do that, I might as well take a look at this computer. No point in us both wasting our time.''

Michael looked back at him sharply but decided they were too tired to start arguing; and in any case, there were far more important things to be done.

''Come,'' said Hans and beckoned John through to the office where they kept their main computer terminal. As he went, he pointed to the telephone on the desk. ''You can use that phone to call your wife. The operator will tell you the code for Britain.''

Michael dialed home, the old Sanderstead number, and waited with a rising feeling of unreality while the phone rang and rang at the other end. At last it was picked up and he heard Margaret's sleepy voice say, ''Two five five one. Who's speaking, please?''

''Margaret,'' said Michael in a stilted voice. ''Margaret, this is Michael. I'm safe.''

''Michael?'' she said, although she knew it was him. And then she started to cry.

''Margaret, please don't cry. I haven't got long to talk. I'm safe.''

''Oh, darling, you don't know how frightened I was. I thought you were dead. I was sure you were dead. And when the Russians started invading Germany . . . I didn't think I would ever see you again. Oh, darling. Are you still in Russia?''

"No, I'm in Copenhagen. Some people—well, some friends—helped me to get out of Russia. John too. He's safe. You could call Sonya and let her know. I'm sure she'd appreciate it. How's Duncan?''

"Oh, Duncan has missed you like anything. Oh, Michael, I've missed you too. I really thought you were dead. I'm sorry I'm crying. Oh, Michael, I'm so glad to hear from you. When will you be home?''

"I'm not sure yet," Michael told her, "but soon. Very soon. Please don't worry. The people I'm with now, they're friends. But I've lost my passport, everything, so it may take some time for me to get back into the country. Listen, I'll call you again as soon as I know anything, I promise.''

"Do you have to go now?" Margaret asked him, begged him.

"I'm sorry, darling. This isn't my phone. But I promise to call you again just as soon as I can. I mean it.''

Margaret said, "This Russian invasion . . . it won't affect Britain, will it? They keep saying on the news that it's perfectly all right and that we don't have to worry.''

Michael took a breath. "As far as I know, you don't. It's all part of some deal that was made between Britain and America and the Soviet Union. I don't think the Germans are very happy about it, but apparently it's going to make World War Three a lot less likely. I mean, that's all I know. I've only heard the same kind of news that you have, and I'll be home soon.''

"Oh, do hurry, won't you, darling?''

An odd and mischievous picture came into Michael's mind: a picture of Rufina standing in front of the mirror at the Rossiya Hotel, naked, her crimson-nippled breasts cupped in her hands, her pubic hair black and shaggy. She was the only girl Michael had ever known who didn't shave under her arms. Somehow that seemed faintly unhygienic and dangerous.

"Yes," said Michael. "Yes, I'll hurry. Give my love to Duncan. Tell him I miss him.''

At that moment the office door opened and a fiftyish man

in a crumpled linen suit walked in, unshaven, with bruised cheekbones, and demanded, "Where's Hans?"

"I'm on the phone," said Michael.

"I can see that," the man retorted in a dry American accent.

"Darling, I'll have to go," Michael told Margaret. "Please believe me, I'm going to do everything I can to get home as soon as possible. Wednesday at the latest."

He put down the phone. The American stepped into the middle of the room and looked around, his hands on his hips, his middle-aged spread bulging over his belt. "The way things are going, I don't think any of us are going to get home, either now or ever."

"You're looking for Hans?" said Michael edgily.

The American nodded and then held out his hand. "Charles Krogh."

Michael shook his hand and said, "Michael Townsend."

"You know this crowd?" Charles asked.

"Lamprey? Well, yes. They rescued me from Russia."

Charles said, "That figures. They do things like that. They're very . . . what do you call it? Iconoclastic."

He hesitated for a moment and then said, "Breakers of icons. The world has always badly needed people like that."

Then he frowned at Michael and added, "Why did the Russians want anybody like *you*?"

TWENTY-SIX

John said, "This is it. The Klarlund and Christensen computer."

On the screen in front of him, the green words hovered, "Klarlund & Christensen IBM 2000 ready," with a flashing cursor. John had contacted the computer through the telephone modem connected to his own IBM keyboard, although he was still faced with the task of penetrating the database relating to Nicholas Reed. He punched in, "Personnel File— Nicholas Reed" but the computer flicked back with "Security Error—Ready."

Charles came into the office closely followed by Michael. He shook hands with Hans and nodded toward John. "Is this your computer expert? How's he getting on?"

"Well, he has just started," explained Hans. "The data we are looking for will be well-concealed by passwords and codes."

John sat back. The flashing green letters on the computer screen were reflected in his glasses. "We're lucky," he said. "The computer's giving me another try at keying the right password. Some high-security computers give you only one shot and if you fluff that, even if you mistype, they close down on you and won't let you in for anything."

"How can you possibly find out the password?" asked Charles.

"Logic," said John and punched in, "Run all redundant passwords." There was a moment's pause and then the computer printed out three defunct passwords no longer secure: "Whipple. Pratt. Howe."

"Well, well," said John, taking off his glasses. "Just the kind of code you would have expected from a firm of architects."

Charles said, "What's this . . . Whipple, Pratt, Howe?"

"My dear chap," John beamed, turning around in his chair, "Whipple, Pratt and Howe are varieties of trusses."

"Trusses?" Charles demanded. "You mean *surgical* trusses?"

Tired as he was, Michael couldn't stop himself from laughing. John said petulantly, "*Constructional* trusses, for bridges."

"All right," Charles acceded. "But what purpose does it serve to know what all the old passwords were?"

"In this case," said John, "it might do us rather a lot of good."

"Rather a lot of good," Charles mimicked sarcastically in a British accent, "Listen, expert, why should this computer have told us what all the old passwords were anyway? Aren't they just erased when they're changed?"

"Not always," said John. "Quite a few companies use a cycle of ten or a dozen passwords and store the passwords they don't happen to be using at any particular moment in the computer's memory. All they have to do to change the password is to key 'Change password' and the computer automatically selects the next one. This is very low security but good enough for most ordinary companies that don't have anything very vital to conceal."

Michael said quietly, "What are you going to do now?"

John shrugged. "As far as I remember, there are only five main nineteenth-century bridge trusses. Five, or perhaps six. If that's what they've chosen, today's password must be one of two or three remaining types of trusses."

Charles shook his head. "This is unbelievable. Bridge trusses. Who the hell knows about bridge trusses? I didn't even know bridges *had* trusses."

Michael said, "John . . . well, he's interested in that kind of thing. You know, engineering, electronics. Anything technical. He's quite a genius in his own quiet way."

Charles patted his pockets looking for cigarettes. "He must be," he remarked, not altogether sympathetically.

"Let's try 'Bollman,' " John suggested and punched it in. The computer flicked up "Security Error—Ready."

"Looks as if it's giving me one last chance," John remarked. "The trouble is, they rarely give more than three. Even the staff people at IBM get only three whacks at their database."

Charles looked at Michael and pulled a face. "I practically got killed for this, I hope you realize."

Michael glanced at him and saw the stress lining the corners of his eyes, tightening his mouth. "We practically got killed too, if you don't mind."

Charles lit a cigarette, blew out smoke. "I don't mind, for Christ's sake. Just tell your friend to get his act together and find out what the hell's going on here."

John nervelessly punched in "Fink," the last type of bridge truss he could think of; it was a span of three inverted triangles strengthened with six right-angle triangles. There was a moment's pause, and then, equally nervelessly, the computer printed out all of Nicholas Reed's personnel file. Age, 31. Salary, 4,800 DKr a month. Address, 27, Istedgade. And then, at the very end of the list, "Ready."

"Ready?" asked Michael, leaning over John's shoulder and peering at the screen. "Ready for what?"

"Ready for another question," said John. "Whoever stored this program stored something else besides."

"But what do we do? If we don't know what we're looking for, how can we log onto it?"

John punched in "Fink" again. The computer replied with "Security Error—Ready."

"Another password," said John. "But this time something quite different." He punched in "List previous passwords," but the computer responded with "Security Error—Ready."

"What do we do now?" asked Lev, who had been sitting in the background quietly smoking.

"Well," said John, "there's nothing we can do short of poking and probing around to see if we can get some inkling of what the next password might be."

"And how long will that take?" asked Hans. "That's presuming we can do it at all."

John made a face. "Hours, maybe days. Maybe weeks. Maybe never."

"Just a minute," put in Charles. "In the last message I got from Peter Secker, he mentioned something about 'the old code.' "

"The old code?" asked Michael. "What's the old code?"

"We had code names when we were both working for the CIA. They were based on old baseball nicknames. I was Sea Lion after Charley Hall, the pitcher; Peter was Charlie Hustle after Pete Rose, who played for the Reds."

Hans laid a hand on John's shoulder. "Do you think this is worth a try?"

"We could do worse. It depends on what sort of a hurry you're in. If it's wrong, the computer could block us out completely and refuse to let us back in. It would be safer to try another way around."

"You say days or weeks? We don't have time," Hans replied. "Tonight the Russians are camped but tomorrow they will be on the move again. Come on, let's try it; it's as good a chance as any."

John punched in "Charlie Hustle—Run."

The display screen immediately went blank. Hans threw up his hands in despair. "Now we have lost it," he said.

"No, no, wait a minute," said John. "Give it a moment."

They watched the screen for thirty or forty seconds. Then suddenly the words "Found Charlie Hustle" appeared, with the word "Loading" flashing underneath them.

"That's it," said Charles triumphantly. "The old code. The old nickname. Damn it, I haven't seen that name in years."

Abruptly the screen began to fill with information. They stared in silent fascination as the extent of Peter Secker's knowledge about the Copenhagen Agreement was steadily revealed to them.

"A rearrangement of political geography was first suggested when Gromyko visited Washington in 1984 to talk to Reagan. In succeeding months, the Joint Chiefs of Staff and the Soviet *Stavka* were given the task of working out a method by which this could be done without at any time exposing either side to unacceptable military risk. Eventually, with the cooperation of the United Kingdom, an agreement was drawn up whereby the Soviet Union would take over Scandinavia and the whole of Europe excluding Spain but including Italy. The Soviets were particularly anxious to have Rome within their sphere of influence because of increasing Roman Catholic dissidence within their own borders and because of the opposition of the Pope to the puppet regime in Poland. In return for Western Europe, the Soviet Union would withdraw all financial and political support from Communist groups in South and Central America and the Caribbean, as well as any Communist cells within the United States and Canada. The Kremlin would also cease supplies of arms and military finance to Middle Eastern and African nations, in particular Libya and Angola."

The terms of the agreement, even when summarized by Peter Secker, ran into thousands and thousands of words. Charles was staggered by the complexity and the detail of it. It included fresh negotiations on fishing rights, fresh limits on international and territorial waters, new exchange rates and banking agreements, unprecedented trade and tariff arrangements, and precise definitions of civil rights within the area that would be described as "Soviet Europe."

"How did he get ahold of all this stuff?" asked Michael in amazement.

"He was a good agent," said Charles, lighting a cigarette. The room was beginning to grow dense with smoke now and John had to take out his handkerchief and dab at his eyes.

At the very end of the summary, however, there was a terse paragraph that startled all of them. A line was left blank and then the cursor rushed out the words, "There has been a further secret negotiation between the United States delegates and the Soviet delegates only. The Soviet delegates were deeply concerned about the United Kingdom becoming a kind of 'Cuba in reverse' and a continuing threat to their security. After several days of talks, the Soviets were persuaded to dismantle their naval base at Spitsbergen and to curtail submarine activity in the Atlantic, in exchange for which they will be allowed to completely take over the United Kingdom. This is to be done without informing the British government, although I understand that Communist subversive elements within Britain will be given advance warning so they can disrupt the movement of troops and generally sabotage Britain's defense systems. The United States will of course withdraw all cruise-missile warheads and at the eleventh hour evacuate all USAF bases. In the event of—'' and there the printout ended.

They stood silent for a long time, staring at the screen. John said, "He must have been interrupted. I expect he was going to send the whole message to you over the phone but he didn't get a chance to key the telephone modem instructions.''

Michael said in a constricted, shocked voice, "The Russians are going to invade England too? I can't believe it.''

"You can believe it all right,'' said Charles dryly. "Peter wasn't the kind of guy who makes things up.''

Hans smoothed back his hair. "It seems that we have come across the greatest double cross ever perpetrated, doesn't it?''

"I have to call Margaret,'' said Michael. He went back to the main office and picked up the phone. John switched off the IBM terminal and came after him. "After you,'' he said "I want to warn Sonya. And my mother, of course.''

Michael dialed the number. There was a long pause and then a continuous whining noise. He dialed again. Another pause, another whining noise. He tried dialing the operator.

"Excuse me, I'm trying to get through to a number in England.''

"I'm sorry, sir,'' the operator told him. "All international lines have been disconnected because of the emergency. No calls out of Denmark are being permitted for the time being.''

"But I called England only half an hour ago.''

"I'm sorry, sir. No international calls are now permitted.''

"But this is essential! It's an emergency!''

"The lines are disconnected, sir. There is no way I could place the call for you even if I wanted to."

"What about telegrams?" Michael demanded.

"I'm sorry. We are handling no international messages, telegrams or telex."

"Then what can I do?"

"You will have to wait, sir. Again, I'm very sorry."

Michael hung up. "No luck?" John asked and Michael shook his head. "They won't handle any international calls at all."

Hans came in and stood watching them, his arms folded. "What will you do, then?"

"I don't see that I have any choice. I'm going to have to fly back to England right away. That's if you can arrange it for me."

Hans said, "We can't take you privately, I'm afraid. But we will see what we can fix up with SAS. Give me some time."

The girl called Krysta brought in a large tray crowded with mugs of hot black coffee. They sat down in the office together, Michael and John and Lev and Charles, tired and tense, feeling the effects of having at last discovered too late what was happening all across Europe. They had a deep sense of frustration, a deeper sense of fear, and yet somehow their discovery of Peter Secker's report had come as an anticlimax too.

Charles said to Michael, "You got a family? Kids?"

"One boy."

"Well, that's where you'll want to be, isn't it? Back in England taking care of your boy."

Michael slowly rubbed his hands together. "How do you fit into all this? Are you one of them? Lamprey?"

"I used to work for Uncle Sam, quite a few years back. This is supposed to be my peaceful retirement. But, well, I have personal reasons for being involved. Those Russians iced some friends of mine. Peter Secker was one. A Danish guy named Jeppe Rifbjerg was another. Roger, he was still another. Then there was . . . somebody very close to me."

He took a deep drag at his cigarette and blew out a thin, long stream of smoke. "The end of the world, you know; that's only a definition."

In the other room they could hear Hans talking on the phone. Then there was a quick knock at the office door and the girl called Krysta came back in. "Inge is here," she told Lev.

"Inge Schültz?" said Lev, getting up from his chair. "Well, at last I shall have the pleasure. I have spoken to her on the telephone but have never met her in person. Is she alone?"

"No, she has the Russian with her."

"The Russian? You mean Nikolai?"

"No, the Russian marshal, Golovanov."

Lev whistled. "She brought Golovanov here, to Copenhagen? She's here now? This is astonishing! Show her in! Hans, come off that phone. Inge Schültz is here with Marshal Golovanov!"

Inge came in first. She was wearing a black beret, dark-tinted glasses and a black summer raincoat. Charles stood up and watched her in fascination as she stalked across the office, tugging off her black-kid gloves. She left behind her a waft of Balmain.

Behind her, dressed in a gray raincoat that fit him across the shoulders but was four or five inches too long for him, came Marshal Golovanov, looking disgruntled and tired. He was closely followed by a young man with both his front incisors missing, wearing a sagging corduroy jacket and carrying a UZI machine gun.

Hans came out of the inner office. He laid his hand on Michael's shoulder and said, "No success with a flight for you just at the moment, my friend. You may have to be patient. All international flights at the Kastrup airport are grounded. Every airline. My friend at SAS says they have been ordered by both the Americans and the Soviet Union to stay where they are for the safety of their passengers."

"What about a boat?" asked Michael. "Is there any chance of getting a boat? Damn it, I'll swim all the way if I have to."

Golovanov asked Inge in Swedish what Michael was talking about. Inge told him and he replied emphatically, "All boats attempting to leave the European coast are going to be turned back by the Baltic fleet. They will not be fired upon, just turned back. Of course they will be sunk if they refuse to do so. And as for driving, well, that would be impossible. The roads are completely blocked with military traffic, as well as with refugees."

Hans crossed the office and kissed Inge on both cheeks. "How are you, my dear? You did well to bring this fish in."

"More of a bear than a fish," said Inge with that Arctic smile of hers. "An angry bear too. He says I betrayed him. He says I used his body and then stole what was inside his mind."

"Well, well," said Hans, walking around Golovanov with his hands on his hips and grinning at him. "A real-life Hero of the Soviet Union. *Zdrastvuytye*, Marshal."

Golovanov said nothing. Hans asked Inge, "Doesn't he speak?"

Golovanov grumbled, "*Mne nuzhen perevodchik.*"

Inge smiled. "He is being rude about your Russian, I'm afraid. He says he needs an interpreter."

Charles came over and looked Golovanov up and down. "Tell him I'm an American," he asked Inge. "Tell him I've heard a lot about him. Tell him I used to work for the CIA. As far as the CIA is concerned, he's quite a character. A *bol' shoy sir.*"

"Who is this?" Inge asked Hans.

"Ah, I must introduce you," said Hans. "This is Mr. Charles Krogh. He has somehow become entangled in this affair. He has helped us immeasurably tonight."

Inge inclined her head, keeping her pale eyes fixed on Charles. "How do you do, Mr. Krogh. I regret that American slang does not translate literally into Russian. Marshal Golovanov is not flattered by your attempt to describe him as 'a big cheese.' "

Hans said, "Sit down, we'll have some coffee." He turned to the boy with the machine gun and said, "Niro, stay outside for a while. Let Tomas get some rest. Krysta will bring you some coffee, and maybe a sandwich if you're hungry."

Inge unbelted her raincoat and slipped it off. Underneath, she was wearing the same tight leather jeans as before and a thin gray-cotton sweater under which her large breasts moved in a way that made it obvious she was wearing no bra. Charles found her quite disturbing: her face, her body and that young, calculating coldness he had seen in some of the finest agents he had ever worked with. It was a special flaw in their humanity, a black hole where their emotions should be, an utter lack of sentiment. He crushed out his cigarette and made a point of sitting beside her on the white-leather sofa, as close as possible.

Hans said to Inge, "Translate this for me, will you? Tell the marshal that we have discovered tonight all the details of the agreement reached between the United States, Britain and the Soviet Union. We know everything. Tell him we also know that the United States and the Soviet Union have agreed between them to sacrifice Britain too."

Inge glanced at him and said quickly, "Is this true?"

Hans nodded back toward the inner office. "It was all on the computer. Nicholas Reed found out everything. Unfortunately, he was surprised by the Russians before he could put the information through."

Inge hesitated and then told Golovanov what Hans had said. Golovanov nodded soberly and then shrugged. "You are, of course, far too late. In fact, you have made matters worse. It was obviously because you kidnapped me that they started Operation *Byliny* one week early."

"What are you going to do with him?" Charles asked Hans. "The Russians may be advancing slowly but even so, they're going to be marching up Vesterbrogade by lunchtime tomorrow. It strikes me that it's going to be pretty embarrassing to be caught with an abducted Soviet marshal on our hands."

"We will kill him," said Hans matter-of-factly.

Charles looked at Golovanov and Golovanov looked back at him. In Golovanov's slitted Slavic eyes, Charles perceived something he hadn't seen for years. It was the curiously disconcerting deadness of a man whose spirit has somehow been broken, of a man whose pride has deserted him and left him fearful of every hour that passes.

"Who interrogated him?" he asked Hans.

Hans said, "Inge. She is one of our best. She has a nose for a man's special weaknesses."

"What the hell did you do to him?" Charles asked her.

Inge smiled. "Do you want me to give you a practical demonstration?"

Charles slowly shook his head. "No. I don't really believe I do."

TWENTY-SEVEN

The Soviet Army began to move west again at a few minutes after four o'clock on Monday morning. Huge diesel engines coughed and belched smoke. Wheels and tracks began to grind forward. Many of the main roads had been cleared of civilian traffic during the night and the tanks of the 1st Guard Tank Army sped all the way through to the outskirts of Dortmund in less than three hours.

Overhead, huge An-22 transports shone in the morning sunlight, ferrying in mobile rocket launches, troops, spares and ammunition. Occasionally a small formation of MiG-21 air-superiority fighters would thunder overhead, turning and climbing before they reached the gradually rolling-back "carpet" of Western airspace. There were hardly any British or American fighters left in Germany now, and Operation *Byliny* was gathering momentum without any hostile incidents between Eastern and Western forces, but the jets flew over to encourage the troops on the ground and to give the Soviet Air Force some active part to play in what was now turning into a huge but routine movement exercise.

Ahead of the advancing army, the fear mounted. The roads through France were so crowded with German refugees that the President of France had been forced to order all border posts closed and guarded. The Channel ports were overflowing with masses of terrified, bewildered people of every

351

Western European nationality; hungry, confused and betrayed. But no ferries or hovercraft were running to England, and any small private boats that attempted to sail across the Channel were turned back by Soviet destroyers.

By nine o'clock, after talks between the Danish government and the Kremlin, the Soviet Army sent one tank division and one motor-infantry division across the Danish border at Flensburg and landed a division of infantry from the troopship *Kursk* at Pakhuskaj in Copenhagen's Frihavnen. Soviet troops were also being put ashore at Skeppsbron in Stockholm, and two troopships were anchored in Oslofjorden, waiting for final arrangements for landing from the Norwegian government.

In the office of the Frederiksberg Paper Company on Thorvaldsensvej, they heard the church bells begin to ring all over Copenhagen. Most doleful of all were the bells of Vor Frue Kirke, the cathedral, echoed by the Helligåndskirken, the Church of the Holy Ghost. There was no traffic in the streets even though it was a Monday morning in summer, and there were scarcely any pedestrians. A temporary curfew had been ordered over Radio Denmark to allow the Soviet troops to land as quickly as possible, without interference.

Charles was standing by the window of one of the offices, staring out over the green copper rooftops of the city, listening to the bells and thinking of Agneta. Inge came into the office and stood behind him, watching him. He could sense that she was there. He could smell her perfume. But he didn't turn around, and he didn't say anything.

"Well," she said, approaching him slowly. "They're here."

"Yes," he replied.

"Is it the end of the world?" she asked.

He shook his head. "It's history repeating itself. History is like a severe case of gas."

"You're very philosophical," she said sarcastically.

"I've lived in Copenhagen a long time. I've got a lot of friends here. Barkeeps mostly, but still friends. They remember nineteen forty, when Hitler marched in here. April ninth, nineteen forty. It was the same old story. The Germans were here to 'protect' the Danes from Allied aggression. The Danes decided it was suicide to fight back. At least King Christian did. You can't blame people for wanting to keep their hides intact. And here it is, happening again.''

He was quiet for a moment; then he looked up toward the east. "You see those clouds? I always think of Copenhagen when I see clouds like that. They kind of remind me of ships, and islands. The lost ghosts of what Denmark used to be.''

Inge touched his shoulder as if she were trying to remember something. "You should not be so sentimental. This is not a sentimental world.''

He made a face. "You don't have to tell me.''

Without any hesitation, Inge kissed him on the cheek. He raised his hand to his mouth and looked at her, trying to figure out why she had done it.

"I like you, that's all,'' she said, answering his unspoken question.

"Well, I guess I like you too.''

"Aren't you going to ask me, 'What's a sweetheart like you doing in a dump like this?' ''

"Sure, if that's what you want.''

She smiled. "I was a delinquent. I was in porno movies when I was thirteen. Lolita movies, they call them. Well, they're banned here now; they're banned almost everywhere except in Holland. And when the Russians take over, of course they'll be banned forever, everywhere. The Russians are very prudish.''

"Is that a good thing or a bad thing? I'm not so sure that thirteen-year-old girls ought to be appearing in porno movies. I'm not so sure that thirteen-year-old girls ought to know that porno movies even *exist*.''

"I don't know,'' said Inge. She touched his shoulder again, stroked it absentmindedly, then suddenly turned away. "Most of the time, when I was doing it, I liked it. But I lost something, and I'm not talking about just my virginity. I lost—I don't know—any capacity to care.''

Charles gave a slight shake of his head. "Nobody ever loses that, not completely.''

Inge looked at him for a long time with calm, inquiring eyes. Then she said, "Do you want to make love to me? If I asked you, would you do it?''

"Yes,'' said Charles.

"I don't believe you. You would have been more of a man if you had said no."

"I would have been a liar. I gave up lying when I left the CIA."

She laughed. At that moment, Hans looked in at the door and said, "We are going to have to do something about Golovanov."

"I thought you were going to kill him," Inge said tonelessly.

"Well, yes, we are. But we must do it now and then leave as quickly as possible. The SPETSNAZ will be here soon."

Charles tightened his tie. "Wait a minute," he said. "Let me talk to him."

"You want to *talk* to him?" asked Inge. "All that needs doing is to put a bullet in his head." She pointed a finger against her right temple and imitated a pistol hammer with her thumb. "*Do svidanya*, Timofey."

Charles knew that Inge was deliberately trying to shock him. He went through to the small office where they had kept Golovanov imprisoned during the night. Inge followed him. Golovanov was sitting dully in a chair as if he were a cancer patient waiting for news of his latest X ray. He looked up and sniffed when Charles walked in.

"Do you want a handkerchief?" Charles asked him. "*Bumajnye plotky*?"

Golovanov raised his hand and said, "*Nyet, spasibo*." He looked desperately tired.

Charles drew up another chair and sat down close to him. He was fascinated by Golovanov's uniform, by his insignia, and by the simple fact that he was a marshal of the Soviet Union. In all the years he had worked for the CIA, Charles had never had an opportunity like this. It was like an SOE officer being granted an interview with Hitler.

Inge sat close by, translating. Charles said, "You and I can do each other a favor."

"What favor?" asked Golovanov, averting his eyes.

"A very considerable favor. You realize these people want to shoot you."

"They might as well."

"What are you saying?" Charles asked him, spreading his arms. "The Soviet Army is already landing troops at Pakhuskaj, not ten minutes from here. The cavalry has come to the rescue! And you sit here quite content to be shot?''

"Do you have a word in your language for 'disgrace'?'' asked Golovanov with a trembling chin.

"Yes,'' said Charles. "And we also have a word for 'futile.' Not to mention a word for 'bananas.' ''

Golovanov frowned. He turned to Inge and asked her a long and heated question in Swedish, German and fragments of Russian. Inge eventually turned to Charles and said, "He thinks you are mad because you keep talking about things like 'cheese' and 'bananas.' ''

"Tell him bananas means crazy,'' Charles growled.

In broken Swedish, Golovanov said, "What is the favor we can do each other?''

"Simply this,'' said Charles. "We can let you live and in return, you can tell your friends out there that it was we who rescued you from your kidnappers.''

"That would be a lie,'' Golovanov replied.

"Of course it wouldn't,'' Charles protested. "Just because we happen to be the people who kidnapped you, it doesn't mean that we can't rescue you from ourselves.''

Inge translated this to Golovanov and while she did so, Golovanov regarded Charles with a serious, baleful face. When she had finished, he said simply, "*Banan.*''

Charles told Inge, "I don't think you have to translate that.''

Just then Hans came into the office. "I've had another call from my friend in SAS. Apparently the Russians are allowing out one plane only . . . for American and British diplomatic staff. This was part of the Copenhagen Agreement, he says. The plane will land first at London, then refuel and go on to New York.''

Michael was standing behind Hans in the doorway. "Did he say what chances there were of getting us on it?''

"Very little, I'm afraid,'' Hans told him. "The Russians have already secured the Kastrup airport and nobody is being allowed anywhere near.''

Charles stood up. "Well I for one would very much like to get a seat on that plane.''

"Can't you try?" asked Michael desperately. "Surely there must be something you could do."

Hans slowly shook his head. "My friends, if there was a way . . . but now I have to be thinking about my own people too. The Russians are here and I have to make sure that my colleagues melt away and that all of our safe houses are dismantled."

"There is a way," Michael insisted.

"Sure there's a way," Charles agreed. "We head for the airport in a hijacked taxi, machine guns blazing, and demand to be flown home. What could be simpler?"

"No," said Michael. "You seem to be forgetting that we have one of the highest-ranking officers in the whole Soviet Army sitting right here. If *he* can't get us on that plane, who can?"

Charles pursed his lips approvingly. "The kid has imagination, I'll give him that. What do you say, Hans?"

Hans said, "Very, very risky, my friend. How can you rely on a Russian? He would only have to make the wrong gesture and you would all be dead."

There was a bustle and a small commotion outside. Then Niro appeared, the boy with the gappy front teeth and the UZI machine gun. He was pushing in front of him Rufina Konstantinova, who was looking red-eyed and exhausted. There was a bruise on her left cheekbone and her mouth appeared to be swollen. She saw Michael and stopped where she was but when he said, "Rufina . . ." she turned her head away.

"What's been going on?" Michael demanded. "Has she been beaten?"

Hans looked him up and down. "Does it matter to you?"

"Yes, it damn well does matter to me," Michael told him.

"She is KGB, my dear fellow. She was trying to enslave you for the rest of your life, attempting to take you away from your family. Now, with her active assistance, her own people have taken over most of West Germany and Scandinavia, and by the end of the week, there won't be any Europe left. Your wife and children will be prisoners of the most oppressive political system the world has ever known. And you are concerned because we bruised her face a little?"

Michael said, "It doesn't matter what she or her people have done; that doesn't give us the right to behave just as badly."

Charles lit a cigarette and without taking it out of his mouth, said, "Bull . . . shit."

Michael turned on him hotly but Charles waved his hand at him to cool down. "Listen, pal," Charles told him, "all the time that you've been making your toys in cloud-cuckooland, there's been a war going on. A real war with real guns and real people torturing each other and dying and you name it. Now I know all about you English people and your sense of fair play and what's cricket and what isn't, but if you want to survive in this war, you have to be slightly vicious. You don't have to be a psychopath or anything like that as long as you're sharp and quick and you're prepared to hit the other guy when the other guy hits you. And let me tell *you* something: the most vicious intelligence agents of all I ever knew were British. They had a flair for it. A combination of sneakiness and sadism. I guess they learned it at Eton. So . . . don't let's be too sympathetic here, okay?"

Michael flushed with anger and embarrassment but Hans said, "This is no time for such posturing, my friends. Believe me, Mr. Townsend, Mr. Krogh is not the tough nut he is trying to pretend to be. But this doesn't matter. Your most important consideration is whether you wish to try to get to the airport with Marshal Golovanov or whether you wish to try to escape with the rest of us."

Charles turned to Inge. "Tell the marshal we're going to drive him to the airport. Tell him that as soon as we get on that diplomatic flight, we'll let him go."

"But what then?" asked Inge. "Once we have released him, he could immediately order the plane grounded and have us arrested."

Charles smiled and shook his head. "Tell him we're taking his compatriot, Miss Konstantinova here, along with us as a hostage. She's coming on the flight. And believe me, if that plane even so much as falters, even if the toilets don't work, she's going to get her head blown off."

Golovanov jerked his head toward Rufina. "I am a marshal of the Soviet Army. What makes you think that I care whether this girl lives or dies? During the war I sent hundreds of men to their death. Hundreds. And women too.''

"Couldn't we take the marshal himself as hostage?'' Michael suggested.

"No,'' said Charles. "With him on board, the Russians wouldn't even let us taxi to the end of the runway. Besides, I doubt if the U.S. diplomatic staff would let us take him on the plane either. The U.S. has made a deal with the Soviets, remember? They won't want to upset the apple cart by helping a bunch of gangsters like us kidnap a full-fledged Hero of the Soviet Union.''

"Then we have no real guarantees,'' said Michael.

"You want guarantees, go to the Institute of Good Housekeeping. Miss Konstantinova here will have to do.''

"I will not help you,'' Golovanov said through Inge.

"It would be better for you if you did,'' said Charles.

"I would rather die first.''

Charles checked his watch. The glass was so scratched that he could scarcely see the hands. "What time does this plane leave?'' he asked Hans.

"You have an hour,'' Hans told him.

Charles went across to Niro and unslung the UZI from his shoulder. He slammed back the cock and then pointed the muzzle directly at Golovanov's nose. Golovanov didn't even flinch, didn't even draw his head back.

"Now, are you going to take us to the airport or not?'' Charles demanded.

Golovanov looked up at him intently. "No,'' he said. "And you may count on that.''

Charles squeezed the safety catch at the back of the UZI's pistol grip, releasing it. "Okay,'' he said. "If that's what you want, I'm going to redecorate this office with your brains.''

Inge said, "He won't do it, Mr. Krogh. He will accept death rather than do what you tell him to. He is more than stubborn.''

"Then what the *hell* are we going to do?'' Charles asked her.

"Leave him to me for a moment,'' said Inge.

"You mean alone?''

"Yes,'' Inge insisted. "Just for a while.''

Charles released the UZI's safety catch and handed the weapon back to Niro. "Beats me," he said to nobody in particular. "I thought *I* was stubborn."

"Perhaps that was why they didn't appoint you a marshal in the Soviet Army," smiled Hans.

They trooped through to the main office, leaving Inge alone with Golovanov. On the other side of the room, John and Lev were talking together. John was trying to explain to Lev how to prepare a simple household-accounts program for his home computer. Since Lev had neither a house nor a home computer, the whole exercise seemed more than faintly irrelevant.

Michael went up to Rufina and stood in front of her for a long time, saying nothing.

"You don't have to apologize for your friends," said Rufina.

"They beat you."

"They did worse than that. But our training prepares us for such things."

"They didn't—?"

She looked away. Niro kept his eye on her, his machine gun raised, although even if she attempted to run away, there was nowhere for her to go.

Rufina said, "You want to hear that they raped me?"

"Did they?" Michael asked. His skin felt cold all over, as if he had been electrocuted.

Rufina was silent. Michael reached out and tried to take her arm but she tugged it away.

"You should go back to your wife and child," she said. "You do not know anything about loving a woman like me."

Michael didn't know what to say. She was still beautiful in spite of her bruises, a martyred angel. But she was beyond his reach. He knew that he would have to go back to Margaret and Duncan and the small house in Sanderstead.

"May I kiss you?" he asked her.

She stared at him. "Why should you want to do that?"

"I don't know. Because I feel guilty about what they've done to you. Because I still care about you even if I can't have you. Because . . . well, I don't know. I do care for you, very much. I never met anybody magical before, if that doesn't sound too sappy."

"Magical?" she asked him. She hesitated and then she came closer and lifted her face to him. He leaned forward and kissed her gently on her swollen lips. She didn't close her eyes but watched him as he kissed her. Michael found it strangely disconcerting, as if he were being examined under a microscope.

"Do you know what they did to me?" she said. "They pushed a wine bottle up me, base first, and then they boiled a kettle of water. They said that unless I talked to them, they would fill the bottle with boiling water."

Michael turned around in shock and stared at Lev. Lev, not realizing what Rufina had been talking about, frowned back at Michael and then shrugged. John was saying, "From then on, only the transactions you type in on the keyboard are going to be printed."

"Your precious friends," said Rufina. "They are just as bad as the KGB. Worse in a strange sort of way because they always pretend they are so honorable and so humanitarian. And you, what do you do? You ask me for a kiss."

She made the word "kiss" sound like something unimaginably mean and degrading.

The door opened and Inge reappeared. Charles said, "Well? What happens now?"

Inge said, "What happens now is that we hurry. We have less than an hour to catch that plane."

"You mean that Golovanov will take us?"

"Golovanov will take us," said Inge. "So let us make haste."

"Well, well," Charles said. "I don't know what you did to him. Maybe you don't want to tell me, but it sure worked."

"Yes, it worked," Inge smiled. "And, no, I don't want to tell you."

Hans said, "We have a gray Volvo parked in J. M. Thiles Vej, just around the corner. You can use that. I would suggest that you take a right onto H.C. Ørsteds Vej and drive straight to Kastrup. The Russians will probably have cordoned off the city center by now."

Hans went through to the next office and returned with the car keys as well as a UZI machine gun that he handed to Charles. "Try not to use it," he said. "I am giving it to you only to make you feel better."

Charles shook his hand. "You people have done more than was expected of you. I hope you realize that."

Michael and John said good-bye to Lev, who had decided to stay. "My fight is here, among my own people. There must always be those who struggle against the Politburo from within."

John went over to Rufina. He took off his glasses, folded them and tucked them into the breast pocket of his jacket.

"We may not get the chance later," he told her.

"The chance for what?" she asked him coldly.

"Well," said John, "simply to say good-bye."

She looked at him scornfully. "I suppose you want to kiss me too."

John shook his head. "I simply want to say I'm sorry. It's just a pity we couldn't have met at another time. You know, under better circumstances." He looked and sounded like a junior-high schoolboy.

Rufina closed her eyes as if she wanted to fall asleep right where she stood and never wake up. "I am too tired for wishes," she said.

It was then that Marshal T.K. Golovanov appeared, rubbing his freshly unfettered wrists, short but muscular and stocky and with a bearing that commanded their attention.

"*Kotoriy chas?*" he asked.

"*Pyat' minut desyat'*," said Inge.

"We should go, then." he said.

Because he was Russian, Lev went down to the street first to make sure there was no Soviet infantry around. The others waited in the outer office, Golovanov stiff and correct, Inge standing silent beside him. Charles kept a custodial eye on Rufina, his machine gun angled in the crook of his arm. He had never had a machine gun before, although he had been trained in its use, and he felt extremely dangerous and rather raffish. Michael and John said nothing to the others or to themselves. They had both begun to realize that the longer this game went on, the less qualified they were to play.

Hans said while they waited for Lev, "I want to advise you of some things. When you get on the plane, if you do, make sure not to tell any of the British or American diplomats that you know about the Copenhagen Agreement or any of its terms. That would make life very perilous for you. You must behave as if you are nothing more than ordinary tourists who have been unfortunately caught up in the Soviet advance and all you want to do is to return home.''

Five minutes went past and Lev still did not return. Charles said, ''We're going to miss that plane anyway unless he gets his ass together. What's holding him up?''

Golovanov remained impassive. John began to gnaw at the side of his thumbnail, something Michael had often seen him do when faced with a particularly difficult computer problem. Charles lit another cigarette and made a lot of noise blowing the smoke out.

After ten minutes, Hans said to Niro, ''Go down and see what's keeping Lev. Maybe there's a Soviet patrol outside.''

Niro slung his UZI over his shoulder and went down the corridor to the elevator. Hans called after him, ''Take the stairs, just in case.'' Niro waved an acknowledgment without turning around.

They waited with increasing tension and impatience. After a further five minutes, there was no sign of Niro either. Charles said, ''This is ridiculous. It's like the ten little niggers. One went to see what the fuck was going on and then there were five.''

At length there were only thirty-five minutes remaining before the plane was due to leave. Charles turned to Hans and said, ''What do we do? Risk it? I don't see that we have much choice.''

''It could be that there are Russians down there,'' said Hans. ''It is possible that both Lev and Niro have been captured and that the bastards are standing around waiting for the rest of us.''

Charles went across to the window and peered down into the street. ''I don't *see* anything. No BMPs, no trucks. The whole street's deserted.''

Michael said, ''For God's sake, we've got to try. Otherwise that plane's going to take off without us.''

Charles nodded. ''You're right; we've got to try. Is everybody ready?''

Hans put in, ''This is not safe, Mr. Krogh. All you people could be killed.''

"Sure," said Charles, "and tomorrow's Tuesday."

Michael looked at his watch, the one Margaret had given him for his birthday. There were only thirty-one minutes to go and the Kastrup airport was at least a half-hour's drive. He could almost imagine the plane on the runway, warming up. Even though the office was air conditioned, he was sweating, and he urgently wanted to go to the toilet.

"Wait for just one minute," said Hans. "Let me send Tomas down. Tomas!"

"Jesus," said Charles, fretting. "We're going to be spending the rest of our lives under the Red flag at this rate."

Tomas appeared, a burly young man of twenty-five or twenty-six with a wispy blond mustache, carrying a UZI. Hans spoke to him quickly and he went off to see what had happened to Lev and Niro. Michael took the opportunity to go to the office bathroom. Afterward, washing his hands, he stared at his face in the mirror and thought: God, what's happening to me? What's happening to the whole damned world?

When he came out of the bathroom, Tomas had returned. "There's nobody down there, nobody that I can see. I don't know what happened to Lev and Niro."

"Maybe they had to make a run for it," said Charles. "In any case, that's it, we're going. Michael, you ready? John? How about you, Marshal Golovanov?"

Inge said, "The marshal says that he is always ready."

"Do you think we'll make the airport in time?" asked Michael.

"Too goddam bad if we don't," snapped Charles.

With Charles leading the way, they walked quickly and quietly along the gray-carpeted corridor. All the other offices in the building were silent: Radio Denmark had warned everybody to stay home, to keep off the streets and to adopt a "dignified and correct demeanor" toward the occupying forces. The bitter irony was that the newscasters used exactly the same words they had used when the Germans marched into Denmark in 1940. "Dignified and correct."

They reached the elevator. "I'm too old for the stairs," said Charles and pressed the button. The elevator arrived almost immediately because there was nobody else in the building to hold it up. They stepped inside and Michael jabbed the button for the lobby. Charles was fidgety; Golovanov remained as calm as he could, his hands clasped in front of him as if he were standing in Lenin's Tomb on May Day.

The elevator reached the lobby. There was a moment's pause, then the doors opened. And there he was, waiting for them. Tall, hideously scarred, his eyes as blank and compelling as switched-off television screens. Novikov, barring the doorway to freedom. *Krov' iz Nosu*, old Nose Bleed.

"Shit," said Charles. He pulled back the hammer of his machine gun and raised it.

But Golovanov caught hold of the gun's barrel and said in English, "Wait." Then he spoke to Inge in that curious hodgepodge of Swedish, German and Russian that they had always used in their private conversations.

Inge said, "The marshal does not want any violence. He does not want this man Novikov hurt. He will continue to take us to the airport; he is sure that Novikov will not cause any problems provided we can take him with us."

"I'm not riding in any car with that monster," rapped Charles.

Michael took Charles' arm. Hans, during the night, had told him what had happened to Agneta, Roger and Jeppe Rifbjerg. "Charles," he said, "listen. We don't have much time left. Let's just play along with it for now."

"I could waste that monster in five seconds flat," Charles snarled. He was so emotional about killing Novikov that he was trembling.

"Oh, yes?" asked Inge caustically. "And in five seconds flat you would attract a whole division of Russian infantry. Be calm. You were a professional once. Show that you can be a professional again."

Charles wiped his mouth with the back of his hand. He lowered the UZI and said, "Let's go. Let's get out of here before I change my mind."

Golovanov stepped forward and spoke quietly and authoritatively to Novikov. The Russian assassin several times bowed his head and grunted in reply. Charles circled around them, looking edgily out the office doors at Thorvaldsensvej and then turning and smiling at Inge, Rufina, Michael and John as if they were all on a college outing and the bus was late.

At last Golovanov said, "If we go now, there should be no problem."

"Thank Christ for that," Charles breathed.

They left the office. An incongruous party on the strangest of days, they crossed the pavement and turned left into J.M. Thiles Vej. Just as Hans had told them, the Volvo was waiting. And lying on the pavement next to a green-painted railing were the bodies of Lev and Niro, black-faced from strangulation, the wires still maliciously tight around their bulging necks.

Charles jerked up his UZI again. "You see what kind of a beast this thing is?" he barked, waving the gun at Novikov.

Inge had tears in her eyes but she said, "Go on. We have only twenty minutes left."

They climbed into the Volvo, with Michael driving. Awkwardly, he U-turned and drove south in the direction Charles pointed out for him. "In a minute we'll run straight into Enghavevej, and that's E-Sixty-six, which goes straight to Kastrup."

The streets were deserted. There were no Russians, no Danes, nobody. Copenhagen looked as if it had been swept by a plague. They passed the huge Carlsberg brewery, crossed the main railway line and then drove over Sjaellandsbro. Glancing north up Sydhavn, Charles saw six or seven Soviet amphibious assault craft ploughing up the slate-gray water in formation. The sky was the same color as the buildings, dove-gray, and melancholy. Good-bye, Copenhagen, he thought. Good-bye, Agneta.

Novikov sat hunched in the back of the car, but he never once took his eyes off Charles. Charles, for his part, never took his eyes off Novikov, nor the muzzle of his UZI. Golovanov sat with his arms folded, as reserved and quiet as a taxi passenger. Rufina sat by the window, nervously tugging at her hair and glancing around for any sign of Soviet combat troops.

"Step on it, for Christ's sake," Charles nagged Michael. "This isn't a funeral. Not yet anyway."

They reached the Kastrup airport with six minutes to spare. As they sped up the approach road, they encountered their first Soviet troops: fifteen or sixteen soldiers from an airborne assault battalion, their khaki-colored Mi-26 helicopters still parked within view. Three of the troops stepped into the roadway as the Volvo came up to the airport perimeter, and they flagged it down.

"The airport is closed," one of them said in Russian.

Golovanov heftily wound down his window. "To me, soldier, nothing is closed. Stand aside immediately."

The soldier recognized with horror the uniform of a marshal of the Soviet Army and snapped to attention. When his companions saw what he was looking at, they snapped to attention too.

"These people are friendly diplomats who are to be flown out on the special diplomatic flight," said Golovanov. "You—I want you to find me an escort straightaway and take us out to the aircraft. You—I want you to go to the control tower and make sure the flight is held until all these people are safely aboard."

"At once, sir," the soldiers replied.

The perimeter gates were opened for them and Michael drove the Volvo out across the concrete, following the frantic wavings of one of the airborne troops, who had decided to guide them on his motorcycle.

"That *putz* is going to fall off if he isn't careful," Charles remarked, trying to be laconic but only succeeding in sounding strangled.

They rounded the terminal buildings and there it was: a 747, engines already started, in the colors of the Scandinavian Air Systems, blue and white. There were four or five baggage handlers around the steps as well as three Soviet officers and half a dozen Soviet troops. Michael drove the Volvo right up to the plane and parked.

The Soviet officers approached as they climbed out of the car. Then Golovanov heaved himself out of the backseat and the officers' confident forward step went instantly into reverse, like in a country dance. They saluted in flurries and stood aside in silence while Golovanov approached the steps of the aircraft.

A Soviet major came forward and saluted. "Comrade Marshal, this flight is about to leave. I am afraid that all the authorized passengers have been accounted for."

Golovanov said harshly, "These people are to leave on this flight, and that is that. I will regard any further comments as insubordination."

A warm May wind whipped across the airfield. The 747's engines built up to a thundering whistle. The Soviet major licked his lips and glanced toward the control tower and then looked back at Golovanov. He knew Golovanov from his picture in the Red Army magazine, and of course the Soviet news agencies had put out no bulletins about his abduction.

"Very well," he said at last. "Board your passengers. But make it quick, please."

With relief Michael and John began to mount the steps of the 747. But then Michael turned around and saw that none of the others were following.

"Come on," said Michael hopelessly. He knew for some peculiar reason that they weren't going to come, that none of them had ever intended to come. "Rufina, come on."

Rufina smiled sadly and turned away. The West was not for her. Especially not with a man who had to go back to his wife and child in a suburb of London.

Marshal Golovanov didn't even look up. To him the West was anathema, no matter what risks he was going to have to take when he announced to the Politburo that he had been lost and now was found. And with an intense shock, Michael realized that Inge wasn't coming either and that he had developed the maturity to understand why.

Inge wasn't coming because Inge had bought their freedom with her own body. Inge hadn't tortured Golovanov into agreeing to escort them to the airport. She had simply promised that she would stay with him, as his concubine, for as long as he wanted her. And why not? He would give her everything she wanted, a *dacha* in the country, perfumes, furs, and she would be no more a prisoner of her own destiny than she had ever been.

And Charles? Charles was lifting a hand, waving, saying, "Just a minute. Hold it a minute. I forgot something."

Michael watched Charles walk back to the Volvo, open the back door and root around under the seat. At the same time, Novikov tried to open the other door of the Volvo and obviously found that he couldn't. Michael couldn't hear any-

Graham Masterton

thing because of the 747's rumbling engines but he could see that Novikov was beating against the window of the car in a desperate attempt to get out.

Charles stepped away from the Volvo and Michael saw with a photographic clarity that he was holding the UZI machine gun. Because Charles had his back to the Soviet soldiers, none of them could see what he was doing. Golovanov was actually smiling for the first time since Michael had met him, and Inge was lifting her face toward the wind like a fashion model.

The UZI's cyclic rate wasn't as terrifyingly fast as the Ingram; it was only six hundred rounds a minute. But it let fly with a burp that startled everybody, and then another burp, and another.

The first burst shattered the rear windows of the Volvo and splattered the splinters of glass with blood. The second burst penetrated the seats, the doors, and the body until sponge rubber and flakes of paint were flying everywhere.

There was a pause. Charles walked around the back of the car with the elegance of a male ballet dancer waiting while the prima ballerina completes her solo.

He's got timing, thought Michael. Beautiful, elegant, experienced timing. He knows when it's time to kill, and he knows when it's time to die.

A bloody hand emerged from the broken window of the Volvo and tried to grasp the bodywork so it could help to heave Novikov out. It was like a mutilated crab, a creature with a life of its own. But then Charles fired again, a short burst, straight into the Volvo's fuel tank.

The car exploded with a dragonlike roar. Inside, it was a brilliant hell of funneling orange flames. For a second—only a second—Michael thought he could see someone flapping his arms in there. But then the black smoke began to tumble out and pile into the sky and Charles turned away; it was obvious to everybody that the act of vengeance was over. *Krov' iz Nosu*, the burned and resurrected man, had burned again.

An SAS stewardess appeared white-faced at the open door of the plane and said, "Sir? Come, we have to leave now. Please, straightaway! We are late already."

Michael and John made the last few steps up to the plane. But then they heard a series of crackling explosions and an extraordinary moan, and they couldn't help but turn around.

Novikov, blazing, had somehow struggled his way out of the car. He was standing on the concrete runway, ablaze from head to foot, and the crackling explosions were the sounds of his body fats burning. He took one step toward Charles and then another, although God only knew how he could tell where Charles was because his eyeballs must have burst long before he got out of the car.

Charles screeched at him, a long, long screech of hatred and revenge, and sprayed the remainder of his machine-gun ammunition up and down the giant's body.

Novikov jerked, trembled and fell. He lay on the concrete burning, and Charles walked over to him and watched his flesh blacken and his fingers curl.

It was then that one of the Soviet officers stepped up to Charles, unfastening his leather holster and taking out his pistol. He shot Charles once in the chest without even breaking his stride and then shot him again in the side of the head.

Charles heard a thundering noise. It could have been the 747; it could have been the sound of his own blood rushing through his brain. It could have been his accumulated memories, released at last. He opened his eyes and saw that the world was sideways, and very shadowy. He must be lying on the ground, his face against the earth. He wondered why he was there and why he couldn't breathe.

He didn't think about Agneta. Instead, he thought about his mother tucking him up in crisp white sheets, and the pale light of winter shining gently through his nursery window.

Somebody was kneeling beside him, a white-haired woman.

"Mother," he said with lips that could scarcely move.

TWENTY-EIGHT

David Daniels was finishing his coffee when the Canadian inspector came into his cell and stood there frowning thoughtfully, jingling his keys. The inspector had a ruddy face—the face of a man with incipient heart disease—and a ginger-colored mustache. He said nothing for a time.

"Are you going to charge me?" David asked.

The inspector shook his head. "I've been given other instructions."

"What other instructions?"

"I've been instructed to hand you over to two gentlemen from the Federal Bureau of Investigation. They're waiting for you outside."

David put down his coffee cup. "But this is Canada. The FBI has no jurisdiction here."

"All the same, that's what I've been told."

"But you don't understand," said David. "They're going to kill me."

The inspector rubbed the palms of his hands together as if he were rolling out tobacco. "I'm sorry, my friend. Those are my instructions and I have to obey them."

"I want to see a lawyer!" David demanded.

"You haven't been charged."

"But if I haven't been charged, you can't hand me over to the FBI."

370

The inspector smiled faintly. "You want to try me?"

They brought David his jacket and returned his wallet to him. He stood in the entrance hall of the police station, which smelled strongly of lavender wax, and signed a form saying that all his possessions had been returned to him. The desk sergeant had made two crosses on the form where he should sign.

Two officers escorted him out of the glass swinging doors and down the steps into the sunshine. There was a light wind from the west. Across the street a gray Buick was parked; two men in sports coats and gray slacks were waiting beside it.

"Get into the car, please," one of them instructed David. He had an unctuous face and a voice to match. David climbed into the backseat of the car and sat there without saying a word. The FBI men got into the front, slammed the doors and started up the engine.

They drove in silence through the streets of Oakville. When they reached Highway 5, however, instead of turning back toward the United States, they took the ramp marked "Toronto." David leaned forward and said, "Where are you taking me? This goes to Toronto."

The FBI man in the passenger seat turned around and winked at him incongruously. "You have more friends than you think, Senator Daniels."

"What does that mean?" asked David suspiciously.

"It means that there are people who want to keep you alive."

"Then you're not FBI?"

"Oh, we're FBI all right. But then the director of the FBI doesn't necessarily see eye to eye with the present administration over this business of Russia taking over Europe, and there are plenty of other organizations that don't feel too happy about it either. The churches, for one, and all those ethnic groups that have ties with people in Europe, like Jewish and French and Italian and Swedish and Dutch."

Still suspicious, David said, "It's happened; the Russians have taken over. What choice do we have? We'll never get them out of Europe now, not without a full-scale war."

The FBI man shrugged. "Maybe you're right. But there are lots of people who aren't about to take this lying down.

They're going to fight it, first by fighting this administration and then by fighting the Russians. Maybe there will be a war. Maybe there *needs* to be a war.''

David sat back. "Where are you taking me?" he asked again.

"We're taking you where you were headed, to Vancouver. That's where we're sending everybody whose life is at risk. Later on you'll be able to come back to the States and help to straighten out this mess.''

"Aren't you supposed to take me back with you?" asked David.

The FBI man shook his head. "We were supposed to take you out and blow your head off. That's what's happening to a lot of people who know more than they ought to. All we have to do is go back to Washington and tell them you've been wasted.''

"Won't they want some proof of that?"

"Sure, and we'll give them your wallet with all your ID. You won't be needing it anymore anyway. From now on, you're Walter Ross. David Daniels is floating around in Lake Erie, a bullet hole in the back of his head.''

David said nothing. The FBI man turned around again and told him, "Things are happening already, believe me. Jewish youth groups are forming into guerrilla gangs. The churches are organizing a peaceful noncooperation program, urging nonpayment of federal taxes, that kind of thing. Our roots are in Europe, you know? We're not going to sell out our roots. You don't get rid of your grandparents, do you, just because it costs a lot of money to take care of them.''

David said, "Do you think it'll work? Do you think people really care that much as long as America is safe? Just remember, this means the end of the Cold War. No more political confrontation. No more worry about nuclear attack. That sense of security is going to be hard to argue against.''

The FBI man who was driving said, "It all depends on your sense of family, doesn't it . . . and your loyalty to where you came from. If you ask me, this administration doesn't have any loyalty to anybody.''

"Well, I think you're wrong," David replied. "It *does* have loyalty, although I personally believe its loyalty has been misguided. It has loyalty to the United States and to every American child who won't have to grow up in the shadow of the bomb the way we did. It has loyalty to the American Way, to prosperity and to a chicken in every pot."

He watched the Canadian countryside go speeding past, sunlight and shadow, and then he said, "The trouble is that peace and prosperity don't add up to much if you win them at the expense of somebody else's peace and prosperity. We stopped living on an island a long time ago. The day we entered World War Two, we committed ourselves to Europe's future and Europe's freedom. Not just for forty years, not just for four hundred years, but for all time."

The FBI man said with another wink, "You give a good speech there, Senator."

David smiled tiredly. "It's my job."

During that same Tuesday, the Soviet Army advanced through the whole of West Germany and by late evening had penetrated into Holland as far as Groningen and into Belgium as far as Liege. In the south they had encircled Switzerland and had crossed the Alps into northern Italy. General Abramov expected to be in Rome by eight o'clock the following morning. After a slow start, Operation *Byliny* was progressing well and the push to the Channel would be completed by Thursday evening, half a day ahead of schedule. Already the airborne assault force that would land in Britain on Friday was being driven through to the front so it would be ready to take off from Calais as soon as the port had been secured.

General Abramov had learned from Hitler that to hesitate in his attack on Britain would be fatal. Mind you, he thought to himself, things had been different in those days. He had already received a "categorical assurance" from the British TUC that all its members would be out on strike when the assault force landed and would give the occupying forces its "best cooperation."

In Washington at lunchtime, the President called for Morton Lock, his National Security Adviser. The President had abandoned a desk-top lunch of cheeseburger and salad and was stirring a cup of black coffee as diligently as if he expected it to curdle like cheese.

"Sit down, Morton," he said. Then he put down his coffee spoon and said, "These are uncompromising times, Morton."

"Yes, sir."

"You know that none of the decisions we have had to make have been easy. You also know that they have been irrevocable. We have changed the world, Morton, and there is no going back."

"I understand that, sir."

The President looked down at his coffee and said more to himself than to Morton, "I just hope that history judges us fairly."

Morton didn't reply. He could sense that the President had something else on his mind.

At last, with that characteristic little nod of his head, the President said, "I have to tell you that Senator David Daniels died this morning, unexpectedly."

"They caught him?"

The President didn't answer that. "I have a sacred duty, Morton, a sacred duty that was entrusted to me by the free democratic will of the people of this deathless nation of ours. For that reason, the decisions I make, whether they are ultimately proven to be right or wrong, must be mine alone, unaffected by partisan pressures. Do you know what I mean?"

"I think so, sir."

"Well, I'm sure you do, Morton. In the case of David Daniels, for instance, you might have been able to say that if anyone had linked his connection to certain leaks in national security with the fact that he was once close to my daughter, that person could have used that connection, no matter how tenuous it might have been, to his own material or political advantage."

Morton made a baffled sort of expression and shrugged. "I guess so, sir."

The President stood up. "Let me just say this, Morton. David Daniels is now the late David Daniels. Nobody can prove anything about anything. For your own sake, let it stay that way."

Morton watched the President closely. For the first time

since his appointment, he saw the face of a man who believed without question in the presidency, a man who had come to not only understand the greatness of his position, but to embody it. He had become not just the President, but the presidency itself. Such a man was not unassailable. No man was. But he was far more dangerous to deal with than a man who saw the presidency as nothing more than a job. He would kill without a qualm to protect himself because as far as he was concerned, anybody who conspired against him personally was conspiring against America.

Morton left the Oval Office and went back to his own office. He locked the door, went to his desk and opened the bottom drawer. He took out a fifth of Old Crow and a heavy-based whiskey glass and poured a large drink. To the future, he thought to himself. To a nation that was greater than all of them, a nation that would outlive all of them in spite of their mistakes.

He raised his glass and quoted, "*At genus immortale manet, multosque per annos. Stat fortuna domus, et avi numerantur avorum.*"

"But the race remains immortal, the star of their house is constant through many years, and the grandfather's grandfathers are numbered in the roll."

The rest of what happened can be found only in history books because those who knew the truth about the Copenhagen Agreement and Operation *Byliny*—those who survived, that is—were never able to tell publicly anything of what they knew. Probably the least-distorted account can be found in *The Soviet Liberation of Britain* by P. Budenny and Walter Greene. The military side is admirably described in *Byliny! The Bloodless Revolution*, issued by the London office of the Politburo Information Service.

Marshal Golovanov was retired and now lives with his wife Katia in a small village outside Moscow. There have been photographs of him feeding pigs, mending fences and smiling into the late-autumn sunlight.

What happened to Inge Schültz nobody knows. Nor was there any trace of Rufina Konstantinova. Some stories say that Miss Konstantinova was promoted. Others say that she was shot. After the annexation of Europe and Scandinavia, there was a total clampdown on military and political information that has yet to be lifted.

John Bishop, after three months back in England, was found in a garage in West Croydon, sitting in the front seat of his six-year-old Ford Fiesta, dead from inhaling exhaust fumes. Michael Townsend now works for the Soviet Computer Complex at Hemel Hempstead.

On the last weekend of May, Michael Townsend returned home and wrote in a small notebook the following words and then hid the notebook in the chimney breast of his son Duncan's bedroom in Sanderstead.

"Today we drove to the Hog's Back to watch the Soviet airborne assault troops parachute down over Aldershot. The Prime Minister had already agreed to a 'no-hostility' pact with the Soviet Union and so there was no real need for the drop, not as a military strategy, but I suppose there was something to be said for it as a propaganda spectacle.

"The roads were jammed all the way from Kingston and when the first Soviet transport planes came over, everybody stopped and got out and just stood there in the road and on the verges, watching them, silent. Hundreds and hundreds of huge planes, thundering so loudly you couldn't hear yourself think. Then the parachutists came out by the thousands. They looked like the seeds of dandelions blown all over the countryside, thousands of them. When the last of them had landed, people got in their cars and went home. Margaret was crying."

In November he wrote:

"I thought about what I had seen for a long time afterward, and I still think about it now. I think I understood that what I was seeing was the final triumph of lies over the truth, the final triumph of indifference over active decency, and the folly of giving away even an inch for the sake of a quiet life.

"I walk home now, of course (can't afford a car), and as I come up the road and see the lights in all those suburban living rooms and hear the televisions gabbling in Russian, and as I turn around and look at the valley behind me, dotted with lights, and hear the commuter trains rattling back from London, well, I feel sad for all of us, and not even particularly glad to be alive."

It is David Daniels, however, who should have the last word. From a shack near Coquitlam Lake, close to Vancouver, he wrote the following message on a Christmas card to his second wife Helen, although he decided in the end not to mail it. "It is snowy here, and very still. There are four or five hundred of us hiding among the woods and the lakes, patient and determined. It would be very easy amidst this snow to forget that the rest of the world even exists, that there is anybody alive but us, and us alone. But we are never alone. There is a family out there, a family of men and women and children, of brothers and sisters; and their freedom and their future are our concern. I see a long and difficult fight ahead of us to undo what has been done. I doubt if I shall live long enough to see it finished. But there is nothing on this earth of greater value than freedom, and to lose one's life in the pursuit of freedom is the happiest sacrifice."

BESTSELLING BOOKS FROM TOR

☐ 58725-1 *Gardens of Stone* by Nicholas Proffitt $3.95
   58726-X   Canada $4.50

☐ 51650-8 *Incarnate* by Ramsey Campbell $3.95
   51651-6   Canada $4.50

☐ 51050-X *Kahawa* by Donald E. Westlake $3.95
   51051-8   Canada $4.50

☐ 52750-X *A Manhattan Ghost Story* by T.M. Wright
                                                 $3.95
   52751-8   Canada $4.50

☐ 52191-9 *Ikon* by Graham Masterton $3.95
   52192-7   Canada $4.50

☐ 54550-8 *Prince Ombra* by Roderick MacLeish $3.50
   54551-6   Canada $3.95

☐ 50284-1 *The Vietnam Legacy* by Brian Freemantle
                                                 $3.50
   50285-X   Canada $3.95

☐ 50487-9 *Siskiyou* by Richard Hoyt $3.50
   50488-7   Canada $3.95

Buy them at your local bookstore or use this handy coupon:
Clip and mail this page with your order

TOR BOOKS—Reader Service Dept.
49 W. 24 Street, 9th Floor, New York, NY 10010

Please send me the book(s) I have checked above. I am enclosing
$_____ (please add $1.00 to cover postage and handling).
Send check or money order only—no cash or C.O.D.'s.

Mr./Mrs./Miss _____

Address _____.

City _____ State/Zip _____

Please allow six weeks for delivery. Prices subject to change without
notice.